FRAGILE MINDS

FRAGILE MINDS

Claire Seeber

WINDSOR
PARAGON

First published 2011
by Avon, a division of HarperCollins*Publishers*
This Large Print edition published 2011
by AudioGO Ltd
by arrangement with
HarperCollins*Publishers*

Hardcover ISBN: 978 1 445 85908 8
Softcover   ISBN: 978 1 445 85909 5

British Library Cataloguing in Publication Data available

Printed and bound in Great Britain by
MPG Books Group Limited

For Fenn and Raffi, again.
All my love, always.

And in memory of my beloved grandpa,
Roy Livingstone Holmes.
Lemonade lollies forever.

ACKNOWLEDGEMENTS

Ten years ago, I made a documentary that involved filming briefly in London's biggest lap-dancing club. I am no prude, but I was shocked at the state of some of the girls backstage. In particular one young girl stuck in my mind afterwards: she had implored me not to film her because, as a trained ballerina, her parents thought she was on 'ballet tour'. It was during the culture of various female journalists championing these new clubs, showing off about paying for dances alongside their male partners. I doubt they'd have been so keen if they'd witnessed what I did—none of which made it onto the screen due to the frankly threatening and misogynist male management. Doubtless there are women who do enjoy this job; still, although we could only show the 'up' side on screen, there is most definitely a down side too.

Sincere thanks to psychiatric nurse Danny Pont for his insight and knowledge; to ex-Chief Superintendent John Ricketts for help with police procedure—some of which I have ignored—any errors are entirely my own; to Helen Clarke for her ballet and osteopathy expertise; to Flic Everett (sorely missed at the moment), Judy McInerney, Guy Ware and Phyllice Eddu for listening patiently as ever; to Bethy, my mother, Tiggy, Nicola and Pippa for the reading, the PowerPoint, the photos and the love; to Jim for teaching me Proctor's Rule of Escalators, and helping with the male psyche; to Kate Bradley & everyone at Avon for editorial eyes, support and lunch (especially Zoë Clarke); to

Teresa Chris for agent-ship beyond the expected. For a few reasons this has at times been a painful book to write, and I'd like to thank my fantastic friends and family for catching me as I fell.

'Whoever takes one life, takes the world entire,
Whoever saves a single life, saves the world
entire.'

The Talmud

'No rescue? What, a prisoner? I am even
The natural fool of fortune. Use me well.'

King Lear, Act IV, Scene VI

PROLOGUE

There are plenty of beginnings, but only one end to my story.

At the police station in the small country town, they brought me tea and toast, but I didn't touch it; I pushed it away. I didn't trust them. Any of them, any more.

My feet were cut and bleeding; I didn't care. They matched my sore hands. In my head I was still running, and the road was cold and rough beneath my naked feet and I didn't care. The pain pushed me on. I was a streak of white light in a black surround, and then you were beside me, only you couldn't keep up, so I leant down and carried you, light as thistledown, in my arms. No one could stop us; I would run and run and run—

Someone was behind me. I could feel my heart beating, I could hear the blood thumping in my ears, I could feel the breath squeezing through my ribs and out of me; I couldn't outrun them.

My feet were hurting badly now and I no longer felt invincible, I could hear the sobs pushing out of me as the car slowed and a blue light flickered across the road between the sand dunes, and the sea hissed to the left of me: 'Don't stop, Claudie, or they will get you.' But I was weak now, too weak—

The man held my arm gently. He was wearing a uniform and he said, 'Are you all right, love, you're freezing.' And he led me to the car with the blue light on top, and made me sit in the back.

And then they brought me to the building in the town, and said another man, a man they called

Silver, wanted to talk to me.

I didn't give him time to sit when he came in. I had waited too long already.

'Something's not right,' I said, too fast, almost before he came through the door.

He leant on the wall in his shirtsleeves, hands in his pockets, and looked down at me. His expression was quizzical but I was relieved that he didn't look amused. He looked tired, perhaps, but not amused.

'I see. Are *you* all right though, Claudie?'

I kept my hands in my lap beneath the table, where he couldn't see me tearing at my own skin.

'I—I'm not sure.' I eyed the toast warily. 'I think I will be OK.' If only they'd stop poisoning me.

He sat now, directly opposite me. There was a black tape recorder on the table between us, but he didn't switch it on. His eyes were a little hooded; they narrowed slightly as he studied my face.

'Have we met before?' he asked.

'I don't think so.'

'You look a little familiar.'

I shook my head. There was a pen on the table; he turned it round neatly, and then gave me a slight smile. 'So, Claudie. In your own time, I need you to tell me why you're here. How you came to be all the way out here. Did someone bring you?'

'Yes,' I nodded. 'And something's not right,' I repeated, slowly this time. I could feel the shiny crescent moon of skin missing from my thumb where I'd stripped it raw.

'What?' he said now. His accent was Northern. 'What's not right?'

'I can't—it's hard to explain.'

We locked eyes. Still he did not condescend to me; he didn't look at me as if I was mad. He just waited, dug in his trouser pocket for something.

'That sounds stupid, I know.' I was trying to order my mind. My thumb throbbed. 'I mean, I can't quite put my finger on it.'

'On what?' He was handsome. No, not handsome even, kind of . . . debonair. Like he'd stepped from a Fred and Ginger film; his cuffs so white they almost shone.

'I think I might have done something bad. The Friday before last.'

'What kind of bad?' he asked. Long fingers on gum; waiting to unwrap it. He sat back in his chair and looked at me patiently. I could smell his aftershave. Lemony.

'Very bad,' I muttered.

'Do you know my name?' he asked.

He felt me falter. I shook my head.

'It's DCI Silver.' It was an inducement. 'Joe Silver.'

A short, stocky woman walked into the room now and stood behind him. She smiled at me, a kind, reassuring smile. I recognised her, I realised. I'd met her before. A woman with funny coloured hair.

'And what happened to your face, Claudie?'

Automatically I raised my hand to my cheek. 'Berkeley Square.'

'Berkeley Square?' He sat up straighter. 'The explosion?'

I nodded.

'OK, Claudie.' He flicked the gum away into the wastepaper basket and smiled again. He must have kids, I thought. He is used to waiting with infinite patience. His teeth were very straight, almost as white as his cuffs. 'Why don't you start from the beginning? Who brought you all the way out here?'

I think I might have done something terrible,' I repeated. I took a gulp of air: I met his eyes this time. 'I think—I think I might have killed a lot of people.'

THURSDAY 13TH JULY
CLAUDIE

It was such an ordinary morning. Afterwards that seemed the most marked thing about everything that followed, that it started as any day that encapsulates absolute normality. Not particularly sunny, not particularly cold—a day on which people get up and eat toast, choose underwear and shoes; argue about walking the dog or taking the bin out, kiss their children and their partners goodbye; catch the 8.13, jostle for space with the same anonymous faces they jostle with every day. A day on which people go about things in exactly the same way as always; not realising life might be about to change forever.

And for me, it was one of the all right days. A day when I had managed to roll out of bed, step out of the house; walk, talk and function. Not one of the pole-axed days. Not one of the splitting days.

One of the all right days.

I got to work early because the yoga teacher hadn't turned up at the Centre. I walked through the back streets of Marylebone, enjoying the relative quiet of Oxford Street, free of the tourists and maddened shoppers, at one with the street cleaners and the other Londoners not yet soiled for the day by the city.

I wandered up the front stairs of the Royal Ballet Academy in Berkeley Square, between the great white pillars and the huge arched windows, soaking in the ambience of the old building. I loved my job and the Academy was grand enough to warrant its

1

distinguished title, training some of the greatest ballet talent in Europe.

'The Bolshoi are in.' My colleague Leila shot past me on the stairs, following a gaggle of chattering students. I caught up with them at the glass wall to watch a little of the guest stars' technical demonstration, watching a sturdy Russian male fling the Academy's young Irish ballerina Sorcha into the air during the *Sleeping Beauty* pas de deux. By the rapt look on the couple's faces, I guessed it might not be all they'd be demonstrating later.

A small, dark first-year student called Anita sat against the back wall, limbering up, watching Sorcha like a hawk. One of Tessa's protégées, I had yet to see her dance, or treat her for any sort of injury myself, but she had a rather glowering intensity that I found unattractive. Her face in repose was simply a down-turned mouth. And recently, I'd noticed that she'd begun to trail Tessa in a way that verged on pathological.

'He's gorgeous,' a girl in a blue leotard breathed, fugging up the glass, 'and look at his arms. His lifts are effortless.'

'He can lift me,' her plain friend said, sticking her bony chest out. 'Any way he wants.' They both giggled.

Down in the office, Mason was as always safely ensconced behind her desk, keeper of the back-room. God only knew where she had found this morning's ensemble: a kaftan in vivid black and orange swirls that entirely swamped her skinny frame. I wondered, not for the first time, if anyone else ever thought she looked like a female version of the transvestite potter Grayson Perry.

'You're early,' Mason said. The sleeve of her

2

kaftan trailed patiently after the raddled hand flying across the keyboard. 'As the esteemed Mr Franklin once said: *"Early to bed and early to rise, makes a man healthy, wealthy and wise."'*

'Indeed,' I grinned. Mason's ability to quote at long and tedious length was legendary, though I was sure she made half of them up. 'Let's hope he was right.'

'Tessa's looking for you.' She glanced up, one pencilled eyebrow disappearing into her glossy fringe. 'Seems a little—anxious.'

As I was changing into my tunic in the staff changing room, Tessa arrived, slightly breathless, her limp a little more pronounced than usual. She looked oddly harried and her spotted hairband was tied too loosely so wisps of fair hair were escaping.

'Morning. Everything OK?' I noted the roses of high colour on her cheeks. 'Mason said you were after me.'

'I—Claudie. I must just catch my breath. Sorry,' she mumbled. She sat on the bench beside me, clutching her tortoiseshell walking stick.

'I've got that book you wanted to borrow, by the way,' I said, 'the Elizabeth David. Don't let me forget to give it to you now I've—'

Tessa startled me by grasping my hand so hard it made me wince. Her breathing seemed very fast as she peered over my shoulder, dropping her voice.

'I need to talk to you, Claudie.' The Australian accent she normally fought to hide was broad today, and something in her tone made me frown. I'd never seen Tessa so tense, although her behaviour in the past few weeks had seemed different, somehow; erratic, even. Recently her star as the Academy's top teacher had slid into the descendant

3

after an ugly incident involving an irate mother and her hysterical daughter; the board were looking into it and Tessa refused to talk about it, but I'd put her unease down to that. 'In private, I mean.' She looked over my shoulder as if she was expecting someone to materialise.

'I've got a full schedule this morning,' I was apologetic. 'They're all overdoing it at the moment apparently, poor loves. End of term in sight, I suppose. Can we talk later?'

'Lunchtime?'

'I'm—I've got an appointment at lunch.' I grimaced. I was aware we hadn't spent much time together recently. 'Sorry. I can't really—how about tea this afternoon?'

'I'm not sure I can wait.' Tessa was blinking strangely, moving to the door. 'I'm—I really need to—' she trailed off as she pushed the door ajar and scanned the corridor.

'What's wrong, Tessa?' I followed her gaze; through the crack, I glimpsed Anita Stuart trailing Sorcha and the Bolshoi dancers up the stairs to the girls' changing rooms.

'It's just—I've been—oh God.' Tessa let the door swing to, biting her own fist. 'I really wanted to tell you before—'

In a blast of surrealist kaftan, Mason arrived, music swelling and dying down again as she opened and shut the door. Behind her in the corridor I saw my first student waiting outside my room.

'Ladies. Don't mind me.' Mason began sticking up audition notices onto the central notice-board. I knew she was all ears.

I looked back at Tessa; her hands fluttered at her sides like long white butterflies.

4

'Look, can we grab a coffee at eleven?' I suggested. 'I'll have about fifteen minutes between sessions.'

'Yes please.' Tessa tried to smile, but I thought I saw her bottom lip tremble slightly. 'Oh, and can you shove my kitbag in your locker? I've mislaid my keys. Stupid, really.'

'Of course.'

Her light eyes were over-bright as I took the bag from her, her mascara oddly clumpy for someone usually fastidious. I felt torn, but Billy McCorkdale was leaning against the wall, only eighteen and already all testosterone and attitude. Starting treatments late meant the whole day became a logistical nightmare.

'Problem?' Mason perked up. 'Can I assist?'

Tessa tried that smile again. 'No, no.'

Later, that smile haunted me.

Later, my abiding memory was that it was one of fear.

THURSDAY 13TH JULY
SILVER

DCI Joseph Silver was just about to step into the shower at the sports club when his work mobile rang. He felt particularly disgusting at this moment, sweat dripping down his back, his t-shirt saturated, having just thrashed it out with his colleague DI Lonsdale in a match that was ostensibly part of the station tournament, but was really about Serious Crime vs Homicide. And in fact, even more so in this instance, about proving the North/South divide was well and truly alive and breathing. Lonsdale stood for everything Silver despised in the force; a supercilious Southern bastard with a daft goatee who drove a Volvo, wore ever-clean Timberlands, and bleated about his paternity rights every other day.

Silver ignored the phone. It rang off, and then immediately started again.

He swore quietly and fumbled in the pocket of his neatly folded trousers, tentatively holding the phone to his sweaty ear, trying not to soak it. 'Silver.'

'Guv.' It was DS Lorraine Kenton, the newest member of his team. 'Sorry to bother you, but Malloy's on the rampage.'

'Go on.' Sweat trickled down his cheek and dripped onto the filthy floor. Silver suppressed a fastidious shudder. He might have just proven that the North bore tough and tenacious sportsmen who were unafraid to slam their own bodies into brick walls in the name of gamesmanship, but he was also the same copper who couldn't abide mess and dirt. OCD, his ex-wife Lana called it, invariably to wind him up, though she wasn't too far behind him in the cleanliness next to Godliness stakes. Not that either of them had ever followed the God bit—but their house had been truly sparkling.

'Just a quick one.' Kenton cleared her throat. 'Missing girl, Misty Jones. Malloy wants to use the GMTV and Crime Live! appeal tomorrow morning for her.'

'Why?' Silver tasted the salt on his own lips. 'It's meant to be for that Down's Syndrome lad.'

'Bobby Elwood. I know. I did say that. But the thing is,' Kenton cleared her throat again, a habit

6

Silver was beginning to recognise as a nervous one, 'Malloy thinks Misty Jones is more—'

'Don't tell me—photogenic. Pretty, is she?' Which meant his boss thought they'd get more response to the appeal, which meant a quicker result, which meant better statistics. 'Brilliant.'

'Is that—are you being serious, sir?' Kenton asked nervously.

'I'm being entirely sarcastic, Kenton. Which is the lowest form of wit, someone once told me. Poor retarded lad traded in for pretty lass. Have we even looked into the case properly?'

'Not really. Flatmate reported it. Can't trace the family.'

'But it's a fait accompli, as those learned French say. Doubt I have much choice, do I?'

Kenton looked at her email inbox, where the GMTV producer had just mailed her to thank her for the Jpeg of the missing girl, and asking for a few more details. Favourite pet, younger siblings, anything that would help the nation's heart bleed. None of which Kenton could immediately answer.

'Er—'

'That was rhetorical, Kenton. Who the hell is Misty Jones anyway?' Down in the shower room, Silver could see Lonsdale approaching. He wanted to get into the shower before his competitor. He didn't fancy chit-chat from a cheating Southern bastard with a wispy chin who'd quibbled over every point.

'Look, if Malloy's given you the word, then do it, kiddo. We'll have a chat in the morning. Or at the weekend, any road. I'm off tomorrow.'

Reason not to be cheerful no. 87. Silver shoved his phone back into his sports bag and made for

7

the shower. He might just have won, but he had no desire to engage in back-slapping camaraderie with a secretly seething colleague, or be invited to go for a drink, which he'd only have to turn down. He was knackered, and his mood was dark. Bed and solitude called.

THURSDAY 13TH JULY
CLAUDIE

Tessa didn't show up at eleven and by lunchtime, I'd been distracted by a first-year student falling in class and a possible elbow fracture. I forgot about my friend and her earlier anxiety as I hastened to sort the subsequent hospital referral, and then to reach my own appointment in Harley Street.

Rushing back to the Academy at the end of the lunch hour, almost late for my next student, I found Anita Stuart lurking outside my room, her feet sketching movement on the spot as someone down the hall played the opening suite from Prokofiev's *Romeo and Juliet* score over and over.

'Have you seen Tessa?' she demanded, fiddling with a small silver dove on a chain round her neck. She was a little surly, as ever, and her rather lazy left eye gave her an unfortunate lopsided look.

'No, 'fraid not.' I unlocked my door. 'She's probably in class, no?'

Anita was clutching something, a pamphlet of some description. I caught the words 'Redemption' and 'Light' before she shoved it in her pocket.

'She's not,' Anita scowled. She smelt odd; it seemed familiar but I couldn't place the scent. 'I

8

thought she might be having lunch with you.'

'Sorry. Can't help.' I let myself into my room, relieved to get away from the scowl and the odd smell. But Anita was too fast.

'What's she said to you?' She stuck her foot in the door so I couldn't shut it behind me.

'About what?' I frowned.

'About—' She stopped and stared at me. Thought better of it, perhaps. 'Never mind. But if you see Tessa, tell her I'm looking for her.'

'Yes, Madam,' I muttered at her departing back. What an unpleasant girl, I thought, and closed my door behind her.

*   *   *

At five, as I was signing out, I had a quick look for Tessa, but she wasn't in class or in the staffroom. I needed some fresh air now, my back was aching from standing for so long, and I was dying for a cigarette. I searched my bag for a nicotine patch, applying it with a sense of slightly defeated relief.

'Seen Tessa?' I asked Leila, who hadn't, and Mason, who immediately raised her non-existent eyebrows in an entirely suggestive way.

'What?'

'She was ever so stressed. I heard her on the phone. I was trying not to listen but—' Mason's letterbox mouth snapped shut dramatically. 'Well.'

'Your speciality, not listening.' Leila winked at me. 'Walls have ears, eh, Mason?'

'Let's just say Tessa was more than a little fraught. She was meant to be covering Eduardo's 4 p.m. but she made some sort of excuse and just left. Jenny had to do it.'

9

Leila and I exchanged glances. Mason was unperturbed.

'She's not best pleased, shall we say. Jenny. Still, *"The busy man is troubled with but one devil, the idle man by a thousand."'*

'Oh dear.' I gathered my things, feeling guilty I hadn't found Tessa earlier. 'I hope she's OK.'

'Oh, Claudie,' Mason barked as I opened the door to leave. 'I completely forgot. She left you a note.' As she bent to retrieve it from the pile on her desk, Mason knocked over her coffee, soaking everything with dark brown liquid. 'Oh, damn and blast.'

After a bit of wrangling, Mason passed me the soggy bit of paper, but it was almost pulp already. I could just make out the words *'Take'* and *'the necklace'*. The last word in the paragraph looked like it was possibly *'Sorry'* with a big curly y.

I held it to the light but it was no good, it was illegible. I balled the note, tossing it in the bin. From the set of Mason's expectant head, I could tell she had read it, she was dying to be asked; but I wouldn't give her the satisfaction. If it was important, Tessa would call me, I guessed. 'See you guys tomorrow.'

'Ta ta for now,' Mason sniffed. 'Don't do anything I wouldn't with that gorgeous Rafe. I know what MPs are like.'

'Leaves me wide open then,' I grinned at her, shouldering my bag, and left.

The summer afternoon was warm and the air outside seemed to almost shimmer. I suddenly felt more cheerful about life, almost euphoric even. Things were going to get better. They simply had to.

I had no idea of the level of my delusion.

*   *   *

But on the bus to meet Rafe, stuck at red lights, I felt less than euphoric and increasingly racked by a headache. I stared out at an *Evening Standard* billboard on the street which read '**Dancer, 20, Missing or Dead?**'; but the words moved up and down with alarming speed as I tried to focus.

Disoriented, I was jolted into a memory that terrified me. I felt like I had last year; my self fracturing into pieces—but it couldn't be happening again—could it? I was over the worst, surely? I leant against the window, my head pounding so badly now I thought I might actually throw up, and I thought vaguely that maybe I should get off the bus before it was too late—only the idea of walking right now seemed a little like scaling Mount Everest. I looked down onto the pavement, onto the worker ants of London, and my phone was ringing in my bag. I tried to pull it out, the flickering lights in front of my burning eyes bewildering me until I felt like I was losing consciousness.

*   *   *

I woke in the dark, almost dribbling, absolutely freezing, my hands curled round my bag strap so tightly I had to fight to unfurl them. I could hear voices, and then Rafe was there, peering down at me, saying, 'Oh my God, Claudie, what's happened?' And I found I could hardly speak, I was so disoriented, but I managed to croak something about my head, and he was saying, 'Oh Christ,

11

you're frozen, how long have you been here?' and practically carrying me up the few stairs to his flat. He gave me a warm drink of something tasteless, and laid me down on his sofa with a cashmere blanket—it was so warm and homely that I drifted off again.

FRIDAY 14TH JULY
CLAUDIE

I came to in the early hours caught in the desperate state between sleep and consciousness; hearing frantic voices whispering in the dark, a woman's voice too now, and I thought perhaps it was Tessa, and then I realised I *was* dreaming.

When I woke properly about six, Rafe had already gone. He was a gym addict, and there was a note, telling me to help myself to anything I wanted, and that he'd see me later, and he hoped I was feeling better.

The headache had gone, but I didn't feel better. I just felt frightened. I'd lost a few hours from last night; I remembered leaving work, being on the bus and then—what? Waking in Rafe's porch; being carried into the flat. An overwhelming sense of anxiety pulsed through me. Images from yesterday flickered through my mind, like a camera shutter opening and closing too fast. I sat on the sofa, my head in my hands, and tried to breathe.

Was it happening again?

I washed my face and hands beneath the expensive lighting in Rafe's stark bathroom and, trying to calm my tousled hair, I opened the medicine cabinet above the basin, looking for what Rafe called 'product'. A packet of Well Woman tablets fell out. I picked them up, frowning. Next to them, a pink electric toothbrush, and a jar of Clinique night cream.

I shut the cabinet door, and walked into his bedroom. It all looked the same as ever, until I opened the drawers by the side of the bed. There was a pale blue hairband and some expensive hand cream.

It underlined something I had been avoiding . . . that Rafe and I were really only a stopgap. Meeting by chance at the Sadler's Wells charity do in January, it had always felt a little like I was one of his pet projects; that we were keeping each other warm on cold winter nights.

But now it was summer.

Grabbing my stuff, I ran down the stairs and buzzed myself out, the fortress door slamming behind me. I stood at the top of the shiny steps to the street. A milk float trundled slowly down the deserted road, and a ginger cat cleaned its ears discreetly as it sat beneath the frothy mimosa tree; it looked at me with disdain and then carried on licking. And I remembered Tessa's soaked and illegible note in my hand yesterday afternoon and I had this sudden overriding feeling that I should be somewhere, and I felt a rising panic, because I just didn't know where.

FRIDAY 14TH JULY
KENTON

How the hell she had ended up having to do this alone, she would never know. Cursing quietly, DS Lorraine Kenton backed the car into the small space, knocked the adjacent Audi's mirror and then looked around guiltily to see if anyone had noticed. It had taken over half an hour to find a parking space because the bloody NCP was shut for some reason, and she was seriously over-tired and crochety. She'd slept badly because all night she'd kept dreaming that she'd forgotten what she was meant to say in the TV studio and no one would tell her the lines so she just sat frozen in fear on the famous cream sofa of Crime Live!, opposite the immaculate ice-maiden presenter who stared at her blankly.

At six, Kenton had woken with relief, before realising with horror she really *did* have to go on TV today. In an effort to rouse herself, she'd drunk too much black coffee in a foolish attempt to get those little grey cells working and thrown half a mug of it down her new white shirt, which meant she had to plump for the crumpled stripy one. She didn't have time to iron it because she'd nicked the fuse out of the plug last week for her hairdryer, which had been unused for at least two years prior to her first date, on the Southbank, with Alison from the dating website *Guardian* Soulmates. Now the only consequence of all that coffee was a mismatched outfit and a horribly pounding heart, her brain exactly as slow and sludge-like as when

14

she'd first woken.

The television studio was on a small side street off Berkeley Square. Kenton checked the A-Z and, grabbing her jacket from the back seat hoping it would cover the crumpled stripes, wondered for at least the forty-eighth time this morning why the hell she'd volunteered to replace Gill McCarthy from the Press Office when she had become 'unavailable' at the last minute yesterday evening (for unavailable read: had just found out her boyfriend in Organised Crime was screwing McCarthy's number two, Jo Reid, who wore a wanton look, too much red lipstick and her dresses practically slashed to the waist. Obvious, maybe, but Kenton could definitely see her appeal).

Her phone rang. Her pounding heart slowed and sank. It was DI Craven.

'I'll meet you there, pet,' he said. 'At Audley Street. Running slightly late.'

'Really? I thought I was—' Kenton collected herself, 'I didn't realise you were coming too.'

'Boss thought you might fuck it up,' he said smugly, and hung up.

Kenton counted to ten slowly and then dug her iPod out to begin the walk west, shuffling the wheel for the Meditation CD Alison had rather shyly suggested she try for stress.

'Breathe deeply. Now imagine yourself in a safe, secure place. Somewhere you are entirely comfortable,' the man's voice droned unconvincingly. 'Perhaps you are in a childhood—'

Someone pushed Kenton so violently from behind that she stumbled, just righting herself in time before she fell; her iPod hitting the pavement hard.

15

Before she could pick it up, she was pushed again. Heart racing, she turned to see who her attacker was, but they had run on. There was some sort of commotion on the far side of the square behind her, beside the big Swiss bank—but she was too far away to see exactly what it was; the railings round the green blocked her view, so she could only see the edge of the building site beside the bank. About fifty metres away, a woman in a burqa stood on the edge of the pavement, about to push a buggy across the road. Now the woman began to run towards the group of people at the bus stop.

As Kenton neared, adrenaline flooding her veins now, she could hear shouting and then another, more eerie noise: a high-pitched wail not unlike the keening of the bereaved at an Arabic funeral.

A bus pulled in, blocking her view again; and then a woman was screaming and shouting something unintelligible and Kenton saw people on the bus look out, and then stand up, a man pointing, pointing out of the far window and then—

All was chaos and noise and white, exploding light.

FRIDAY 14TH JULY
CLAUDIE

I stood on the quiet street outside Rafe's flat. The church clock on the green struck seven, and a double decker slid into place at the bus stop in front of me. Unthinking, I climbed on. I didn't check the destination, I just slapped my Oyster card on the reader like it was a dead fish, and I sat in the first seat I came to.

I kept thinking *I need to be somewhere* only I couldn't seem to collect my thoughts; and when I did manage to assemble them a little, I found I was thinking of Ned, and then of Will. I fiddled anxiously with my locket, realising I had a sudden urge to see my husband. Oh the sweet irony: an irony Will would not thank me for.

The old lady beside me smelt high, as if she'd been ripened especially for months. She kept grumbling about the driver, on and on she droned. 'He's trying to scare us, that lad, you mark my words, it's because they don't learn to drive here, they learn in Africa, too many holes in the roads, those jigaboos.' After a few minutes, I said, 'I'm afraid I don't share your horrible opinions,' and I moved to the back, stumbling against the other commuters who stared at me with empty eyes.

We reached Russell Square. Tessa; that was it; that was what I had to do. I changed buses and boarded a new one. It seemed to take forever to reach Oxford Street where we became one in a line of nose to tail buses, crawling at tortoise pace— something was holding us up, but we couldn't see what; until eventually I knew, I knew I had to get off the bus NOW. I began to smash on the doors until the other passengers stepped back in fear, until the driver thought I was truly mad, and gave in, and let me off.

And I ran, ran, ran towards Berkeley Square.

FRIDAY 14TH JULY
KENTON

Somehow the bus protected her. Forever after she would be grateful; she would look on London's famous red double decker as some kind of lucky charm; some kind of talisman to her.

Instinctively, Kenton had hit the floor when the explosion ripped through the north side of the square. She had lain motionless on the pavement with her hands over her head for a minute or two, until the noise settled, the rumble stopped, and there was quiet across the square. A strange pocket of silence in the city, broken only by the incongruous sound of birdsong.

And then a new noise began. Now it was the alarms that filled the air: the cars, the shops and flats; the electrics triggered by the huge explosion. There was thick dust swirling in the air, making Kenton cough as she thought absently of 9/11 and the survivors staggering about covered in white like ash-covered ghosts.

She tasted it in her mouth and spat a few times, trying to find some moisture. She stood slowly, trembling, and began to walk towards the mutilated bus that had inclined fatally to the right, towards the crying and the wailing—towards the devastation, glass crunching underfoot. Her inclination might be to run back, but she knew it was her duty to go forward. She stopped for a moment, and breathed deeply and then pulled her phone from her pocket to ring for help. Afterwards, she couldn't remember the conversation, or whom she spoke to, but soon after, the air was filled with police sirens.

Nothing could prepare her for what she was about to witness. In her mind's eye, she imagined her late mother, smiling with encouragement from her usual place at the kitchen sink. 'You can do it, Lorraine,' she heard her mother say, snapping off her yellow Marigolds. 'That's my girl.'

The smell of burning filled the air as Kenton stepped over something, walking towards the bank in the far right corner. She looked again: it was a hand. She retched into the gutter; the pavement nearest the bank was red with blood. She held her phone tighter. She looked for the first ambulance. She saw another mutilated body. She kept breathing. She didn't retch this time.

A blonde woman was lying on her back, face bloodied and blackened, one foot extended gracefully; glassy eyes open. Dead. Most definitely dead. Another woman lay at a right angle to her; this one was alive, whimpering in terror and pain. Kenton knelt beside her gratefully.

'What's your name?' she asked.

'Maeve,' the woman whispered. Her face was entirely drained of colour. 'Maeve O'Connor.'

'You're going to be all right, Maeve.' Kenton had no idea if the woman would be all right but it seemed the thing to say. 'Where does it hurt?'

Desperately Kenton looked again for an ambulance. Where the hell were they? She held the woman's hand, and she tied her belt round the woman's bleeding leg. Then she spoke to a young man; a builder from the neighbouring site. He seemed delirious, worried he'd lost his hard hat; his face was speckled with shrapnel cuts. Other people were coming now; moving amongst the dead and injured. Kenton looked up. The front and side of the Hoffman Bank were gone; it looked naked, like a half-dressed man. The building site beside it had lost its front hoarding; gentle flames licked the side of it. The dust flew in the air.

When the ambulances finally arrived, and the police cars and fire engines, and there were no injured left to talk or tend to, Kenton sat on the kerb in the debris until she was moved off, like any other member of the public, and after a while, she wept.

FRIDAY 14TH JULY
CLAUDIE

I came to in St Thomas's A&E, on a bed in a curtained cubicle, with no memory of what or who had brought me here. Concussion they said, but I'd be fine. I'd collided with a cyclist ten minutes— quite literally—after the 'major incident' that had apparently just shut central London. I couldn't remember any of it, but the cyclist lay in the next cubicle with a twisted knee. My head was hurting even more than it had last night, and I kept trying to say I didn't know what had happened, but they thought that was normal. I wasn't sure they were listening; they kept saying it was just shock. And the pain, it was different to last night; a dull throb, and the nice nurse who had treated me delivered me to the waiting area, and patted me on the head like a well-behaved puppy. She propped me up with a print-out on concussion and a vial of painkillers, and told me to hang on, someone would be here soon.

'You'll be all right,' she said, in an accent that was probably Nigerian. Her bobbed wig was slightly askew; I wanted to straighten it. 'You got a hard head, child. Praise the Lord you were not nearer the incident.' She glanced up to where God obviously resided. 'Go well, Claudia. And don't forget to ring through for your results in a few days.'

The consultant's single concession to my confusion and mention of blinding migraines had been to give me a blood test.

'The confusion is probably partial concussion.' He looked about ten, slightly nervous, hardly old enough to have left school, and his ears protruded at alarming right angles. 'Which is what you must watch for now. Tell your family, OK? Re: the migraines, well, I haven't got time to do a full set of bloods now,' he filled in a form, which is what he *had* to find time for, 'we're too stretched. But let me just do a test for your hormone levels. It could explain a lot. We'll have to wait for the results of course.'

And I hadn't been in a hospital since that terrible day two years ago, the day that Ned had finally given up on life; and it was even worse than I remembered. There was an air of flattened panic throughout the building and everyone who entered through the sliding doors seemed almost shifty; they would check the room quickly to see who else was here as if they were casing the joint: the walking wounded, the traumatised. A constant stream of ambulances arrived in the bay outside the doors; the seriously injured were whisked

21

somewhere we were not allowed. After a while we all averted our eyes because it was simply too much.

And the sirens; the sirens were a constant chorus of the morning, screaming through the stultifying air. The doctors and nurses walked with a different tread, faster, and they seemed different to how they would be in a normal Emergency Room; quicker, more energised. Frightened.

About an hour after I had been led to that shiny orange chair, my younger sister trotted through the doors at a fair pace, like a circus pony, anxious to perform.

'Oh, thank God!' she said. She was almost breathless with fear and excitement, her fair hair tumbling around her broad, friendly face, only missing its circus plume. 'Are you OK? Isn't this awful?'

'Thanks for coming, Nat.' Gingerly I stood, clutching my medication and my bag. 'I know you're busy.'

'Of course I'd come.' Her face was flushed and she had put her pink lipstick on crooked. 'Who else would? Though I didn't want to bring Ella into the zone, you know, the danger zone,' and I almost laughed. 'I left her with Glynnis next door. Such a nice woman. She understood.'

What exactly Glynnis had understood, I wasn't sure.

'We'd better get out of here quickly.'

'It's not Afghanistan you know,' I said, but perhaps it was; perhaps this crisis that I did not understand yet was the start of something truly terrible. Natalie rolled her eyes, guiding me towards the car park now.

'Well, who knows what it is yet, Claudia? They

haven't said. They're saying nothing on the radio, just that it was an explosion, and don't go into town. The traffic's appalling. Oh God I was so worried, it's right beside your work isn't it? Thank goodness it happened so early.'

'I should have been there,' I said. *I should have been there, I should have been there.* 'I was on my way in.'

'You should? Oh my goodness, Claudia!' she exhaled noisily. 'You must be in shock. I would be. Your poor face. I've got a thermos of tea in the car.' My ever-efficient little sister, the prize-winning Girl Guide, the soloist chorister, the parent rep. 'You know, I can't stop watching the news. It's so horrific. We need to ring Mum. Let's get home.'

FRIDAY 14TH JULY
SILVER

Despite it being his day off, Joseph Silver woke at 5.15 a.m. Despite or because of . . . Habit was a forceful thing, he thought sourly, burying his head beneath the pillow. Silver loathed his days off, hated having time to think; he would happily spend the whole time unconscious until it was time to go to work again.

Naturally this morning, try as he might, sleep eluded him until eventually he emerged from the Egyptian cotton he'd replaced his landlady's cheap polyester with, and lay on his back in the bed that was too soft, that sent him precariously close to one edge each time he rolled over. His upper arm was bruised from smashing into the squash court wall last night, so it was hard to get comfortable. Hands beneath his head, he stared at the ceiling, at the damp patch near the small window. And then at the framed photo beside him. He knew the picture intimately, the Dales rolling gently behind the figures in the foreground, the wide open space of his own childhood calling him, his children's carefree faces beaming out at him, gap-toothed grins, dimples, freckles like join-the-dots. A photo pored over too many times now until it almost meant nothing. He knew it almost as well as his own face, but that brought little relief from the homesickness he so often suffered.

Silver rolled away from the three grins. Missing the children was a constant weight, like knees on his chest; a pain he fought every bloody day alongside the guilt, a guilt that called him northwards again but that he had not yet succumbed to. He wondered idly what Julie was doing today and then acknowledged that he didn't really care. She had a good body ('nice rack', Craven would say and everybody else would tut and roll their eyes) but nothing much to say. She'd giggled a lot when they went to that dreadful wine bar last week and talked about police dramas. In particular, Lewis's sidekick Hathaway, who was played by a Fox, who apparently *was* a fox: until Silver had had to grit his teeth. And later the sex was fine but not good enough to warrant that incessant gurgle that she thought was alluring but really wasn't; that reminded him more of water going down a plug hole than anything else. Not good enough for him to call her on his day off—and anyway he thought he remembered her saying she was away, on some middle management course this week, which no doubt meant trust exercises of the sort that involved falling backwards and catching one another before getting pissed in the identikit hotel bar and waking up hungover and horrified next morning beside a married colleague.

Silver allowed himself a wry smile and briefly debated going to the gym, but for some reason the soulless space in the station basement held little appeal today. He swung his legs out of the bed, his bare feet meeting the polished floorboards, rubbing his short hair impatiently with both hands until it stood on end. He felt confined and caged and suddenly incredibly depressed.

Philippa's tribe were all still in bed, which was a rare piece of luck. In an effort to cheer himself, Silver spent the next hour drinking coffee in his landlady's huge kitchen, the early morning sunlight spilling through the old sash windows, and booking a holiday in Corfu for the kids' October half term. Lana had actually agreed to it last time they spoke, albeit reluctantly, and he wouldn't take the risk of asking again; he knew it was now or never. Eventually a ping from his email said he'd succeeded: three grand poorer maybe but still, the proud owner of one package holiday with perks.

Philippa plodded into the kitchen now, yawning, rubbing sleep from her almond-shaped eyes, and switched the kettle on. He raised a hand in greeting as he dialled home: the kids would be about to leave for school. He missed the boys, they'd left already, but Molly was breathless with excitement, despite Lana's low tones chiding her to put her shoes on whilst she talked.

'Come *on*, Molly.'

He heard the dull exasperation in his ex-wife's

tone and his fist clenched unconsciously, wondering why the hell she couldn't just let him have this time, why she couldn't relax for one moment. But he still managed to absorb the pleasure in his youngest child's voice, words tumbling over each other about the plane, about beaches and ice cream and staying up late. Halfway through the excited patter, as Philippa padded out to the hall to start screeching at her kids who were not getting up, his mobile rang.

Kenton's name flashed up.

'Hang on, kiddo,' he said to Molly and answered the mobile. 'Silver.'

'Sir,' she was stammering; he could hardly hear her words for the jarring dissonance of sound behind her. 'There's been an incident. An explosion.'

He spoke to Molly quickly. 'Mol. I'll call you tonight.'

'OK.' For once he'd fed her enough for her to be happy to hang up. 'Thanks, Daddy. Love you.'

'Where are you, Lorraine?' He stood now.

'Berkeley Square. I was on my way to the TV place.'

He could hear pure terror in her voice; sensed her trying to suppress panic.

'Are you OK?'

'Yes. But—I don't know what to—' She was fighting tears. He could hear car alarms jostling for air space. 'What to do.'

'Call Control.' Silver tucked the phone beneath his ear and reached for the remote, snapping the television on. Nothing yet. 'I will too. And don't do anything stupid.'

He rang Control; they knew already. He hung up.

His phone rang again. It was Malloy.

'You'd better get down here, Joe. It's a fucking disaster.'

An appalled Philippa stood behind him as they watched the images begin to unfurl on the television. The tickertape scrolling on the bottom of the screen 'Breaking News'; the nervous presenter, the ruined bank, the burnt bus, the smart London square now home only to distress and panic. Silver felt that familiar twist in the belly, the lurch of adrenaline that marked crisis.

'Oh dear Lord,' Philippa whispered. 'Not again.'

Eyes glued to the screen, mobile clamped to his ear, Silver watched for a moment. The buzz, the rush; what he lived for. Julie and the stinking gym and the irritation Lana caused him faded entirely. He spoke to his boss.

'I'm on my way.'

FRIDAY 14TH JULY
CLAUDIE

At Natalie's neat little house in the suburbs, Ella at least was happy to see me, demonstrating her hopping on one leg, her fair curls bouncing up and down, chunky and solid as her mother but far more cuddly.

'Good hopping,' I admired her. 'Can you do the other side?' But she couldn't really, despite gallant efforts.

'Please, Auntie C, can we play Banopoly?'

'Banopoly?' She meant Monopoly. 'Of course. I'd love to.'

'You can be the boot if you like,' she said kindly, swinging on my hand. I agreed readily, because I felt like an old boot right now, and it suited me just fine to not think about real life for a moment.

'Claudia's hurt, Ella,' Natalie said, but her heart wasn't in it. She was so transfixed by the television, by the rolling news bulletins, that she wasn't concentrating on either of us, so Ella and I sat in the kitchen, away from the television, and had orange squash and digestives as we set the Monopoly board up. In the end, I was the top hat and Ella was the dog, and I let her buy everything, especially the 'water one with the tap on' because I knew if she lost, her bottom lip would push out and she would cry. And I found if I didn't move too suddenly or dramatically, the pain in my head was just about bearable.

At twelve o'clock Natalie washed Ella's hands and face and took her round to her school nursery for the afternoon session.

'Will you be here when I get back, Auntie C?' Ella asked solemnly. 'We can watch Peter Pancake if you are.' And I smiled as best I could and said probably. She had once informed me that my complicated name was actually a man's, and she had long since stopped struggling with it.

'Of course you'll be here,' Natalie snapped, 'where else are you going to go?' and we looked at each other in a way that meant we were both acknowledging the reason why I wouldn't be anywhere else.

'And of course, we want you here,' Natalie managed a valiant finish, retying her fussy silk scarf under her chin.

As the door shut behind them, I slid open the

28

French windows and stood in the garden and tried very hard to breathe deeply like Helen had taught me. Natalie's pink and green garden was so well regimented, just like everything else in her life, that it felt stifling. The air was heavy, rain was on its way, and a strange hush seemed to have descended. Everyone staying inside and a hush that had settled over the whole city—as if we were all waiting. I felt very small suddenly; tiny, a mere dot on the London landscape.

I made myself tea and I put a lot of sugar in it, and then I tried and tried to ring Tessa, but she wasn't answering; her phone wasn't even on. No one picked up at the Academy either, so eventually I gave up, and switched on the News again.

MASSIVE EXPLOSION IN CENTRAL LONDON scrolled across the bottom of the screen, and a reporter who looked a little like a rabbit in the headlights informed viewers nervously that Berkeley Square had been hit by some kind of explosion but at the moment no one knew if it was a bomb or a gas main that had blown up. There was no more information, but then numbers were listed for those worried about friends or family; and we were all asked to stay at home.

'Do not attempt to travel in central London. As a precaution, police have shut down all public transport systems for the moment. We reiterate, it is only a precaution, but the advice is to please remain at home unless your journey is absolutely necessary,' the dark-skinned reporter warned us gravely, before throwing questions to a sweaty terrorism expert who began to hazard guesses at the cause of the explosion.

My phone rang again. This time I did answer it,

praying it was Tessa.

'Claudie. I've been so worried. What the hell's going on?' Rafe sounded furious. 'I thought you'd be here when I got back.'

'London's gone mad,' I said quietly. 'It's all exploding.'

'Never mind that—what the hell happened last night? I waited for you in the restaurant, and you never came, and then there you were, on my doorstep, frozen and practically unconscious. Were you drunk?' He was accusatory.

'No,' I replied. 'Definitely not drunk.'

'What then?'

'I can't remember, Rafe. I just—I had this terrible migraine, and then—'

'What do you mean you can't remember?'

Now was not the time to tell him about the splitting. In fact, I was realising there was never going to be a time to tell him about it. And yet, I was terrified that I was sliding backwards, back to the place I'd gone when Ned died, when my world had caved in and the nightmare became reality.

'Rafe, one thing—'

'Yes?'

'Who is she?' I stared at my bare feet. The ground beneath them was shifting again and life was not going to be the same now, I realised. My silver nail varnish was very old and chipped. I must do something about it, I thought absently.

'Who?'

'The owner of the pink toothbrush. In the bathroom cupboard.'

'No one.' There was a long pause. 'It's not what it looks like. I mean, she's just an old friend.'

'Yeah right.' I felt so tired I could hardly speak.

30

'She stays sometimes when she's in town. That's all.' He was both contrite and angry in turns, as if he hadn't quite decided the best form of defence.

'It's fine. Look, I've got to go, Rafe. It's up to you what you do.'

'Claudie—'

I hung up. I tried Tessa again. Nothing.

I was frightened. I was fighting panic. Why couldn't I remember this morning clearly? I debated ringing my psychiatrist Helen, but I wasn't sure that was a good idea. I couldn't go running to her every time something went wrong. And she might think I was deluded again, and I wasn't sure I could bear that.

I switched the News on again, the explosion still headlines, the first pictures I had seen. A bus lay on its side in hideously mangled glory, like a huge inert beast brought down by hunters. The newsreader emitted polite dismay as I stared at the pictures in horror.

'Speculation is absolutely rife in the absence of any confirmation of what exactly rocked the foundations of Berkeley Square this morning at 7.34 a.m. Immediate assumptions that it was another bomb in the vein of the 7/7 explosions five years ago are looking less likely. Local builders were working on a site to the left of the square, the adjacent corner to the Royal Ballet Academy, on a new Concorde Hotel. The site is situated above an old gas main that has previously been the subject of some concern. The Hoffman Bank has been partially destroyed; at least one security guard is thought to have been inside. So far, Scotland Yard have not yet released a statement.'

At least, thank God, the Academy seemed

31

untouched by the explosion. I tried Tessa one more time, and then Eduardo; both their phones went to voicemail now. I turned the News off and went upstairs, craving respite. I heard Natalie and Ella come in, Ella chattering nineteen to the dozen. I felt limp with exhaustion. I'd tried so hard to stay in control recently, and yet something had gone very wrong.

In the bathroom I rifled through Natalie's medicine cabinet: finding various bottles of things, I took what I hoped was a sleeping pill. I went to the magnolia-coloured spare bedroom with the matching duvet set, shut the polka-dot curtains against the rain that had just started, and invited oblivion in.

FRIDAY 14TH JULY
KENTON

Silver had insisted DS Kenton was checked out by the paramedics, but she knew that she wasn't injured, only shocked. He wanted her to go home, but Kenton wasn't sure being alone was the right thing. She kept seeing that hand in the middle of the road, bloody and raw, and the body sliced completely in two, and every time she saw it, she had to close her eyes. She felt numb and rather disconnected from reality; she sat in the station canteen nursing sweet tea and it was a little like the scene around her was a film, all the colours bright and sort of technicolour.

The person Kenton really wanted to speak to was her mother, but that was impossible. So she rang her father, but he was at the Hospice shop in town, doing his weekly shift, and he couldn't work his mobile phone properly anyway, so he kept cutting her off, until she gave up and said she'd call later. She didn't even get as far as telling him about her trauma. She drank the tea and stared at the three tea leaves floating at the bottom, and then on a whim, she rang Alison.

Alison didn't answer, so she left her a rather faltering, stumbling message.

'Hello. It's me.' Long pause. Not wanting to sound presumptuous she qualified: 'Me being Lorraine.' Oh God, now she sounded like an idiot. 'I've been in a—in the—I was there when Berkeley Square, when it exploded.'

She panicked and hung up.

On the other side of the canteen she saw Silver stroll in, as calm and unruffled as ever, his expensive navy suit immaculate, not a hair out of place. She could understand why women's eyes followed him; not particularly tall, not particularly gorgeous, perhaps, but just—assured. Commanding, somehow.

'Lorraine.' He bought himself a diet Coke from the machine behind her. 'How you feeling? Time to go home, kiddo?'

'I don't know.' Her voice was trembly. She cleared her throat. 'I keep thinking about the hand.'

'The hand?' Silver snapped the ring-pull on the can and sat opposite her.

'There was a hand,' she whispered. 'In the road. Just lying there. There were—there were other—bits.'

'Right.' He looked at her, his hooded hazel eyes kind. 'Nasty. Now, look. Go home, get one of the

33

lads to drive you if you want—and call me later. We'll have a chat. Take the weekend off. And you should think about seeing Merryweather.'

'I'm not mad,' Kenton was defensive.

'No, you're in shock. Naturally. And you did a great job, Lorraine.' His phone bleeped. 'A really great job.' He checked the message. 'Explosives officers are at the scene now. Got to go. Call me, OK?'

'OK.' She sat at the table for another few minutes. Sighing heavily she began to gather her things. Her phone rang. Her heart skipped a beat. It was Alison.

'Lorraine.' She sounded appalled. 'Oh my God. Are you OK? What happened?'

Kenton felt some kind of warmth suffuse her body. Alison had rung back. She walked towards the door, shoulders back.

'Well, you see, I was on my way to a TV briefing,' she began.

MONDAY 17TH JULY
CLAUDIE

I woke sweating, like a starfish in a pool of my own salt. A bluebottle smashed itself mercilessly between blind and window, its drone an incessant whirr into my brain. It had been a long night of terrors, the kind of night that stretches interminably as you hover between sleep and consciousness, unsure which is dream and which reality.

'Where are you? Where are you? Why are you not answering? I'm scared, Claudie, I can't do it, Claudie

34

. . .'

My heart was pounding as I tried to think where the hell I was. I tried to hold on to the last dream but it was ebbing away already, and fear was setting in. Momentarily I couldn't remember anything. Why I was here. I was meant to be somewhere else surely—I just couldn't think where.

I had spent the weekend at Natalie's, against my better judgement but practically under familial lock and key. Natalie was truly our mother's daughter, and I'd found the whole forty-eight hours almost entirely painful. She had fussed over me relentlessly, but it was also as if she could not really see me; as if she was just doing her job because she must. In between cups of tea and faux-sympathy, I'd had to speak to my mother several times, to firstly set her mind at rest and then to listen to her pontificate at length on what had *really* happened in Berkeley Square, and whether it was those 'damned Arabs' again. And all the time she'd talked, without pausing, from the shiny-floored apartment in the Algarve where she spent most of her time now, and wondering whether she should come over, 'Only the planes mightn't be safe, dear, at the moment, do you think?' I'd kept thinking of Tessa and wondering why she didn't answer her phone now.

Worse, it had poured all weekend, trapping us in the house. The highlight was Ella and the infinite games of Connect 4 we played, which obviously I lost every time. 'You're not very good, are you, Auntie C?' Ella said kindly, sucking her thumb whilst my sister scowled at her 'babyish habit'. 'Let her be, Nat,' I murmured, and then Ella let me win a single round.

The low point was—well, there was a choice,

35

actually. There had been the moment when pompous Brendan drank too much Merlot over Saturday supper and had then started to lecture me on 'time to rebuild' and 'look at life afresh' whilst Natalie had bustled around busily putting away table-mats with Georgian ladies on them into the dresser. I had glared at my sister in the hope that she might actually tell her husband to SHUT UP but she didn't; she just rolled table napkins up, sliding mine into a shiny silver ring that actually read *Guest*. So I sat trying to smile at my brother-in-law's sanctimonious face, thinking desperately of my little flat and the peace that at least reigned there. Lonely peace, perhaps, but peace nonetheless. After a while, I found that if I stared at Brendan's wine-stained mouth talking, at the tangle of teeth behind the thin top lip, beneath the nose like a fox's, I could just about block his words out. For half an hour he thought I was absorbing his sensitive advice, instead of secretly wishing that the large African figurehead they'd bought on honeymoon in the Gambia (having stepped outside the tourist compound precisely once, 'Getting back to the land, Claudie, and oh those Gambians, such a noble people, really, Claudie; having so little and yet so much. They thrive on it') would crash from the wall right now and render him unconscious.

The second low came on Sunday morning, just after I had turned down the exciting opportunity to accompany them to the local church for a spot of guitar-led happy clapping.

'Leave Ella here with me,' I offered. My head was clearer today, not as sore and much less hazy than it had felt recently. The paranoia was receding a little. 'It must be pretty boring for her, all that God stuff.'

'Oh I can't,' Natalie actually simpered. 'Not today. We have to give thanks as a family.'

'What for?' I gazed at her. She looked coy, dying to tell me something, that familiar flush spreading over her chest and up her neck and face. I looked at her bosom that was more voluptuous than normal and her sparkling eyes and I realised.

'You're pregnant,' I said slowly.

'Oh. Yes,' and she was almost disappointed that she hadn't got to announce it, but she was obviously wrestling with guilt too. 'Are you OK with that?'

'Of course. Why wouldn't I be?' I moved forward to hug her dutifully. 'I'm really pleased for you.'

Natalie grabbed my hands and pushed me away from her so she could search my face earnestly. 'You know why. It must be so hard for you.' A little tear had gathered in the corner of one of her bovine brown eyes. 'I—I'd like you to be godmother though,' she murmured, as if she was bestowing a great gift. 'It might, you know. Help.'

'Great,' I smiled mechanically. And I was pleased for her, of course I was, but nothing helped, least of all this, though she was well-intentioned; and I knew it was impossible for anyone else to understand me. I was trapped in my own distant land, very far from shore; I'd been there since Ned closed his eyes for the last time and slipped quietly from me. 'Thank you.' And I hugged her again, just so I didn't have to look at the pity scrawled across her face.

'If it's a boy,' she started to say, 'we might call him—'

I heard an imaginary phone ringing in my room upstairs. 'Sorry, Nat. Better get it, just in case—' I disappeared before she could finish.

Whilst they were at church, I gathered my few bits and pieces and wrote her a note. I was truly sorry to leave Ella, I loved spending time with her, but I needed to be home now. I needed to be far, far away from my well-meaning sister and the suffocating little nest she called home.

And so here I lay, alone again. In the next room, the phone rang and I heard a calm voice say *'Leave us messages, please.'*

My voice, apparently; swiftly followed by another—male, low. Concerned. I attempted to roll out of bed, but moving hurt so much I emitted a strange 'ouf' noise, like the air being pushed from a ball. I lay still, blinded by pain, my ribs still agony from where I'd apparently fallen on Friday. When it subsided, I tried again. Wincing, I stumbled into the other room, snatched the receiver up.

'Hello?'

'You're all right.' The accented voice was relieved. 'Thank God.'

'Who—who is this?' I caught my reflection in the mirror. Round-eyed, black-shadowed; face scraped like a child's. My bare feet sank into the sheepskin rug I hated.

'Claudie. It's Eduardo. I didn't know if you'd be there. Your sister called. I thought you might be away.'

'Away?' My brow knitted in concentration. 'Eduardo.' I made a concerted effort. Eduardo was head of the Academy. In my mind I conjured up an office, papers stacked high, a man in a grey cashmere v-neck, big hands, dark-haired, moving the paperweight, restacking those papers. 'Oh, Eduardo.' I sat heavily on the sofa. 'No, I'm here. Sorry. I think I—I find it hard to wake up

38

sometimes.'

I had got used to a little help recently, the kind of pharmaceutical help I could accept without complication.

'I'm ringing round everyone to check. You've obviously heard what has happened?'

'About the explosion? Yes,' my hands clenched unconsciously. 'Awful.'

'Awful,' he agreed. 'They have only just let us back into the school. But—well, it's worse than awful, Claudie, I'm afraid.' I heard his inhalation. 'There is some very bad news.'

Bad news, bad news. Like a nasty refrain. I stood very quickly, holding my hands in front of me as if warding something off.

'I'm sorry.' I sensed his sudden hesitation. 'I should have thought. Stupid.' He'd be banging his own head with the heel of his hand, the dramatic Latino. 'My dear girl—'

'It's OK.' I leant against the wall. 'Just tell me, please.'

'It's Tessa.'

'Tessa?' My cracked hands were itching.

Tessa, with her slight limp and her benign face, her hair pulled back so tight. My friend Tessa who had somehow seen me through the past year; with whom I had bonded so strongly through our shared sense of loss. My skin prickled as if someone was scraping me with sandpaper.

'Tessa's dead, Claudie. I'm so sorry to have to tell you.'

Absently, I saw that my hand was bleeding, dripping gently onto the cream rug.

Emboldened by my silence, he went on. 'Tessa was killed outside the Academy. Outright.' He

39

paused. 'She wouldn't have known anything, chicita.'

'She wouldn't have known anything,' I repeated stupidly. My world was closing to a pin-point, black shadows and ghosts fighting for space in my brain.

'I'm so sorry to have had to tell you,' he said, and sighed again. 'I am just pleased for you that you are not here this week. It is a very bad atmosphere. I think it's good your sister has arranged for you to have this time off.' I hadn't had much choice in the matter: Natalie had taken over. 'Try to rest, my dear. See you soon.'

Tessa was dead. Outside the birds still sang; somewhere nearby a child laughed, shrieked, then laughed again. The rain had stopped. Someone else was playing The Beatles, *Lucy in the Sky with Diamonds*; Lennon's voice floated through the warm morning, like dust motes on dusk sunshine. Death was in the room again. I closed my eyes against the cruel world, a world that kept on turning nonetheless, a sob forming in my throat. I imagined myself now, stepping off the bus, fumbling with the clasp of my bag, raising my hand in greeting, happy to see her . . .

The birds still sang, but my friend Tessa was dead—and I couldn't help feeling I should have saved her.

TUESDAY 18TH JULY
SILVER

7 a.m., and Silver was exhausted already. It had been a horrendous weekend; the worst kind of police work. Counting the dead, identifying and naming the corpses: or rather, what was left of them. Recrimination and finger-pointing and statistics that meant nothing. Contacting the families, working alongside the belligerent and somewhat over-sensitive Counter Terrorist Branch; waiting for the Explosives Officers who were struggling due to the amount of debris caused by the Hoffman Bank partially collapsing, hampered by torrential rain all weekend.

Images stuck to the whiteboards at the end of the office made him wince; the carnage, the tangle of metal, strewn rubber, clothing, the covered dead and the walking wounded. The life-affirming sight of human helping human—only wasn't it a little late? Too late to make a difference: one human had hated another enough to do this—possibly . . . A gas leak was still being mooted, but Silver knew the drill, knew this was to prevent panic spreading through the city, another 7/7, another 9/11, the stoic Londoner weary of it all already. The Asians fed up of ever-wary eyes, the Counter Terrorist Branch overworked and frankly baffled. How *do* you keep tabs on invisible evil that could snake amongst us unseen? Silver was hanged if he knew.

He yawned and stretched as fully as his desk allowed. That bastard Beer was calling him, whispering lovingly in his ear over and again. He

41

needed a long cold pint, smooth as liquid gold down his thirsty aching throat. He swore softly and checked the change in his pocket. Out in the corridor, he bought himself his fifth diet Coke of the night and unwrapped another packet of Orbit. Distractions. He wished he felt fresher, more alert, but he felt tired and rather useless. However much he preferred work to home, he wished himself there now, asleep, oblivious to the world's inequities. Leaning against the wall wearily, he drank half the can in one go.

Craven popped his balding head out of the office. 'Your wife's on the phone.'

'Ex-wife,' Silver said mechanically.

In an exercise of male camaraderie, Craven grimaced. 'Sorry. Ex-wife.'

Silver checked his expensive Breitling watch. Following Craven, he leant over the desk for the receiver. It was early even for her.

'Lana?'

There was a long silence. He rolled his eyes; he thought he heard a sniff. Lana never cried.

'What is it, kiddo?' he tried kindness. He had ignored so many things recently, he was stamping all over his 'emotional intelligence' apparently; the intelligence they'd been lectured on recently at conference.

'Don't call me that, Joe,' Lana snapped. 'It drives me bloody mad.'

Some things never changed. And he didn't have time for emotional intelligence anyway. He relied on gut instinct.

'Sorry.' He almost grinned. 'What is it, Allana?'

'I saw her on the News.'

The hairs on his arms stood up. Not this again.

42

'I couldn't sleep so I got up. It was GMTV,' she was breathless and angry. 'She was just there, smiling. A photo. I saw her, Joe.'

He'd thought they were through this. 'Don't be daft, Lana.' Through, and out the other side. He dropped his voice to little more than a whisper. 'We've been over this a million times.' Persuasive, comforting. 'It's not her. It can't be.'

'On the News. I was watching about the bomb.'

'Explosion,' again, he corrected automatically.

'Explosion. Whatever.' Her distress was palpable. 'They had a separate item about missing kids. She's a dancer. I saw her face.'

'Whose face?' He knew who; but he needed her to say it, needed to hear the name.

A gulp, as if she were swallowing air. 'Jaime. Jaime Malvern.'

'Lana. Are you drunk?'

'Nooo,' the vowel was a long hiss, drawn-out. 'I am stone cold sober, Joseph. But it's her. As sure as eggs is eggs.'

They used to laugh at that expression. They used to lie in bed, legs intertwined, and do all the egg expressions: 'Eggs in one basket, don't count your chicken eggs.' They were young, they were in love. They thought they were hilarious. 'Teach your grandmother to suck eggs.'

Neither of them was laughing now.

'Lana. It can't be Jaime, you know that. She's dead, kid—sweetheart. She's been dead a long time now.'

'I know,' she howled, and the pain in her voice pierced him in the old way. 'I know she's bloody dead, Joe.'

Of course she did. Of course Lana knew this

43

better than anyone.

'But I saw her, Joe. I'm not mad, and I'm not drunk. Not yet anyway. I saw her.'

He stood now. 'Lana. Don't. You've done so well.'

But she'd gone. He was talking to the air.

*   *   *

Silver didn't believe his ex-wife's claims that she'd seen Jaime; he'd heard it a million times before. Allana had been haunted by Jaime's face every day for six years, obsessed since the accident—since the afternoon that changed their lives forever. The afternoon that ruined Lana irrevocably and finished Jaime's forever.

Silver had tried his damnedest to bring his wife back to the present, tried and failed; he'd grown used to Allana's distress and his own guilt. He'd attempted every tactic: therapy, rehab and finally anger, until eventually he knew she was beyond reach. He mourned his lost love—for too long; until finally the mourning turned to indifference as he accepted he could no longer connect. No one could really pierce that layer of pain; not even her own children.

Silver hung up the phone feeling weary of battle. Tired and flat, he was ready for his bed—but something nagged at him. Draining the final backwash of diet Coke and crunching the can in one hand, he sat at the computer and quickly scrolled through the gallery of faces that flashed up. First the missing from the explosion: a photo album of mostly smiling anonymity, gathered quickly by frenetic journalists, posing for graduation, wedding, family snaps. Mothers, sons, nieces, nephews. Many of the families still waiting for their worst fears to be confirmed. The mess that is identifying devastated bodies after fatal accidents. Fourteen dead; the death toll still rising.

He called up the general Missing folder. Nothing. Allana was mad as ever. Not mad, he corrected himself; obsessed. Yawning until his jaw ached, Silver reached the final screen—and then—on a separate page, that face.

With a violent stab of recognition, he clicked back; pulled her up to full-screen. Slightly blurred: pretty little heart-shape, vulnerable baby face— and yet oddly tough too. Long blonde curls, widely spaced light eyes, blue maybe, too knowing for their years. Leaning into another darker girl whose face had been cropped off.

Christ.

Lana *was* right. He felt a finger of cold horror hook the back of his collar. She looked just like Jaime Malvern. But she couldn't possibly be. Jaime was long dead. Who then was this girl? A doppelganger?

A ghost . . .

TUESDAY 18TH JULY
CLAUDIE

Someone woke me, banging at the door, banging and banging until I let them in. I was so groggy I could hardly see; looking at the face on my doorstep out of one sticky eye.

Francis.

'You didn't come last night,' he said, 'and then I heard about Tessa, poor angel. Mason called.'

Bloody Mason. I bet she couldn't wait to spread the news.

'So I came to you. I brought chai.'

He walked past me into the flat, his thermos of tea wafting fragrant scent into my living room. But I was a little perturbed. He'd never been here. *Why* was he here? Had I arranged it, and forgotten this too?

On Monday, after Eduardo's call, I had gone back to bed and hidden. I couldn't move, couldn't function. I lay on the bed, on top of the duvet, entirely still, until I slept again. I dreamt of Tessa. I dreamt of Ned. I feared I was going down again. I had this overriding feeling I should have saved Tessa. I couldn't save my son—but I could have saved my friend. What had she been so scared of? I kept thinking of the lost hours before Rafe's; the thoughts went round and round until I felt like screaming.

'It's not good to break the treatments,' Francis said now, perusing the room. 'Let me pour you tea, and then lie on the sofa and relax. I brought my needles.'

Francis was the acupuncturist and hypnotist Tessa had introduced me to when I fell off the smoking wagon; when I couldn't sleep after Will left, when the migraines got so bad. I was a mess. I'd been a mess since Ned. 'He's amazing, Claudie, really; he has the hands of a genius,' Tessa said, and so I gave it a go. Actually, I suspected Tessa was slightly in love with him, although she'd never confessed as much. She'd met him on a yoga retreat in the Cotswolds last year, I thought, and extolled his virtues ever since; in the way people who are falling in love want to use the name of their newly beloved all the time, so did she, only I feared her love was not reciprocated. Still, half the staff at the Academy were now using Francis, including a once-sceptical Mason, so Tessa's enthusiasm had done him no harm.

Francis was certainly a unique individual; dark hair with a mullet and a deeply cared-for goatee beard, black discs in his tribally pierced ears, a shark tooth round his neck but pushing fifty, I suspected. He was friendly and empathetic, but I couldn't for one moment see the sexual appeal Tessa obviously did, though his needles undoubtedly worked.

I drank a little of his revolting tea out of courtesy and took my jewellery off first as Francis always requested. He believed the metal interfered with my chakras and who was I to argue? I hardly knew what a chakra was. And perhaps the acupuncture would help clear my head now. I put my necklace on the sideboard and lay down on the sofa.

'You're not wearing a nicotine patch are you?' he murmured as he measured my arm with his own hand, and inserted two needles near my elbow.

'No,' I shook my head.

'Good girl.' Francis chose another needle from his little box, and jabbed suddenly. A searing pain shot through my wrist.

'Ouch!' That had never happened before.

Francis looked troubled and took the needle out. I thought his hand was shaking a little.

'I'm so sorry, Claudia.' He stroked his beard. 'My own energy is a little depleted today, I fear.'

'No worries,' I said, but I was nervous now.

He took a fresh needle and jabbed again—and the same searing pain shot through me.

'Ow!'

He stared down at me, needle in hand, and I gazed back at him with apprehension. 'Why's that happening?' I asked anxiously, looking at the spot of blood welling from my wrist.

'I'm not sure. It could be hitting a chi path, 'specially if you're feeling unwell.' He stroked his beard again until it began to look pointed. 'Something feels off kilter to me.'

My vague headache was taking a more severe hold and suddenly I felt violently ill. He was an alien presence, smelling so sickly of patchouli and lavender; and the stupid whale music he'd put on in the background seemed unbearable now.

'Can you take them out?' Panic was building in my chest. I was going back to a place I never wanted to revisit. 'The needles. I really would like you to—'

'Of course, Claudia. Be still for a moment.' He removed the first two needles as I tried desperately to calm my breathing.

'I'm so sorry,' Francis shook his head, melancholy now. 'This so rarely happens. And it is inexcusable if it is my fault. But as I say,' he held his hands above my head now, not touching me, just hovering over my hair, 'as I say, if you are poorly, then your paths can get so blocked that it causes pain. And I do feel a blockage.'

'Right.' I stood now, wishing his hands far away from me. 'I need to go out now. Thank you for coming.' I walked to the front door; held it open. 'It was very kind.'

'Something is not right, Claudia.' He stepped

48

through the door, gazing at me. 'I sense it in your system. Is there anything you've changed? Your diet maybe, or—'

'No,' I almost shouted. 'Nothing. Really.'

'And I did want to talk about Tessa with you. To celebrate her spirit—'

'Another time, OK?' I shut the door firmly and leant against it, my heart thumping painfully.

What was happening to me?

*   *   *

Tessa had fitted no mould. Unconventional; gentle but outspoken, it was as if she had been born in the wrong era, out of her time. Push her back through the decades by forty years, and it would have seemed right. She revelled in beauty; the whiteness and the thread count of a tablecloth; the cylindrical shape of a water glass; Grace Kelly's frocks. She dressed simply, in silks and cottons more expensive than my rent. The way she pulled her hair up and back was reminiscent of Margot Fonteyn or Lynn Seymour, not of the dancers' styles today. She was anachronistic, misplaced—and hiding some deep hurt.

We'd met on her first day at the Academy. I was just back from compassionate leave, unsure if I could now hold down a job. I had retreated into myself wholly. I absorbed myself in work as best I could, but I was still raw as butcher's meat on the block.

That morning during a break I had found the staffroom empty and I'd hunched into the corner chair, restraining myself from running; desperately repeating the mantras I had been taught, which were apparently meant to see me through the times of despair.

Tessa burst in, her long black skirt trailing dramatically, her spotted hairband wrapped tight round her fair hair. She exuded excitement.

'Coffee?' she offered, resting her walking stick in the corner whilst she wrestled with the jar of Nescafé. I indicated my full mug.

'Thanks, I'm OK.' I bit back the tears that had been threatening to fall.

'Tessa Lethbridge, new from Melbourne.' She poured the boiling water into her polystyrene cup. 'God, the sense of history in this place. I can't believe I'm actually here—er—'

I looked at her. She was waiting for me to tell her my name, I realised. I met her eyes, and they were kind.

'Claudie. Claudie Scott. I'm one of the physios.'

'Well, Claudie Scott, the sense of heritage and beauty in this building, my God,' she whistled low and long. She sounded so much more Australian then. 'We are privileged beyond belief, aren't we?'

'I guess so.' I had never really looked at it like that.

'You English. You don't know you're born half the time. I mean, look at this place, just look, Claudie, and give thanks.'

I just gazed at her. She looked back, frowning slightly now.

'Sorry. Are you OK?' She swiped up her cup now and sat in the chair beside me.

'Yes.' I nodded my head. The tears fell. I despised myself. 'No. I don't know.'

'Oh, Christ.' She pulled her chair nearer. 'Me and my big mouth. There's me all revved up and you're

50

crying in the corner. Wanna share?'

'If you don't mind,' I wiped away the tears, 'not really right now.' I looked at her face, so worried now, and I tried to smile. 'But thank you.'

But there was something about Tessa that did make me want to share, and eventually I did. An openness we uptight British lacked, perhaps, a warmth, or just a basic human instinct for being there, and it drew me to her until we forged a proper friendship. We ate lunch in small brasseries down the side streets; we talked of ballet and books and, sometimes, old boyfriends. We both liked Jean-Luc Godard and Tati; we cooked from Elizabeth David. We went to the ballet—our favourite busman's holiday, or to watch French films; inevitably I forgot my glasses. We didn't talk family often; it was unspoken and safely off-limits most of the time, but after a while, I discovered that she too had lost a child; two in fact, when her only pregnancy ended in early tragedy, and it led to a strong bond. We both had huge holes in our lives that needed filling, but we let them lie quietly beside us. Tessa, with her limp and her stick; her passion bubbling below a benign surface; with a love of ballet more intense than any I'd ever known before.

It was Tessa who I'd come to depend on in the darkest, bleakest hours. It was Tessa who had encouraged me to listen to my heart when my husband Will left, to not follow him to a place I didn't belong. It was Tessa who had found me Francis when I couldn't sleep. It was Tessa who knew what loss was like; it was Tessa who answered the phone in the middle of the night when I felt I couldn't wake my oldest friends any more, though I saw her a little less once Rafe was around.

It was Tessa who had gone now. Dead.

It was I who, once again, was left behind. Who couldn't help fearing that in some way, I had helped her to her death. I clutched the necklace she'd bought me; I racked my brain. If only I could remember why. And if only I knew *why* I couldn't remember . . .

TUESDAY 18TH JULY
KENTON

Silver had insisted she take the weekend off, but by Monday night, Kenton had been champing at the bit to get back to work. The horrific images had begun to fade a little, and she had listened to Alison's calming tape at least five times until frankly, she thought the images were probably increasing manifold in her supposedly relaxed mind. Severed limbs and the like strewn across the 'safe place' of her childhood, a long beach in Dorset with good fossils and an ice-cream van selling cider lollies on the cliff. It had been difficult keeping busy with not much to do.

On Saturday she had driven down to see her father in Kent, who had worried her rather by referring to her at least twice during the visit as 'Lilian', which had been her late mother's name. She had taken him to Waitrose, which was a real treat in her eyes. She had picked up some lovely ginger cordial and a fantastic Beef Wellington—but Dad had just grumbled that it wasn't what he was used to, and then grew apoplectic about the prices, so in the end she had given up and taken him down to Aldi.

On Sunday the rain had been Biblical, as her mother would have said, and Alison came over for lunch: Beef Wellington, green beans and lumpy mash. Cooking really wasn't Kenton's forte, but Alison had been nice about it all, even about the sticky toffee pudding, which had more stick than toffee and had been impossible to get off the bloody pan for days after; the custard that was in turn both liquid and powder. Kenton had kept sneaking looks at Alison's pretty round face, slightly troubled now as one dark curl caught in the zip of her borrowed cagoule, as they had prepared to walk along the canal after lunch.

'Here, let me,' Kenton had said, and she had been both nervous and exhilarated as she helped free her hair, and she had wanted to stroke Alison's face. Her skin was like alabaster, her mum would have said, and Kenton had wondered for the tenth time that day what Alison saw in her, in her own pleasant blunt-nosed face that no one could ever call pretty. Alison had slipped her hand into Kenton's and Kenton had felt a kind of pride that she hadn't for years, since Diana Grills had kissed her behind the science block after the Sixth Form disco. Before Diana had blanked her and got off with Tony Hall half an hour later, leaving her broken-hearted for the first but not the last time in her life.

'How are you feeling?' Alison had asked, and Kenton had grinned and said, 'Happy.'

'That's nice,' Alison had smiled too, but then looked more serious and said, 'But I meant about work. You know. The bad dreams.'

'All right,' Kenton had became gruff. She didn't

like to show her weak side.

'It's OK to be freaked out,' Alison had said gently, and she'd held Kenton's hand tighter, as if she could feel that Kenton had been about to relinquish hers. 'We can talk about it if you like.'

'It's just part of the job,' Kenton had said, and Alison nodded, and said, 'Yes I can see that.'

There'd been a pause. Then two Canadian geese had flown overhead in perfect symmetry; they wheeled and turned course together over the rooftops.

'Amazing,' Kenton had shaken her head. 'How does one know where the other is about to go?'

'Not sure,' Alison had looked up into the sky. 'Synchronicity, I guess.'

They had walked on in silence for a bit.

'I'm going back tomorrow,' Kenton had said eventually. 'Or Tuesday. See how I feel.'

'You do that,' Alison had said, and squeezed Kenton's hand.

*　　　*　　　*

And so, by 8.15 a.m. on a damp Tuesday morning, Kenton was back at her desk, papers stacked neatly. Not exactly raring to go, perhaps, but looking forward to putting the trauma behind her, and getting on with the case. She had been in Berkeley Square herself; now it was of paramount importance to find the culprit and lay it to rest.

TUESDAY 18TH JULY
CLAUDIE

I switched off the landline, so they rang my mobile instead.

Natalie first. I didn't answer the phone.

I tried Tessa's number. Just in case. Just in case it was all a big mistake, I tried it. Nothing.

I lay on the sofa. I stared at the ceiling.

Rafe rang. He was at the House of Commons; he sounded pretty keen to hear from me, but I didn't answer the call. I wasn't sure what I wanted to say yet. I couldn't help feeling like I'd been a challenge to him and he didn't want to admit defeat.

I got up again and ate some stale Jammy Dodgers. I threw a dead spider plant away I'd always disliked. Its dead leaves trailed from the bin like fingers.

I tried Tessa again. The silence was deafening.

I paced the flat. I had that feeling again that someone was watching me from the corner of the room. I was fighting the paranoia and the memories of what had happened so dramatically to me when Ned died. I *had* to find an answer to this mess.

Helen rang. 'Call me, Claudie, please. I'm worried. You've missed an appointment.'

I looked at my photos, I turned the big one of Ned back up again. Sometimes it hurt too much to look at him, but now I stared into his laughing eyes. What should I do?

My head was beginning to ache again; I was becoming my headache. Why couldn't I remember Friday morning?

55

Listened to the rain outside. Got dressed, turned on the television.

There was yet another news conference taking place, headed by the Commissioner of the Police; blindly I stared at it. Next to him sat a bullet-headed man with the bluest eyes, grim-faced, glaring at the cameras, and beside him a gently weeping woman, face in her hands, and a plain middle-aged man wearing gold-rimmed glasses and an expensive but nondescript suit, his receding grey hair pushed back, talking about the Hoffman Bank and how they would rebuild despite the tragedy. After a while, the Commissioner stopped talking and the bullet-headed policeman called Malloy was asking for the public's cooperation as confirmation was still awaited re bomb or explosion, and our patience whilst they worked on the difficult task of identifying the missing and wounded as quickly as possible. Once again help-line numbers were flashed up.

An unsmiling photo of Tessa floated behind the man's head.

'One of the confirmed dead was ballet teacher Tessa Lethbridge,' the bullet-headed man said vehemently. 'We need these deaths not to go unmarked. If you know anything at all about the events of Friday morning, if you saw anything, were in the area, please, don't hesitate to get in touch. You will be doing your public duty.'

Now the weeping woman began to talk about her missing brother. I turned the television off, rubbed my aching head fretfully. Fear was building in me until I felt like I might explode. I banged my head desperately with my flattened palms, palms that were itching desperately, the eczema flaring again.

Why could I not remember? Why did I feel like I had done something very bad?

I returned to the sofa. The sun set over the rooftops, sliding into cloud, tingeing the sky with a pink luminescence. I felt an ache like a hard stone in my belly. I couldn't cry any more. Something was very wrong and I didn't know what. Tessa was slipping into the darkness, and she didn't belong there.

TUESDAY 18TH JULY
SILVER

Silver had stared at the girl's face for what seemed like an age, and then called up her name. With a flash of relief he saw that it wasn't Jaime Malvern. *Misty Jones, 20*, the name read. The girl Malloy had bumped Bobby Elwood for; reported missing at the end of last week, just before the explosion by a worried flatmate and friend, Lucie Duffy. No other details yet. He sat behind the desk, head in hands, trying to laugh at himself. Ridiculous to think it could have been her.

Silver had debated calling Lana and reassuring her—but he didn't; he simply couldn't face it now. He clocked off; glad to see Kenton back at her desk, brave lass, and then fought his way through the traffic wondering for the thousandth time why exactly all Londoners seemed so imbued with rage, glowering and swearing in their vehicles. Silver put on his CD of Duke Ellington and managed to maintain his calm by imagining his kids on the beach in Corfu. At a set of lights, he pulled up next to an elderly Rastafarian swaying to music by Burning Spear, crumpled spliff in hand. He smiled politely at Silver, his beard grizzled against his darker skin. Silver nodded back.

In the lively house in New Cross that was presently home, Silver retreated to his attic room and ate a bowl of cornflakes sitting on the bed. He slid his boots off and lay down on the chintzy bedspread, fully clothed, sick with tiredness, thanking God most of his landlady's noisy tribe were out.

When Silver had first come to London three years ago, when Lana had fully recovered, he'd stayed in the Section House nearest the station. But he'd found the boxy little room and the cool anonymity depressing after the noise of a large family home, and when one of his constables moved out of Philippa's, Silver took over the large attic room as an experiment. He'd been expecting to stay for a few months at most, but somehow, a year or so later, here he still was. It was cheap and predominantly cheerful; Philippa cooked for him, which meant his tolerance of chilli pepper was impressive now; plus living here meant he could afford the small cottage at the base of the Pennines that sat empty for ten months of the year; that he planned to make home one of these days. Before too long, he told himself. For now, he felt comfortable where he was.

But tonight there was no rest to be had. Each time he shut his eyes, Jaime's face floated in the ether, her name whispering through the red blood that thumped in his ears.

He dozed for a fitful hour and then he was back up again. It was dark now and he could hear the younger children below, the jolly and incessant jingle of the Wii. He called Craven.

'Any news?'

'Nope. None of the Islam-a-twats are holding their hands up—yet, anyhow. Fucking monkeys.'

'No call for that, is there, Derek?' Silver said lightly. 'Need a favour, actually.' It pained him to even ask.

A sigh. 'Go on.'

'I need some details on a missing person. Girl called Misty Jones.'

'*Misty* Jones? As in Clint?'

'Clint?' Silver switched the kettle that lived on the table in the corner of his room, and wiped the surface down. It was spotless already, but he wiped it anyway.

'Eastwood. *Play Misty For Me.*'

'Oh right.' He pulled the coffee off the tray. 'I'm not a big Western fan personally.'

'Not a Western. More—creepy. About a bunny boiler with big tits, I seem to remember. Anyway,' Craven ate something noisy down Silver's ear. Crisps, by the sounds of it. 'Misty. Kind of a made-up name, don't you think?'

'Maybe.' He didn't want her to be made-up: she *had* to be Misty. Flesh and blood and real; nothing to do with Jaime. 'That's what I need to find out.'

'I'll have a dig around.' Craven finished whatever he was eating with relish. Was the man actually licking his fingers? 'Get back to you as-ap.' He pronounced it as two words. Irritating. He did irritate Silver, a lot. All faux-jollity, resentment and latent bigotry, big belly spilling over a thin crocodile-skin belt.

'Cheers, pal.' Silver hung up. His emotional

intelligence might be out of kilter, but his gut instinct was working hard now at least. He had tried to convince himself all afternoon that things were all right—but he knew deep down something was definitely wrong.

TUESDAY 18TH JULY
CLAUDIE

In the evening, I managed to open the front door to my best friend Zoe. Good old Natalie had rung her, and despite all my best protestations she had been insistent that she'd cook paella and sit with me tonight. Zoe had a new Spanish boyfriend called Pablo and was learning Spanish cuisine for his benefit, which was infinitely preferable to the toasted cheese sandwiches she normally lived on. She arrived at six in her latest incarnation—Zoe was the eternal chameleon when it came to men—Capri pants immaculate, ingredients spilling out of the wicker basket she lugged up to the flat, neat auburn ponytail and gold hoops swinging from her ears as she unpacked her wares, black eyeliner flicked above her watchful eyes. We drank white Rioja and didn't talk about the explosion, apart from the plaster on my cheek. We talked about love; she was thinking of moving to Barcelona to be with Pablo.

'Hmm,' I mused. 'It means your babies will play for Barca and not Man U. Your dad will be devastated.'

'My mum will be relieved, that's all I know. She knows my clock is ticking.' She shot me a quick look.

60

'It's fine, Zoe,' I murmured, staring into my cloudy glass. 'Don't worry about it.'

'So,' she said brightly, 'how's it going with that nice Rafe guy? Will you be moving into Number 10 together soon?'

'It's not going.'

She stared at me.

'Are you joking?'

'No.'

'I thought he was good for you.' She looked so disappointed, I almost felt guilty. 'And so bloody successful.'

'*Good* for me?' I drained my drink. 'Like Vitamin C or broccoli?' I thought of Francis's botched attempt earlier at making me feel better. I thought about my new fears that the disassociation I'd experienced after Ned's death was returning. I wondered whether to mention it to my oldest friend.

'You know what I mean.'

'Do I?' I stood to stack the plates.

'Don't be difficult, Claudia.'

'I'm not, really. It's just—it's meant to be love, not—not health.'

Zoe gazed at me until I felt uncomfortable. 'And it's not love?'

'No. It was company. And I'm fine on my own.' Though I had definitely felt a little more protected since I'd met Rafe. I pushed that thought away.

'Are you?' She stared at me until I nearly squirmed.

'Yes. Even though I did quite fancy opening the door in my nightie on Election Day.' I chucked a prawn shell in the bin. 'I'd have made sure I got my hair done first though.'

61

We gazed at each other for a moment and then began to laugh, almost hysterically, so I had to sit down again and catch my breath.

'It's not funny,' I gasped in the end.

'No, it's not.' Zoe wiped her eyes with some kitchen roll. 'And you could do with a good haircut actually. You do look a bit—dishevelled at the moment. Slightly—Worzel Gummidge.'

'Oh thanks a lot.' She was revving up for a lecture, I could tell. I changed the subject. 'It's just—it was all wrong. Me and Rafe. I think he's been seeing someone else, anyway.' I stood again.

'Really?' she frowned.

'Yes. And the funny thing is,' I considered it for a moment, 'I couldn't really care less.'

'That's what worries me.'

'I mean, he's nice and everything, but—'

'But he wasn't Will,' she finished for me.

I plonked the plates into the sink.

'I heard he's back you know,' she said, and I felt ice in my belly. 'Will, I mean.'

'Did you?' I said casually. I hadn't. I was still furious with him.

'Claudie,' Zoe looked at me all seriously, her dark eyes almost beseeching, 'I really think it would be a good idea to—'

The phone rang and I snatched it up gratefully. It was a policewoman called DS Lorraine Kenton from Holborn.

'We have some routine enquiries following the death of your colleague Tessa Lethbridge.'

I felt the cold kick of guilt and sorrow again.

'Is there a suitable time we could meet please? Where will you be tomorrow or Thursday? It won't take long.'

Unnerved, we arranged a time and place and I hung up the phone. Zoe had busied herself in the kitchen and was manfully grating nutmeg over baked peaches, her middle knuckle bleeding into the sauce.

'Ouch! What I was going to say about Will was—'

The phone rang again.

'Blimey, you're popular,' she glared at me as if I had arranged the call to stop her probing.

'It'll be that policewoman wanting to move the time.'

But it wasn't.

'Claudia,' the voice said, and I wasn't sure I recognised it. It was low and threatening, angry even. 'If you are there, you know you shouldn't be. Time is running out.'

They hung up before I could reply.

*   *   *

With shaking hands, I tried to call the number back, but of course it was barred.

'Who was that?' Zoe asked, and I stared at her stupidly. Behind her the sky was melting into darkness.

'Some complete nutter,' I tried to joke but it didn't seem very funny.

'Are you OK?' She peered at me, running hot water into the sink. 'You've gone terribly white.'

That voice. I'd heard it in my dreams.

'Yes I'm fine. I'm just going to wash my hands.'

I went in to the bathroom and leant my hot head against the cool bathroom tiles. *Did* I know that voice? It was probably someone just winding me up. My hands were trembling as I looked through the

63

little basket on the shelf for my pills. What would Helen say? Breathe deep, breathe into the panic.

I held on to the basin, and looked into the mirror, shocked at the sight of me. My shoulder-length hair was unbrushed and rather like hay with roots; my eyes seemed a darker brown than normal, black almost, and slightly wild. Half my face was still hidden beneath a great plaster; I slowly peeled it off. The dirty marks from the tape made me look like a panda and my skin beneath the dressing was almost translucent. I stared at myself, trying to come back to the moment. I had the strange sensation I should be going somewhere right now. I shook my head and swallowed the pills, scooping water from the tap like a man in a desert.

Zoe was calling me from the other room.

'Claudie. Listen. They're saying someone has taken responsibility for the explosion.'

She'd switched the radio on whilst she did the washing-up; the Northern tones of the presenter were crisp and precise as he announced:

'We can reveal that earlier today a letter was sent to the BBC claiming the explosion in Berkeley Square was entirely deliberate and down to their organisation, although no names were given. However, the package contained a banner that read DAUGHTERS OF LIGHT: FOR PURITY. New Scotland Yard have refused to comment at this juncture, saying only that they receive many numbers of false claims every day.'

'Sounds pretty far-fetched to me.' Zoe pulled the plug out with a resounding squelch. 'Daughters of Light, my arse; creating mayhem and killing everyone.' She dried her hands on the oven gloves for want of anything better. 'I'd better get going, darling, if you'll be all right? Said I'd Skype Pablo later.'

'I'm fine,' I mumbled. I looked down, clenched my fists, then unclenched them. I forced myself to speak. 'Actually, I'm—I'm a bit scared, Zoe.'

'Why?' She stepped closer, peering into my face as if she could read my thoughts that way.

'I think—' I took a deep breath, 'I'm worried it's happening again.'

'What's happening?' She took my hands in hers, her neat little nose slightly wrinkled with worry.

'The splitting. I'm worried—' I tried to smile. 'I'm worried that I'm having—an episode.'

'Like last time? I thought it was under control now?'

'So did I.' I freed my hands and busied myself with the dishwasher for a moment. Zoe waited patiently. 'It sort of feels like that, but different.'

'What does?' I could sense her struggling to understand. 'Tell me.'

'It's like—I had this weird thing last week. I found myself at Rafe's and I—the thing is, I couldn't remember how I'd got there.'

'Have you told the doctors?'

I shook my head vehemently. 'No. I don't want to get locked up again. I'm not mad, Zoe, I know I'm not.'

'Of course you're not,' she soothed me like a child.

'But why can't I remember?' I frowned at her. 'I know that the day before the explosion Tessa was panicked—'

'Oh, bloody Tessa.' Zoe had never gelled with Tessa, and I'd secretly always wondered if she was a little jealous of our friendship. 'I mean, I'm sorry

65

she's dead—but she was a loose cannon, Claudie.'

'A loose cannon?'

'I don't know. Maybe that's harsh. But there was something not quite right about her, if you ask me.'

Which I hadn't.

'But she was trying to tell me something, Zoe, and I don't know what. And then the explosion. I was in town and yet, it's just so confused in my head.'

'You'll be telling me next that you did it,' she joked.

I stared at her.

'Claudie,' there was an urgent note suddenly in Zoe's voice. 'You didn't do it, for God's sake. That was a joke. Not a very good one, admittedly.'

'I know,' I tried that smile again. 'But something's wrong somewhere.'

'Look, perhaps you *should* see the doctors again.' Zoe's phone bleeped. 'Tell them you're worried.'

'Perhaps.' There was no way I was admitting this to the doctors. And anyway, confused as I felt, I knew this was not *exactly* the same as last time.

Zoe checked her message. 'Pablo,' she grinned ruefully, her face lighting up.

'Ah, young love. Don't let me keep you from Skype.'

'If I can still speak after all the vino. My Spanish is still crap, though my swear words are coming on a storm.'

At the door, Zoe swung her wicker basket onto her arm like Little Red Riding Hood—though I imagined it was more Penélope Cruz she was channelling.

'Let me know what they say, Claudie.' She kissed me and took my hands in hers. 'The doctors.'

'I will.'

66

'And talk to me, won't you, if it gets really bad again.'

'OK,' I mumbled, trying to pull away.

'And promise me one thing.'

'What?' but I already knew what Zoe was going to say.

'Promise me you'll call Will. I think you may need—' she trailed off.

'What?'

'Nothing.' She frowned. 'It just worries me. You being alone again.'

I reached around her to open the front door. 'Don't worry about me. I'm fine. I like being alone. And I'll think about it.'

But right now, I had more pressing things on my mind.

WEDNESDAY 19TH JULY
SILVER

Silver woke feeling hungover, which was ridiculous because he hadn't had a drink for five years, three months, four weeks and—well. His fanatical counting of the days AA-style had dissipated a little in the past year or so, but old habits did die hard, it appeared.

Five minutes after arriving at work, Malloy called him in; bantered about the squash tournament briefly, and 'that ponce Lonsdale', and then asked Silver to head up part of what was now being referred to as Operation Nightingale.

'You've probably heard, Al-Qaeda's little friends have put up this new website since the explosion, celebrating the death toll. It's a fucking travesty.' The top of Malloy's bullet-shaped head was practically quivering with outrage. 'But the fucking knobs who run the worldwide web say they have no jurisdiction to shut it down. And the Muslims are *not* taking the rap for this, though they're having a damn good laugh about it, so Counter Terrorism are about to pass it over. Got enough on their plate apparently; they'll give us one dedicated officer to work with us and that's it. And now we've got this fucking stupid "Purity" pony to deal with that's been leaked to the press.' Malloy flung a typewritten letter onto the desk in front of Silver; he scanned it quickly.

To those who perpetuate the suffering in this world:
It is time you saw that things must change, that we cannot continue ad nauseam to ruin our planet, to never take the blame. We need to purify: we are purifying for you all. Be warned, Berkeley Square is only the beginning.

'Nutters, no? Any other developments?' Silver folded the letter and sat opposite his boss.
'I've just found out that there was some sort of tip-off on the Friday morning; some bird rang to say there was going to be a "major incident southeast of Oxford Street". If the press get hold of that, we are for the fucking high jump.'
'Who dealt with the call?'
'It was passed over to SO15, but the operator thought it was a hoax. Said the woman was slightly hysterical and she thought she was a crazy.

68

And fucking Explosives are taking forever, and they're so reticent to actually confirm anything, it's doing my head in.' Malloy fiddled with his Police Benevolent Fund paper-clip box in a way that suggested he wanted to slam it through the wall. He was highly agitated; more so than Silver remembered seeing him. 'The bank wants to sue, the building firm are terrified they're going to lose everything and British Gas are cacking themselves. Plus we've hardly managed to retrieve any CCTV footage at all, surprise fucking surprise. So far only one of the cameras that survived the blast seems to have even been switched on. I wonder why the fuck we bother really.'

Malloy dropped the paper-clip box and opened a DVD package on his desk, fiddling with his laptop for a minute, his stubby fingers clumsy on the keys, swearing quietly. 'Christ. Technology. Makes me feel prehistoric. Right, here we go.'

The picture was visible now.

'See, this little thing arrives at the Academy around 6.47.'

Silver watched a short teenage girl in a beanie hat enter via the front stairs, holding a gym bag. At 6.49 another taller woman, using a stick, walking as quickly as her limp allowed, came out and, standing at the top of the Academy stairs, made two calls, scanning the square as she did so. Then she went back into the building.

'Tessa Lethbridge possibly? TBC. About five minutes later, the girl comes back outside, apparently to have a cigarette. Then this courier bike arrives,' Malloy pointed at the screen, 'and hands her this package; she goes back inside at 7.03.'

Silver found the flickering footage made him feel almost seasick.

'Now look.' At 7.08 a white car drove up, an old Golf, stopping outside the Academy, the driver apparently on a mobile phone.

'Who's that?'

'No fucking reg of course, from this angle.' Malloy cracked his knuckles. 'But we need to identify him.'

Two minutes later a couple of builders in hard hats and yellow high-visibility jackets walked past the Academy, presumably heading for the Hotel Concorde building site in the adjacent corner.

On the other side of the road, a figure in a full-length burqa pushed an empty pushchair to the edge of the pavement, then began to cross the road. Silver found he was riveted despite his slight nausea. A car passed through frame, then a black Range Rover. The figure in the Golf saw the girl come out of the Academy doors again, holding up a hand in greeting as she ran down the stairs to the pavement, and then a figure follow behind her, but before their identity was revealed, a double-decker bus pulled in front of the camera, obscuring any view.

Another thirty seconds: and the picture went white.

'What the hell—' Silver sat back, intensely frustrated, as if he'd just missed the end of his favourite soap opera.

'Exactly. What the hell? The only people visible to us in the square and they hardly look like your typical group of fundamentalists do they?'

'Except burqa-girl.'

They replayed the video. This time Silver noticed the way the girl smoking a cigarette outside of the

70

Academy, who had accepted the courier's parcel, was pacing back and forth as she waited. He watched again as the woman in the burqa seemed to react to something behind her.

'Of course, burqa-girl might be totally unlinked.' Malloy scratched his head, his grey crew-cut like burnt stubble in a field. 'It's just she seems obvious to me. Why's the pushchair empty? It's just a foil, surely. But Counter Terrorism disagree. And upstairs, they're so fucking paranoid about inciting religious hatred at the moment, they won't say boo to a goose, which don't help.'

'But then,' Silver rubbed his face wearily, 'there's no actual evidence from any of that, that *any* of them are directly linked to the explosion.'

'No, of course. But what the fuck *were* they up to?' Malloy slammed the laptop lid shut with a thump. 'Strike 'em off the list, and I'll be happy. We need to find all of them: the courier bike and the bloke in the car, burqa-girl, and the dancer. And fucking pronto. Christ, Joe,' he stood up and then sat again. 'We've got fourteen dead, the fucking world's media breathing down our necks, not to say the Commissioner and everyone at County Hall. I'm setting you up a new team; take Roger Okeke and Tina Price for now.'

Silver felt the surge of adrenaline that came with a new investigation. Okeke was good; young and baying for blood; Price was new but came with good reviews from Southampton. And now Kenton seemed back on track after her initial shock. It was shaping up to be a nice little team. Except, perhaps, for Craven.

'While we wait for Explosives to pull their heads out of their tiny little arses, we need to identify who

71

this little lot are,' Malloy's blue eyes were burning, 'and what the fuck they were up to before they got blown to kingdom come.'

Silver felt enthused for the first time in weeks.

'Get on with it, Joe.' Malloy's attention was already distracted by an email. 'And take the CCTV footage with you. You need to liaise with Counter Terrorism. I need fucking results, and I need 'em yesterday.'

*   *   *

Five days on from the bombing, the phones in the office still rang incessantly: frantic relatives who hadn't seen loved ones for weeks or even months and were now beginning to panic. The vast divisions of family became more obvious at times like these, Silver knew; loved ones ignored for years suddenly became the world's nearest and dearest. The help lines were so busy they kept jamming, and eventually some of the Traffic team had to be seconded in to answer calls.

Lessons had been learnt from 7/7 and the chaos that had ensued then, but for the Met, a disaster like this was still a nebulous mass that was hard to manage. They had to think on their feet; very often, frustratingly, they had to chase their own tails.

When Silver returned from Malloy's office, Kenton was filling in the whiteboard at the end of the room with today's date and updating the lists.

MISSING, PRESUMED DEAD

Silver called Kenton over.

'How are you?'

'Fine, sir.' She practically stood to attention. He grinned. He liked this girl; despite her dodgy hair, she was as solid as her stocky frame; diligent—with fire in her belly.

'Here's some CCTV footage of the bombing. I think you should take a look, if you can cope with it? See if you recognise anyone.'

She paled slightly, but nodded at the same time. 'Sure.'

'Did you see Merryweather?'

'Not yet.'

'Well. The facility is there if you need it. Don't forget.'

'Thanks.'

'By the way. Misty Jones.' Silver straightened his cuff with nonchalance. 'The girl you were going to Crime Live! about. Have you got details of whoever reported her missing?'

'Girl called Lucie Duffy, I think.' Kenton frowned. 'Flatmate, and yeah. Everything filed in the A drive, under Contacts.'

In the safety of his own office, Silver called the mobile number listed. A girl answered sotto-voce, piano music thumping in the background; he explained who he was.

'I'm in rehearsal, I can't really talk now,' she murmured.

'I need some more details. Why you think your friend's missing.'

'I'm on lunch in an hour. Can I call you back then please?'

'Where are you, Miss Duffy?'

'Covent Garden. Royal Opera House.' She had a small, rather husky voice. 'Tech run for *Swan Lake* at 4 p.m.'

Silver had no idea what she was on about. He unwrapped another stick of gum. 'I'll meet you there. One o'clock.'

'Fine. Ask for Rehearsal Room 3.' She hung up.

Silver should have sent one of his team; Misty Jones was nothing to do with Operation Nightingale, and he had more important matters at hand. The beauty was, though, no one would stop him. Before he got on with the bigger questions in hand, he had to satisfy himself that Misty Jones had no connection with Jaime Malvern.

*　　　*　　　*

Silver sent half of his team out on various dead and missing enquiries, including tracing the family of Australian ballet teacher Lethbridge, one of the first to be identified, who were proving elusive. Kenton and Craven were given the CCTV footage and the task of beginning to identify those featured. Silver wasn't sure they'd work together well, but Kenton was a good foil for the bull-headed older policeman—if she could bear his outdated chauvinism. Now Silver headed out himself. Parking up near Holborn he walked the last half mile. Rehearsal Room 3 was on the top floor of the Royal Opera House; he was in good enough shape to jog up most of the stairs without being out of breath. Or much out of breath anyway, he thought ruefully, on the top step.

Through the glass-paned door he watched a slight mixed-race girl with dark plaits being whisked up into the air by a strapping youth in shorts so tight they made Silver wince. The ballerina's back arched until she was curved almost fully into a circle, her short practice skirt rippling as one strong shapely leg extended gracefully before her. Silver had not

74

the first clue about ballet and even less interest, but even he could recognise this as impressive. Lana would have enjoyed it. He remembered Molly trundling round the church hall aged five in her little pink leotard with a tummy swelling gently over her frilly skirt, constantly wobbling the opposite way to everyone else as the *Dance of the Sugar Plum Fairy* was crashed out on the ancient piano, and he grinned. Happy days. Lana had high hopes for her only daughter—bright lights, big cities; chances she'd never had—chances a relentless diet of reality talent shows had rendered seemingly attainable. Hopes that most definitely weren't ever going to be fulfilled by flat-footed Molly in the performance arts.

Satin-clad feet firmly back on the ground, Lucie Duffy had a quick discussion with her partner, who was annoyed about something. He was wiping his face on his muscled forearm, gesticulating and swearing in heavily accented English. Lucie placated him, stroking and patting him gently on the chest, before she caught Silver's eye through the glass door.

She padded over with a towel round her neck, smooth caramel cheeks faintly pink, still panting slightly. Sweat had collected in the cleavage of her silver leotard and there were damp patches beneath her pert bosom as if someone with wet hands had placed them around her breasts. Silver looked away.

'Sorry. Bit out of breath.' She blinked up at him, her huge grey eyes framed by doll-like lashes. 'We've really got to nail this today or we're in trouble. Kiko is fed up with me.' She blinked again, bottom lip almost quivering; like a true innocent.

'He's such a flipping perfectionist. He hates the way I lean in for the lifts.'

You're as innocent as Reggie Kray, Silver thought. And a good actress to boot.

'Looked all right to me,' was what he actually said.

'Thanks. God, I'm going to be bruised all over.' She held her diaphanous skirt aside and pulled down her leggings a little to study her thigh. She was a sexy little thing, sinewy and hard-bodied, and she absolutely knew it. Silver looked away again.

'Kiko doesn't half like to hurl me around,' Lucie bit her lip with neat white teeth, as if Kiko was a very bad man whom Silver should immediately chastise.

'Look, I don't want to keep you,' he said. 'But is there somewhere quiet we can talk?'

She indicated a small room along the corridor. There was a drinks machine against the wall and a series of old posters of Norma Shearer and Nijinsky on the wall. Silver followed her in.

'Do you want something?' she indicated the machine.

'No, thanks. Can you tell me about Misty?'

'Have you found her?' Lucie looked up at him, her voice breaking slightly.

'No.' Silver sat at the table. 'But it would help to know why you think she's missing.'

'She hasn't been home since the start of last week. Even before the bomb went off—'

'Explosion.'

'Whatever,' she shrugged. 'Terrible, isn't it? We trained at the Academy, you know.'

'We'd already put a missing alert out on her by last Friday morning.' He thought of the girl

76

in the beanie hat on the CCTV footage. But she had been tiny, and from her description, he didn't think Misty Jones was that small. 'Is there any reason, incidentally, she might have gone near the Academy that day?'

'Not really.' Lucie leant against the table, and unwound the ribbons of her ballet shoe. 'I don't see why; we graduated over a year ago. But she'd been hanging out with some strange types recently. We'd—' She stopped.

'What?' He was impatient now.

She peeled the pink satin back from her foot, wincing. Her big toe was bleeding, the blood thickly congealed between nail and skin. Silver felt faintly sickened.

'No pain, no gain,' she widened great grey eyes at him, and bit that bottom lip again.

'You were saying—about Misty.'

'We had a bad row. Last Tuesday, I think. Then I went away for a few days. But I don't think it's relevant.'

'Why the row?'

'She was acting like a prat.' Her face hardened as she spoke the harsh word. 'I got fed up with her.'

'In what sense?' He imagined arguments about make-up and clothes.

'Let's just say, she'd got in with the wrong crowd. She was lying to everyone. She even refused to answer to her proper name.'

Silver felt unease settle over him like a fine layer of dust. 'Misty Jones?'

'Misty Jones was just a stage name that she used.' She leant forward slightly, affording him a glimpse of that buoyant cleavage. 'Since she, you know, got into the clubs.'

'Clubs?' Silver needed to cut to the chase.

'You know. Tits and arse.' Lucie flashed a lascivious smile at him and he saw the girl behind the mask. 'What little girls are made of, apparently. There was no telling her though. Just cos she didn't get the breaks I did.'

But Lucie Duffy didn't really think she'd got a break, Silver was quite sure. She thought she'd earned her place in the sun. He'd rarely met someone her age so assured of herself.

'And if Misty isn't Misty,' he cleared his throat, 'what's her real name?'

'Sadie. Sadie Malvern. Misty was her stage name.'

Silver felt his stomach roll. Of course. Jaime's big sister. He cursed his stupidity. How could he have forgotten her? Lana had been half right after all. And yet he was not surprised. Even since he'd seen the face in that photo, he'd known something bad was coming.

'Why didn't you give her real name when you reported her missing?' He remained deadpan.

'She'd changed it officially. Poor Sadie.' Her cloying concern was unconvincing.

'What about her family? Did you contact them?'

'I never met them. I don't even know where they live. Just,' Lucie pulled a funny face, 'you know. Somewhere up North. She never mentioned them except to say they think she's on ballet tour; she's never told them about the club, I don't think.'

Something about her manner smacked of disingenuousness.

'If you can think of any other reason she might have not come home, I need to know,' Silver tried hard to focus. 'What about boyfriends?'

'No one in particular, I don't think,' she sniffed,

78

pulling a disgusted face. 'A few no-marks she was dating. Oiks.'

'I'll need their details.'

'OK.'

'How did she get into the clubs?'

'Not sure. Quite a few of the girls do it, you know. Easy way to make money.'

If you like taking your clothes off in front of lascivious men for a living, Silver thought dryly. 'Who introduced her to it though?' he pressed. 'You must have an idea.'

'There was some guy who came to the end of term shows when we finished, I think. Gave her and a few others his card. Promised her fame and fortune, that type of thing. She's a bit gullible, our Sadie.' Lucie shrugged lightly; looked at him curiously. 'Why are you so bothered?'

'I'm not, kiddo,' he smiled pleasantly. 'I'm just doing my job.'

Lucie Duffy stood up and moved nearer him, one hand extended slightly; she was so near he could smell the sweat mixed in with the scent of her deodorant. For a strange moment he thought she was going to place that small hand on his crotch— but she didn't. She gazed up at him.

'Something's troubling you, Mr Policeman,' she murmured so he almost had to bend to hear. 'Can't I help?'

'I'll be in touch.' Silver took a swift step backward. 'Let me know immediately if you hear from Misty.'

Lucie smiled. 'Oh I will.' She seemed to be enjoying this. 'Let's just pray Misty is sitting there safe and sound with her chicken chow mein when I get home tonight.'

But her concern was unpersuasive. As he lolloped

down the stairs two at a time, Silver thought he'd never met anyone who seemed more excited by the apparent disappearance of a friend.

WEDNESDAY 19TH JULY
CLAUDIE

The phone woke me with a nasty start at 8 a.m. I held my breath, but it was only Rafe, still seeking forgiveness apparently.

'Claudia, if you do not ring back by lunchtime, I'm coming round between sittings.' His voice softened. 'I saw the thing about Tessa in today's paper. Such a tragedy.'

I couldn't help feeling his persistence was more to do with being thwarted than anything more sincere. Rafe did like his own way. Pulling my jeans on, I went down to Ahmed's on the corner; I bought *The Times,* a copy of *Vogue* for the sheer normality of it, a can of Fanta and a Flake, craving sweetness and comfort. I left the shop quickly before Ahmed's wizened mother could appear through the beaded curtain and ask about my face, which she'd then refer to every day for six months. I hadn't been out of the flat for two days, I realised, as my feet trod the filthy pavement, and the colours of the day were bright and unreal, piercing my tired brain; as if the rain had washed London clean for once.

I sat beside the open window and drank my drink through a twirly elephant straw I'd found at the back of the cutlery drawer. I breathed in the fresh air, the smell of blossom, the scent of hope; I tried to avoid the tower block that sliced the sky

80

in two before me. I felt a little more normal today; my head wasn't aching and I felt clearer, but my craving for a cigarette was building again. I had to start denying my fears. I wouldn't let it happen again, if it was. I'd fight it every step of the way this time.

I read my stars in *Vogue*, clinging to some vestige of my old life. I looked at the pedigree girls striking odd angular poses, all legs and big hair and surprised eyes. I pulled my own blonde scarecrow-do back and tied it with an elastic band that had held yesterday's post. Then I scanned the newspaper headlines briefly; they mentioned the 'Daughters of Light' claim, but I turned the pages until I found the picture of Tessa, taken from a series the *Sunday Telegraph* had commissioned of the Academy last year, including Lucie Duffy. The picture showed intense concentration on Tessa's bony face as she oversaw a class of seniors, black practice skirt flowing from her tall, lean form. I read the tribute. Darcey Bussell had given some flowery comments about the Academy and its brilliant teachers. Prima ballerina Natalia Vodovana had praised Lethbridge's style, which made me smile wryly as I remembered Tessa's disparaging views on Vodovana's 'showy style and forced line'.

And Lucie Duffy, who had graduated last year and was rocketing up the Royal Ballet's ranks, was quoted: 'Tessa Lethbridge was the best.' I remembered Duffy and her friend Sadie; pretty, spiteful dancers, all about themselves. Sadie, blonde, Northern, tough and horribly bulimic, living in Duffy's shadow, never reaching the potential of her friend and room mate.

81

I shut the paper and finished the Flake, tipping my head back to pour the last crumbs into my mouth. I couldn't have been less like the girl in the technicolour poppy field if I tried. I tried to focus on positive memories, as Helen had taught me. Zoe and I on the beach in Goa last Christmas. Tessa listening; Tessa laughing over crème brulée at Mimi's. Ned's hand in mine. Ned's little hand in mine. Ned's hand, slipping through mine . . .

They didn't work: the positive memories. They never did. The incision was too deep. His hand in mine, clutching so tight—and I, I had let go. I had failed fundamentally as a mother.

Savagely, I pushed the thought away. But the pain when it came was unbearable, like my soul was thrashing around for a refuge—only there wasn't one. I wanted to pull my hair out, scratch my eyes out: to lacerate myself with pain.

I got up and put another nicotine patch on. I felt better immediately; the craving calmed. I rang the office and left a message for Eduardo, asking if I could come in for a shift or two. I didn't want to sit here any more, alone with my thoughts and the guilt that was accumulating. I'd be better back at work, occupied; if I sat here any longer alone, I might fall back down. I loved my job; it had been my passion for years, working with the human body, helping people to heal. It had saved me when I had been flailing; it bridged a terrible void.

I filled the old metal watering can at the kitchen sink; I kept seeing myself on the bus on Thursday. Why could I not remember getting to Rafe's? Where had I been? I was frightened that I was slipping backwards, that was the truth. I contemplated ringing Helen.

As I watered the window-boxes out on the balcony, the scarlet geraniums bright against the overcast sky, the telephone rang again. A swan flew across the canal, brilliant against the murky waters, and landed with elegance.

I thought it would be my boss but it wasn't.

'Claudie. It's nearly time.' There was a long pause and a sigh. 'We're waiting for you now.'

I felt a fierce twist of fear. Transfixed, I gazed at the light blinking belligerently on the machine. I heard the click as the phone was cut off.

Savagely, I pulled the phone out of the wall, dislodging a small cloud of plaster in the process. Someone was angry with me, and I didn't know why. I had the strangest sensation that my life was shrinking down to this moment—and I had two choices. Run, or face it.

*   *   *

In the bathroom, I scrabbled around for my last few pills. Then I lay on my bed, in the dark, fiddling with the locket on the necklace Tessa had given me; thinking, thinking.

Friday morning was all such a haze still. I had got on the bus outside Rafe's; I had started towards work. I had this strange idea that was forming, that Tessa had needed me; that I had been summoned . . .

Thinking, thinking—I fell into a doze.

Dreaming. Tessa and Ned, dancing in a poppy field . . .

My bedroom door was opening and I was screaming, screaming and—

My sister stood in the doorway, clutching an

83

orange Le Creuset casserole dish, blinking rapidly like a worried rabbit.

'Oh my God.' I sat bolt upright on the bed, my heart thudding. 'I nearly had a heart attack. How the hell did you get in?'

'I borrowed the spare key from Mum's,' she said brightly. 'I was so worried, Claudia, you haven't been answering your phone.'

'Haven't I?'

'Don't be silly. You know you haven't.'

I didn't remember her ringing.

'And I bet you haven't been eating either. I know you, Claudie Scott.' She put the dish down on the chest of drawers and opened the blind. 'Come on, hoppity-skip. Out of bed with you. I'll put the kettle on.'

She breezed out of the room, retrieving her casserole dish and proudly bearing it before her like a precious icon. At least she was a better cook than our mother.

'Hoppity-skip?' I muttered to myself. 'Dear God.' But I got out of bed and followed her into the living room, like a child.

'Your hair needs a brush,' she said reprovingly, from her station at the kettle. 'And a trim. I'm surprised you can see out of that fringe. And your roots are showing.'

'Nat,' I slumped down at the table. 'When did you turn into Mum?'

'Probably when I became one. Now, Earl Grey or builders? Or green. Now that's very good for you, I've read. Cleans your digestive tract. I'll make some green, and we can have a nice chat.'

'Do we have to?' I groaned. 'I think my digestion's all right, honestly.'

84

'I just wanted,' her bluster subsided for a moment, 'I wanted to check you've been looking after yourself actually.'

Suddenly she was less sure of herself.

'Did you?' I gazed at her. We never talked about my mental state. Natalie found it too shaming.

'Yes.' She was too bright. 'Now, your lovely psychiatrist has been on the phone. Helen, isn't it? Ever so worried she can't get hold of you. Has it—' The brightness was fading; she was struggling now. 'Has it happened again?'

'What?'

'Come on, Claudie.' She flapped around with the teabags, banging cupboard doors. 'You know what.'

'You mean, have I disassociated from reality again?' I thought of my lost hours. 'I don't know,' I said truthfully.

'Right.' She looked supremely uncomfortable.

'Actually,' I changed tack midstream. I couldn't do this with Natalie. 'I don't think it has.'

She couldn't handle it, that much was obvious. Not many people could. Not even my husband, Will—so why put them through it? My own mother had been distraught at losing her three-year-old grandson, but more distraught, I feared, at my own descent into hell. 'Thank *God* Phillip's not here,' I heard her tell my auntie Jean once, 'it would have destroyed him to see her like this.' They'd expected me to be strong, and I failed them too.

'No. I'm fine,' I said. I put some cream on my sore hands for something to do.

'Good,' she looked infinitely relieved. 'Also, Mum's been calling. Can you just ring her back, Claudia? I mean, Portugal is not the other side of the world, is it, love, and she's not coming back for a while apparently, not unless you need her, she says. Just give her a bit of reassurance, and she'll leave you alone.'

My little sister and I stared at each other, and then slowly I smiled. Perhaps Natalie did understand a little.

'Sure. I will. Perhaps I'll go out and see her.' The idea of the sun on my weary bones suddenly seemed enticing, although my mother's incessant chatter and home cooking did not.

Natalie reached across me for the sugar bowl.

'Gosh, what's that smell?' she wrinkled her nose. 'It's really horrid.'

'Probably me,' I joked, but she didn't smile.

'My sense of smell's gone crazy. Must be the hormones.' She sniffed the air like the small alert dog she sometimes reminded me of. 'It's really weird. Like something burnt.'

'Oh,' I fingered the locket round my neck. 'Might be this. It's a native African herb. Tessa bought me some for my birthday, says it protects you. Old lady's fingers, they call it.'

'I'm not surprised.' She pulled back from me. 'It's disgusting. Get rid of it, you hippy.'

'I can't,' I said miserably. 'Tessa's dead, Nat.'

Natalie looked down and stirred her tea carefully.

'Yes,' she said quietly, 'I know; I saw. I'm so sorry, Claudie.' She put her hand over mine. 'It's the last thing you needed.'

And for a while we sat there, side by side at that old table, tied together not by choice, but by familiarity; by something more even. From necessity. And all the while the phone was unplugged, looking like an evil plastic toad, squatting malevolently on the coffee table. At least it couldn't ring.

WEDNESDAY 19TH JULY
SILVER

His ex-wife was at the hairdresser's in Frogley when Silver called. He could hear the chorus of hairdryers in the background, imagined the girls moving in perfect choreographed precision in front of the long mirrors, whilst the immaculate Allana scrutinised her manicure critically. Her shell-pink nails that were never chipped and certainly never naked, her hair all caramel and tawny, streaked within an inch of its life. They had been a well-matched couple in this respect at least; both beautifully turned-out at all times, until Lana had her breakdown, and even then she'd managed perfect hair. It was only beneath the surface things had been so different than they seemed.

'Lana,' he twiddled with a biro on his desk. 'The girl in the photo. The girl you saw on TV.'

'Jaime,' she said, calmly. 'It was Jaime. I knew it.'

'Don't be silly. It's not Jaime,' he took a deep breath. 'Jaime's dead, Lana, we both know that. But it is—it's Sadie Malvern. Her big sister Sadie.'

'I know who Sadie is,' she said. She didn't miss a beat; she was still calm. He didn't know what he had been expecting; for her to lose it, start crying and screaming. Of course she didn't. 'Sadie was in the car that day too, Joe.'

'So,' what else was there to say? Sadie was still alive. Jaime was long dead, but then, Lana had only killed one sister. Sadie had survived; traumatised

87

but alive, and now she was missing. That at least was nothing to do with the Silvers. 'I just wanted to set your mind at rest.'

Lana said something that he couldn't catch, the noise in the salon increasing behind her as she spoke, a cacophony of women's voices fighting the hum of the dryers.

'I can't hear you.'

There was a pause; the sound of the salon door opening and closing. He saw her now on the narrow high street, pacing.

'My mind's never at rest, Joe. It's never been at rest. Not since that day.'

'I know, Lana,' he sighed. 'But try not to go back there again.'

'Where?'

'To that dark place. To all this self-flagellation.'

She hung up.

*   *   *

Now Silver had satisfied himself that Lana's worst nightmare hadn't come true, there was no reason for him to have any more to do with Sadie's disappearance. He could easily pass it back over to his colleagues and be done with it; he had more pressing matters at hand.

But the situation really bothered him. Seeing Sadie Malvern's face again after all this time, well, it flipped the proverbial can of worms wide open: and now they were out, they'd be bloody hard to recapture. Right now, in fact, they were slithering all over the damn place. He couldn't just leave it now to others.

As Silver retrieved his suit jacket from the

hanger on the wall, Ian Kelly stuck his head round the door. He'd been seconded for the week from Fraud; Silver had only seen him once or twice since the Finnegan baby case. Silver felt a fleeting twinge of nostalgia for the feisty Jess Finnegan, whose baby son Louis he'd helped recover after a kidnap attempt two years ago.

'Come and have a drink with me and Lorraine,' the portly DI was as pink-faced as ever. 'Be good to catch up.'

Leaning against the fruit machine in the pub whilst Kelly queued for a round that included the wholly un-thrilling prospect of a pint of tepid diet Coke, Silver called Julie against his better judgement. When she didn't answer, he left her a short message, but before he'd even pocketed the phone, he felt ashamed. There really wasn't much to be said for a relationship entirely based on sex, whatever Craven or some of his younger colleagues might have felt. Silver sighed heartily. Maybe, at the grand old age of forty-five, he was getting old. He thought briefly of Jessica Finnegan. There had been an undeniable attraction between them, but Jess had been married still to the despicable Mickey, and neither Silver nor she had been ready for anything serious. Plus Jess, for all her tough façade, had been far too fragile to mess around with. But Silver had been drawn to her more than any other woman since Lana. He wondered where Jess was now.

The truth was he was tired of being alone—but he never met anyone who really excited him, not the way Lana had excited him once, before she slipped from reality. Silver suppressed another sigh and joined the others at their table. Briefly they

89

discussed the latest claimant of the explosion.

'They really do all crawl out of the woodwork, don't they? And it might be weeks before all the dead are identified.' Kelly spilt peanut crumbs down his front. Silver winced at the mess. 'Just like 7 bloody 7. It's a fucking logistical and DNA nightmare. *"Can I borrow your precious Lisa's toothbrush, Mrs Smith, because we think she might have been blown to high heaven but we can't tell cos she's in bits."* Christ.'

'Don't,' winced Kenton, hunching her square shoulders, and Kelly looked apologetic.

'Sorry, love.'

'We've already got one possible mix-up.' Kenton sipped her pint most daintily for such a well-built lass. Not for the first time Silver wondered why exactly she dyed her hair *such* a similar shade to Heinz tomato soup. 'Australian ballet teacher from the Academy calling herself Tessa Lethbridge. Can't find her documents at the moment.'

Something chimed in Silver's head. 'The Royal Ballet Academy?'

'That's the one.' Kenton wiped foam from her top lip, where just the faintest trace of dyed moustache was visible. 'Turns out the best. Thank God the damage wasn't worse. They've reopened already.'

Silver frowned, thinking of the sassy little ballerina he'd met that afternoon. What had Duffy said? *'We trained at the Academy, you know.'*

'I met a dancer today at Covent Garden.' He poked the lethargic slice of lemon down into his pint of brown syrup. 'Girl called Lucie Duffy.'

'Of course! *That's* why I knew her name,' Kenton said. 'Beautiful ballerina. So natural for such a young 'un. The new Bussell, I reckon.'

'Bit of an aficionado, are you?' Silver grinned at her, and the policewoman was struck as ever by the lazy lopsided smile. If she hadn't preferred the ladies, Kenton would definitely not have been the only woman at work who held a small torch for the solitary DCI. 'Can't see you in a tutu.'

'No you blooming well can't! No, it was Mum who loved all that. Took her to *Sleeping Beauty* for her birthday last year. It was Duffy's first solo role, as the Lilac Fairy.' Kenton changed the subject, a lump forming in her throat, scared she was about to show weakness over her late mother. 'What's her story then?'

'Still not sure if Misty's just off on a bender, or has really disappeared.'

'Oh yeah?' Kelly perked up at the prospect of death. 'Who is she?'

'Inconveniently,' Silver folded his crisp packet very neatly, 'she's got two names. Misty or Sadie, depending on the persona. Misty's the bad girl, from what I understand. Lap-dancer. A far cry from Sleeping Beauty, I fear.'

'Girl with two names. Interesting. Where did she dance?'

'Not sure. Duffy didn't know.'

'Sugar and Spice is the most infamous club.' Kelly's eyes followed a buxom blonde carrying a dripping pint. He reminded Silver of a hungry dog who knew he had no chance of snaffling the bone. 'Boss is desperate to pin something on the bastards. They're bent as arseholes down there. Nasty bunch with a habit of getting away with bloody murder. Literally.'

'*Are* arseholes bent?' Kenton deadpanned.

'What little girls are made of!' Silver clapped his

hands to his forehead. 'Of course, that's what Duffy meant. Misty was dancing at Sugar and Spice. How bloody stupid.'

'You know, it's probably a coincidence, the Academy thing.'

'Maybe.'

Kenton looked at her boss, who was draining his diet Coke. For a moment, their eyes met. He gave her a half-smile. Was it her imagination, or did he seem unusually tense?

Silver was saved from her scrutiny by the beep of his phone: Julie responding wholeheartedly to what she called a 'booty call'. He had a strange image of stripy-topped burglars carrying sacks of loot. Not a good sign, surely.

'Gotta go.' He stood, brushing down his trousers, the crease as razor-sharp as ever. 'See you tomorrow.'

He left the pub, cursing internally; he was not going to be able to leave the Misty thing alone. There were too many coincidences turning up today—and he owed it to the Malverns, that much he knew. He'd be pleased if he never saw the poor parents again, but still, he knew he owed it to them to find out what the hell was going on with their surviving daughter.

WEDNESDAY 19TH JULY
CLAUDIE

The police tape flickered in the dusk breeze on the north side of Berkeley Square, the new hoardings hiding the chaos behind. Nearer the Academy, one lamppost was twisted and bent mournfully to the left, as if it had bowed its head and given up. The pavement was blackened slightly—and that was it. There were no other signs of the tragedy that had erupted here last week.

Averting my eyes, I trudged up the Academy's front stairs, past the white pillars and the great arch windows, feeling none of the usual pleasure I gained from the beautiful old building. After nights of troubled dreams and broken sleep, my body felt heavy, my eyes gritty with tiredness. Only the strains of Tchaikovsky from the practice studios were soothing as I hurried towards the office, the patter of feet as students ran from one class to the next.

Natalie had finally left after I'd pretended I was going to lie down again, but instead I'd caught the tube into town. I'd been hoping everyone in the office would be gone, but Mason was still ensconced behind her desk; she was on the phone when I walked in and nearly dropped the receiver in her hurry to get rid of her caller.

'Claudie! How are you?' She stroked down her glossy black fringe. 'What are you doing here? I thought you were on holiday.'

'Did you?'

'Have you heard from the police? Asking questions about Tessa?'

'Yeah.' I headed straight for my pigeon hole that sat beneath the Ex-Student Performance board. Lucie Duffy: *Swan Lake*, it announced, Royal Opera House. Amanda Curran and Sarah Planer: *Giselle corps de ballet*, English National Ballet; and so it went on. The Academy liked to keep proud tabs on its protégées.

'What do you think they want?' Mason's eyes were wide with complicity. 'Isn't it sad?'

'Horrible,' I agreed, retrieving my post. Out of the corner of my eye, I could see Mason flattening the perfect fringe again. I braced myself for a pearl of wisdom.

'Tragic. *"Noble souls, through dust and heat, rise from disaster and defeat the stronger."* But you know, I was saying to Eduardo yesterday,' she cocked her head on one side like a ruffled blackbird, 'I always felt something might go wrong for her.'

'That's a strange thing to say.' I rifled through the memos and offers for physio equipment, chucking most of it straight in the bin.

'I mean, she was a bit odd, wasn't she?' Mason stared at me disingenuously. 'Oh—sorry! Silly of me.'

'What do you mean?'

'You were such good friends, weren't you? I did tell that nice policeman yesterday. But you know, I never could quite see what you saw in her personally.' Mason's hands were too thin, raised veins like tube tunnels surfacing through skin as she put the lid back on her pen. 'I mean, I know you shouldn't speak ill of the dead, but really—'

'You're going to anyway.'

She pursed shiny lips. 'Well. She was a snooty cow sometimes.'

'Mason!' I protested. Usually I found Mason's child-like honesty refreshing. In her bizarre ensembles, with her twig-like legs ending in T-bar shoes, dressed at least ten years too young for her age, she often got away with things others wouldn't. Now though, her scathing words seemed inappropriate.

'Well, she was. Thought she was better than the rest of us.'

I was tuning out. I stared at the whiteboard, at my schedule.

'I'll go to her funeral, and pay my respects,' she stood now, 'but I won't tell lies about her. As Mark Twain so rightly said, *"Truth is the most valuable thing we have."* You know, it was a good thing you didn't come in that day. Or you know—' She threw her hands up in the air dramatically. 'You could have been blown to smithereens like poor Tessa.'

'Mason! For God's sake.'

'And you know little Anita Stuart is missing too.'

'Is she?' I was shocked by the news. I thought of her surly little face the day before Tessa died; her foot thrust against my door to prevent me shutting her out. 'Are you sure?'

'Suspected dead,' Mason's voice dropped to an almost gleeful whisper as she pulled her poncho on. 'I'm going to get caffeine. I've got a ton of paperwork to catch up on. Can I interest you?'

I looked back at the date of the accident, Friday 14th July. I wasn't down to work, but I had been on my way in to the Academy. Fear crept up my gullet.

'You look terribly peaky, you know, darling.' Mason was gazing at my face. 'What's happened to your poor cheek?'

'Just a scratch.' I pushed my hand through my hair, thinking desperately. 'I'm fine. Have you got the key to the changing room, please, Mason? I've forgotten mine.'

Grumbling slightly, she unzipped her bag and dug around for the keys. 'Put them back in my drawer.'

I waited until she was out of sight down the corridor and then I let myself into the changing

95

room. My hands were slightly shaking as I fumbled in my pocket for the key to Tessa's locker I'd just pinched from the board in the office, fuelled by some kind of desperate hope that there would be some clue to my ill feeling about Friday.

But someone had got there before me. The small metal door was hanging off and the locker was empty, though I ran my hand round it anyway to check.

There was a sudden noise, and I jumped, banging my head on the metal corner.

Mason stood behind me.

'God you scared me.' I felt like a naughty schoolgirl.

'I forgot my purse. What are you doing?' she said curiously.

'I—I lent Tessa a book. I just wanted—I just thought I'd get it now. As I was here.'

'Oh.' Mason cocked her head again. 'I see. Well, you're too late, I'm afraid. Police took everything, actually.'

I pushed the door half-shut. 'Right.' I wished I'd stop feeling guilty. 'Well, never mind.'

Mason kept staring at me until I felt shifty. I began to follow her towards the office—and then suddenly I saw Tessa in front of me last Thursday, telling me she'd lost her key. Tessa's kitbag was in *my* locker, wasn't it? How the key came now to be on the office board, I didn't know. But whatever the reason, she had shoved her stuff in with mine on Thursday. I didn't remember her having retrieved it again.

I stopped walking. Mason turned round and stared at me. In the outer office, the phone in her bag began to ring. She hesitated.

'It might be your next date,' I suggested helpfully. Mason's love-life was the stuff of legend; three on-line dates a week in the search of true love, trying to forget her feelings for Eduardo, who was absolutely gay. 'You don't want to miss it.'

'Might be,' she turned to retrieve it. Heart thumping, I whipped my own locker open and pulled Tessa's half-empty bag out of it, shoving it as best I could into my own bag. I shut the door, heading through the office. Mason was now deep in rapt conversation.

'See you,' I mouthed at her, leaving the keys on her desk, and started down the corridor.

'Wait—' she hung up the phone. 'You're not going to believe this.'

'What?'

'That was Eduardo. He's been with the Governors today. He's having absolute kittens.'

'Why?'

She was stringing her news out deliberately now.

'Someone from the board read Tessa's obituary, and called her family in Australia to pass on condolences.' Her whole face shaped into a moue of astonishment.

'So?'

'They were astounded.' Now Mason was blazing with something like triumph. 'Her family, well— they saw Tessa this morning in Melbourne.'

WEDNESDAY 19TH JULY
SILVER

Joe Silver was calculating exactly how soon he could leave Julie's without mortally offending her—although as he'd finally realised he'd happily never see her again, perhaps it didn't matter if he did. He'd swung by for a coffee and a nightcap, which when you don't drink alcohol, really did mean coffee. It had taken him approximately eleven minutes to realise that he didn't want to lay his nightcap anywhere near Julie, ever again. He took a swig of his coffee and steeled himself to leave.

'All right?' Julie giggled and sashayed over to the stereo where she put a CD called *Lovers' Ballads* on. Silver groaned internally as he watched her pulling her skin-tight skirt down over her voluptuous curves, straightening the folds, before starting to sway on the spot to Marvin Gaye.

'Cares of the world on your shoulders tonight, lover.' She began to undulate towards him, kicking her stilettos off. 'Let me help you forget, babe.'

Silver was dying inside. Forcing a weak smile as Julie undid the top button of her pink shirt, while licking her lips suggestively, he knew he had no one to blame apart from himself.

His phone rang: it was Matty, his middle child. Silver flipped it open with such alacrity he caught his own finger in the fold.

'How do, kiddo?' Silver grinned into thin air, ecstatic to hear from his son for not entirely pure reasons. 'Been to football? How's that tackle coming along? I must say, those Blackburn—'

'Dad,' Matty cut him off. 'It's Mum.'

'What's Mum?'

'She's gone.'

'Gone where?' Silver sat up on Julie's fake leather sofa.

'I mean, she's not come home,' Matty's normally even tones were distressed; he suddenly sounded very young. 'Not since this morning.'

'When did you last see her?'

'Before school. She didn't even remember to collect Molly from Gran's.'

'Have you called her mobile?'

Julie had stopped dancing and was glowering at him now. He ignored her, sticking his finger in his ear against Marvin's crooning.

''Course,' Matty was indignant. 'But it just rings and rings.'

'Where's Ben?'

'He's took my skateboard and gone down to Chasers. To see if she's there.'

'*Taken* your skateboard,' Silver said automatically, but his heart missed a beat. He imagined his kids, confused and alone whilst his ex-wife sank Bacardi on a leather-topped stool in the local wine bar, drinking until she could hardly stagger in her three-inch heels. 'Are you on your own with Molly?'

'Gran's here,' Matty muttered. 'She made me eat peas.'

'Can you put her on, mate?'

'I hate peas.'

'I know, lad. Squash them down and push 'em under your fork. Always worked for me.'

'I tried. She sussed me.'

'Look, Matty,' Silver was very gentle; he didn't

99

want to upset his son any more than he already was. 'Just get your grandma, OK, and then we'll have another chat in a minute.'

Lana's mother Anne arrived on the line.

'Joseph.' She was curt.

He pictured her now, stiff and proper, beige twin-set beneath beautifully coiffed fair hair, every inch her daughter's mother. She had still not forgiven Silver for leaving Allana, even though it was indisputable that her daughter had been ruined largely by her own actions, and was temporarily beyond all reach. Anne could not get past the fact that Silver had been the drinker before Lana, that she had followed his path and then stuck steadfastly to it alone, even after he had found sobriety some years ago. In Anne's eyes, Silver was the arch-villain.

'Anne. First off, are you all right to stay with the kids?'

'Of course.' She dropped her voice. 'I'm very worried though.'

'I know you are,' Silver soothed, his mind ticking furiously, 'but Allana's a big girl now, Anne. And it's not like this is the first time.'

Four years ago, just before their marriage broke down irretrievably, Lana had gone through a stage of disappearing at lunchtime, usually into Leeds, usually to get hammered in one of the big hotel bars. It was only afterwards that Silver had discovered she had also been using the hotels to sleep with his pal Ray Steen from Yorkshire's Vice Squad. At the point that Lana got back in a car for the first time since the accident and drove herself home, thankfully without passengers this time, taking out half the front garden as she arrived

100

home, Silver had taken compassionate leave. She was lucky not to have been jailed for Jaime's death anyway, and in exchange for Silver, having battled his conscience for a while, managing to persuade the local force to quietly look the other way, Lana had gone into rehab at the Phoenix Centre in West Yorkshire. Silver struggled to keep the family going—with a little help from his sister Nicky, and later Anne, when she had recovered from the shock of Lana's ignominy.

'She hasn't done it for years,' her mother said plaintively. 'She's been so much better. So why now?'

Silver thought with sinking heart of the phone call he'd had with Lana earlier. Apparently she wasn't reacting well to Sadie Malvern's disappearance.

'Anne. Let me make some enquiries. She might just have been held up.' They both knew this was untrue.

'But where?' Anne's voice quivered slightly. Her daughter's shame had been utterly her own too, in the tight community they lived in, though Anne had stuck absolutely by her daughter, enduring the whispers on Frogley's every corner until they had at last died down, replaced by fresh scandal.

'Is—is she driving?'

'Yes.'

'Right.' His heart sank further. Lana had only just got her licence back. 'I'll call you back. Can you put Matty back on for a sec, please.'

'Matty!' he heard her call.

'Oh, and Anne—'

'Yes?'

'Go easy on my kids, would you. Give 'em ice cream or something nice,' he tried to joke. 'Let them stay up late. Just don't give 'em a hard time right now.'

'I'll thank you, Joseph, to remember I brought up four of my own.' She was predictably terse. 'I think you'll find I've got a damn sight better idea of what's good for *my* grandchildren than you have.'

Matty was back on the line before Silver could protest. He reassured his son as much as he could, promising he'd call back in a while to speak to Molly and Ben.

'Mum's probably just shopping in Leeds. It's late night tonight, remember. Probably getting more shoes, meeting a pal. You know what she's like.'

'Yeah probably.' Matty, bless him, tried to laugh along with his father. 'She hasn't got enough high ones. I did tell her.'

The bravado broke Silver's heart.

But as Silver rang the station to ask for a track and trace on Lana's number plate, he had the horrible feeling that his mother-in-law was absolutely right. Anne probably did know best— and anyway, what earthly use was he to his children all the way down South?

WEDNESDAY 19TH JULY
LANA

Because the sky was so big.

Because the sky stretched above her, so vast, so cavernous—and she was so tiny; so very tiny. She had been staring at it from the beach for hours, the pale milky-blue sky, for what seemed like hours. And in the end she picked herself up, herself and her empty polystyrene cup with the small coffee stain the shape of Italy on the side. She picked herself up and she was freezing. Her body was ramrod straight because she was tensed against the biting wind; she stood and a great gust buffeted her and she walked towards the sand dunes, away from the flurried sea, away from the sky that went on forever, the chalk marks of cloud swept across it.

She knew they would be waiting for her but she found now she didn't care. She had been thinking about this for months now, she realised, only she had never really acknowledged her feelings, her fears. But now she was here, it seemed so obvious—absolutely crystalline.

She could hear their voices briefly, clamouring for her, clamouring like tiny hungry fledglings waiting to be fed—and then it all went quiet. Shockingly quiet. Just the roar of the sea and the wind in her stinging ears. Her children's voices dampened, like someone had just lashed a great blanket across them.

She didn't know where she was going. When she saw the man silhouetted on the cliff, she still didn't know where she was going. She just knew she wasn't going home.

THURSDAY 20TH JULY
CLAUDIE

By Thursday morning, my head was absolutely thumping again; the pain making me nauseous and the fear creeping in again like a stealthy spy. I wanted to smoke, and the nicotine patches were doing little for my craving. I felt hazy and tired; trying to clean the flat to keep myself busy, but I had to keep sitting down during the hoovering. When the doorbell rang my inclination was not to answer it—but the ring was insistent. I held my breath. It rang again. Whoever it was wasn't leaving. I peered out of the window; a police car was parked behind next-door's van.

Somehow I'd forgotten they were coming.

'Ms Scott? We'd appreciate a moment of your time as discussed. It's about Tessa Lethbridge.'

I had no choice, so I let them in. A policeman called Craven, whom I felt an instant distrust for. Balding, overweight and supercilious, he pushed past me into the flat. A woman called Kenton. Short, wide and neat, with the bright eyes of a squirrel and bizarre-coloured hair, she shook my hand. They sat at the scrubbed pine table and refused the drinks I offered them.

I thought uncomfortably of my discoveries in Tessa's bag yesterday at the Academy. I had dismissed Mason's big announcement as her usual flair for the dramatic and histrionic. On the bus home to Kentish Town, sitting on the upper deck, I checked through my booty. A pair of soft block ballet shoes; a black and white spotty hairband of the kind Tessa always wore. Half a packet of jaffa cakes. A DVD of Baryshnikov teaching *La Sylphide* and, stuck to the cover as if by mistake with an old bit of Sellotape, a yellowing cutting from *The Telegraph*; a piece about the Lehman Brothers bank going down, and the Hoffman Bank stepping in, led by a man called Ivan Adanov. Finally, reaching into the depths of the bag, right at the bottom, was a set of keys and one glossy little card for some

104

club called Sugar and Spice, with an illegible name scrawled on the back.

I read and re-read the clipping from *The Telegraph*: a dull piece about how the misguided actions of money men had taken down the bank, and where those now out of work were likely to go next. Why would Tessa have had this in her bag? Maybe she'd invested some money somewhere; it wasn't the kind of thing we'd ever talked about. The idea of Tessa as speculator was hard to imagine.

Turning the article over in my hands, I noticed a faded pencil-written line in the margin; I squinted at it in the fluorescent bus light. *'Here comes the chopper to chop off your head.'* It rang vague bells. Was it a poem I'd learnt at school, or perhaps a nursery rhyme? My heart clenched uncomfortably at the thought of nursery rhymes, and when I'd got home, I'd shoved the bag into a kitchen cupboard.

'How can I help?' I asked now, sitting at the other end of the table. 'I hadn't actually known Tessa that long.'

'Handy,' I thought the policeman called Craven muttered. The woman shot him a look.

Craven fiddled with a plastic cigarette he'd pulled from his shirt pocket. His fingers were fat and clumsy; he was almost guilty of a comb-over. 'We have a few questions. There's been a development.'

I felt my chest tighten. 'Do they—do you know who it was?'

'Who it was?' Was he being deliberately obtuse? I couldn't tell.

'You know. Who set the—the bomb off? I heard something on the radio.'

'We're still not even sure yet,' said DS Kenton carefully, 'whether it actually was a bomb.'

I scrunched my face up; it made my sore cheek throb. 'I thought someone had claimed responsibility now. Something about "purity and light", I read?'

She smiled patiently. 'We're here about Ms Lethbridge.'

'Right,' I pondered this. 'So how can I help?'

'Tessa Lethbridge,' DI Craven glanced down at a pad he'd placed on the table earlier. 'How well did you know her?'

I thought about this for a minute. 'Well, we only met last year. But we became quite good friends.'

I saw her long hand stretching towards mine across the void. Offering something I'd lost.

'Yes, that's what Eduardo Covas said.'

I winced at the mauled pronunciation of his name.

'So—' I tried not to appear rude. 'I'm not sure what you're driving at, I'm afraid.'

'It's just—we've had several calls today.' His phone bleeped. He broke off mid-explanation and began to read a text.

I sensed Kenton trying to hide her irritation.

'It seems—' she continued now as he remained distracted. 'It appears that your friend and colleague might not have been quite whom she said she was.'

I shook my head. 'I don't follow.' I looked at the red-headed woman for help; I thought uncomfortably of Mason's big announcement yesterday that I had dismissed as her usual histrionics. 'What do you mean, not who she said she is? Was,' I corrected myself, pointlessly. 'Tessa was a first-rate ballet teacher. She came from the Royal School in Melbourne two years ago. She

106

danced with the best.'

'No, love.' God, he had an unfortunate manner about him, this man. 'Tessa Lethbridge is still safely in Melbourne.'

'She's alive?' I felt a rush of euphoria. Mason hadn't been making it up. 'She's not dead after all?'

'The *real* Tessa Lethbridge is alive. Very much alive, if a little ancient—and Down Under. I spoke to her earlier. Unfortunately, your mate,' he actually smirked. 'Your mate, I'm afraid, is very much dead—and very much a Jane Doe.'

'He means,' Kenton cut in quietly, 'that we cannot at the moment identify the dead woman, the woman who taught at the Academy. All we do know right now is, she's most definitely not Tessa Lethbridge.'

I stared at the two of them; my head spinning.

'That's why we're here. To see if you are able to shed any light on the matter.'

'Only judging by your face, I'd say not, eh, Lorraine?' Craven stood now. He picked up a silver-framed photo. 'Cute kid.'

My hands were itching.

'Also we are interested in understanding Tessa's movements on the day before the explosion. Thursday 13th July. She missed some of her afternoon classes—'

'And Mason Pyke tells us you were meant to have lunch together.'

'No,' I shook my head, 'she's wrong. We weren't—I had an appointment.'

'An appointment?'

'Yes.'

They gazed at me until I realised I was going to have to qualify myself.

'In Harley Street.'

'With?'

'With—' I took a deep breath. 'With my psychiatrist.'

'And her name is?'

'Is it relevant?' I clenched my fists. Now they would judge me.

'Every detail helps, Ms Scott, in case we have to verify anything,' Craven attempted a smile, sitting again.

'Helen. Helen Ganymede.'

'And why do you see her?'

'I see her because—' I didn't want to share it with them, but they looked like they'd settled in for the day. I took a deep breath. 'Because I briefly suffered psychotic post-traumatic shock syndrome.'

'Because?'

'Because,' I stuck my fingernail into a bloody fissure on the back of my hand, 'my son died.'

*　　　*　　　*

I had fought long and hard against seeing Helen, largely because Will, in his final act of husbandly benevolence before shipping out of the country and my life, had found her on my behalf. I'd seen enough doctors during the past year, many against my volition when I'd been briefly sectioned. I felt therapised beyond belief. But in the end, after much coercion from my mother and Zoe, and because Helen was the best in her field, I had agreed to see her once, six months ago.

And here I still was. Despite my reticence, it had been all largely positive so far, and I had felt gradually healthier in mind if not in spirit. My spirit

108

was mortally wounded; my heart utterly broken.

On the Thursday before Tessa died, the day she wanted to talk to me so badly, during my lunchtime appointment, Helen and I had run through my week, the fact that it had been a fairly good one, the best in a while.

'And the disassociation. It's still decreasing?' Helen met my gaze with her level one, her pale eyes still striking despite the deep lines around them, her smart suit immaculate and particularly severe today. For some reason though, it highlighted her rather ethereal grace. 'Have you had any remote moments in the past week?'

I took a deep breath. I still found it hard to countenance; to admit something I suffered was akin to madness.

'No,' I shook my head. 'No, none that I've been aware of. It's been pretty good actually. Thank God.'

The disassociation, when it happened, was terrifying. Or the absence of memories; perhaps that was what terrified me. It had begun two years ago when I came home from the hospital alone, without my son; crippled with grief and afraid, too guilty to live. Over the next few months, it had developed to the stage where I wouldn't remember where I was. I would slip from consciousness but I would remain conscious; leaving those around me unaware of my state. At its height, I could have whole conversations with people and the next day I'd not remember having seen them at all. It was blocking, Helen had explained, the mind shutting down to protect itself.

'I think it's subsiding, you know—'

My phone suddenly beeped mid-flow.

'Sorry,' I reached to turn it off, glimpsing Tessa's name on the display. 'It's just my friend Tessa.'

'Interesting that you left your phone switched on today, Claudie. Is there any reason?'

I did wonder sometimes why therapists liked to look for the hidden meaning in everything.

'No.' I hesitated. 'I must find her later though. She was worried—she said she had something to tell me.'

'And have you been avoiding her, Claudie?' Helen's gaze was direct.

'No,' I said, but I felt my fingers curl on my knee involuntarily.

'Are you sure? You can be totally honest here, you know that. It's a safe space.'

'I haven't. But I have to say—it's just—' I paused for thought, and my hand went up to my necklace, the gift Tessa had bought for my birthday. 'She's been a little frenetic recently. Out of character. And I did feel guilty today that I didn't have time to talk when she needed me. I've seen less of her recently.'

'Because?'

'I don't know. I've been busy.' And perhaps, if I was honest, I'd needed her less.

'All guilt is suppressed anger, you realise,' said Helen mildly. 'So why do you feel guilt? Are you cross with her for needing you?'

'No,' I shot back. Then I contemplated her words. 'I should be there for her. She has helped me so much. She understands what grief is.'

'All I would say,' Helen blinked at me kindly; she'd mislaid her glasses earlier and I thought I was probably just a blur to her. 'I'd just say that negative energy is not—not very good for you right now.'

110

'Are you saying someone needing me is negative?'

'No, absolutely not, Claudie. But you must stay attuned to your own instinct. It will tell you who is best to be around.'

I nodded. Helen brought clarity when often I had none. 'I do try.'

'So.' She swept her greying hair back and checked her gold watch. She had beautiful hands, Helen, the hands of a pianist, slim and elegant. 'We need to finish up. How've the migraines been?'

'Not so bad.'

'And the no smoking?'

'Hard,' I pulled a face. 'But those patches you gave me have helped.'

'I'm so glad. They're invaluable, as I know all too well,' Helen was a little rueful. 'It's the hardest drug to beat, nicotine, as I've learnt to my cost!'

She stood now and walked me to the door, her navy trouser suit remarkably uncreased, expensive court shoes whispering across the floor.

'Thanks.' I slipped my jacket on. I hated to outstay my welcome; I tried to always remember that I paid for my time here. That Helen was a therapist, not a friend.

'You're very welcome. I'll see you next week. Have a good one. And remember, follow that heart.'

'I will, thanks.' I ran down the stairs feeling almost cheerful.

*   *   *

'Thank you, that's fine.' Kenton sighed almost inaudibly; whether at me or her belligerent partner I wasn't sure. 'If you think of anything else, Claudia,

111

love, can you call me please? On this number.'

She slid a card in front of me. I had an urge to stroke the shiny white of it, but I didn't. I just nodded. I debated telling them about the two anonymous phone calls I'd received, but I didn't know what I'd say. I thought of Helen. It had occurred to me that she might say I'd imagined them.

It had occurred to me that maybe I had.

'We'd appreciate your help. Always hard, when a corpse has no name.' Craven smirked again, and picked his trousers out of his arse. 'They could be anyone. Let ourselves out shall we?'

Kenton paused by the front door. 'Anything at all, love,' she repeated. 'It all helps.'

Craven turned as the woman went down the stairs. 'It's funny,' he stared at me, 'I thought it was our boys in Iraq and Afghanistan who suffered from PTSD?'

'Anyone can,' I mumbled as he lumbered away. 'It's not exclusive, I don't think.'

But he had gone. After a while, I shut the door and stood with my back against it. I would not cry. I glanced down at the crumpled *Times*, on the floor by the sofa. All that time, all those espressos and glasses of red wine and all that courage I had somehow drawn from Tessa; all those walks in Hyde Park and St James's, all those talks into the night; that quiet confidence she exuded, so self-possessed, so put together. All that had been fake. All the time she had told me she understood how I felt about Ned—and now this. I had been betrayed by the woman I had so quietly relied on.

And if Tessa was not Tessa, who the hell was she then?

THURSDAY 20TH JULY
SILVER

Silver spent the day alternately fielding calls from his increasingly frantic family and Malloy, who was now so beside himself with frustration at Explosives' refusal to commit to the cause of the blast that he'd taken it upon himself to bark down the phone at Silver's team each time he was thwarted.

'How's the ID coming on?'

'We've traced the beanie girl's identity. The bad news is, she's missing too. She's a first-year student called Anita Stuart. According to her mother she was in early to have an extra-curricular class with a teacher because she had an audition to train alongside something called—let me just check.' It sounded like a group of stroppy teenagers to Silver. 'The Bolshoi?'

'Which teacher?'

'The nut-job one who is proving not to be who she said she was. Lethbridge who is not Lethbridge.'

'Right. So find her. The girl Stuart.'

'We're trying, guv—if she's still alive. I'm pretty sure she's not though, or she'd have come forward by now. We have at least seven unidentified dead still and we're sifting through DNA matches. Good news is,' he tried desperately to talk it up, 'we have tracked the courier. Polish lad called Lev Kowal. He was bringing a costume delivery from the Parliament Hill area, he says.'

'Does it check out?'

'He delivered it to a girl fitting Anita Stuart's description. We're checking the other end.'

'Thank fuck *someone's* off the list. And burqa-girl? Please tell me you're a bit fucking nearer *her*? She's got to be our number one, yeah?'

'Not necessarily,' said Silver carefully. 'This "Purity" claim could be more sinister than it first appeared. Kenton's checking out something called the Purity Alliance now. They have links to an underground movement called Daughters of Light, who apparently believe we are corrupting the earth, and they're certainly not benign. Well, obviously, or they'd not be making claims to mass murder. Radicalised hippies, it seems.'

'I don't care if they're fucking Hitler fucking Youth,' Malloy howled. 'Just get me some hard fucking evidence, Joe. I'm doing my pieces here.'

That much was obvious.

'Yes, guv,' Silver said quietly. 'We are doing our best.'

'Well your best, DCI Silver, your best at this precise moment,' Malloy's voice had gone dangerously quiet, 'ain't good enough.'

*   *   *

Kenton brought Silver an ice-cold diet Coke and a mass of clippings about various groups who were linked to the far-left organisation the Empathy Society and the more recently formed Purity Alliance. They'd been around since the early 1970s but had never got up to any more mischief than a few road-blocks outside various vivisection factories, a demonstration that had turned nasty on the Salisbury plains when developers had cut down a small wood to build a supermarket, and a homemade bomb of sorts set off on the Cornish shores to protest against trawlers ruining the seabed. Why they would suddenly blow fourteen people up in central London remained a moot point, but finally Explosives had come back with confirmation that it was a suicide bomb.

'Can't see it, can you, boss,' Kenton shook her head as they sifted through the cuttings. 'Not this little lot.'

Silver reached over for a cutting about a guy who had formed a splinter group. *BENEVOLENT SOCIETY SPLITS: NICE GONE NASTY?* read the headline. It talked of how the leaders of the Empathy Society had fallen out over ethics and one member, known as the Archangel, had led a small group of dissidents away from the main group to set up on their own. He was also linked to the splinter group Daughters of Light. The article about the Empathy Society, written in 1998, read:

'Born in America, literature graduate and sometime sociology lecturer Michael Watson's prime concerns included the growth of narcissistic individualism and the damage it was doing to today's society as a whole.'

It also talked of a beautiful girlfriend who had left her aristocratic family to follow Watson to the ends of the earth, apparently.

'To the despair of her family, heiress Rosalind Lamont acts as Watson's number two, recruiting the youth of today: students, the disaffected and those with money to burn for the cause. As yet the group have done no particular harm, but ex-member Robert Norman recently spoke out against them. "They are zealots and they despise anyone who does not agree with their creed, although their creed is undoubtedly extremely confused. They are clever with their brainwashing techniques: they make you believe you

115

are acting in the interest of the world, they persuade you your family is bad and keep you from seeing them. Thank God I realised in the end that they are simply power-crazed."'

A small photo of Michael Watson showed him to be dark, dreadlocked and heavily bearded. There was a blurred photo of a teenage Lamont in a school lacrosse team, but it was so tiny her face was a mere smudge. It was not much to go on.

Silver tossed the cutting down again onto the pile they were assembling. 'Never heard of them. Have you?'

Kenton shook her head. 'Can't say I have, guv. Classic disaffected middle-classes with too much time on their hands, if you ask me.'

Craven arrived as they were rifling through the rest.

'Fucking stupid hippies,' he spat, looking over Kenton's shoulder. 'Could all do with a good wash if you ask me. Now, I've got a *proper* result for you.' He swung back on his heels, looking incredibly pleased with himself. 'That teacher, Lethbridge.'

'Yeah?' Silver looked up at him now.

'I've ID-ed her on the CCTV.'

'What CCTV?'

'There were another couple of cameras in the Embassy next to the Academy. One of the buggers was actually working.'

Silver absorbed this. 'So, Lethbridge—?'

'Yeah. It's at 6.49 a.m., before the explosion. She exits the Academy, and makes a call at the top of the stairs. She checks her watch. Then she makes another call and goes back in.'

'The famous tip-off that was ignored?'

'Who knows? Later we see her exit the Academy

116

behind Anita Stuart, a couple of minutes before the explosion.'

'And then what?' Silver was excited.

Craven looked deflated. 'The camera range doesn't extend down onto the pavement there unfortunately, guv.'

Silver stood now, paced to the other side of the room and back again. 'Can you get me the tape? I want to see for myself.'

'Right you are,' Craven smirked at Kenton, who was starting her trawl through the cuttings again. 'You can always rely on old Derek here to bring in the goods.'

'Really.' Kenton wasn't rising to it and didn't so much as look at him.

Craven was waiting. It pained Silver, but he prided himself on being fair. 'Nice work, Derek. So the mysterious Lethbridge might be in some way connected to the explosion. Still, we've got to ID her properly, and tie up all the others too. Keep on it.' Silver crossed the room again. 'Run a check on this Watson character and the heiress girlfriend, can you, Lorraine? Find out their whereabouts today.'

'And what are you going to be doing, boss?' Craven was finding it hard to keep the sneer from his voice.

Silver thought of his lost wife. 'I'm going to be across the whole damn lot, Derek.'

THURSDAY 20TH JULY
CLAUDIE

The walls of the flat felt like they were starting to draw in, so I forced myself out and went to pick up milk, eggs and bread from Ahmed's. Standing in line, automatically I looked down at the children's comics, then looked away again.

Outside the flat, I fumbled around for my key. The sky was glowering and overcast, the street unnaturally dark and deserted, no one was around. The door key was caught in a hole in my jacket pocket; the harder I pulled, the more tangled it became and I just couldn't seem to free it. My heart was beating ever faster until I realised I was actually frightened. The strange phone calls had rattled me more than I had realised and when a figure suddenly stepped out beside me from the dusk shadows, I jumped, dropping the eggs.

'Bloody hell,' I swore softly, stepping over the viscous splatter to open the door as quickly as possible. 'You scared me.'

'I know you like your eggs scrambled,' Rafe joked, 'but that's taking it a bit far.'

'Hilarious.' I almost fell through the door as it finally opened. I tried to shut it quickly behind me before he followed me in.

'Claudie—' Rafe stopped it with his foot. 'Wait. Please.'

'Why are you here?' I ducked under his arm and turned to face him now. He looked as handsome as ever, totally guileless, although he was no longer clean-shaven, his dark face almost bearded now with stubble, rings of tiredness beneath his eyes.

'You know why I'm here. For you, darling. I couldn't get away before, or I'd have been here earlier. It's murder at the Commons.' He rolled his eyes comically. 'Almost literally. In-house war.'

'You'd better get back there.' I turned away again. He had all the patter. I was shocked at how raw I felt at the sight of him.

'You're hurt.' He caught my arm. 'I realise that.'

'It's fine. OK?' I shook him off. 'Just go home.'

'I've been really worried.'

I smiled at his gall. I wasn't prepared for this now. I wasn't sure what to do, what to say.

'See? We're meant to be together.' Rafe's boyish face relaxed for a moment, his thick chestnut hair falling across his eyes. He opened his arms just a little, stepping towards me.

'You don't really believe that,' I said quietly. Neither of us did.

'I'm sorry,' he cajoled. 'You have to believe *that*.'

'Why do I?' I flattened myself against the door-jamb, out of his reach, my smile already faded. 'We're about as meant to be together as—as Cameron and Clegg. Please, Rafe. Just go.'

'I can explain about the stuff in the flat.' He pushed his hair back, his forehead furrowed. 'It was a—a misunderstanding.'

'A misunderstanding?' I was incredulous.

'She's just an old friend,' he muttered. 'She stays when she's in town.'

'Don't worry.' I looked down at him from the top step. 'Rafe, really. I've nothing to say because there's nothing to say.'

We stood there, Rafe and I, in the middle of my little street, and I closed my eyes. I saw the past year reel back through my head like an old film, jerky and in slow motion, and I thought:

I should tell you that you've hurt me because I trusted you. How your presence enabled me to get out of bed every day when I thought I never would again; when the pain was so bad I could barely breathe. You showed up and you stayed and you slowly pulled me through, dragging me from the abyss incrementally until my feet found solid ground. For that I will always be truly grateful.

But had I ever really seen Rafe in my future? Not so very long ago I genuinely hadn't cared if I even *had* a future. Without Rafe, God knows where I'd have ended up. I was finding it almost impossible to admit that he had been important to me, now that he had hurt me too. I had spent so long suppressing my pain I had pushed myself into some kind of emotional limbo.

We'd met at Sadler's Wells on a freezing January night. I had dragged myself to the Academy's charity fund-raiser after a couple of sessions with Helen, during which she had firmly told me that I had to act as if I wanted to keep on living, even if I felt like I was dead inside. Even if I felt pierced with guilt every time I laughed, or so much as smiled. Even if I felt I was betraying Ned's memory.

Rafe was at the do in an official capacity, a junior minister in the Department of Culture, and he had made a speech that was funny and entertaining. He was a captivating storyteller, and afterwards, as Tessa and I chatted quietly on the periphery of the busy room, Rafe had introduced himself. Tessa had been called over by Eduardo to meet a rich benefactor and I was left with the junior minister who was charming whilst I was shy and awkward, still weighed down with my own grief. After a minute or two of polite chit-chat, Rafe had fetched me a drink.

It was almost unpalatable white wine, and I'd wrinkled my nose at it and then tried to hide it because it was rude when he'd been kind enough to fetch it for me. He'd laughed, and cracked a joke about warm Chardonnay for the Bridget Jones generation, and then we'd both admitted we were dying for a cigarette.

'I haven't smoked for years. Not since I was a student,' I was rueful. 'Not till quite recently.'

'So why now?'

'I—it was—' I found it almost impossible to voice the truth. That I had lost my son. That my son had died. That I didn't care what poison I put in my body; that I would quite happily follow him.

'Could I tell you another time?' I managed eventually, and Rafe smiled and said of course, and we went and shared a cigarette outside, stamping our feet against the cold, watching our own breath join the smoke curling up into the freezing air. We talked about why he had got into politics—'to save the world' apparently. And when he asked me out, a few days later, although Tessa had discouraged it ('you can't trust a politician, Claudie' she'd frowned), Zoe, typical PR girl, had loved what he stood for (or maybe what he could do for her, who knew?), a Tory swung to "new" Labour—and it had been easy to listen to her. Helen had not been so sure I was ready for a new relationship, but she was guarded about her own views, making it clear that it must be my choice what I did. And so I began to 'date' an MP.

Rafe was a curious combination of social ease

and mercurial moods. Sometimes I found him too glib, but he was very easy-going about life, whilst passionate about his job, and was often away for whole weekends at his constituency in Norwich, which suited me just fine. I needed light relief and human warmth, not the next grand passion.

For a long time, I had imagined myself as a very deep wound, gradually growing shiny skin across the bloody mess beneath. I had begun to heal, slowly, infinitesimally. But there would *always* be a bloody mess beneath; that was the truth, for the rest of my life.

I took a deep breath and opened my eyes again. 'Let's go and get a drink then,' I said slowly. Perhaps I should be braver. Perhaps I should try to tell him how I had really felt.

Together we went to a little Ethiopian restaurant round the corner on the high street. We didn't hold hands, but our arms brushed as we walked, and I thought, this is what I will miss, the easy intimacy I'd found with this man.

We sat at a little formica table with one wilted freesia on it, and it was so steamy we both had to take our jackets off. A long-faced boy with a puny moustache and skin as dark as bitter chocolate brought us coffee so strong it made my heart kick.

'I know it looks odd, Claudie,' Rafe said. 'But I want you to believe me.'

'We're grown-ups,' I shrugged, tracing figures of eight in the sugar I'd spilt. 'You're free to do what you like.'

'Claudie!' he expostulated. 'We both know that's not true.'

I was surprised by the depth of his emotion.

'It's made me realise,' he caught my hand now,

and for a moment I actually thought tears might flood his brown eyes, 'I don't want to lose you.'

The tears were an illusion. I tried my best to concentrate; but a part of me felt so detached I could have been in the other room. He let go of my hand.

'Frankly, Claudie, half the time I don't think you give a toss about me anyway. And that's the problem.'

'That's not true,' I mumbled, but I was worried it was.

'Oh come on,' attack was the best form of defence, of course. 'It's like you're bloody devoid of emotion, Claudia.'

'Oh,' I said. I rubbed my sore eyes with the heels of my hands. A lethargy had settled over me after I'd come out of hospital the last time. I had fought it hard this past year; I'd tried to come out of my shell, to stop protecting myself from any form of external life, but recently I'd felt so strange again. I shook my head, impatient with myself. 'Yes OK. I can see that I might come across like that sometimes. And I do try not to, really.'

'I mean, Christ knows, I understand you've had a horrible time.'

'A horrible time?' I repeated, almost puzzled.

'The worst. Like I did when I was growing up. Losing my parents so suddenly. You know, I can help you. And you can't define your life for all time because you lost Ned—'

I didn't want to hear him say the name. I stood violently, my chair scraping loudly across the silence. The long-faced boy stared at us blankly and turned up the volume on the TV in the corner. A studio audience applauded wildly and

123

incongruously in the empty room. And then a face I knew stared out at me; Sadie Malvern. 'Missing girl' the text read beneath it. I saw Rafe's eyes flicker to the screen. He was a 'sucker for a pretty face'—his words, not mine.

I felt my stomach knot. Had she been caught in the explosion too? I looked back at the screen, but her image was gone.

'I'm going to go now.'

'Claudie.' Rafe chucked money on the table and followed me out into the night. It was a relief to get out of the heat. 'Sorry. That was shitty of me. I just mean—I can't reach you sometimes.'

'So you decided to fuck someone else?' I was starting to feel anger now, which was some kind of release at least.

He looked like a small schoolboy now, bereft and guilty.

'I wasn't. I'm just—I'm not very good at commitment.'

'It's OK, Rafe.' We were at my front door now. I walked away from him slowly, stepping over the broken eggs now smeared into the pavement, up the front stairs. 'I don't think I am either any more. Sorry if you've found me hard work. I probably am.'

'Give me another chance, Claudie,' he pleaded, but I knew that his heart wasn't in it. We were both going through some sort of motion.

I gazed at him; at his hangdog look, at his lithe body and his immaculate designer clothes. He had provided comfort when I was desperate, a port in a storm when Will had decided to go—but we weren't right for each other, I knew that much. He had known sorrow too, orphaned at an early age, and he had empathised. He had been a pair of warm arms in the night, and he hadn't minded when I sobbed myself to sleep occasionally. He wanted to heal me, I could feel that, because that's what he did; fixed things. Suddenly I saw him for what he was. Some kind of charming charlatan. I looked at him, and then I opened my front door and walked away— and Rafe let me go.

Slowly I climbed the stairs with the milk and bread I'd bought earlier. The doorbell rang one disconsolate time. We both knew I wouldn't answer it. It was over.

In the dying light I looked out of the window and I contemplated the truth for a moment. I'd become so good at suppression; I was only half myself these days. Somewhere, in the far reaches of my brain, I knew that by hiding it all, I'd never recover properly from anything. And Helen—what would Helen say? Oh she'd have a field day about this when she found out. She'd warned me I'd be better on my own for now . . .

If she found out. I could choose what to tell her. Just like Tessa had chosen to lie . . .

I scrabbled in the kitchen cupboard and retrieved Tessa's things. I picked up the business card from the club and tried to decipher the name scribbled on the back. *Paul Piper*, I thought it read, which meant precisely nothing to me.

Which Tessa was real? Had she draped herself in the persona I'd known, wrapped it round her like a disguise—or was that the real woman despite the stolen identity? It was time to do something about this mess.

I shut the door behind me, and headed into town.

THURSDAY 20TH JULY
SILVER

Silver let himself into Philippa's as quietly as he could, in the almost vain hope that the whole household would be asleep. He slipped off his boots by the front door, planning to make tea in the large, cosy kitchen and contemplate what to do about Lana, unassailed for once by argument, the blip-blip of a Nintendo DS or some unedifying Dub-step. But the gentle throb of Bob Marley coming from the end of the hall announced that Philippa at least was still up. Abandoning the tea idea, he began to creep up the stairs. After the shrill dressing-down from Julie, followed by the tears and recriminations when he said gently he thought it was best they stopped seeing one another, he'd had his fill of women tonight.

'Leticia?' he heard the creak of the kitchen door opening. 'That you?'

He swore silently. 'No, P, it's me. Joe.'

'I told her to be in by ten.' It was half-past. 'Flipping kids.'

Leticia, Philippa's middle daughter, was going through what could only be described as a hormonal stage. She'd hit thirteen hard, retreating to her messy pink bedroom when she was in the house, where cast-off clothes were scattered across the floor like small islands. Or she sat at the large kitchen table scowling, iPod earphones stuck firmly in whilst she surfed the net endlessly, usually on Facebook. Speaking to her was generally pointless; occasionally she'd manage a monosyllable or a forced smile that never reached her heavily mascara-ed eyes. The fact that Philippa was on Leticia's back the whole time only served to ratchet up the general tension.

And yet despite all the sulks and slammed doors, Silver knew what a lovely girl Leticia really was; he could see she was merely lost in a wilderness of uncertainty about life. He thanked God Molly was still a few years from the angst-ridden adolescence that was so overwhelming Leticia. It probably wouldn't be long though . . . Silver felt the knot of anxiety in his gut tighten as he thought of his own family.

The track and trace on Lana's car had rendered nothing so far. Silver was still praying that she'd simply parked up somewhere, got horribly smashed and was sleeping it off. If she didn't surface by the morning, though, he'd have to act.

'Do you want me to go and have a look for Leticia?' he asked her mother now.

Beneath her neatly coiled corn-rows, Philippa's wide, jovial face was unusually serious, her dark eyes troubled, but she shook her head.

'Thanks, Joe, I appreciate it, but she's down the road at Marlon's. She's just pushing me over this time thing. I'll give her till eleven and then I'm down there, if you don't mind holding the fort. Fancy a cuppa?'

Silver debated the fug of a kitchen. He knew if he chose, he could discuss his worries about Lana with Philippa and, as single-parent-extraordinaire, she'd be a good sounding-board. But he feared the reality of voicing his fears.

'I'm knackered, P.' He started back up the stairs. Then he changed his mind. It was good to talk, wasn't it? He had to remember that sometimes. 'Maybe just a quick one, then.'

Philippa was drinking rum, but she knew better than to offer Silver any. She switched the kettle on whilst he yawned at the kitchen table, rubbing his eyes with the heels of his hands.

'Bad day?'

'Long day.'

'Any nearer the truth?' She plonked a cup of tea in front of him and pulled over the red biscuit tin from the middle of the table. 'What's the word on Berkeley Square today?'

'I'm more worried about my errant ex-wife right now, to be honest,' he lifted the lid. 'She's gone walkabout again.'

'Oh dear.' Philippa glimpsed the empty tin. 'Little sods! That's three packets in two days.'

Silver groped around for the last crumbs. 'I think she's drinking again,' he muttered.

Philippa had had her own issues with an ex-husband who was an addict; boy-man Marlon, the eternal loafer and weed smoker. But Silver seriously doubted that the ever-efficient Philippa had been the one to lead Marlon down the slippery slope into addiction; whereas he lived every day with the knowledge that if he had not hit the bottle so hard himself as he ascended a stressful career ladder, just like his own father had, his wife would have been unlikely to follow. If he had not ignored her whilst in a whisky haze, she might not have met Ray Steen every Monday at the Majestic. And if she had been happier and more sober then Jaime Malvern might still be alive, and Lana might not have disappeared into the ether herself.

'Why's life so complicated, eh, P?' He ate the

crumbs of a custard cream with despondence.

'Joe, you take too much on your shoulders, man. Drinkers—they make their own choices, no?'

'Maybe.' He shrugged, unconvinced. 'It's a hard habit to beat though.'

'You did it.' She knew he still attended the occasional AA meeting after he'd left an address list open on the family computer once. 'And she's a grown woman. Just like Marlon's a grown man—or pretends to be.' She pulled a face, almond eyes indignant. 'Some people, they just find it hard to deal with life. With responsibility. But you can't live it for her, Joe.'

'I've hardly been doing that though, have I? I've left her up there with the little 'uns whilst I get on with stuff down here.' He'd said it. It almost winded him, but he'd said the thing that was pressing into his brain, that was hurting him most. He exhaled.

'You've been earning a crust and helping the nation to boot.' Philippa sucked her teeth. 'Come now, Joe. Stop beating yourself up. You're doing good; doing something important. You're following your path. And you know your kids love you.'

'I know I don't see enough of them.'

She laid a warm hand over his, her skin dark against his own tanned hand. 'There's time, Joe. You can rectify your mistakes. Remember that.'

She was a wise witch, this woman, he thought, grinning at her remorsefully. 'I hope so, P. I really hope so.' He yawned and stretched. Leticia still wasn't back. 'Do you want me to sit up with you till she's back?'

She glanced at the clock. 'No. I'll give her another fifteen minutes. And then—' she mimed wringing a neck, 'I'll give that father of hers what for.'

129

'I'm going to hit the hay then. Give me a shout if you're going out, and I'll keep an ear open.'

'Appreciate it, Joe. I'll see you tomorrow.'

Philippa shook her head as she listened to him lollop up the stairs, pursing her generous mouth as she dumped his mug in the sink. He was a good man, Joe Silver, of that there was no doubt. Even if he was a little distracted from time to time by his expensive clothes and unsuitable women. That Julie! My God, what a pain; far too desperate to win the attractive Silver over. Philippa held no hope for Julie at all after an awkward Friday night drink in her kitchen a few months ago; she was obviously just another dalliance for a lonely man who still mourned his marriage. As for the children issue—well, Philippa might have her own opinions when it came to fathers and child-care—but Silver would come to the right conclusions soon enough, of that she was pretty certain. He wasn't terrified of a *little* self-reflection, as so many men were—though he was still a selfish child at heart, like them all. Philippa expected no more of the male species, and her cynicism ran deep. She drained her last centimetre of rum and checked the time. Where the hell was her disobedient daughter?

As Silver hit the bed, he heard the slam of the front door downstairs announcing Leticia's arrival home. He could sleep easy now. But exhausted as he was, Silver found it impossible to doze off. Thoughts of Lana and the rolled car outside Hebdon Bridge six years ago haunted him; and eventually when he slept, he saw his ex-wife pirouetting through the fields with a muscle-bound Ray Steen, Molly panting behind in bloodied ballet shoes, reaching out in vain to her mother.

He woke sweating at 5 a.m., and put another call in for the track and trace.

Still nothing. He lay in bed, staring at the ceiling. If Lana wasn't back by lunchtime, he was going home.

THURSDAY 20TH JULY
CLAUDIE

In the cab that smelt of old sick and new air freshener, I stared out of the window as the London night slid by, turning the little pink and black card for Sugar and Spice over and over in my hand, feeling the embossed tassels on the huge breasts of the cartoon girl on the front. Passing under a street light, I gazed down at her lascivious wink as she curled one arm above her head.

As we pulled onto the high street, I had leant forward and tapped the Asian driver on his back.

'Can you take me to this place please? It's in London Bridge.'

I thrust the card at him. He swore and swerved, nearly taking a female cyclist out.

'Yeah all right, love,' forcefully he pushed his arm back against my hand. The girl on the bike was busy flicking him a V. 'I'm driving. Just tell me where you want to go.'

'It's called Sugar and Spice.'

'The titty bar?' he sounded incredulous. 'Are you sure?'

I wasn't at all sure. 'A *titty* bar?'

'Yeah, you know. Lap-dancers, pole-dancers, that type of thing. Girls with no clothes on.'

'Oh I see.' I took a deep breath; I had no idea what I was going to do once I arrived. 'Yes, there please.'

He eyed me in the mirror. 'Are you one, then?' he asked doubtfully. 'A dancer?'

In my old green parka and jeans, grazes still covering half my left cheek, I hardly looked like the girl on the card.

'No. I'm just—' I looked down at her sly come-hither leer. 'I'm just looking for a friend.'

Muttering, he swung the cab towards London Bridge.

*   *   *

There had been a time that whenever I'd crossed the Thames I'd been amazed by the night beauty of this great city, at the skyline and the mix of new and old. Only gradually, it had begun to feel different . . . recently it had felt too crowded; full-up, no sky left, electric light cancelling out the black. No room for anything except artifice, Rafe had said to me sadly one day, citing a need to get back to basics some time soon to save us all. 'We'll be living in a crater soon.'

On the edge of London Bridge, beneath the arches, I paid the surly driver. In an ironic twist, Sugar and Spice was situated opposite Southwark Cathedral, between McDonald's and a bike store; it had a big black door, a bigger, blacker doorman with an earpiece and a curly-lettered gold-plated sign—all of which looked thoroughly uninviting to me.

'You're not going to get seen looking like that.' The doorman folded his gloved hands before him, his face implacable. 'I'd go home and come back when you're feeling better.' He didn't bother looking at me when he spoke.

'I'm perfectly fine, thanks, and I don't want a job.' I tried a winning smile. I realised I hadn't smiled properly in days; it almost hurt my face. 'I've come to see Mr Piper.'

He did look now. 'Mr Piper?'

'Yes,' I smiled harder. 'Mr Piper. Is he here?'

'Never heard of him,' the man shrugged.

'He's expecting me,' I lied.

'Not here, he ain't.'

'Oh.' I didn't believe him. 'Maybe I got his name wrong.'

'Maybe you did.'

'I was told he was the man in charge.'

'You was told wrong.' He had all night, apparently.

'So,' I tried the useless smile again, 'could you help me, please? What is the *right* name?'

I was interrupted by a short, fat man like a cannon-ball in a dark pinstripe suit pushing past me with a rather dumpy blonde in tow, all leopard skin and scarlet lipstick and a cloud of cheap perfume. The man eyed me quickly and looked away derisively.

'Tell her to beat it,' he instructed the doorman, jerking his head at me and clamping Blondie's wrist in his meaty paw as they descended the stairs. He was American, with comb-marks in his slicked-back hair; so fat that his sagging belly strained tightly against his blue shirt, and he had a nasty little moustache that could only be reminiscent of one person. 'Not our type. At all.'

'I have told her, boss.' The doorman folded and

133

re-folded his gloved hands, looking at me as if to say *I told you so*.

'Don't be mean.' The blonde, whose chest was as inflated as the American's ego obviously was, stopped on the step below me and sniggered, her over-blown top lip protruding over little teeth. 'I'll give her a lesson, if you like.'

'That, cherry pie,' the American tweaked her nipple lasciviously, 'I'd love to see.'

'I was looking for Mr Piper, actually,' I said loudly, sickened by his temerity. 'Do you know him?'

'*Mr* Piper? Who wants to know?' The American dropped the blonde's hand now and stared at me. Oil seeped from the deep creases and acne pits on his face. I held his gaze.

'Me. I—I have an appointment, actually.'

It was the American's turn to smirk. 'Really?'

'Yes, really. I won't take up much of his time.'

'I'll say, honey. You're,' the American glanced at his ostentatious watch, 'only a week too late.'

'What do you mean?'

'No Piper here, honey.' He spelt the words out like I was deaf. Or stupid.

'Oh.' I was thoroughly confused. 'Well, I can come back.'

'You do that.' The American ran a fat finger down my good cheek. His breath smelt of old meat. 'You're a good-looking broad, or you might be out of all that shit.' Without warning, he pulled my coat open. 'Good tits.'

I lurched backwards, standing on the blonde's bare toes in the process. 'Ouch,' she protested, digging her nails into my hand to push me off.

'Come back when you've cleaned up,' he leered.

'Get your roots done. You never know. We may even have a job for you.'

'Come *on*, Larry.' Blondie scowled at me. 'I'm dying for a wee.'

'Sure thing, cherry pie.' But he didn't like being hurried by her, that much was clear. He pushed her hard in front of him so she stumbled slightly in her spindly stilettos, grabbing the railing just before she fell. She pouted up at him, and then thought better of complaining. I looked at her again. There was something vaguely familiar about her.

'Sorry, Larry,' she simpered. 'Weak bladder!'

'Yeah. You and the rest of those tramps downstairs.'

Charming, I thought, as they disappeared into the club. He was horrible, and he had a vile energy about him that fouled the air even after he'd gone.

I turned away. Now what?

FRIDAY 21ST JULY
SILVER

For the fiftieth time since Wednesday, Lana's phone clicked straight through to voicemail without ringing. Silver chucked the receiver down, threw his drink can in the bin and called Kenton in.

'Any joy, kiddo?'

'Not on Michael Watson, not yet, guv, no.' Her squirrel eyes were less bright than usual as she admitted defeat. 'Directly after he set up the Purity Alliance he was living in India, Mumbai I think, hanging out with some Sanyasins.'

'Some who?'

'You know. Baghwan and orange clothes and Rolls Royces? Encouraged to sleep with each other and sometimes their children, and break their own legs in therapy to find themselves. That kind of liberal thing.'

'Marvellous,' Silver rolled his eyes, and noted with annoyance he'd got diet Coke on his pristine cuff. 'And then?'

'Possibly involved in running one of those trendy teepee campsites apparently down in Devon, about five years ago—but it's long since moved on.'

'Trendy teepees?' Silver thought nostalgically about camping in the drizzle and the sheep-shit in the Lake District when the children were small. Lana, of course, had never come; she would have rather died first. Nowhere to plug the hairdryer in. 'Christ. And now?'

'Not sure,' she cleared her throat. 'But we'll find him, don't worry.'

'And the posh girlfriend?'

'Rosalind Lamont? I'm going to talk to someone who was attached to the Empathy Society later. Acted as some kind of secretary, woman called Jan Martin, runs a café now down in Spitalfields called the Vegetarian Oven. They've all lost contact though. Not spoken since around 2007, according to her.'

'Wild-goose chase, no doubt.' Silver sighed heartily. 'It's a bit bloody preposterous isn't it? These so-called do-gooders doing harm.' He opened the top drawer of his desk and retrieved his electric shaver. Kenton gave a half-smile. It'd be a bad day, the day Silver didn't shave. He switched it on, then switched it off again as he thought of something.

'Any joy from the Sadie appeal?'

'Just the usual nutters.'

'Parents?'

'Phone's been cut off. Local uniform are going round. Again. No one ever answers the door apparently.'

Silver wondered if it would be someone he knew making that house call. With an effort, he turned his thoughts away from the Malverns.

'OK, thanks. Keep on the Watson thing. We need to eliminate him.'

'Sure, guv.' Lorraine Kenton turned to leave, then turned back, hands dug deep in her trouser pockets like a schoolboy, clearing her throat. 'It's probably none of my business—but is everything OK?'

Silver walked to the window and looked down at the station yard where a couple of Vauxhalls were being washed. It was humid today, the sky sagging with unspent rain, and he felt tired and below par after a disturbed night's sleep.

'My ex-wife's missing.'

'Missing?' Kenton looked worried.

'Well, I say missing, but that might be a bit dramatic. She didn't come home again last night apparently—not for the first time in her life, it must be said. She had a bit of a—' He snapped the blinds shut, and then opened them again. 'A drink problem. She's been sober a while, but—'

'Old habits die hard,' Kenton finished for him.

'Exactly.'

How hard, Joe Silver knew exactly. The long, cold pint, the whisky chaser glinting gold on the bar; the alcohol that would take the pain away, the bitter-sweet annihilation. The morning after, dry mouth, cold sweat, clear clean panic followed by self-loathing—followed by the only cure—another drink.

'Kids all right?' Kenton asked gruffly. Personally, she didn't really see the point of kids, but still . . .

'They are for now, their grandma's there, but if Lana doesn't turn up by lunchtime, I'll have to go back.'

'Boss'll understand.'

'Yeah, guess so.'

Didn't look good though, the disappearing alcoholic wife; of that he was fully aware. It would be ringing all sorts of alarm bells in the promotion department. Silver worried that he'd be taken off the Op immediately if he told Malloy—though his gut was telling him he should relinquish the responsibility now anyway; his concentration simply wasn't good enough. The Sadie Malvern thing was bothering him to a ludicrous degree and the reality was, he needed to solve it for his own ends. He had it firmly in his head now that he owed the poor family.

And much as he adored his kids, he loathed the idea of Frogley right now, and that was the truth. He hated the village, he felt the stone walls closing in on him every time he drove down the winding main street. Worse, the guilt lacerated him. He didn't want to admit that he was terrified of going home.

The desk phone rang. Silver eyed it warily.

'Want me to—' Kenton indicated the phone.

'No, it's fine. You go on.'

She quietly closed the door behind her as he picked up the receiver.

'The track and trace, boss, on the Peugeot; we've got a spot.'

'Go on.' Silver sat.

'Beach car park, Wednesday afternoon, about five.'

Beach. The bleak sea; hungry and unforgiving. His heart twisted. 'Abandoned?'

'No. Leaving the car park. A couple.'

Silver frowned. 'A couple?'

'Yeah, bloke and a blonde woman, long hair.'

Lana. With a man. He felt relief: and something else, something intangible.

'Right. Cheers for that. Do me a favour, can you run another track and trace in about an hour?'

He called his mother-in-law. 'She was seen leaving Forth Harbour Beach at five yesterday with a man. The cliff car park.'

'Thank God.' He heard the break in Anne's voice. 'But with who?'

'Don't ask me, Anne. I'd be the last to know. Is she seeing someone?'

'Not that I know of.'

They were tight, Anne and Lana, thick as the proverbial thieves, drinking tea all morning, setting the world to rights; shopping together in town most afternoons. Strange if Anne didn't know. But then, if Lana was off the wagon again, she'd hide everything from her mother she could; she'd managed to in the past.

'Let's give it to the end of the day, yeah? If she's not back by then, I'll drive up tonight. OK?'

'Right you are,' Anne sighed deeply. 'Oh, and Joseph—'

She was going to thank him, he could sense it.

'Don't mention it, Anne.'

'I was going to say, Matthew's room is dead tatty. You really could give it a lick of paint next time

139

you're up. And he needs a haircut. Long hair on boys is ridiculous. And have a word with Ben about those pictures on his walls. Girls, you know. Not many clothes on. I mean, really, that Jordan. All inflated. Not nice.' She sniffed. ''Specially not with our Molly in the house.'

With that, she was gone, and Silver was left, grinning into thin air. Some things never changed, and for once, he was relieved. It made life a little more secure.

*   *   *

Silver had a quick meeting with Counter Terrorism, who were now more distracted than ever after a new threat to British airspace had just been reported by American and Saudi intelligence.

'I just can't see that Berkeley Square is anything to do with any of the Al-Qaeda factions.' DCI Lynne Murray pushed her hand through her short, dark hair like a woman on the edge. 'Not their style, and we'd know by now if it was them. They like to lay claim. It's something domestic, if you ask me. Some nutter much closer to home.' She chucked her coffee cup in the bin and missed, coffee splashing up the wall. 'Bollocks. I'm so bloody stretched it's unreal, and now the bloody Yanks are kicking off again.'

Half an hour later, Silver had a briefing from the Explosives team at Bow Street. The bad-tempered head of the department, Leo McNulty, leafed through a batch of images from the scene, sucking his greying moustache in a way that turned Silver's stomach.

'A fucking badly made suicide bomb, Joe. In a

bag. Not a vest or a belt. Nails galore. Which makes it harder to tell you who detonated it.'

Silver didn't ask why it had taken so long for them to determine what was pretty obvious from these pictures. McNulty said it anyway.

'Fucking rain hampered us, and the amount of debris and asbestos from the bank. Health and Safety have gone fucking mad, especially after all the civil suits following 7/7 and 9/11.'

'Any way of telling yet who our bomber was?'

McNulty spat into his own bin. Silver tried not to wince.

'I'll let you know asap, all right?'

FRIDAY 21ST JULY
CLAUDIE

All night the name Piper had rattled round my head like a toy train on a track, interspersing dreams where I was dying in a lift-shaft. When I woke up, my head was pounding. I went to the bathroom to take a pill but I realised I had finished the bottle. When though? I couldn't remember. A sob built in my chest. I had to hold on; to get through this, just to find out about Tessa and what I'd done. Then . . . well, who knew? The future seemed an indistinct and unimportant blur.

Finally, I made the call I had been avoiding. My dependence on Helen scared me sometimes: I tried to cope without her as much as possible, but I was frightened. Please God don't let me be losing it again.

'I'm sorry I missed my appointment yesterday,'

141

I said, when she picked up, and I heard my voice crack. 'I'm not—'

'What is it, Claudie?'

'I don't feel too good right now.'

'That's OK, Claudie. Can you come to me today? I'll make time for you.'

'I don't think I can move, Helen.' The admission was torturous to make. I fought back the tears. 'I'm sorry. I'm really sorry.'

'Don't be. You hang in there. I'll see if I can shift some appointments.'

I breathed out.

'I'll call when I'm on my way.'

I just sat, staring into the middle distance, listening and thinking. A sudden distant bang, the whirr of someone's mower. Next door's piano. People living as if nothing had changed.

I watched a spider slowly encroach on me across the ceiling, and I thought about Tessa again. Why would anyone lie about who they were? Because they wanted to hide something, I supposed, or because they wanted to be what they were not . . .

Whatever the reason, somewhere there was an answer to why Tessa lied, and more crucially, an answer to my part in her death.

I wiped my eyes and forced myself into the shower. I had to find some clarity before this headache killed me.

When I got out the phone was ringing. Dripping onto the rug, I picked it up, steeling myself. I wouldn't be intimidated.

It was Will.

'Are you OK?' he sounded faintly annoyed. 'I've been worrying about you, Claudie. Why haven't you rung me back?'

'I didn't know I was meant to,' I said. A spider's shadow was magnified three-fold behind the pale blind. It must be spider season.

'Don't be so obtuse,' he snapped. 'I left you loads of messages.'

'Did you? I haven't spoken to you for over three months.'

'You have.'

Oh God. Had I?

'I didn't get the messages.'

'Well there's a surprise.' His sarcasm stretched down the line.

'I will just hang up if you're horrid,' I warned. 'You know I will.'

'Oh that's grown up,' he mocked. He was always nasty when he felt guilty. 'Hang up then.'

I deliberated for a moment. 'What do you want?' I said eventually.

'I want to know you're OK.'

'I am OK.'

'You sound—spacey.'

'I've just had a shower.'

'It's ten o'clock,' he sounded mildly outraged. He was a lark, Will, up with the dawn chorus.

'So?'

'So, why aren't you at work?'

'Week off. Courtesy of my dear sister.' I thought again of Friday; of the fact I apparently hadn't had a scheduled shift—and yet I'd been on the way to work. My hands started to itch.

'Can we meet?' I could hear the tension in Will's voice.

I sat down on the sofa, pulling my towel tighter. 'I don't know. I'm not sure if—'

'What?' he prompted.

'I'm sorry, Will.'

'Look,' my husband said. 'I've got to come into town tomorrow. I've got a meeting at St Pancras. We could have some lunch.'

There was a pause.

'I'd like to see you,' he said softly.

'I'm still pretty pissed off, Will.'

'Why?'

Another pause. Was he serious?

'Because you left,' I said eventually. It was hardly rocket science.

'You could have come.'

'I couldn't. I couldn't leave London. You knew that.'

'But he wasn't here any more, Claudie,' Will sighed. 'Ned wasn't here any more.'

'So?' I was stubborn. 'He was to me.'

'And now you're pissed off because I tried to help you?'

'I didn't need that kind of help.' He had found me Helen when I was on my knees; but at the time I had only felt he had interfered. Abandoned me, although I had been unreachable, perhaps; and then interfered to ease his conscience. Oh, the ironies of separation. No one knew me better than this man. But I couldn't see him, not now, anyway. And he had been weak. Weaker than me, maybe, I was realising recently. He had cut and run. He had not sat beside me when Ned breathed out for the last time. I had been alone, uselessly willing my tiny son so desperately to hang on, my mother in a taxi that arrived too late, my husband—my husband pacing the streets of London, unable to countenance his own pain. Freefalling into unimaginable grief, I hadn't registered his actions

144

at the time: but when he chose to flee later, I was astounded.

'Listen,' he said. 'I've got to go. Clients waiting.' He was a designer in a small firm. 'Call me later. Let me know. And, Claudie—'

'What?'

'Just be careful, Claudie. Take care of yourself, I mean.'

Futile platitudes. But something he'd just said suddenly clicked.

'OK,' I muttered. *St Pancras.*

'Proper care.' I could hear someone calling him. 'Hang on,' he was shouting.

'I'll call you,' I lied. Anything to get him off the line. 'I swear.'

Messages, he had said. I looked at the answer-phone that I had not listened to for days; I clicked it on. There were two from my mother last week, from Portugal: one about coming to London for shopping; one about my sister's birthday. One from Rafe on Thursday night, trying to track me down. One from a loan company offering to help me with debts. Two from Will. And then Tessa's voice, tense and low. I froze in the centre of the room.

'What happened to you, Claudie? Are you OK? You said you'd come; I stayed here all night. Oh God. I don't know what to do. And,' the noise of traffic, a beeping horn in the background, 'I just wanted to say,' another pause, tearful now, 'I'm sorry.'

I found myself checking the room almost guiltily in case anyone else had heard. I went back to the machine and hurriedly replayed the message, my hands shaking. Friday morning, 6.50 a.m. Her voice

145

urgent and distressed. What did she mean? Why couldn't I remember where I should have been? I banged the side of my head frantically with the flat of my hand.

I wiped the message off, and opened the cupboard, scrabbling around for the bag I'd shoved in there yesterday, searching for the keys I had found in Tessa's bag. My hands were shaking as I swung them round the small bejewelled ballet shoe. A tiny silver key; the key to a locker. *Property of St Pancras* was stamped on it in little letters. I'd thought nothing of it, but now—now . . .

Above my head now, the spider was black and blot-like on the ceiling. I couldn't wait for Helen. I had to get to St Pancras now.

*   *   *

Outside, the noise of the street seemed riotous and the colours hurt my eyes. Ahmed on the corner loading up his fruit and veg boxes with gaudy tomatoes and oranges. Guy over the road lovingly washing his old Renault. The postman in shorts, whistling as he walked down the street. Tentatively I shut the front door behind me. I stood stock-still for a moment, clasping Tessa's key, the cold metal warming in my clammy hand. I heard sirens in the distance. *'There's a nee-nor, Mummy.'*

I was already sweating, beads springing on my top lip. Panicking slightly, I turned to go back and then Helen came round the corner, brow slightly furrowed with concern, greying hair very pale against the black jacket she wore; leather despite the heat, smart velvet trousers swooshing across the dirty pavement. She had come, and now I was going to betray her effort and run out on her. Instinctively I pressed myself against the door, heart hammering. She hadn't seen me yet; she had stopped to pop her A-Z back in her bag.

Swiftly I turned the opposite way, speeded to a jog before she saw me. Frantically I flagged down an oncoming black taxi and jumped in before she caught me. It was vital that Helen didn't catch me. I knew she would think I wasn't lucid. We'd have to do the delusions chat again and she'd suggest medication; maybe I'd get sent back to hospital. My stomach churned like I'd drunk five litres of coffee: I was totally awash with adrenaline, which made a change from the torpor I had felt recently. I asked the driver for St Pancras and caught my breath as I sat back in the seat, feeling almost jubilant.

The jubilation subsided pretty fast.

I couldn't remember the simplest of things; I could barely remember my breakfast. My head throbbed; my heart ached, but I would find out why Tessa had lied, and where I should have been to meet her before she died.

FRIDAY 21ST JULY
SILVER

'Mum sent a text,' Matty said breathlessly, and he sounded so pleased. 'This morning. She's really sorry. She said. She's sorry, Dad, she just weren't feeling too good, and she had to get away for a day or two.'

Matty's grammar always slipped when he was over-excited.

147

'Wasn't,' Silver corrected, standing in the corridor outside McNulty's office. 'Wasn't feeling too good. Did she say anything else?'

'She said she'd be back soon.'

'Good lad. Let me call you back in a minute.'

At that moment Silver despised his ex-wife. He despised her with every fibre of his body.

He rang her mobile. She didn't answer, so he left her a short, sharp message telling her exactly what he thought. The stupid, heartless bitch. He'd climbed out of the guilt pit and was back on solid ground.

Then he rang his son back.

'I'll be up at the weekend, I promise. Either late tonight or tomorrow morning. How you doing with your peas?'

'Gran's stopped giving 'em to me. I can nearly do a kick-flip on my skateboard. And,' he was jabbering with excitement, '*and* I beat Ben's score on Mario Game Kart, Dad. He's gutted.'

'Atta boy. And wear your helmet on the board, yeah?' Silver never thought he'd be the kind of man who'd worry about what he'd once regarded as over-protective measures, but overnight it had happened to him, as his love for his own children burgeoned, along with the best of them.

'*And* Ben keeps kissing that Emma Burton girl behind the kitchen door. But Gran won't let them go up to his room and—'

There was a commotion in the background. Silver waited.

'Molly wants to talk to you.'

Molly was in tears. 'Can you come home, Daddy, please? I miss Mummy. And Gran doesn't know how to fish-tail my hair properly.'

'I know, sweetheart. I will come home.' Silver felt the cold clutch of guilt in his belly. 'Just got to finish something up here, and then I'll be back, I swear.'

Silver went to see Malloy. He updated him on events and Counter Terrorism's rather fraught cooperation, and then he explained in as little detail as possible what had happened at home, as far as he understood it. His boss was a tough but fair man, if a little volatile, with two children of his own although, unlike Silver, he also had a doting wife who had always kept the home-fires well stoked.

'No worries, Joe. You do what you've got to do.' Malloy sighed heartily. 'The kids'll need you. Just keep me posted on when you'll be back.'

'Will do. Cheers, guv.'

'Fuck knows who'll take over while you're gone though. That bunch of muppets can hardly manage the proverbial piss-up.'

Silver left Malloy's office with a heavy heart. He checked his watch. He wanted to see Tessa Lethbridge's flat; he needed to chase Michael Watson's whereabouts, and to make some headway with where the hell Sadie Malvern might be. When he headed back up North, he'd go and see her parents, and he wanted as much information under his belt as possible before breaking any sort of bad news.

Out in the main office, Tina Price was waving frantically at him as she took a call on the public line, her angular dark bob swinging madly as she did so.

'Someone claiming responsibility for Berkeley Square,' she mouthed, jabbing at the receiver she held.

'Again?'

149

SOUNDS SERIOUS she'd written on a piece of paper that she was holding up now.

Silver picked up the extension to listen in.

'It's taken you a while hasn't it?' The voice was assured, slightly American and definitely synthesised; croaky and mechanical. Soulless and eerie—and impossible to tell whether it was male or female at this juncture.

'Sorry sir?'

'You've been very reticent to confirm that it was definitely a bomb that caused the devastation.'

'Do you have information for us?'

'It's not the Purity Alliance, I'll tell you that.'

Was that a slight stutter Silver detected?

'So do you know who it was?' Tina said.

'Yes, my love, I do.'

'Who?'

Silver shook his head wearily. This was just another loon with delusions of grandeur.

'It was the bank we were after. The Hoffman Bank. So greedy. Did you know they are responsible for the deforestation of 96 million square feet of rainforest? The leeches will take it all.'

'Really?'

'Get a fucking trace.' Silver stiffened and beckoned to Okeke. 'Now.'

'We're on it,' the younger man hissed back.

'So my girls sorted it. And we will make you all pay. Pay for the unnatural taking of the land and the ruination of this beautiful world.'

'Your girls?'

The hairs on the back of Silver's neck went up.

'The Archangel whistles, and they come. I whistle, and they follow. My Daughters of Light.'

'Follow you where exactly?'

'Everywhere, from Hamelin to Harrods. Harrods may be next. All those greedy shoppers. Consumers have gone mad.'

'Are you planning another attack?'

Silver could see the perspiration on Tina Price's brow. He winked at her. 'Good job, kiddo,' he mouthed, 'keep him going.'

'Are you all listening? Do I have Scotland Yard's full attention? I'm so pleased. Remember, we're alive and remain and shall be caught up together in the clouds.'

'We've got a trace,' Okeke leapt up.

'Coming to find me?' the voice laughed. 'I don't think so.'

The line went dead.

'It's a fucking pay-as-you-go mobile. Somewhere near Upper Street.'

'Put everyone in the area on alert.'

But it was useless, they all knew that much.

Silver's heart was thumping. At least they had something; something was better than nothing. He called Kenton over.

'You busy?' Silver grabbed his jacket from the hanger on his office coat stand.

'Seeing the radical Jan Martin at five o'clock for leads on Lamont and Watson. Not looking forward to it actually. She sounds pissed off. *And* posh. My worst combination.'

'Fancy a visit to Sugar and Spice after we've interviewed Lucie Duffy?'

He could have sworn Kenton's face lit up.

'The club? Not half!'

'All right, Lorraine. Calm down.' Silver straightened his collar in the glass. 'I didn't mean as

151

a customer.'

'No problem, guv,' she flushed, following him out. 'I knew exactly what you meant.'

FRIDAY 21ST JULY
CLAUDIE

The taxi pulled into the rank between King's Cross and St Pancras stations. I thrust the money into the driver's hand without waiting for change and sprinted into St Pancras.

It was buzzing with the anticipation of a thousand travellers; expensive luggage, lovers forced apart, families reunited, weary businessmen. A tramp asked me for change; I had none.

It took me a while to locate the public lockers in the glossy new station, which were at the back beside a bakery and the Ladies, and longer to locate no. 209. There was a young couple dressed all in black passionately entwined in front of the section I needed. I waited as patiently as I could manage for about three minutes, tapping my foot on the tiles, but when I realised they had no intention of letting each other go, I asked them politely if they wouldn't mind just moving slightly. The girl, skinny and dark, raised a tear-stained face to me before pushing her head into her Goth boyfriend's neck so hard that I thought they might become surgically attached.

'*Oui*,' she shrugged. '*Bien sur*.' They moved infinitesimally to the left so I could just about open the locker door, and began kissing again.

I had to bend to slide the key in, my heart beating ridiculously fast. It opened smoothly, and

152

I crouched down to search inside. Within seconds I felt crushing disappointment as I realised it was empty. All this—and nothing. The police had obviously got here before me—though I wondered how they'd know about the locker if there was only the key on the ring as evidence. But whatever the truth, the answer to the real Tessa Lethbridge wasn't here. My hands shaking, I slid them round the locker for a final search in some desperation, unwilling to believe that I had come here for no purpose.

My fingers made contact with something smooth and my stomach contracted: thank God. I pulled it towards me. It was an A5 photo, the ballet school students of 2010, a few of the girls' faces ringed with blue biro. I felt an involuntary shiver. Amanda Curran; Sadie Malvern; Lucie Duffy. The new girl Anita Stuart. Favourites of Tessa's, that much made sense.

I smoothed the photo out against my knee, and their bland faces gazed up at me; Sadie Malvern scowling, red-haired Amanda Curran smiling, Lucie Duffy smirking, a blue halo of biro around each of their heads. I turned the photo over. On the back was written 'The Queen of Hearts, she had some tarts'.

I remembered Tessa saying that Sadie would never go far. 'She brings too much baggage, that one,' she shook her head as we sat in the staffroom one day, watching a tape of a rehearsal. 'I had so much hope for her; technically she is brilliant, but she can't lose herself when she dances. She is too conscious.' She paused the DVD. 'Not like Lucie and Manda.'

I had seen very little of Sadie Malvern myself;

she wasn't one of the dancers who tended to hurt herself, and she was a tough cookie, so I'd only treated her once or twice. She had broken her arm badly as a youngster in some kind of car smash, and it had set badly. Plus I knew she had some sort of eating disorder from the frailty of her structure, but although I always alerted Eduardo when I spotted it, not eating was absolutely rife amongst the girls. There was little to be done before they actually started collapsing in class.

I pushed the photo into my bag and checked the locker again. There was something else, shoved right up against the back wall; I reached in and pulled it towards me. A thin book, a leaflet almost, on African plants. I started to flick through it, spotting words scribbled in the back pages, but before I could absorb anything, out of the corner of my eye I saw someone approaching. Quickly I pocketed the book in my parka and began to shut the locker door. I was worried that a station official had rumbled me and was about to ask how I had come by the key. But that was ridiculous—I could be the temporary owner of the key; they would know no better.

I began to stand, ready with a string of excuses— and then something was flying at me, the weight of a body, and I was so shocked that for a moment I didn't know what to do; I didn't move fast enough. I felt myself falling, I was going down again, and the man too. As I tried frantically to find my feet, to stand again, I felt hot fingers on my ankle. Glancing down, I saw meaty knuckles tattooed with strange symbols.

I kicked out with all my might and pushed myself off the floor and away from the hand. Stumbling

154

forwards, I smacked my head on the lockers and for a moment I stood, bewildered, listening to a voice scream, and I realised the scream was coming from the French girl who had been kissing her boyfriend.

I glanced at the boyfriend and I thought that he was bleeding, and crying and shouting, and I realised I had to start moving before it was too late. A tall, thickset man in a leather coat was behind me, cursing in a language I didn't recognise. He was nursing his wounded hand that I had kicked, and then he was reaching his arms out for me, his dark woolly hat pulled down very far over his forehead. I pulled myself together and I ran, ran, ran for my life through the crowds, the tourists and bemused commuters, tripping over a thousand matching wheelie cases, and all the while, the girl behind me was screaming.

*　　*　　*

My first instinct was to make for the cab rank, but when I rounded the corner there was a long snaking queue, so I turned tail and pelted down the Euston Road until a bus passed that I could jump on.

Bent double, fighting to breathe, I travelled to the junction with Euston Station and then jumped off and into a black cab. No one was behind me. I had apparently lost the man back at the station, but I was frightened now, really frightened. What the hell was going on?

I stared at the photo from the locker; at Lucie Duffy's smug little face. I knew from the office that she was at the Royal Opera House rehearsing for the gala performance of *Swan Lake*. Perhaps she would know something more about her mentor

155

Tessa. I tapped on the driver's glass.

'Would you take me to Covent Garden, please?' I needed to get to the girls in the photo, that alone seemed clear.

Lucie Duffy and I had never hit it off amazingly well; she was born to be a prima donna and that was all there was to it. Fully aware she was talented above and beyond the rest of her year; to be dancing a solo role at the Royal Ballet at nineteen spoke of phenomenal success. Yet she lacked the humility to make her likeable, certainly when it came to other women. Men, well, that was different. Lucie liked men. But she couldn't be bothered with her own sex, apart from her little coven, and I had also discovered, she didn't like being touched. She suffered badly from cartilage problems with her left knee, and I had treated her a lot throughout her two years at the Academy. But despite all the time she'd spent on my table, she could barely raise her eyes to meet mine, let alone make conversation. Her classmate Amanda Curran was very different. Manda was charming, open and chatty, but Lucie didn't have time for a mere physiotherapist. And there was something not quite right there, I sensed: a fear, almost, of someone getting too close.

Arriving at the Royal Opera House, I ran up the front stairs so fast I lost my footing and banged into the chest of a dark-haired man in an expensive suit coming the other way.

'All right, kiddo?' he said, steadying me, and I nodded, pushing my scarecrow hair out of my face—'My fault'—and ran on.

I was surprised to see Lucie in the foyer, wrapped in blue angora, on her mobile phone. She was

156

waiting for the lift, and I called to her before she was swallowed up into the bowels of the building.

'Lucie!'

She turned, uncomprehending, looking through me as if I was not there, phone clamped to her ear.

'Claudie Scott,' I reached her side now, slightly breathless. 'Physio from the Academy. Used to treat your knee.'

'Oh hi, Claudie,' she smiled tightly, and a look I couldn't fathom crossed her pretty face. Triumph, perhaps. 'Hang on, would you. I'll see you later, my darling,' she murmured into the pale-pink phone. 'My big prince.' She snapped it off and pocketed it. 'If you're after a comp, you'll have to talk to Mason. I gave her my entire allotment of freebies.'

'No, it's fine thanks.'

'You've lost weight,' she said almost accusingly. She looked me up and down and then smiled properly.

I smiled back. 'How is your knee?'

'It's holding up. At the moment, anyway.' Lucie pressed the lift button again urgently. 'Bloody lift. Kiko'll be going mad.' She turned to me, suddenly all consternation and great grey eyes. 'God, did you hear about Tessa? How freaky! I'm a bit annoyed actually. I look like a right idiot.'

'Why?'

'All those quotes I gave the papers, about her being an inspiration. And she'd been lying the whole time. I mean, why would you?'

'Yes, well. That's why I'm here actually.'

'Oh?'

I had her attention now.

'I'm trying to understand *why* she lied. I found this photo.' I dug it out of my bag. 'It belonged to

157

her. Look.' I pointed at the blue biro circles around her and the other girls' faces. 'Do you know what this means?'

'Oh my God.' Lucie wrinkled up her little nose. 'That's really creepy. Why the fuck was she doing that?'

'I don't know. I kind of hoped you might. Do you know who the Queen of Hearts is?'

Lucie shoved the photo back at me. 'Haven't got a clue. And I don't want one either. I'm really pissed off with her, silly cow. I mean, I know she's dead, but honestly.' The lift doors slid open and Lucie practically jumped inside. 'I trusted her. I told her things—' She broke off.

'What kind of things?' I prompted.

'Just things. Never mind.'

'Have you got Sadie or Manda's numbers?' I asked, slightly desperately, placing my arm against the door to stop the lift leaving.

'Manda's round the corner at the Coliseum. And Sadie—' she stooped to press the button inside, 'Sadie's missing, poor thing.'

'Missing?' I gaped at her. And then I had a flash of the television in the restaurant last night with Rafe. I hadn't absorbed it properly.

'Sorry, but I'm in a rush. Are you all right by the way?' she smirked. 'You look a bit—mad.'

The door slid shut in my face. I couldn't help feeling, as I walked away, that the last look on Lucie's face had been one of victory.

FRIDAY 21ST JULY
SILVER

They went via the Royal Opera House to see Lucie Duffy, who wasn't answering her phone. Kenton stayed in the car to take a call from the Yorkshire police about the Malverns, whilst Silver asked Reception to call the young dancer down this time. He didn't fancy watching her contort that lithe little body this morning. Standing in the huge foyer, Silver flicked through leaflets about dancers digging graves on stage, and a performance from Japan featuring nuns, nudity and soft porn. Bizarre, what they called art.

Lucie appeared five minutes later, as pink-cheeked as yesterday but wrapped in a long, blue cardigan today.

'Any news?'

'Nope,' she shook her head, lowering her lashes so he couldn't see her eyes, wispy tendrils of damp hair curling into her slender neck. 'I tried the most recent idiot last night. Roberto. Hasn't seen her for weeks, he said. There was another one, Mikey. I only met him once. I left him a message but he hasn't called back yet. There was an older guy I met once—but—'

'But what?'

'I can't remember his name. A one-night stand, I think. He was foreign I think.'

Silver wasn't surprised; he'd had no joy with the boyfriends either.

'But I think she'd lost interest in men recently,' Lucie said, looking faintly appalled.

'Really? Are you worried, Lucie, about your friend?' Silver was genuinely curious. This girl was difficult to read: both hard and soft; not necessarily in the right places.

She pouted. 'Of course I am. What do you take me for?' She looked up at him, narrowing her eyes now. 'I'm not heartless, DI Silver.'

'DCI Silver,' he corrected automatically.

'Ooh, very important.' She tapped his chest with a dainty forefinger. 'Do you have a uniform?'

'Only for special occasions.' He sighed internally. Men were meant to be the uncomplicated creatures sexually, but actually, in his experience, women weren't so far behind. It was just what happened the morning after that they seemed to differ on. 'I think we have to assume your friend Sadie might be in trouble. I'm on my way to speak to the manager of the club she danced at. It was Sugar and Spice, was it?'

'There were a few actually. But yeah, it was mainly the big one at London Bridge, I think. Sugar and Spice.'

Every copper in London knew the huge lap-dancing club, which was fast becoming renowned globally. Started in Moscow by a Russian oligarch with mafia connections, the London venue had opened five years ago and had cultivated a celebrity clientele and much media furore—until a gangland shooting behind the building two years ago had threatened the club with closure. Everyone used it: bankers, politicians, barrow-boys and aristocrats; footballers and female journalists who considered themselves cool because they wrote clever articles proclaiming their support. They boasted of tucking tenners in dancers' G-strings and whistling them on with the lads. Silver found the journalists tiresome; he felt that if they actually knew the truth of it, it would be a very different matter, as yet another girl died of her crack habit or was coerced into a gang-bang by the pimps in charge of the clubs. That was the real story they needed to be reporting.

'And all things nice.' Lucie stretched like a cat, exposing the curve of her small breast as her blue cardigan fell back.

'Excuse me?'

'What little girls are made of. Sugar and spice, and all things nice. Not like you nasty boys,' she pouted. Silver suppressed a grin. She was irrepressible, this girl. He pitied any boyfriend of hers.

'Poor Sadie,' she sighed unconvincingly. 'Sexy Sadie. She didn't seem very happy and it's not where she wanted to end up, though I do have to say—'

'What?'

'She loves the money.' Lucie wrinkled a distasteful little nose. 'On a good night, she makes more than I do in a week. Comes home with all sorts, new Mulberry bags, Gina shoes, the lot. Those City boys love to splash their money about. And she loves to boast to everyone. A few private dances and—bingo! Some of the other girls—' She stopped, biting her full lower lip.

'Some of the other girls?' Silver prompted, trying to read her look.

She shook her head. 'Oh, it's nothing. Really.'

He gave Lucie a minute, but she obviously wasn't going to elaborate.

'Right. Well, let's pray she's just off spending a bit

of that hard-earned cash.' Silver had had enough of Duffy for one day. 'Cheers, kiddo. Let me know if you hear from her.'

'You don't think something, you know, something really bad has happened, do you?' Her grey eyes suddenly brimmed and she blinked them back girlishly. Silver felt guilty for his harsh appraisal of her. She wasn't much older than Ben, his seventeen-year-old; a child at heart.

'Let's hope not. I'll stay in touch.'

As he left the building, a pretty, dishevelled blonde ran into him on the front stairs.

'Sorry,' she mumbled, seeming slightly unsteady on her feet, her brown eyes bruised with tiredness, tangled hair all over the place. 'My fault.' She clutched her green parka around her, though it was a warm day.

'All right, kiddo?' he asked, but she was already well past him, up and into the building. He headed back to the car, heart heavy, where Kenton was still absorbed on the phone, scribbling notes furiously. Sadie was officially missing, Anita Stuart still hadn't materialised—so that made two of them. Three maybe. If Lana hadn't turned up in the next few hours, he was headed for home.

*   *   *

At Sugar and Spice in London Bridge, Kenton and Silver were shown downstairs into the dimly lit main club and asked to wait for a man called Larry Bird. A curvy waitress was sent over to ask them what they'd like to drink, her shiny platinum hair-piece more elaborate than one of Molly's dolls. They both asked for water.

'Whew. It's bloody hot in here, isn't it?' Kenton took her sky-blue tank-top off, a decadent piece of clothing for her. It clashed horribly with her hair. 'To stop the girls getting cold, I guess.'

'Hardly. It's to get the punters to buy drinks,' Silver said. He felt dispirited and tired, and Lana's face revolved constantly in his head.

'Guv,' Kenton said.

'Yep?'

'Why are we here?'

'Misty Jones, Kenton,' Silver was abrupt. He didn't want to have to explain himself now. 'Just trying to join the dots.'

Kenton shrugged. 'Fair enough.'

The club had been open for about an hour and a black girl with a figure like an egg-timer was performing a lackadaisical dance to Michael Jackson's *Beat It*, a song far more energetic than she was. She wobbled round the pole a few times, her huge breasts swinging high enough to make Kenton wince. A group of middle-aged businessmen drinking champagne clapped enthusiastically as she stuck her hands down the front of her silver G-string and simulated lazy masturbation. Silver looked away. Near the door to the Ladies, a fragile-looking brunette leant against the wall, wearing Perspex stilettos, knee socks and a see-through baby-doll dress. Silver beckoned her over, and she undulated towards them as best she could for someone so thin.

'Sit down, please,' he asked her politely. Kenton moved round the red velvet banquette to let the girl sit. 'What's your name?'

'Gigi,' she intoned in an Eastern European accent. Close up, she looked ill; her pale skin

163

almost translucent, thick make-up failing to hide a huge cold sore on her top lip. 'Would you like a private dance?' She motioned to the booths that lined the main floor that were separated by curtains. In one, Silver could see two girls performing a lesbian routine for a couple of City boys; one girl crouched over the other's body, pretending to lick her washboard stomach.

'No thanks, love.' Kenton shifted uncomfortably. 'We're police.'

'Really?' The girl looked unperturbed. 'Police some of my best customers.' She put her emaciated hand on Silver's thigh. 'Very nice uniform sometime.' Her skin was very hot; he could feel it through the fabric of his suit trousers. He smiled politely and removed the hand. Her scarlet fingernails were horribly chewed.

'Yes, really,' he said. 'Do you know a girl called Sadie? Pretty, medium height, blonde, curly hair. Blue eyes.'

'No,' she said immediately without even considering it.

'Or maybe not Sadie. Maybe Misty.'

This time the girl shifted in her seat. 'I don't think so.'

Silver and Kenton exchanged looks.

'Are you sure about that?' He pulled out the photo of Sadie he'd brought with him and showed it to Gigi. She cast a desultory look at the photo before shrugging, but she had begun to bite one non-existent fingernail.

'Well?' Kenton snapped. Her patience was wearing thin. 'This girl is missing. This is serious.'

'Maybe I saw her.' Her dark eyes flicked from side to side like a snake's as she checked who was around. A fat man was waddling towards them, slicking his hair back in the dim light, a chunky gold bracelet glinting on his thick wrist. Gigi registered him and then looked back at the photo.

'No,' she said loudly, pushing it away now. 'No I do not know this girl. I never seen her here.'

She was frightened, that much was obvious, and she was also lying, but Silver knew this was not the time to push it. As the man arrived beside them, Gigi stood and cuddled up to him, towering over him in her five-inch heels.

'Larry,' she said, simpering like a small child. 'You looking good, Larry.'

He was most definitely not looking good.

'Yeah well,' Larry sniffed, grabbing a handful of Gigi's scrawny arse. 'You're looking thin. You back on the gear, sweetheart?'

'Of course not.' She blinked doll eyes at him coquettishly. It was painful to watch. The more Silver gazed at her, the more her face looked like a death's head. Larry grabbed her arm now, checking for track-marks; Gigi pulled it back.

'Larry,' she purred, but she was nervous, 'you know I am good girl now. I see you in office, yeah?'

Larry sighed elaborately.

'I show you how good I am.' Gigi ran her bony hand across his crotch with a hint of exhausted promise.

Kenton looked down at her knees, biting her lip.

'OK. Wait for me there. And don't fucking lose another inch off those tits or you're out.' Larry let the girl go so suddenly she staggered slightly, sniffing wildly as she collected her purse from the table. 'No tits, no job. Consider yourself warned.'

'Ciao,' Gigi tried a little-girl wave at Silver as she

165

weaved her way towards the door. He held a hand up in response.

'What a mess,' Kenton muttered under her breath.

'Yeah, fucking girls,' Larry agreed, wiping his forehead with a handkerchief. 'If they get too ugly or too high, they're straight out.'

'Pardon?' Kenton stared at him.

'We're the best fucking club in town. We can't have dogs here. We've got a reputation to uphold.'

'*Dogs?* Excuse me, but really,' Kenton's words were tumbling over one another, 'it's exactly that sort of attitude that damages young—'

'Lorraine,' Silver murmured. 'Let's just leave the lecture for now, shall we, kiddo?'

'Yes, guv,' she muttered, but she shot daggers at the American, who, oblivious, was beckoning a waitress.

'We're looking for this girl.' Silver showed the photo of Sadie Malvern to Larry. 'She's missing.'

The fat man considered the picture for a moment, holding it in unwieldy fingers. He was sweating in the heat, an unchecked droplet rolling down his pock-marked cheek and bouncing off the glossy paper. Kenton shuddered.

'Pretty broad,' he smirked. 'I'd give her a job.'

'That's my question. *Did* you give her a job?'

'I don't remember them all,' he shrugged. 'They come and go.'

'I'm sorry, sir,' Silver adjusted his cuff minutely. 'I'm going to have to ask you to be more specific than that.'

'Really?' Larry looked up at him.

'Really.'

The two men stared at one another.

166

'OK, sure.' Larry shrugged again. 'Let me have another look.' Silver was patient whilst the other man pretended to reconsider. 'Yeah, OK.' He returned the photo. 'She may have danced for us once or twice.'

'Do you keep records?' Kenton asked, barely civil.

'Sure. We keep lists and till receipts when the girls check in for the night.'

'Till receipts?' Kenton shook her head, not understanding.

'They pay for the privilege of dancing, at the till in the changing room.'

'*They* pay?'

'Like I said, lady, it's the best club in town. They choose a name, and they pay their £100, they keep the tips, and everyone's laughing.'

As she opened her mouth to speak, Silver silenced Kenton with another look. Now was most definitely not the time to unleash her feminist principles.

The young waitress brought the champagne Larry had ordered now, bending over him to expose a deep cleavage, trailing her talons down his arm as she poured him a glass.

'Thanks, baby,' he smiled at her, his button eyes disappearing into his oily dough face.

Kenton looked like she was about to spontaneously combust.

'So, when did you last see her?' Silver asked.

'Hard to say. Few weeks probably. Like I say, they come, they go. She wasn't one of the best.'

'She was a highly trained dancer,' Kenton snapped.

'So? As long as they know how to shake their

booty, I couldn't care less if they trained with Britney Spears.'

'That's hardly what I meant.'

'Oh?' He stared at her. 'What did you mean?'

'Never mind,' Silver intercepted. 'So she definitely hasn't been in the past week?'

'Definitely not. I've been here every night.'

'But you'll double-check,' Silver said firmly. 'Now.'

The American sighed. 'But I'll double-check, now.'

'And you won't mind if I ask the girls. Check if anyone's seen her?'

'It's crappy for business—' Larry broke off, defeated. He certainly did mind, that was clear; but he had no option. Huffing and puffing, he heaved his great bulk off the banquette, and headed back to the office, where perhaps the emaciated Gigi could soften the blow of police presence in the club. Or blow the man softly—Silver grinned at his own wit.

As Silver and Kenton approached the changing room, a line of around fifteen girls queued at the door, chatting idly, texting on pink phones, preparing for the next, busier shift. A muscular Eurasian girl in a vest top and jeans was on the till just inside the room, taking the money.

'Brandy,' a small curvaceous redhead in a powder-blue tracksuit passed her cash over.

'The other Brandy's in already,' the cashier said, without looking up.

'Bollocks.' The redhead sighed. 'Paige then.'

'Paige it is.' The cashier rang up the hundred pounds and jotted her name in a notebook. 'Next!'

Silver stopped the redhead as she dumped her

bag at the long mirror and showed her Sadie's picture. 'Do you know this girl?'

'Who wants to know?' She eyed him warily. Her freckles were so infinite the pale skin between was almost entirely hidden.

'I do.' He flashed his badge.

'Shit.' Her yellow cat eyes narrowed as she looked him up and down, weighing up her options. 'Yeah, I do,' she said in the end, reluctantly. 'That's Misty. What's she done now?'

'Nothing. When did you last see her?'

'Not for a bit.'

'Can you remember when? It's important.'

She thought about it for a moment. 'Maybe two weeks. Maybe last week, actually. I had flu; she was in on my first shift back. I remember cos she gave me some painkillers. She kept boasting about going away. She was getting on my tits actually.'

'Going away where?'

'Dunno. Somewhere flash. Some hippy dippy expensive place.'

'What kind of place? With who?'

'I really don't know. We weren't that close.' She kicked her trainers off and started unzipping her tracksuit. 'Sorry, but I'm on at three.'

'What did you mean, what's she done *now*?'

'Nothing.' She peeled off her t-shirt, revealing large rose-coloured nipples.

Silver averted his eyes. 'You must have meant something.'

She reached over for her corset, brushing her breasts deliberately against his arm. He stepped back.

'She'd had a warning. From Larry and the big boss.'

169

'For what?'

'For snorting coke in the toilet.' She squeezed herself into the lacy black number. 'Half the girls are bang on it, but it don't do to get caught, you know. Misty got careless.'

'So what happened?'

As she struggled with the clasp on her top, her gaze was distracted. Silver glanced round; the Eurasian girl was standing behind him, hands on hips.

'I dunno. Ask Larry. It's not my business.' The redhead sat and extended one leg almost up to her ear to pull on a thigh-high patent black boot. 'We keep ourselves to ourselves, know what I'm saying? We've got bills to pay, mouths to feed.'

A gorgeous black girl bounced into the room now and chucked a load of business cards in the bin. Silver recognised her as one of the girls simulating lesbian sex in the booth earlier. 'Fucking losers. Like I'm going to fuck one of them for nothing.'

'Er—Linda!' the brunette in her bra and knickers next to Paige pointed furiously at Silver. 'Old Bill.'

'What?' the girl giggled, her wrap falling open, her eyes an alarming green colour, from contact lenses Silver assumed. 'I'd do you though, darling. Love a boy in blue.'

Silver hid his grin badly, fishing out his card to hand to the cashier.

'Right, well,' he said stoically, passing it over. 'If anyone thinks of anything else, give me a call, yeah?'

'I will,' the redhead said quietly, standing up now and manoeuvring her breasts to the front of the dress so they spilt over the corset, pink nipples just visible. She took another card from Silver and held

170

Silver's eye, biting her lower lip provocatively. 'If I think of anything at all, I'll call.'

*   *   *

Kenton had been watching a small, compact girl with the most enormous breasts shimmying up and down the pole, hair like Cleopatra, eyes like the dead, pretending to lick her own nipple.

Despite herself, she couldn't stop laughing as they left the club. 'They're not shy, those girls, are they?'

'Nope. But I'm surprised at you, Lorraine, especially as you were coming over all Mary Whitehouse on me there.'

'They're still pretty—' Kenton paused.

'Hot?'

'No,' she retorted, but Silver saw the flush flood her face again. 'Anyway,' she changed the subject quickly, *you* looked like you were in your element.'

Silver unwrapped a stick of gum with absolute nonchalance. 'I did not.'

'Oh yes, guv.' Kenton opened the car door. 'You did!'

FRIDAY 21ST JULY
CLAUDIE

Round the corner at the Coliseum on St Martin's Lane, I bought a *Big Issue* from the bald vendor who looked as downbeat as I felt, and waited at the Stage Door for Amanda Curran. To my relief, she was far friendlier than her classmate had been.

'I'm finished for a few hours,' she said, slipping

171

her snowy tutu off and shoving it into her kitbag. 'Shall we grab a coffee? I'm starving.'

We sat outside at the café on St Martin's Lane and I showed her the photo that Lucie had been so disturbed by. As usual, Amanda's red hair was pulled tightly back from her funny pale face; tiny rosebud mouth, large forehead and protuberant blue eyes making her look a little alien. But what she lacked in beauty, she made up for in charm and character.

'I don't want to be horrid, but I always thought Tessa was a little strange, to be honest,' Amanda confided, ordering a double espresso and no food. As a concession, she unpeeled a banana she'd taken from her own bag, but then laid it down again without taking a bite.

'In what sense?'

'I'm not sure exactly.' She lit a cigarette, and offered me one.

'I'd love to but I'm quitting.' I tapped my arm, indicating a patch. 'Or trying to, anyway, with a little help. Not much fun.'

'No. I should try,' she agreed, looking at the picture again. 'Yeah, Tessa. Just a bit odd. Like, sometimes, in class, she would tell stories that just didn't quite add up.'

'Like what?'

'Well, once she said she'd danced with Nureyev. But she couldn't have done, could she? He was really sick by 1990, and she would have still been training in Australia.'

'If she even was Australian.' I resisted the temptation to bury my face in my hands. 'I don't know. I guess it's not impossible she met him.'

Amanda shrugged. 'There was other stuff.

A world record for pirouettes, or something ridiculous. And always some kind of drama. It's hard to explain really.' She added four sweeteners to her coffee, pushing the photo back to me. 'I found her—you know—very highly strung. And then she kept asking me round to her flat for dinner in my last few months at the Academy.'

'Really?' I was surprised. She'd only asked me once or twice, and we'd been firm friends; we usually ate out. I thought she enjoyed her privacy. I was beginning to seriously question my relationship with her; I had felt such a strong bond when she had told me she had lost her own children during a premature labour, but it seemed now a friendship built on quicksand. In fact, I was beginning to question every decision I'd made in the past year.

'Yeah, a few of us. Lucie and Sadie both went. And Meriel Steele, before she left.'

I vaguely remembered Meriel, a mousey little girl with an out-of-proportion bosom that the boys had loved to tease her about, who'd dropped out after two terms, citing exhaustion. As far as I knew, she'd given up dancing and returned to her family in Devon.

'Why didn't you go?'

'I—I don't know. I just didn't fancy it, I guess. And when I started going out with Tommo, Tessa got really funny with me. She didn't really like the boys.' She looked at her watch and forced herself to eat a bite of banana. 'He'll be here in a minute; he'll be pleased to see you.'

Strong, jolly Tommo from the Ukraine, with the soulful eyes and a physique to die for.

'Why was that? Not liking the boys?'

'"*Big ugly brutes*" she used to call them, and I

173

think she was only half-joking.'

I thought uncomfortably about my occasional underlying worry that Tessa had felt a different kind of attraction to me than I had towards her.

'Though I did meet a male friend of hers once.' Amanda stubbed out her cigarette. 'Bit of a weirdo,' she pulled a face now. 'Don't tell Tommo about the fags,' she grimaced. 'He'll kill me.'

'Who was he?' I was confused. 'Tessa's boyfriend?'

'Not sure really. He took us out to lunch once. Older man. Bit—serious.'

'In what way?'

'Kept staring at us all the time. Talked a lot about the politics of nature, which I didn't understand a word of, to be honest. Celebrating the naked human form, being at one with nature—but then talked about money for the rest of the time. How he could make us rich. Talked about raising money for the cause, which made me switch right off. Gave us all a number to call if we were interested.'

I thought of Tessa's fascination with Francis.

'Did he have a beard? Earrings?'

'No, definitely not. Very ordinary. Older. Slight accent, I think. Expensive clothes, but a bit of a bore, I do know that much. He called Tessa a funny name.'

'What?'

'I can't remember now,' she frowned. 'Something like—like from a poem or something. She gave us all some stinky herbs to burn for good luck that day. I chucked mine away. What are you looking for?' she asked kindly as I pulled things frantically out of my bag, looking for the little book I'd found in Tessa's locker. The African plants. Was there a link?

'Oh, sorry.' Did I seem a little manic? I gave up the search. 'So who went with you?'

She ticked them off on her long fingers. 'Lucie, Sadie, Meriel, Tessa. And me.'

The girls circled in the photo.

'Not Anita Stuart?'

'Who?' She peered down at her banana like it might suddenly bite. 'And he suggested we all go away some time. He invited us all.'

'Away?'

'Yeah, like, some retreat or something in the countryside. Really hippy.' She shuddered. 'Not on your nelly, I thought. I can just about manage a night at Glastonbury with no hot water.'

'Did the others go?'

'I don't know. Don't think so.'

'Do you keep in touch with them?'

'Lucie, a bit, yeah—though she's so busy now, well, you can imagine! It's all lunches at Claridges and first-class tickets to New York. But Sadie, it's a bit sad really. She's pole-dancing, as far as I know.'

Alarm bells rang. 'Pole-dancing?'

'Yeah, I know. Awful. But she earns loads. God knows what she does for it though.' She lowered her voice. 'I think she's got into coke.'

'Lucie says she's missing.'

'Missing?' Amanda frowned. 'Really?'

'Though she didn't seem terribly worried. Do you know who Paul Piper is?' My heart was beating faster.

'Piper?' Amanda shook her head. 'No I don't think so. Should I?'

'Not really. And the man you met with Tessa, what was his name?'

175

'Not sure. Something ordinary, I think. Can't remember it though.' She scrunched her face in thought.

'It'll come back, I expect.'

'He wore glasses, I think.' She looked at me, her pale face serious. 'Why are you so interested in all this, Claudie?'

'Oh,' I felt embarrassed suddenly. 'I'm not really, it's just—it's so strange, that's all. A friend turning out to not be who they said they were. It's really confusing.'

Tommo appeared behind Amanda now, tiptoeing dramatically round the corner of the café, gesturing to me to keep quiet until he placed his hands over her eyes. She squealed in surprise and clamped his hands with hers.

'Silly! You scared me.'

'Sorry.' He leant down and kissed her. 'Hi, baby.'

'Tommo,' she grabbed his hand, 'you remember Claudie, don't you?'

'Certainly do,' he made a mock bow. 'The lady with hands of steel.'

I grinned. 'Always glad to be of service.'

'Claudie was asking about Tessa Lethbridge.'

Tommo pulled a face. 'That old lesbian? I never liked her much. Always forced our turn-out till we hurt our backs.'

I gathered my things. 'Right, well, I'll leave you to it.' As I stood, I had a sudden thought.

'That name he called Tessa, the foreign man. It wasn't—' I turned the photo over and showed her, 'the Queen of Hearts?'

Amanda gazed at the scrawled line, and then up at me with her bulgy blue eyes. 'God, yes, I think it was. So what were we then?' She looked down again at the writing. 'The tarts?' She sniffed. 'Charming.'

I left them nuzzling one another; young lovers, their affection for one another quite obvious—and I managed to suppress any feelings of envy as I walked away. I did look round, once, just before I went round the corner, and for a moment I thought they might have been laughing at me—but I dismissed it as paranoia.

*   *   *

At the bus stop, I didn't feel very well again. My head ached and I felt nauseous and hazy, and above all else, frightened. I found I was constantly checking to see if I was being followed, and I clenched my fists, reminding myself I was out in the open, in the sun, that all was normality. But everywhere I looked, shadows seemed to fall. I got on the bus; concentrated on watching a young woman with her rosy-cheeked toddler in his Mr Men sunhat, carefully wiping away the jam from a doughnut, counting blue cars through the window, his pudgy nose squashed up against the glass in delight.

'Bless him! Makes your heart glad, doesn't it?' an elderly lady in tweed said, smiling at me. 'Have you got any?'

I had to look away. I felt an overwhelming sadness that threatened to engulf me, clamping the heart of me. I was starting to shudder, metaphorically, the very core of me not fitted to my centre any more. I tried to breathe.

It was stupid not to have stayed to see Helen this morning; I needed her common sense and her innate knowledge. She would be able to make it better. I switched my phone back on. Hands shaking slightly, I texted an apology. I'd go and see her now.

FRIDAY 21ST JULY
KENTON

DS Lorraine Kenton arrived at the Vegetarian Oven in Spitalfields around five, troubled by thoughts of the dancers she'd met earlier. Despite being quite taken by Alison and wondering whether they were—rather gingerly—becoming an item, Kenton couldn't stop thinking of the dancer Paige that Silver had just interviewed, those slanted cat's eyes and that voluptuous creamy body. She sighed heavily and checked out the Vegetarian Oven's wares whilst she waited for the owner. There were some extremely stodgy-looking and worryingly yellow Quorn pasties and a mushroom biryani that looked like something her cat had—

She shuddered and moved away.

'DS Kenton?' a shrill voice asked, and an anaemic-looking middle-aged woman with her hair in a striped headscarf appeared from the back room. Her skin was almost as yellow as the Quorn pasties. 'Jan Martin.'

'Jan, hi. Thanks for your time. Is there somewhere we can talk?'

'Yes.' Jan eyed Kenton's extended hand coldly. 'Here.'

It took Kenton less than five minutes to establish that Jan believed all police to be both bourgeois

178

and fascist. She then had to listen to a rant about the Empathy Society and what they had believed in, and how they had been betrayed by the world in general. They had all met at Sussex University apparently, most of them English Literature students, or members of the Socialist party during the late 1980s, campaigning and standing outside Middle England's railway stations, trying to flog their ideals and their paper. Jan had acted as Secretary, expanding the ranks as best she could.

'This world is ruined,' Jan said, her long nose quivering slightly. Her mouth was too small for her face, Kenton noted absently. 'You mark my words. It's only a matter of time before it all implodes.'

Once her diatribe had ended and she'd actually managed to get a word in, Kenton had asked Jan when she'd last seen either Michael Watson or Rosalind Lamont.

'Michael changed his name long ago,' Jan sniffed. 'God knows why he was hanging out with that bloody Rosalind. She really was a prize bitch.'

Aha, thought Kenton. A woman scorned . . .

'So,' she asked pleasantly, 'what did he change it to?'

'Gabriel Oak,' Jan said.

'Why?'

'*Far from the Madding Crowd*?' Jan stared at her like she was completely stupid. 'Thomas Hardy?'

It irritated Kenton beyond belief that she had no idea what the woman was on about and was going to have to ask her to clarify. One more supercilious look from Jan Martin and she might be tempted to shove a Quorn pasty somewhere the sun didn't shine.

'Sorry,' she kept calm. 'You've lost me.'

'He's a farmer, Gabriel Oak. A man of the land. Michael wanted to renounce all worldly goods. He believed our society was about to eat itself.'

As long as it didn't have to eat the mushroom biryani, Kenton thought wryly.

'So he chose his favourite literary character. He was a very charismatic man, Michael. He was also a terrible bloody liar. Capricious as the wind.'

'Right.' Kenton wrote the name Gabriel Oak down carefully, glad to have the time to collect herself as she did so. 'And Rosalind? What happened to her?'

'Don't know, and frankly I don't care,' the woman was petulant as a child, pursing her thin lips.

'You've really got no idea where she might be?' Kenton was patient. 'It would be so helpful.'

'Well, I heard various things. Once, that she ran off with a millionaire, some kind of Freud scholar with an estate in Lincolnshire—that would be just her luck.' Martin's nose quivered. 'More recently, that she'd met a Russian professor of politics, a refugee—but really, who knows? I expect she did marry into money in the end, because she was that shallow. No real morals. And that's what they do, don't they?' Jan stared at Kenton like she was the cause of all the world's grief. 'I mean, that's how the rich stay rich.'

'So she's not with Michael Watson any more?'

'Not as far as I know.'

'And you have no idea where I could look for either of them?'

'Like I said, try Lincolnshire.' Jan got up now from the little table they had been sitting at, and began to restock the fair-trade brown sugar. 'If that's all, I'm really busy.'

Not a single customer had crossed the threshold the whole time they'd talked, and Kenton couldn't blame them—though she was too kind to point this out. Jan Martin's life was obviously miserable enough as it was. She gathered her things.

'I'll take a piece of carrot cake, thanks.' Kenton smiled gamely at the older woman, half-expecting her to offer it on the house.

'That's £3. Please.'

Kenton bit back a retort about the slimy-looking icing and paid the exorbitant sum. She'd claim it back on expenses anyway.

'Well, thanks, Jan. If you do think of anything else,' she popped her card onto the glass counter, 'you know the drill, I expect.'

As she stepped out of the door, infinitely relieved to get away from the acrid smell of Tibetan joss-sticks if nothing else, Jan spoke.

'There was one other thing, actually. Rosalind. Now you come to mention it, I did hear from one of the group that she'd gone to Australia briefly a few years ago. Initially to save the Reef—like she could—and then on somewhere else artsy-fartsy probably. Not sure where exactly. Melbourne, perhaps.'

FRIDAY 21ST JULY
SILVER

So Sadie and Anita were both missing, and that was all there was to it. Sadie might well be away somewhere as Paige had suggested; Silver prayed she *was* safely ensconced somewhere, with one of

181

the 'loser' boyfriends perhaps, in a fug of sex and sweat; but she hadn't crossed a border, according to Kenton's checks—and Lucie had said she'd lost interest in men recently.

He took another call from Kenton just as he was leaving Tessa Lethbridge's flat, which Craven had already visited a day ago. As Craven had reported, there had been nothing of any great interest in the Bloomsbury rental, apart from a few travel documents he'd retrieved, namely an air ticket to New Zealand in Lethbridge's name, for the evening of Friday 14th July—the day of the explosion. They had checked where and when the ticket had been booked; she was travelling alone apparently. Now Silver, who didn't quite trust Craven, was here to double check the flat himself. If she was travelling under the name Tessa Lethbridge, she must also have a false passport somewhere—and possibly her real one.

Silver slipped a photo of Tessa and a dark man out of a frame on the mantelpiece and pocketed it. He noted a penchant for nursery rhymes and children's toys, though to his knowledge she had no children of her own. How whimsical, he thought wryly—how apt for this pretentious ballet world. She was definitely of the hippy persuasion, that too was obvious. Rummaging through a half-packed suitcase on the bed, he looked for a passport in case Craven had missed it, but couldn't find one. He did however find a stack of papers hidden in a ballet book on some bloke called Diaghilev, pamphlets about the Daughters of Light. Bingo. Typical of Craven to miss the crucial.

*   *   *

'The woman, Rosalind Lamont,' Kenton was fighting to keep the excitement from her voice down the phone line. 'She was out in Australia. Melbourne.'

'Right. So you're thinking she could be the mysterious Lethbridge?' Silver clicked the car open, cursing his bad luck once again. He would do anything to stay in London now the leads were starting to pay off. 'Bloody big coincidence if it's not, no?'

'Yeah.'

'Good work, Lorraine. Keep me posted.'

'There's something else, too, guv,' she cleared her throat. 'Just spoken to the family of a girl called,' he could hear her pause as she checked her notes, 'Meriel Steele. She was an Academy student; they've not seen her in nine months. According to the Academy, she dropped out last year, but the family thought she was still there.'

'Christ.' Silver rammed the key in the ignition hard. 'What is it with these fucking families? They never know where their own are half the time.'

Which of course was entirely ironic, given his own circumstances, Silver thought as he negotiated the New Cross one-way system with as much calm as he could muster during a Friday night rush hour. He was finding serenity harder than usual today. A heavy woman with faded tattoos of Winnie-the-Pooh up both flabby arms pushed her buggy almost directly in front of Silver's car as she cut through the traffic, and he braked hard, swearing beneath his breath, placing his hand on the horn. From the safety of a traffic island, the woman mouthed a choice selection of obscenities at him before pushing the baby straight into the next lane

183

of oncoming traffic. Julie London was singing *Cry Me a River* on the stereo; he turned her up to drown out the sound of traffic as best he could.

*   *   *

Leticia was in the kitchen when Silver arrived home, looking for his landlady.

'Mum in?'

'Nah,' Leticia didn't bother looking up from her laptop. 'She's collecting Precious from swimming.'

'Good day at school?' Silver poured himself a glass of juice from the fridge and kicked the door shut. 'Learn anything cool?'

Leticia shot him a withering look. *'Cool?'*

'Sorry,' he grinned. 'Got the wrong lingo have I?'

'Lingo?' She shook her head with disdain, her pink heart sunglasses askance in her little afro. 'What are you, like, ninety-three?'

'No,' he said, still smiling, 'not quite. Not yet.' He grabbed a nectarine from the overflowing fruit bowl and walked behind her towards the door, glancing down at the laptop as he did so. He froze.

'What are you looking at, Leticia?'

'Nothing.' She slammed the lid shut.

'Let me see.'

'No.' She slumped her body over the computer. 'It's, like, none of your business.'

'Well, OK.' He put the glass and the nectarine down on the table. 'But does your mum know?'

'Know what?' the girl muttered, scowling furiously. Silver's heart went out to her. God, it was hard being young today. Life moved too fast to keep up with it.

'That you're looking at those sites.'

184

'What sites?' She sucked her teeth at him. When Silver looked at her, he could see the woman in the child's face, and it scared him.

'Letty,' he used the baby name Philippa sometimes did, 'you know what I mean. They're a bit old for you. That lad I just saw, he was twenty-five if he were a day.'

She rolled black kohled eyes. 'He's, like, seventeen.'

'My eye.'

'Your what?'

'I just mean, you can't believe everything people say on the web. It's easy to make things up. Be anyone you want to be.'

'Yeah, yeah. Tell me something I don't know.'

'Well, if you know it, then why use them? You must meet nice boys at school.'

'I don't.' There was a pause. 'They all tease me,' she muttered.

'About what?'

She grimaced at him, tears glinting in eyes shaped just like her mother's, brandishing her metallic smile in his face. 'Do you think anyone's ever gonna like me, let alone kiss me with a mouthful of this shit?'

'Of course they will,' he frowned. 'You're a lovely lass. There's plenty of time for kissing.'

'Lovely?' One big tear plopped out now, and rolled down her smooth cheek.

'Yeah, Letty. Lovely. Just give it time. You're only thirteen.'

'I'm a teenager.' She was defiant. 'I'm nearly grown-up.'

He thought of his children, waiting up North, no sign still of their own mother, and he sighed.

Standing now, he downed his juice.

'Listen, I've got to go home for the weekend.' Please God it *was* just the weekend. 'Will you tell your mum I'll call?'

Leticia shrugged. 'Sure.'

'And, Leticia?' He bit into the hard fruit.

'Yeah?'

'*Promise* me you won't meet anyone from the internet without speaking to your mum or me first.'

'Ras. You're not my flipping dad.' He heard her suck her teeth as he took the stairs two at a time. He'd call Philippa later and make sure she knew exactly what her daughter was up to.

*   *   *

Silver had just filled the car up at the local petrol station when his phone bleeped:

Meet me at the Soho Hotel at ten; about Misty.

It wasn't signed but there was a single smiley face followed the message. He deplored those smiley faces: Julie had loved them—which made them anathema for Silver.

He checked the time. He'd really wanted to be on the M1 by ten, but he had no choice. He swung the car round, swapped Julie London for Nina Simone on the stereo and headed for central London.

FRIDAY 21ST JULY
CLAUDIE

By the time I arrived at Helen's I was dry-mouthed and slightly shaky and utterly convinced someone was following me. I'd looked over my shoulder so many times as I'd walked the last ten minutes from the bus stop that I had a crick in my neck.

Helen let me in and frowned at my appearance.

'Your hands,' she said. 'I've never seen them so bad.'

I looked down; I'd scratched my skin to shreds somehow. She held my shoulders, her grey hair tumbling over her green cashmere cardigan, a fragile gold chain bearing a tiny flat matryoshka doll around her neck, the skin round her watery blue eyes crinkled as she searched mine. Her house smelt comforting somehow: of baking and roses and Diptyque candles. I'd only been here once before, but today, to my relief, calm pervaded me as I stepped past the stained-glass door. The little gold plaque beside the doorbell read: Helen Ganymede, MA SCs in flowery letters.

'I'm very glad to see you, Claudie.' She let me go and opened the door into her therapy room, ushering me in gently. 'I don't think you are well enough yet to be out there totally alone, without your support systems.'

Rather reluctantly, I told Helen of my fears that someone had followed me here.

'Why?' she frowned, 'why would anyone follow you, Claudie?'

'Because,' I mumbled. I didn't know whether to begin the whole Tessa spiel; it seemed so complicated. But the level of distress it was causing me was immense and, I recognised, debilitating. Speaking to Helen about her might normalise the situation a little.

Helen sat in the wicker chair opposite me and smiled gently, crossing her feet, and I felt myself

187

relax slowly.

'It's been a bit crazy, Helen, since I saw you last time.' I tried to smile, but I felt my eyes start to swim slightly.

'The Thursday before last?' she asked quietly. 'So why's that, Claudie?'

'Because of everything that happened at the Academy.'

'The explosion, you mean?'

I nodded. 'Yes. But it's worse than that.' I told her about Rafe, and then about Tessa and the fact she'd lied. I told her about me attempting to get to work on the day of the explosion, and blanking out, and the fact that I was positive I was meant to be meeting Tessa that Friday morning, yet the details kept escaping me.

I could see Helen struggling slightly to keep up, and at certain points, she asked me to repeat parts of the story. I tried to clarify them as best I could, but it was difficult, because my head had been hurting on and off so much again, and things had been hazy, almost as if I'd been anaesthetised at times.

'Wow,' Helen looked at me, and I felt that calmness again that she brought me. 'I can see why you did call it crazy, Claudie. You must be exhausted.'

'I am a bit,' I nodded again.

'I've read about Tessa Lethbridge in the paper, I'm so sorry. And I'm not surprised that on one level you feel betrayed,' she said, and her placid face seemed almost angry for a moment. 'You put your trust in Tessa, you shared your innermost secrets, didn't you?'

I nodded.

188

'So, it must be difficult to equate that with the fact she lied about her identity?'

'Yes,' I said slowly. 'I do feel betrayed. That's absolutely it.' I was just relieved Helen didn't seem to think I was mad.

'But you weren't the only person she duped,' Helen said. 'It's important to remember that. And she must have been deeply disturbed to have done so. It's hardly a rare occurrence in my field, though, forming a new, more idealised persona. How do you feel about it,' she looked at me intently, 'other than betrayed?'

'Stupid,' I whispered. 'And sad.'

'Well, you're not stupid by any stretch of the imagination.' Helen crossed her legs. 'I did meet her once, you know.'

'Really?' I was astonished.

'She came to me for an appointment; she said you'd recommended me. I explained that I couldn't see two friends. It's not ethical.'

'I didn't recommend you.' I was loath to talk to anyone about my therapy, though I knew I had mentioned Helen to Tessa once or twice. 'I mean, of course I would do, but I didn't tell her to come to see you.'

'Well, with cases like Tessa Lethbridge's, it wouldn't be unusual for her to cross into your life inappropriately. In fact, it'd be par for the course.'

I gazed at her. 'Really?'

'Absolutely. But what concerns me is how it's left you feeling, Claudie. The deceit.'

I contemplated her words. 'Wobbly.'

'Which is natural,' she nodded. 'So how can we rectify this?'

'I'm not sure.'

'No doubt Tessa was very damaged herself, and she picked up that you were absolutely vulnerable. She very likely selected you specially to be her friend. You must acknowledge that it wasn't your fault that you let yourself believe in her. You have been in such a low and sad place. So,' Helen smiled again at me, but her face was sad. 'We'll have to do a little work to repair the damage this revelation has done, won't we?'

'There's something else too,' I said, carefully. 'Like I said.'

'What?'

'I've got a nasty feeling I was followed here.'

Helen contemplated me for a moment. 'We've talked about this before, Claudie, haven't we?'

I blinked. 'Yes, I know.'

'It's likely to happen when you are disassociating, these fears. You are splitting again, to free yourself of the trauma.'

'But a man attacked me.'

'I'm so sorry.' Helen frowned. 'That's terrible. Where?'

'At St Pancras station.'

'Attacked you? Did he hurt you?'

'Well,' I paused. 'He tried to.'

'Why?'

'Because I was clearing out Tessa's locker.'

'Right,' Helen held my gaze. I wanted to look away but I couldn't. 'And you're quite sure he wanted to attack you? Think, Claudie. Don't let your mind go to the obvious, damaged places.'

I thought. I thought so hard it almost hurt. Maybe he hadn't been after me; I hadn't hung around to see. Maybe he was after the French girl, the girl who had still been screaming as I ran. Maybe he'd snatched a handbag, or her purse—

'I suppose,' I said slowly, 'I could have imagined it.'

'Maybe you did. You have before, haven't you?'

'Yes,' I said quietly. I thought about the phone calls. I didn't mention them.

'Can I recommend a book to you?' Helen stood now, and retrieved a book from the big shelf above the dresser.

'Of course.'

'Dr Everdene's work on disassociation is powerful stuff, and it might take some of the fear away too. It'll really help you get a different insight into the condition, how the mind shuts down and takes us somewhere else when we are very desperate. We will talk some more when you come back on Monday.'

'On Monday,' I repeated.

'You can't deal with all this on your own, Claudie,' she was earnest, her eyes full of consternation. 'You need to be supported. Let me help you. It worried me a lot when you sounded so distressed on the phone. How are you feeling physically?'

'OK,' I blinked at her. 'A little tired. Not a good time to give up smoking either,' I was rueful.

'Ah, but you're doing so well. Still using those patches?'

'Yes. They do seem to help.'

'Yes, I've found them effective myself. It's such an on-going battle isn't it? Blasted nicotine. And how have the headaches been?'

'Quite bad. And I've run out of my migraine pills.'

'I can help you there.' Helen opened the dresser and found her prescription pad. As a psychiatrist,

191

she could prescribe as well as listen. 'It's good for you to keep the migraines in check because as we know, the bad heads just cloud your thinking more. It puts you under more stress.'

When I had first seen Helen, she had quickly diagnosed me with psychotic post-traumatic disorder. I had described how I had stood at the kitchen window, waiting for Ned to come home; apparently, on the first day, I had stood for nine hours without moving, until my family called doctors who sedated me and forced me to finally lie down. I didn't remember much of it, but that's what had happened. I had lost whole sections of days, weeks sometimes; I couldn't retain the memories. I had no recollection whatsoever of Ned's funeral, for instance, although I saw the tiny coffin over and over again in my dreams.

Helen had slowly taken me through the reasons the disassociation would have happened, and I had been glad to learn I was not insane. The hospital therapists were quick and dry and dismissive, eager to prescribe huge quantities of mind-altering drugs. Helen, on the other hand, really listened. She had explained the delusions were quite normal and that I would need help and training to free myself of all of them. She was spiritual, shamanistic even, which I had been sceptical about at first, but it had helped me in some way. She had discouraged the terrible guilt I felt whenever I managed to derive any sort of pleasure from my life. I had been bereft after Will had chosen America over our marriage, but she had explained that Will could not deal with the trauma and sadness either and that was his way of coping.

'I think you should try to dismiss Tessa as a wounded soul,' Helen said now. 'Embrace the anger, if there is any. Eventually you will be able to forgive her for what she has done, but it may take a while.'

'Yes.' I looked at her, and I nodded. Anger had not been my prevalent emotion, but I felt a taste of it now. 'I will try, but it's not going to happen immediately. She told me so many lies.'

'Such as?' Helen leant forward, almost knocking into one of the tall carved statuettes beside her. This one was a woman threshing corn, a baby bound to her back.

'Well, like the babies she lost. I mean,' the thought was horrible, 'perhaps—perhaps they weren't even real.'

There was a pause.

'Possibly not,' Helen agreed eventually. 'But she would have needed something to bond with you over loss and grief. To pull you in, as it were.'

'Pull me into what, though?' I stared at her, troubled.

'That, I'm afraid, Claudie,' Helen shook her head gently, 'remains to be seen, doesn't it? Her world, I guess. We can talk about it next time.'

We walked to the front door and she handed me my parka and my prescriptions. 'I'll see you on Monday, yes?'

I nodded gratefully.

'And get some sleep. But don't hesitate to call me if you need me. I'm always here, Claudie.'

I smiled at her. 'I know you are.'

I just didn't know who might be lurking outside.

FRIDAY 21ST JULY
SILVER

Joe Silver hated glitzy places like the Soho Grand with a vengeance. All low lights, over-priced cocktails and constantly teased iPhones. He'd far rather be in the local pub; although actually, since the days of AA, he'd be more likely to be found taking his problems out on a squash ball.

He squeezed himself onto the last corner of the row of tightly packed tables with a copy of the *Evening Standard* and the world's most exorbitant soft drink, stretching his legs out into the aisle and scanning the apparently sophisticated crowd to see if he could pinpoint the sender of the message. After twenty minutes of poker-faced waitresses glowering at his ill-placed legs, depressing stories in the paper about teen stabbings and the lisping posh bloke next to him banging on about sound-scapes and how post-modern Jean-Michel Jarre was, Silver was utterly fed up. He should be halfway up the M1 by now, not trapped in pseud's hell. His head was thumping and there was still no sign of any contact. He stood, draining his drink, when a little voice purred somewhere below his left ear.

'Nice whistle.' The petite redhead from the club stood beside him, wrapped in a tight green silk jumpsuit and beautifully made-up, looking infinitely more elegant than earlier. She stroked his arm. 'Armani? I've never seen a copper with so much style.'

He racked his brain. 'Paige?'

'That'll do.' She stared up at him, her freckles

194

almost luminous in the dim light. 'For now.'

'Drink?'

'Yes, please.' She blinked once, slowly. 'Shall we go somewhere a bit quieter?'

'Such as?' Silver looked around; the bar was heaving.

'I've got a room upstairs,' she moved a little closer. 'Don't want no one listening to my secrets. Know what I'm saying?'

Silver thought he knew exactly what she was saying.

'I'm sure we can talk down here,' he said pleasantly.

She bit her pink bottom lip with her tiny white teeth. 'No.' She looked around quickly. 'If you want what I know, it's got to be somewhere walls don't have ears.'

Her strappy shoes were so high, her voluptuous body was tipped slightly forward, like a ship's figurehead. Looking down at her, Silver was unable to avoid that freckled creamy cleavage. To his irritation he felt a vague stirring of something.

'There's a pub round the corner,' he said, with purpose. 'We could go there.'

'I don't do pubs, darling.' Hands on hips, she waited. 'Not in this clobber. It's upstairs, or I'm going.'

In the lift, Silver leant against the wall, as far from Paige as he could manage. He watched her; she watched her own reflection, seemingly fascinated, preening herself. She was almost feline, her yellow eyes half closed. Any second now, she'd start cleaning behind an ear with one delicate paw. But she was alert like a cat too.

The room she had booked was minimalist and

195

rather sterile, with no proper window, the air conditioning rendering it icy. Paige shivered slightly and then leant over Silver to reach the bottle of champagne she must have pre-ordered.

'Drink?'

'I don't, thanks.'

'Don't be so dull,' she pouted, dripping the bottle across his lap. 'Bollocks to all that on-duty stuff.'

'It's not to do with duty,' he shook his head, 'it's personal preference.'

'Come again?' She stared at him.

'I just—' He didn't have the mental energy to explain. 'I don't like the stuff.'

'Ex-drinker?'

Perceptive. He could like this girl.

'Suit yourself.' She poured herself a long glass and pulled the cord for the ceiling fan, turning the air conditioning down on the wall. 'I love a real fan, don't you? Sort of—Arabian nights.'

'So?' Silver leant against the white lacquer dressing-table. He was starting to feel a little impatient. 'What did you want to tell me?'

The fan's breeze ruffled the flimsy material of the girl's outfit so it became obvious she wore no underwear beneath it. She exuded sex from every pore, but this was work, Silver reminded himself—and he couldn't help feeling he was being manipulated. He sensed Paige had a will of iron beneath her artificial façade.

Paige perched on the edge of the huge double bed, her silk legs splayed. 'Sit beside me,' she patted the bedspread, 'I'm lonely over here on my own.'

'Paige,' Silver ran a hand through his short hair and checked his watch again. 'I'm working, lass. And I've got to get up to Yorkshire tonight on urgent business. Can you please just share whatever it is you know?'

This was not a girl used to being ignored by men; this was a girl used to using her sexuality to her best advantage. 'What if I don't want to tell you now?' Her little face had darkened.

'I'd be immensely grateful if you would.' He smiled at her.

'What's it worth?' She narrowed her unusual eyes at him, ever more cat-like. He had a sudden image of her springing towards him, claws extended.

'Depends what it is,' he said, gritting his teeth beneath the grin. 'Do you know where Misty is?'

'No,' she sulked. 'But I might know who she was screwing.'

'Who?'

'Apart from half of Spice's punters, that is.' She inspected her nails with nonchalance.

Silver raised an eyebrow. 'Surely sex for money is vetoed by the club?'

'Are you joking?' she snapped. 'They practically fucking pimp us out.'

'Right,' no surprises there. 'So—Misty?'

Paige eyed him like he was her prey. He could sense her deciding whether to help him or not. And he sensed something else. A slight unease. Fear, even. 'It's just—' She gave a deep sigh. 'She'd gone a bit—weird recently.'

'Weird?'

'Like, holier-than-thou.'

'You mean, religious?' Silver was confused. A Bible-bashing lap-dancer seemed unlikely.

'No, not really,' Paige shook her head. 'More like, the world needed saving from itself. It was big and greedy and dirty and we were all going to pay the price, that kind of thing. Humanity was suffering, apparently,' she sniffed. 'Silly moo. Ideas she hardly seemed to understand.'

'OK,' Silver was intrigued now. 'And when did that start?'

'Only quite recently, I think,' Paige shrugged. Her nipples were like bullets in the green top; an unbidden memory of their pale pink hue flashed through his mind. 'Since I came back from being ill.'

'Did you ever meet any of her friends? Or boyfriends?'

'Yeah, once or twice. There was one bloke with a funny name. Only it seems to have slipped my memory.' She smiled up at him sweetly and he felt that damned lick of lust again. 'Can you help jog it?'

'Her flatmate mentioned a couple of blokes.' He ignored the unsubtle invitation. 'Lucie Duffy.'

'That stuck-up bitch?' Paige banged her empty glass down emphatically. 'The ballet dancer? She can go fuck herself.'

'I see.' Silver suppressed a smile. They'd be a match for each other, Duffy and Paige. 'You didn't see eye to eye?'

'We didn't see each other full-stop. I only met her once, at some poncey Members' bar a few weeks ago, and she didn't even bother to speak to me at all.' Paige gave a sniff of derision. 'Anyway, this geezer was there. He was called—oh God, I really can't remember. I'm good with names usually.'

'Describe him.'

'Tall. Dressed a bit stupid, like, young for his age. Kind of cowboy hat and boots. Really intense. Amazing eyes though. Like they could see right

198

through you. It felt like I recognised him actually. From telly or somewhere.' She stood and refilled her glass now. 'He got a bit flirty with me, which well fucked that Lucie bird off.'

'You mean Misty?'

'No. I mean that ballet dancer one.'

Silver considered this information. 'But why would Lucie be annoyed if he was Misty's boyfriend?'

Paige shrugged again. She licked her top lip with a little pink tongue. 'I got the feeling they shared stuff, them two girls.'

'Shared?'

'Yeah, shared. You know—clothes, make-up, men.' Paige moved towards him and pressed herself against him now; she was so close he could smell her hairspray. 'Us club girls, we get used to sharing.' She fluttered a strategic hand near his groin. 'Know what I'm saying?'

Silver took a deep breath. 'That's very nice of you, Paige—'

'Nice wasn't necessarily on my mind, babe.' She moved her hand infinitesimally nearer.

Despite her small size and her voluptuous body, Silver found her persistence off-putting. He felt the last vestige of desire trickle away. He stepped back, relieved at his own feelings. 'Another time, another place, Paige, love.'

'There won't be another time,' she scowled at him. She turned to pick up her glittery purse. 'You had your chance. This is dangerous for me. Perhaps you don't realise what those monkeys running the club can do.'

'I'm sorry.' He genuinely was. 'What *can* they do?'

'They're nasty, those Russians. You must know

that.'

'Which Russians?'

'All of them. They don't stand for no shit. Specially—'

'Specially?'

Paige paused, checking her hair in the mirror, hesitating. Eventually she spoke quietly.

'Look, something was going on with Misty. Let's just say—well, she might have got too close to someone.'

'Who?'

'Someone at the top. And you don't mess with the boss, know what I'm saying? Cos if he gets bored of you—well.'

'Are you saying he's done something to her? The "boss"? Who is he?'

Paige gazed at him with something akin to contempt.

'You can find that out yourself, surely? All I'm saying—there was some weird shit going on. He might have—like, passed her on.'

'To who? You've lost me, Paige.'

'Really? I *am* surprised.' She grabbed a cigarette out of her purse and then thought better of it. 'You know, you're starting to piss me off.'

'Sorry.'

'I'm fed up of being bullied. Know what I mean?'

'No,' Silver said frankly. 'Explain, please.'

'Look, if Misty got all la-di-da or if she started talking out of turn—well, they like the girls smacked-up or submissive. But,' she hesitated again, 'I don't know. It was more than that.'

Silver felt his frustration building.

'Paige, I really need your help, love.'

There was a knock at the door. Paige jumped

200

visibly.

'Room service?' a voice said.

'No thanks,' Silver returned smartly. They waited a moment in silence, Paige glaring at the door as if it might suddenly burst open. Silver stood and moved nearer to her.

'Paige, you need to tell me what you know.'

'I don't *know* what I know. That's the point. Like I said.' She was hissing between neat little teeth now. 'There was some weird shit going on, and I didn't want to know. I did my job; I kept my head down and my tits out. But Misty—' She shoved the cigarette box back in her purse. 'There was some woman involved. Something to do with the boss. And that's all I can tell you.'

'What woman?'

'I don't know.' She was almost tearful with frustration herself now.

Silver didn't believe that she didn't know more. She was edgy and scared, far more so since the knock on the door.

'Please, Paige—'

'No more.' Paige stared at him. 'You must get my drift.'

'Names?'

'No names.'

He'd lost her trust.

'Talk to the other girls.' She pulled a sheer cardigan on over her jumpsuit. 'A few have been put in their place the hard way.'

'Right. And the woman?'

Paige ignored him.

'And another thing, Joe Silver,' Paige had her hand on the door handle; she jutted her chin in the air. 'You shouldn't be so ready to judge. Like, what you see ain't necessarily what you get.'

'I don't judge.' But he was lying and they both knew it.

'Still waters, and all that. Remember.'

'I don't understand.'

'I expect you can work it out, if you can be bothered,' she snapped. 'I'm a dancer, not a prostitute.'

'You've been very helpful,' he soothed. 'And I'll send an officer down to the club.'

'Well *don't* for fuck's sake mention me.' A shadow crossed her little heart-shaped face. 'Swear you won't.'

'Paige, lass, I'm not stupid.'

They stared at each other.

'If you need protection—'

'I can look after myself.' She stuck her chin in the air again, and Silver felt a flash of regret that he'd pulled away from her advances. Her sudden vulnerability was much more appealing.

'OK. But you can always call me. And if you remember the boyfriend's name, you'll let me know?'

'Why should I?' Her yellow eyes were cold.

'Because, kiddo,' it was Silver's turn to flex his metaphorical muscles now, 'Misty is missing, and if we don't find her soon, well, God knows what might happen to her. And then how would you feel?'

*   *   *

Silver was just past junction 12 of the M1 motorway, deep in a reverie about what the hell he was going to say to the children about their mother, when his phone rang.

202

He hoped it was Kenton with news on the management of Sugar and Spice, but it was Philippa returning his call.

'What's up, Joe?' she asked. 'No sign of the ex?'

'Not really. Hoping she'll be back soon.'

'Good luck with that, love. You back Monday?'

'Sincerely hope that too.' He remembered Leticia and the internet site she'd been viewing. 'P—it might not be my place, but—I'm a bit worried about Letty.'

'Oh?' her tone was immediately wary. 'What's she done now? Not my bloody credit card again?'

'Not to my knowledge, no. No, it was just—she was surfing the web a little—unsuitably.' He was reluctant to be the one to tell her. Let the girl have her chance first. 'Maybe just ask her to talk to you first.'

'OK,' Philippa sighed deeply. 'Cheers, Joe.'

Within minutes, the phone rang again.

'Don't tell me. I didn't do my washing-up.'

'Not in my place, you didn't. But you're still welcome to.'

Paige.

'Hi there,' he said neutrally. He felt unreasonably awkward. Chastised, perhaps.

'One thing I did remember,' she was talking very quietly. 'Misty—Sadie's boyfriend.'

'Go on.'

She paused. 'Not that you deserve it.'

He gripped the steering wheel tighter. He needed this information badly. 'I understand. And I'm sorry, Paige. Really.'

She couldn't resist it. 'Sure you don't want to come back and find out in person?'

'In another life, lass, I'd be back like a shot.'

Distance equalled safety. 'So?'

'Well you know where I am,' she murmured.

'And the name?' he prompted. 'Of Misty's boyfriend?'

'I heard the name Archangel once or twice, but I don't think he was called that. He was called the Prince,' Paige said triumphantly. 'Told you it was something strange.'

FRIDAY 21ST JULY
CLAUDIE

Anger was building in me now like a pressure cooker. I went to the chemist and filled my prescription and then I sat outside Bar Italia in Soho, trying to feel part of something, watching the Friday night revellers, the couples arm in arm, the beautiful boys and the out-of-towners. I kept thinking about Tessa and why she'd picked me. And then I thought of Natalie, and her ringing Eduardo and saying I couldn't work, and it all started to feel like a conspiracy.

I took one of the pills and eventually my head stopped hurting so much and I fumbled around in my bag for Helen's book about disassociation. And whilst I was doing so, I found Tessa's keyring again and I realised I did know what the other keys were; they must be for her flat. And I felt that swell of anger again, and so I paid my bill and I walked from Soho through the busy streets to the quieter environs of Bloomsbury.

*   *   *

No one answered the door at Tessa's; why would they? I buzzed and buzzed, but no one was in.

I slumped in the doorway. People sneaked glances at me as they passed, the foreign tourists' curiosity less veiled than the locals, and they all thought I was drunk. It was late, why wouldn't I be? I buzzed again, one final futile time. Even with the keys, I found I needed a code to enter, and if I'd ever known it, I couldn't remember it now.

'All right, love. Been in the wars?' I turned to see a short, rotund black lady with a strong West Indian accent, carrying her Tesco bags up the stairs. 'Locked out?'

'Yes,' I said automatically.

She puffed in through the door, and I swiftly followed as she pressed the lift button.

'Cat got your tongue? Or just your cheek?' She pointed at my graze, grunting with satisfaction at her own joke as the lift arrived. I followed her in. 'Third floor?'

'Yes,' I nodded dumbly. It sounded right.

'Thought I recognised you. Tessa's friend.' She unpeeled a Twix in the lift and took one neat bite, then offered me a bit. I shook my head politely. On the third floor, we got out. She stopped outside 55 and looked at me pointedly. 'Haven't seen her for a few days, I been at my daughter's. Tessa said she was going away though. Anywhere nice?'

She obviously hadn't heard the news. I bit my lip. I couldn't tell her now.

'You know one thing—'

I turned back.

She dropped her voice confidingly. 'I'm glad that boyfriend's gone, aren't you?' She didn't wait for a response. 'Not good enough for her, I always

205

thought.'

She shut the door before I could respond.

A shadow lurked in my brain; something hidden, something waiting to emerge from its corner.

Boyfriend. I racked my brain, turning the key over in my hand.

My hand shook slightly: the key slid neatly into the lock. Why would it not?

*   *   *

I don't know what I was expecting, but it wasn't behind that door. The flat was light but airless, humid even, overly fragrant. There was a pungent smell of rose in the air and candles everywhere; incense sticks, faded Tibetan prayer flags hanging listless from the ceiling, pale Venetian blinds down to the floor. It was more messy than I remembered.

I went into the bedroom; it was very plain and white and a great wooden Buddha sat in an empty fireplace, dead daisies in front of him. Tea-light candles in glasses. I caught my reflection in the carved mirror on the wall and grimaced; I looked wan and exhausted and my hair needed a good cut. An empty frame stood beside a framed photo of Tessa, her head in part hiding that of a dark, smiling man with a lion's mane of long hair. Tessa was leaning back into his chest and shoulder, and he was looking down at her, his face partially obscured. I stared at him. It was my acupuncturist, Francis. I'd never realised they'd had a relationship; I thought it was just unrequited love on Tessa's part. But their stance in this picture suggested that they had been lovers.

On the bed was a suitcase, half-packed, some of

Tessa's clothes trailing from it. There was a pair of gold-dipped pointe shoes on the bedside table that I recognised as Lucie Duffy's. I remembered her simpering over Tessa the last day of term. 'Here you are, Tessy,' she'd lisped, handing them over. 'I couldn't have done it without you.' And Tessa had looked so pleased and happy that I'd almost felt embarrassed for her.

Where had she been going with this suitcase?

I turned away. On the mantelpiece, beneath a framed photograph of the entire school, a gauzy shawl covered a framed tract:

THE SUN MAY STILL SHINE
BUT IF YOU DO NOT ACT
SOME DAY SOON
THE END WILL BE THINE

Beside it, there was an illustrated nursery rhyme, with a picture of little girls in mob-caps holding hands that formed an arch above it:

Oranges and lemons, say the bells of St Clement's.
You owe me five farthings, say the bells of
St Martin's.
When will you pay me, say the bells of Old Bailey.
When I grow rich, say the bells of Shoreditch.
When will that be, say the bells of Stepney.
I do not know, says the great bell of Bow.
Here comes a candle to light you to bed,
And here comes a chopper to chop off your head.
Chop chop chop chop, the last man's dead!

It was the rhyme scrawled on the newspaper article about the bank I found in Tessa's belongings.

And on the floor beneath the mantelpiece, there was a child's toy: an old steam train.

The room felt airless: I couldn't catch my breath. I had a memory now, a distinct memory of being at Tessa's, of sitting in the velvet chair in the corner perhaps, or lying on the bed. Of a voice, soothing and caressing me. Had it been Francis?

I bent down to look at the train, reaching my hand out for it. Ned's train. It had disappeared months ago, and I hadn't even noticed. I felt that familiar clutch of guilt. As I pulled it towards me, it knocked against the fireplace, where it upended the heat balloon wedged there to keep out the draught. A cupboard file dropped down, covered in soot, and a load of photos slid out, followed by an envelope marked with some kind of shorthand I couldn't read, and strips of passport photos. I looked down at them. Tessa and Francis. Then I turned the other photos over. A couple of Rafe and me, taken at that Sadler's Wells event. I stared at myself; I looked a little like one of the deer that used to run across the dark road around my parents' village when I was growing up. Huge eyes; startled in the headlight.

And then an old British passport, the blue kind, in the name of Rosalind Lamont. I flipped it open to the front, but the photo was missing, it had been cut out. Still, it must be Tessa's.

So—Rosalind Lamont. That was her real name, then.

As I stood finally, my eyes met something else. There on the mantelpiece: a note. In my handwriting. Hand shaking, I picked it up.

WHERE ARE YOU?

I took the photos of me, and the note, and I left. I slipped the keys into my coat pocket—and then I ran for it. As I passed her flat, the old lady I'd met earlier was carefully parking a plaid shopping trolley outside her door.

'Off again?' She looked surprised, and rather excited. 'You know, I've had a note to call the police.'

'Really?'

'Something about Tessa. You don't know—'

'No,' I said quickly. 'Got to go, sorry.' I headed towards the lift. 'Bye.'

'Bye then. It's good to see you look better than the last time anyway.'

'Last time?' I turned back.

'Thursday night. I think it was Thursday. After *EastEnders*. Last week, before I went to Martha's. You looked really poorly.'

I stared at her, and then I ran to the stairwell at the end of the corridor, belting down three flights to the street. I thought I might have seen a police car sliding into the space behind me. I didn't stick around to check.

FRIDAY 21ST JULY
KENTON

DS Lorraine Kenton was just about to undo the top button of Alison's pink spotted blouse and slide her hand inside her lacy black bra for the first time, accompanied by the plaintive strains of Tracy

Chapman's *Fast Car*, when Kenton's phone rang, making both women jump.

'Bollocks.' It was work. 'Sorry, babe, I'll have to get it.'

Alison smiled, her round face filled with light, and kissed Kenton's hand. 'Get it then. I'm not going anywhere.'

'Kenton.' Kenton leant back on Alison's rather chintzy sofa, winked at her new girlfriend, who was flirtatiously twisting a lustrous black curl round one finger—and then sat upright as she absorbed what the voice on the other end had just said. 'Shit. When?'

She was already standing, making the flame from the vanilla candle gutter in the breeze; hurriedly re-buttoning her own shirt and checking the zip on her jeans.

'What is it?' Alison looked worried.

Kenton slid the phone into her denim jacket pocket. 'Girl's just set fire to herself in the middle of Trafalgar Square.'

'What? Why?' Alison followed her to the door. 'Oh my God.' Her eyes were round with shock. 'Is it another suicide bomber?'

They stared at each other for a second. There was something altogether terrifying about acknowledging the world's atrocities had reached these shores again.

'I dunno. It's bloody scary, whatever it is.' Kenton ran towards the stairs, then turned and kissed Alison's nose. 'Sorry, babe. I'll be in touch.'

And she was gone.

*   *   *

On the way into town, Kenton tried desperately to

reach Silver, but his line was unobtainable. Perhaps he was already up North. She was getting sporadic pieces of information over the police radio; the latest was the perpetrator was a white girl, who had been screaming about Berkeley Square. More of the same, it would seem. The girl who had set fire to herself was dead, but no one else had been seriously injured. Kenton arrived on Pall Mall around eleven. The whole area had been shut off to everyone except the emergency services. Drunk clubbers and frightened foreign tourists thronged the periphery of the area; camera crews and photographers were already collecting. Kenton pushed her way through the crowds and found her boss Malloy, shadowed by Craven, who was chewing on his plastic cigarette. A white tent had already been placed round the remains of the girl and a local constable with big ears and a sweaty, pallid face was explaining to his seniors what he had seen. Beside him two dark-haired students stood, terrified, hand in hand, clutching a camcorder.

'We all thought it was some sort of joke,' the bobby kept saying, over and over. 'Like that—what do you call it? Performance art.'

'Just tell me exactly what she said,' Malloy was patient, but his blue eyes were scorching.

'She kept shouting about the banks and nuclear power and the oil companies and—and corrupters. She kept saying—' The bobby took his hat off and mopped his brow with a hanky. He had huge sweat patches under his arms. 'She kept saying "the corrupters shall pay, they shall pay". And then she was screaming "Get back, get back", and pouring some sort of liquid over her head and the next minute—boom.' He looked a little like he might

211

throw up. 'She went up like a bonfire. Christ.'

'You're in shock, mate,' Kenton was surprised by Craven's gentle tone. 'Go and get a cuppa. We'll talk to you later.'

Malloy beckoned the long-haired students over. They looked terrified.

'Where are you from?' he asked, kindly for him, and they looked at each other and then the girl said, 'Tel Aviv.'

'And you were filming, were you?'

She nodded. 'Yes. I wanted to show to my mother the lions. And then this girl, she was here, and so I filmed her for a minute.'

'We thought it was an—how do you call it. An act?' the boy chipped in now. His hair was longer than his girlfriend's, Kenton thought absently.

'I wish to fucking Christ it had been,' Malloy muttered. 'You'll have to give me that, I'm afraid.' He held his hand out for the camera. The couple spoke to each other in Hebrew.

'When can we—will we get it back?'

'Look, love,' Malloy feigned patience. 'I wouldn't want to ruin your holiday or anything, but a girl has just burnt herself to tiny little cinders, and we need to understand why—and who she was. OK?'

Kenton took their names and contact details, and the camera.

'I'll try and get it back to you as soon as I can,' she murmured quietly. 'Just bear with me.'

*   *   *

They sat in the car and watched the footage, all craning to see the tiny screen. The girl was dressed in a long skirt and coat buttoned to her neck, her

212

hair tightly scraped back. She was white, average height, brown hair, snub-nosed, generously-bosomed. She became extremely agitated as she began to chant 'Corrupters, corrupters.' She worked herself up into a frenzy and then began to open her coat. She had some kind of canister tucked inside the coat, full of a liquid, which she tipped onto her head, before reaching into her pocket for a cigarette lighter. She appeared to pause for a moment, as if she wasn't quite sure of what she was doing—and then she screamed 'The world shall pay the price' one final time. Her teeth clenched almost in a death mask, she ignited the lighter.

Malloy paused the film.

'Recognise her?' Malloy looked at his officers.

'No, guv,' Kenton shook her head, disappointed and horribly disturbed by the image. The severed hand hit her memory like a meteorite; she almost ducked.

'We need to get her photo out there quickly and get her identified. Fuck.' Malloy hit the dashboard with a fist. 'This is fucking craziness. Put the picture out on the wire. Now.'

FRIDAY 21ST JULY
CLAUDIE

Will was waiting outside the flat when I pulled up in the cab, his sandy hair all on end.

'What are you doing here?' I was exhausted. The last thing in the world I wanted to do now was chat to Will about—stuff.

'I came to see you were all right,' he muttered.

'What, at midnight?'

We gazed at each other. He seemed shifty, and I was struck suddenly by my lack of feeling towards him. He wasn't the man I thought I'd married, I realised that now, though it had been a painful journey.

'Can I offer you a drink?' I said politely.

'Go on then.'

The front door was slightly ajar, which was annoying. The young Polish guys who lived beneath me often forgot to shut it; they were always in a rush, and I was always politely reminding them, to no avail.

I pressed the light switch in the hall, but nothing happened. The stairwell was shrouded in complete darkness. 'Bloody hell.' I tripped over the hall rug.

'You want to have a word with the landlord.'

Halfway up, on the first landing, I dropped my keys through the banister. I had a sudden urge to run away; I didn't know what Will was doing here and it was beginning to spin me out.

'You go on up,' I mumbled, making my way back down.

As I opened the street door, unsure where I was going, there was a cry from above me, followed by a massive crash. Heart pounding, I was rushing back up the stairs when a hooded figure came flying past, knocking into me so that I smashed backwards into the wall, hitting my head hard, passing so close I could smell garlic on their breath.

'Hey!' I shouted, grabbing instinctively at the figure's hood, breaking my nails in the process on the rough fabric of their top. But they didn't falter, pushing out into the night. I staggered up and out onto the street but whoever it was had already

214

disappeared into the dusk. As I turned, the glint of silver struck me from the hall's rush matting. I picked it up; a broken chain with a tiny dove. Where had I seen this before?

I heard a groan from above.

'Will—are you OK?' I called frantically, pocketing it and running up the stairs.

By my front door, my husband was staggering to his feet.

'Yeah I'm fine,' he mumbled, rubbing his head. 'Who the hell was that?'

My front door was wide open, and I reached inside and switched the lights on, baffled by the foot-high black letters scrawled on the wall beside the upended book cabinet that lived on the landing. Next to a badly drawn flower was written:

ATISHOO! ATISHOO!
WE ALL FALL DOWN

'God, I'm bleeding,' Will groaned.

I saw the blood on the hand he held out before him, and I felt sorry, knowing it was my fault. 'Oh God,' I said.

'I'll live. It's a nursery rhyme isn't it?' He indicated the wall.

'I guess so.' Tentatively I pushed open the door. 'I'll fix you up, Will.'

'Wait, Claudie.' He pulled me back urgently. 'I don't think you should go in there.'

'Whoever it was has gone.' Gently I tried to free my arm. 'It's OK.'

'I'm going to call the police.' Will looked shocked and pale.

'No!' I said firmly. 'I don't think we need to.'

'Are you mad?' He stared at me. I stared back.

'Maybe.'

'Some guy's just punched me in the head, defaced your property and possibly burgled you. I'm calling them.'

'It's probably just kids, messing around.'

'That wasn't a kid,' Will snapped. 'That was a proper punch.'

'Please, Will.' I thought about that horrible policeman who'd come here to tell me about Tessa. I thought about being dragged into the back of a police car after I'd sat on the wall outside Ned's nursery school in the snow for a straight five hours without moving, a month after he'd died; of the policewoman who had eyed me suspiciously when I'd sat alone in the park once watching the children play in the sandpit. I was bereft, not menacing, but she couldn't see that. No uniforms, not yet. 'Look. Let me just check if anything's been taken, OK? Then we can decide.'

Will glared at me for a moment and then he sighed deeply. 'OK, I won't call the police if nothing's been touched. But if even a hair's out of place, then—'

I turned all the lights on and together we walked through the flat. When we came to the small room where I kept Ned's things, I let Will look inside alone. Everything was untouched as far as I could see, exactly as I had left it earlier.

'I think it might have been someone after the Polish boys downstairs.' I went through to the bathroom to find Will some Savlon.

'Why?'

'They keep such funny hours and I'm sure they're growing weed in there.' I rummaged in the

216

half-empty medicine cabinet. At the back I found a packet of Tigger plasters I'd kept. Tears pricked my eyes and I swallowed hard. 'I can smell it in the hallway most days. It's bloody strong.'

I put the plasters back carefully. Funny how the smallest things can have the biggest effect sometimes. A lump formed in my throat; I couldn't swallow it down this time.

'What's going on, Claudie?' Will followed me in. 'You don't return my calls; Helen rings to say you've been missing appointments—and now this.' He sat on the edge of the bath.

'Helen rang you?' I frowned. How annoying.

'Yes. She wanted to know if you were OK when you didn't turn up. *Are* you OK?'

'I'm fine,' I said automatically, finding a bit of limp cotton wool and dabbing pathetically at his wound with it. 'I just had a bit of a—of a wobble, that's all. The Tessa thing threw me.'

'Tessa? From the Academy? Ow!' He pushed my hand away. 'I think you're making it worse, actually.'

'Probably.' I threw the cotton wool in the bin. 'Yes, Tessa from the Academy. She was killed in the explosion.'

'The bomb, you mean?' Will leant on the door frame. 'I'm sorry. That's terrible.'

'Terrible,' I intoned, carefully washing my hands. 'But it's not just that she's dead. She's also not who she said she was. Can you put the kettle on?'

I followed him out into the sitting room.

'I don't understand.' He filled the kettle at the tap. 'What do you mean, not who she said she is?'

'No,' I agreed. 'I don't really understand either.'

It was as if I was sleepwalking; like I couldn't get

217

my feet back on solid ground ever since the news of Tessa's death and her false identity.

'Why have you come back now, Will?'

'Your eczema's bad,' Will said, looking at my hands. I hid them behind my back.

'It's not.'

'It is. Have you been using your cream?'

'Don't fuss, Will. Why don't you answer the question?'

Will was back in the kitchen, looking for the teabags as I vaguely searched for my hydrocortisone cream on the side. I suddenly saw the frailty in his face that I had started to recognise when Ned first got ill, and I looked away.

'What's this?'

I turned absently, still thinking about Ned.

Standing in front of the open kitchen cupboard, Will held the same framed tract I'd seen in Tessa's earlier, only the glass on this copy was cracked.

THE SUN MAY STILL SHINE
BUT IF YOU DO NOT ACT
SOME DAY SOON
THE END WILL BE THINE

*   *   *

I gazed at it, then up at him.

'I don't know,' I said truthfully. 'I really don't know.'

218

SATURDAY 22ND JULY
SILVER

Silver woke to find his daughter Molly standing beside the bed brandishing a tray. He hadn't slept well, having taken a call at 3 a.m. from Malloy about the burning girl.

'I know you've got family stuff on, Joe,' Malloy had sounded exhausted. 'But this is becoming a nightmare.'

'Do we know who she is?' Silver was bleary.

'No. Had another call from the fucking Purity lot. Bunch of fucking no-mark new-age nutters. And Lynne's lot in Counter Terrorism are coming round to thinking it might be Al-Qaeda's baby brothers after all, the Al-Jazeen branch, in which case this whole investigation will be taken off us, thank holy fuck. Burqa-girl from the CCTV is dead. She was a nanny for the Saudi royals; she was on her way to collect the baby from the mother who'd been rushed into the Rushborne Clinic in the early hours. The chauffeur couldn't get the Merc up the side street because of the roadworks, so he dropped her and the pram in Berkeley Square. Her bad luck.'

'How did we miss that?'

'Because the poor cow's clothes were blown right off her, not to mention her bloody face. Meanwhile the press are on to the fact that we're *still* struggling to identify all fourteen dead a week on, and they're stirring up the shit. The sooner you're back, the better.'

'Breakfast in bed,' Molly said proudly now,

launching the tray at him.

'Woah—careful.' The coffee pot slid precariously across the carthorse's face as Silver, lurching up in bed, still half-asleep, grabbed the tray just in time. Next to the coffee was a singed bit of toast with no crusts, a scraping of orange marmalade, and a whole milk bottle containing less than a dribble.

'Oh, I forgot the butter.' Molly's round face fell. 'I'll just go and get it.'

'Don't worry, lovie,' he said. He moved up in the small bed to make room for his daughter. 'This is grand. Here, sit with me. I'm not that hungry yet anyway.'

When Silver had arrived in the early hours of the morning, he'd found his mother-in-law in Lana's bedroom, so he'd taken the spare. Actually he was glad to avoid sleeping in the room he and his ex-wife had once shared. However relieved he was that they were no longer tearing each other apart, he still found memories of their relationship deeply painful. As they'd stumbled through the divorce process, Silver found it hard to believe that they had once been so close; shared everything from jokes and body fluids to long painful labours and his swift ascent up the career ladder. Somewhere, buried deep, was the knowledge that his job had taken precedence over everything else, that he had sacrificed his wife and marriage for the adrenaline that was chasing down criminals and bringing them to justice. That he started to pour himself ever-larger whiskies each night because of the stress, because that was what he'd learnt from his own father. Lana had followed suit because she had nothing else apart from interminable days alone with three young kids to keep her sane, and a

220

husband who loved those kids but wasn't interested in hands-on fathering most of the time. Silver held this knowledge inside, and every now and then he would retrieve it momentarily to increase his guilt, before burying it again swiftly.

He'd showered and was about to shave when Anne opened the bathroom door, catching him with only a small towel slung round his waist.

'Oh, I'm sorry.' Her neck immediately flushed a deep and mottled red as she slammed the door in her haste to get away. Silver grinned at himself in the mirror. God only knew when Anne had last seen a semi-naked man. He knew he wasn't a bad specimen for his age; the gym and squash court having replaced the pub and all-night lock-ins he used to indulge in, his old beer-gut replaced by not quite a six-pack, but something a little leaner. He must do something about the bloody stupid tattoo on his shoulder that read Lana though.

Five minutes later, there was a tentative knock at the door.

'Lana's on the phone. She wants to talk to you.'

He took the receiver that his mother-in-law thrust round the door, trying not to cover it in the shaving foam that swathed half his face. 'Where the hell are you?' he snapped.

'If you're going to be rude, Joe, I'll hang up.'

'Don't, please,' he interjected quickly. 'Just tell me where you are. Do you want me to come and get you? We've been worried sick.'

'Really,' she said, but it wasn't a question.

'Yes, really.' He felt his toes curl. No one inspired anger in him more dramatically than his ex-wife. 'The kids are distraught.'

The kids were sprawled downstairs on the sofa

with the Wii, rather less than distraught right now, but she didn't deserve to hear that. Anne was hovering like a worried poodle in the background, back and forth she went, back and forth.

'I want to talk,' Lana said.

'OK, good.' He hated 'talking' with a passion. 'Come home, and we can talk as much as you like.'

'I'm not coming home.'

'What?'

'I'll meet you at the Tea Rooms in Skipton in an hour. On your own. I'm not coming back, not yet.' She sighed, long and hard. 'Kiss the kids from me.'

'Right.'

She'd already hung up.

It took him half an hour to calm Anne down enough to get out of the house. Fortunately Molly was going riding with her best friend Shona so she was distracted, and the boys were playing football that afternoon. He'd hear what Lana had to say and then he'd persuade her home where she belonged. And then he'd go on to see the Malverns.

* * *

Within ten minutes of sitting down with his ex-wife, Silver was wondering why he was so daft as to think he'd ever be able to control anything she did, and when he'd ever learn that nothing would ever go to plan when they were together.

Lana had lost weight since he last saw her at Easter, and it didn't suit her. She'd had such good bone structure, but now her jaw looked thin and overly tense, her neck slightly scrawny, and for the first time ever he could see the older woman she would be in a few years. It shocked him in the way middle age constantly did, sneaking up to surprise him. Her hair was a whiter blonde than normal and it seemed too harsh for her face, which was not as tanned or made-up as usual.

She kept piling sugar into her coffee and when she sat down, he'd glimpsed a packet of cigarettes in her handbag, though she'd given up years ago, before she'd had Matty.

'What's going on, Lana?'

'Did you find Sadie Malvern?' She ignored the question.

'Not yet, no.' His heart sank.

'Are you still looking?'

'Yes.' He took a sip of his own cappuccino. Whoever had invented frothy milk should be shot. 'It's not your fault, you know. That Sadie's disappeared.'

'Yes, I do know,' she said flatly. Her manicure was slightly chipped, he noticed, as she curled her hand round the coffee cup. None of this was good, he knew that much. Lana was falling to pieces again before his eyes; the last time she'd let herself go she'd ended up driving the car halfway through the garden fence, semi-conscious on gin.

'The kids are worried about you, Allana, and your mum's going spare.'

'So?' she said. She wouldn't meet his eye.

'Is there—' He cleared his throat. 'Is it someone else?'

'You mean have I been screwing around? Even though I am perfectly entitled to.' She shoved her mane of hair away, out of her face before she answered. 'It's none of your business, but no. That's been your forte recently, hasn't it?'

It was a deliberate swipe for which she had no

real proof. Still, Silver thought of Julie, who'd been calling incessantly since Thursday night, and of Paige in the hotel yesterday, whom in truth he would have bedded in a flash if he hadn't been working. He thought of Jane Gregor from Vice and all the women he'd taken to bed during the past few years whose names escaped him. They had provided momentary solace, a pair of arms in the night, human warmth if you liked—and not much more. And none of them had been Allana, whom he had loved so very much since he was twenty-one and they'd met at her cousin's eighteenth. Allana, shy but self-possessed; quiet but confident of her allure already. Allana, his beautiful, lost wife, whom he'd been completely faithful to until the moment he discovered she'd been seeing Ray Steen. Silver's first mistress had been the whisky bottle, but he wasn't going to start arguing semantics now.

'Lana.' He tried to take her hand, but she wouldn't let him. 'Come back with me, would you, sweetheart? Come and see the kids. I can help you.'

'Help me?' Her forehead creased in disbelief. 'How the hell can you help me? You have never *ever* been here when I needed you. Why would you start now?'

'That's not bloody true,' Silver asserted forcefully, but just like that other memory he lied about, he knew that it was. 'I was here after the accident.'

'You were pissed, you mean.'

'Not as pissed as you,' he snapped, and then instantly regretted it. The colour drained from Lana's face until she was just two staring blue eyes.

'Sorry,' he said, but it was too late. She slammed down her coffee cup and got to her feet.

'I don't know why I expected you to understand.

You don't understand anything except your precious bloody job.'

'Lana, please.' He grabbed her arm and pulled her down again. 'Explain to me then. Where are you staying?'

'With a friend.'

'A man?'

'Why does it matter?' She did meet his gaze now. Her left eye was slightly bloodshot, he noticed now. 'Is it your pride, Joe? Don't like the fact I don't need you any more? That I don't cry myself to sleep every night these days.'

He had a sudden memory of their last night together.

'She's out there.'

When he wakes, it takes him a moment to realise where she is in the room.

She stands by the window, looking out; looking down into the garden. It is still dark, the moon a white ghostly light; a light far more hopeful than he feels. He thinks she has spoken but he's not sure.

'What are you doing?' His voice is the voice of sleep, cracked and bleary, it vibrates up through his torso.

'She's out there. She's out there again.' She turns slightly as she speaks. She looks much younger than her forty-two years. She is wearing a long white nightgown with a high collar that makes her look rather like a Victorian matron, but she is still beautiful. He can see her breasts through the cotton fabric; he looks away. He rubs his eyes with the heels of his hands; it seems too intimate to see his wife's body. She is still beautiful but she is no longer robust. She's fragile now.

'Who?' he says, but he knows absolutely who. 'Who do you mean?' He holds his breath as if she might not say it.

'Her.' She holds on to the long velvet curtain now, she holds it for support. He wonders if she is drunk. He doesn't say it. She was asleep when he came to bed. The sweet smell of alcohol heavy in the room, cloying and invasive.

'Don't be silly, Lan. It's the middle of the night.' He lies down again with that thud of relief that means it's not yet time to rise. He doesn't know how much more of this he can take. 'Get back into bed. It's freezing.'

Slowly she gets back into the bed, folds her hands over her belly, lying rigid and wakeful. He turns onto his right side so he doesn't have to see her face.

He doesn't know it now as he drifts off back to sleep, thinking of the transfer meeting in the morning, thinking of his wife's bereft face. He doesn't know it right now, but this is the last night they will share a bed.

'No,' Silver muttered now, but she was probably right. 'When did you cry yourself to sleep, anyway?'

Again Lana ignored him. 'I'll come back when I'm ready.'

'And what about—' He caught himself in time. He'd been about to say 'What about my work?' but he stopped. 'What about the kids?'

'Do you mean what about their welfare, Joe, or what about who's going to look after them?' Lana picked up her bag and pushed her chair away. 'I'll ring them. And you, Joe, you can worry about their welfare for once. You're their dad. Remember?'

And she was gone, leaving a trail of Nina Ricci and despair in her wake.

SATURDAY 22ND JULY
KENTON

The call had come in about 9.30, partially confirming the news Kenton had feared. It seemed that the annihilated body in Trafalgar Square *was* most likely to be that of the girl called Meriel Steele, the third missing student from the Academy. A girl whose parents had believed she was still happily dancing at the Academy and waitressing at the Dorchester in the holidays. She had, in reality, dropped out of the ballet school last year. To do what though? That remained the question. And what the hell was going on at the Academy that linked all these tragic or missing girls?

Kenton gazed at the photograph of Meriel's broad, sturdy face, her serious dark eyes, and wondered what the hell had happened to drive her to such an extreme act. Someone was going to have to interview Meriel's family and to get a positive ID, and she had a horrible feeling it was going to fall to her. She looked again at the photo. Where had she seen that face before?

She was also waiting for a more recent picture of Rosalind Lamont from an elderly aunt. Both parents were dead and her sister was apparently unreachable in the Canadian wilds. The aunt was in a home in St John's Wood, but the matron said she had a chest infection and was currently too poorly for visitors. Kenton was waiting for the all-clear before she could go and visit her.

Craven walked through the office.

'Busy?' Kenton called. Perhaps he'd go and see

the Steele family for her. 'I could do with some—'

'Poor you,' he smirked and walked on. Kenton gritted her teeth. She pulled the phone towards her, and, muttering to herself, called Silver, wishing for the tenth time today he was back here. Tina Price rolled her eyes at Kenton.

'Talk about a bloody dinosaur,' she muttered. 'I thought his sort went out with the Ark.'

'Hardly,' Kenton muttered back. 'Not the most enlightened place, the Met, sadly. But you'll get used to it.'

'I hope not,' Price pulled a face. Kenton was momentarily distracted by Jo Reid sashaying past in a very tight red dress and seamed stockings.

'Have you seen poor Gill?' Price hissed at Kenton as they watched the press assistant lean provocatively over Roger Okeke to give him a message about a press conference later. 'She's been completely tear-stained all week.'

'Don't blame her,' Kenton sniffed, but she found it hard to tear her eyes from Reid's voluptuous behind.

'I'm surprised they can work together after all that,' Price scowled at Reid. 'Look at that, heading straight for the boys.'

Kenton found the Steeles' home number.

'Can you call the Academy for me?' Kenton asked Price, setting her shoulders and dialling the Steele household. 'We need to speak to the Principal again, asap. Something bad's going on down there.'

'Bad?'

'Yeah, properly bad. I just can't work out exactly what.'

SATURDAY 22ND JULY
CLAUDIE

I let Will stay the night, against my better judgement. He kept on and on about how worried he was about me, and how he wanted to call the police, insistent on taking photos of the graffiti with his iPhone for evidence before I went out and scrubbed it off as best I could, pushing the bookshelves back in front of the faint words. In the end, it seemed the only way to silence him, to stop that 999 call. He slept on the sofa.

There was a single crack of blue in the sky when I woke. It was very early, and I immediately rued the fact that Will was here. I knew he could see into me better than anyone else, and I found it so much easier to be alone these days, shutting myself off from most contact except the necessary. I lay in bed for a while wishing I was back in oblivion, debating my best course of action today. I kept thinking about the man who'd been in the flat last night, and whether it was the same man from St Pancras. For the sake of my friendship with Tessa, I had to make one last-ditch effort to find out the truth—and then I would give up.

I was padding quietly out of the bathroom when Will surprised me in the hall, his hair on end as usual.

'Morning,' I said a little stiffly. 'Sleep all right?'

'Not bad for a sofa,' he yawned. 'St Thomas's Hospital just rung by the way. Said something about results? The number's on the side.' He yawned again, so wide this time I heard his jaw crack. 'Are

229

you sure you're OK?'

'Oh, that doesn't sound good,' I said, nodding towards his jaw. I vaguely remembered some blood test in A&E on the day of the explosion, but it seemed irrelevant now. 'Do you want me to have a look?'

'Maybe later,' he was distracted.

'What is it?' I followed his gaze to the door of the small room. *Don't say it*, I prayed.

'I just wondered—why is the telescope in there?'

'I don't use it now,' I shrugged.

'Why not?'

'Because I stopped looking at the stars.' I walked back into the bathroom to clean my teeth. Will had bought me that telescope for my thirtieth birthday five years ago, when I was pregnant with Ned; it was the best present I'd ever received. Before Ned's birth.

'Why?' He was in the doorway behind me. 'You love all that stuff.'

'Just. Because.'

'Because—' he pushed.

'Because there's nothing up there any more.' I was impatient.

'There's still the same stars. And there's—' He stopped. I glanced at him; I thought I saw the glint of tears in his eyes.

'Don't, Will.'

'There's a star I look at—well. Kind of, you know. Heaven.'

'Oh, come on! You don't believe that.' My anger was immediate and white-hot; I felt it pulse through me. 'You don't believe that for a bloody minute. That's crap.'

'I have to believe it,' he whispered. 'I have to.'

230

I threw the tube of toothpaste onto the basin so hard it splattered against the tiles.

'How can you be so hard, Claudia?' He followed me out of the room. 'It's so weird. It's not you.'

'Don't, Will.' I put my hands over my ears. 'You didn't care before.'

'I did care,' he mumbled. 'I just didn't know how to deal with it. When Ned died—and you knew he was going to die—you knew they said he couldn't get better—'

'Don't,' boiling tears suffused my eyes. That word; I couldn't bear it still. His little body: the fat tummy, the chubby limbs: the life all gone. So final, so—

'Don't ignore me.' He pulled me round forcibly. 'You've closed down so much. It scares me.'

'You didn't want to know. You went to New York.'

'I wanted you to come.'

'No you didn't, not really. And I couldn't.' I couldn't leave my son. His grave. 'You knew why.'

'We could have had another baby.'

'Will. I could barely function. You could barely look at me, let alone touch me. How would we have managed that?'

'Well, talk to me now. You don't look good, Claudie.'

'I can't,' I said miserably, refusing to meet his hazel eyes. I couldn't bear the hurt I'd see there.

'Why not?'

'Because,' I wrenched my hands out of his. 'Because if I let one single little chink of sorrow in, I will go down again. And if I go down again, Will,' I was practically shouting, 'I will never ever get up again. Do you understand? I'm still not convinced

231

my life is worth living any more. If I go down again, it will be the end.'

We stood in the centre of the room, glaring at each other, fists balled, until eventually he shrugged and moved away.

'I'll get going now,' he muttered, sitting to pull his shoes on, and I didn't try to dissuade him. This was why we couldn't be together any more. We were both so racked by our own pain, so wrapped up in it, that we would only end up killing one another if we stayed together. In our own strange ways, we were both fighting for survival. And a year ago Will had chosen his own over our mutual one.

'Can I ask you one thing?' he said quietly, standing now.

'Go on.' I stared at the photo of the three of us that was on the kitchen wall. We were all smiling, smiling fit to burst. I didn't recognise any of us though. That was what scared me most. We had been so happy, and then, in a flash, it was over. Then there was only the two of us left, and an emptiness where Ned had been. Impossible to ever fill again.

'When you—when that strange thing happened to you—' he trailed off.

'You mean when I started splitting?'

'What did it feel like?'

I contemplated for a minute. 'It felt like I had gone away from myself. Like I couldn't remember stuff. Which was a relief, I suppose, at the time.'

'Did you feel—mad?'

'No. It wasn't like madness.' I looked up at him, at his kind, pleasant face, at his sad eyes. At the weakness around his mouth and chin I had not noticed when we first met. 'It was like—necessity.'

232

He zipped up his jacket. He still didn't understand, I could see. He didn't want to.

'You should stop scratching,' he said quietly, as he left, 'you'll scar yourself.'

I looked down at my hands, and I saw that they were both bleeding again.

'Will,' I called, as he started down the stairs.

'Yeah?' He looked back at me, so mournful, with such a look of—with such a look, that my heart turned over.

'I'm sorry,' I bit the tears down fervently.

'So am I,' he said.

'I just—' Miserably, I trailed off. 'I still don't know why it had to happen, Will.'

'Yeah, well,' he said over his shoulder, 'we'll never know.' And he walked out of sight.

*   *   *

Some people, apparently, when they lose someone they love beyond all others, they feel the need to talk about that person all the time. But I was not some people. The only way I could even imagine getting through the rest of my days was by closing down; in public at least. I felt Ned's presence with me virtually every second; he followed me, I took him with me. Sometimes I would turn around quickly, and I would think I saw him from the corner of my eye, laughing in that uproarious way he had; chattering away to himself across the room, playing with his beloved trains. Yet that was no one else's business but mine, and no one else would understand. So why share it?

Initially, when I was so traumatised I couldn't function, and I had to be hospitalised for a while,

Will had been scared by my behaviour, by how far away I seemed. When his project in America had got the green light, he had done little to persuade me to accompany him. Later, he tried to help, he spoke to my friends, to the oldest ones like Zoe, and to Tessa and Eduardo at the Academy, and then he found me Helen. Undoubtedly she had helped, but Will had lost my confidence. It was only latterly that he realised I hadn't been able to help it, and that maybe he should have been more patient. But now it was too late.

*   *   *

In the back of Tessa's book on African plants, there were various obscure scrawls, lines from nursery rhymes, and the words *as you like it* followed by lots of question marks written over and again. I also found another clipping from a paper; a tiny picture of Tessa and a man called Ivan Adanov: ordinary, with glasses, slightly balding. They were smiling at the camera at an official ballet function in Paris, sponsored by the Hoffman Bank. I stared at the photo. I had the feeling I might have met this man once. Something escaped me: something just out of reach, constantly there and yet not there: like a fox's tail slipping round the tree; like the trail of my mother's dressing-gown whisking out of the door.

I opened the nursery rhyme book I'd retrieved from Ned's old box.

'*The Queen of Hearts, she made some tarts all on*
   a summer's day,
The Knave of Hearts, he took those tarts and stole
   them right away.'

Amanda Curran had said she'd heard Tessa called the Queen of Hearts by the man she'd introduced the girls to. The tarts were the girls, I assumed. But why all these nursery rhymes? And who was going to chop whose head off? My own head was pounding now. It was like some kind of code, and I had no idea how to crack it.

I flicked through her little book again. Somewhere, somehow, there had to be a clue. I pulled out the newspaper clipping. The words 'Dear Piper' were written on the back in someone else's handwriting.

If anyone would know who this man in the cutting was, it would be Mason. It was an audition day, so Mason would be at the Academy. I called the office.

'Do you know who Ivan Adanov is?' Mason knew everybody in the ballet world.

'Of course. He was a benefactor. From the Hoffman Bank. When there was a Hoffman Bank. He's retired now, I think.'

'Any idea who Piper is?'

'Piper? Oh indeed. *"Be not another, if you can be yourself"*, as Paracelsus said.'

'Parcel— who?'

'I mean your friend Tessa. She was such a pretender, Claudie, though it saddens me to say so. Not at all who she made out to be. I'm afraid you were blind to it. She must have had a huge inferiority complex you know.'

'Why?'

'I heard her say it. That she was like the Pied Piper,' she sniffed. 'Running a popularity contest with the students.'

235

'The Pied Piper?' I stuttered.

'You know, the Pied Piper of Hamelin. He played a tune that lured the rats away from the town, but it also took all the kids. Tessa used to boast she was like that with some of the girls, that they'd follow her anywhere.'

'Did she?' I sat heavily. 'I never heard her say that.'

'Well, she certainly banged on about it to me,' Mason sniffed. 'Pride always comes before a fall, I warned her, but she took no notice.'

Not *Paul Piper* at all; I'd read it wrong. The Pied Piper, who called the tune, who danced, and they all followed.

SATURDAY 22ND JULY
SILVER

The Malverns lived in an ex-council house on the Rothbury Estate. The small red-brick house had a tired air about it, as if everyone who lived there had rather given up on life; the flowerbeds empty except for a half-grown sycamore sapling that had been left to seed, and a solitary weed or two. The black front door was faded and slightly peeling, a pink sticker for *'Gem Radio, West Yorks' Finest'* stuck in the corner of one pane.

Silver sat in the car outside for a long five minutes. He had not seen the Malverns since he had attempted to attend Jaime's funeral six years ago, and had been stopped at the church gate by Pete Malvern's younger brother, Lee.

'Don't think it's a good idea, pal, do you?'

The thickset bouncer had put a hand on Silver's shoulder, an insistent firmness propelling him backwards. 'Brenda hasn't slept for a week; the poor lass is beside herseln. Seeing you is just gonna drive her over t'edge. You'd better get gone, lad. You're not wanted here.'

And Silver had a sudden recollection now: a memory he'd buried; of little Sadie, who must have been about fourteen but was already sexually precocious, sure of herself, standing outside the church in the driving rain, her arm in a sling, white-blonde curls tumbling over the collar of her navy school coat, dwarfed by her lanky father. She had looked over at Silver from beneath her big, black umbrella, her pretty little face still bruised, and he could have sworn that she smiled. Moments later Silver had done what Lee Malvern asked and had left, heading back to his local pub to drown his sorrows. He walked through the empty Friday afternoon streets in that driving rain. He felt the water on his face and knew he would never be allowed to forget that his wife had killed a girl.

He remembered that there had been a time when he and Lana, on their honeymoon in Scotland in the caravan that belonged to Lana's granddad, had driven it to the top of a hill in a deserted caravan park and made love all day and night to the sound of the rain outside. At some point, for a mad dare, Lana had run out of the caravan and round the field completely naked, laughing and screeching happily until she was soaked, turning cartwheels, her long wet hair sticking to her back like a mermaid's.

But Lana hated the rain now. It had been raining that day, the day she rolled the car; it had made the road more lethal. Now it only reminded her of death.

When Silver rang the Malverns' doorbell, even that sounded muted. There was the yapping of a small dog, and then a woman's voice shouting at the dog, and eventually Brenda Malvern stood there, holding a Yorkshire terrier, which quivered dramatically in her arms.

Silver was shocked by her appearance. She looked old beyond her years, wearing a tatty pink dressing-gown and furry old slippers with the backs pushed down. Her hair was grey and lank, unbrushed over her sloping shoulders, and the corners of her mouth turned down naturally. The dog growled at him and she peered myopically for a moment then said, 'Pete's out. He'll be back around four.'

She moved to shut the front door and Silver moved forwards himself, and said, 'Brenda? My name is Joseph Silver. You might remember me from—' but he got no further because she stared at him with naked horror and began to cry.

'Silver? As in Allana Silver?'

'Yes. Please, I'm so sorry. It must be a shock—but I need to talk to you about Sadie.'

'Sadie?' She stared at him uncomprehending. 'You mean Jaime?'

The dog was yapping again now, picking up the tension from the woman, growling and drooling angrily at Silver, droplets of saliva flying as he twisted his head this way and that, trying to escape from his mistress's arms.

'No, Sadie—' he began.

'My darling baby who that bitch murdered?' the pitch of her voice was climbing quickly. 'That bitch who never served a single solitary day in prison?'

'I'm sorry. We tried to ring but—' Silver said, cursing his own stupidity. Then he heard footsteps, a young man running down the stairs behind the wailing Brenda.

'Who is it, Ma?' the youth said, and he stared at Silver, uncomprehending. He looked like he hadn't seen the sun for a very long time, and he was badly scarred by acne, his hair cut in a complicated and unflattering boy-band style.

'I'm a police officer,' Silver decided to take the other approach. 'I'm here on business, but I knew your—my ex-wife, Allana Silver, she—'

'Allana Silver?' The pale youth eyed him malevolently, placing a protective arm on his mother's shoulder. 'Yeah, I know who that cunt is. We all do, believe me. What do you want?'

Silver was wondering why the hell he had thought this was in any way a sensible idea. But he also knew that these people deserved to be told the truth.

'I've come about Sadie.'

The woman paled, if that was possible, her frightened eyes now slashes of distress in her worn-out face. Silver imagined how he would feel if anything happened to any of his children, God forbid, and he realised that to Brenda Malvern, six years was probably nothing; just more dull days stretching out infinitely, laced with grief and pain.

'What's happened to Sadie?' she asked, her voice trembling.

Silver realised that this was going to be far, far worse than he had ever anticipated. The young man looked at Silver, and then he stepped back, making a decision, pulling his mother gently with him. 'You'd better come in.'

239

'Thanks.' Silver stepped into the hallway, which smelt of wet dog and damp. 'I won't take up much of your time.'

'Let's go in best room.' The youth pushed the door open, and they all sat gingerly on a cream-coloured three-piece suite that still had the plastic covers on. They all looked at the shrine to Jaime, framed pictures; seven-year-old Jaime doing gymnastics, grinning toothily, in her uniform with well-brushed bunches. Never got past seven. Silver could hear that bastard Beer practically yelling in his ear. He smoothed his trousers over his knees.

'Take your shoes off, can you, Colin,' the woman mumbled, clutching the dog to her like a baby, and Silver was amazed she'd even noticed her son was wearing any.

'Ma's a bit house-proud, aren't you, Ma?' Colin said to Silver, sliding his trainers off. For the first time, Silver sensed the desperation in the young man's bearing, and had a glimpse of what it must be like to be left here with this woman's suppurating pain.

'I've just signed up,' Colin must have read Silver's mind. There was a small hole in the toe of his Bart Simpson sock. 'I'm off to ATC Pirbright next week for six months. Training. Can't bloody wait. Hoping I get out to Afghanistan.'

'Good lad,' Silver nodded at him, inwardly appalled. That was all Brenda Malvern needed. Hopefully by the time Colin had trained, the government might have seen sense and actually pulled out of the deadly war-zone, but the idea of losing another child . . . Christ. 'Army needs brave boys like you. But have you considered the police force instead?'

'So, Sadie?' the woman interrupted plaintively, as if she had been forgotten.

'Yes.' Silver's heart felt heavy; he felt like he was wading through boggy mud, his feet sinking ever deeper. 'It's just—I have to tell you—'

'Only I spoke to her last night.' The dog yapped again, and the woman bowed her head and kissed the top of his, shushing him. 'And she were in ever such a good mood.'

'Last night?' Silver stared at her. 'Are you sure?'

'Of course I'm sure. I know my own daughter.'

'Only, we—we've been worried that she was missing. Her flatmate Lucie—she—'

'That little cow?' the woman sniffed. 'Wouldn't trust a word she said.'

'Ma!' Colin was embarrassed. 'Don't be nasty.'

Silver looked at the lad's thin flushing skin and his Adam's apple, sharp as a child's protractor above the grey t-shirt bearing the legend '*Terminator lives*'. A crush on Lucie Duffy? Only to be expected, he thought, with a girl that obviously sexual.

'You've met her then? Lucie Duffy?'

'Yeah. Went down to see Sadie's graduation show last summer. Dead good, it were,' Colin pulled a funny face, 'if you like that sort of thing.'

Lucie had definitely said she didn't know the Malvern family. Silver was right then: she had been lying. Why, though?

'Right. Well, Lucie was worried that Sadie was missing,' Silver went on. 'And another—friend,' he saw Paige's cross little face, 'mentioned a boyfriend. Had a funny nickname. The Prince?'

'No,' the woman was firm, unequivocal. 'She's not missing, and she's got no time for men. Not with all the dancing. Not my Sadie. She's on a, what do you

241

call it?' She stared at him. 'A retreat.'

'A retreat?'

'Yeah. Something about tranquillity and her—finding her inner—oh, what were it, Col?'

'Her inner child she said,' he flushed further. 'Didn't make no sense to me.'

'She were dead happy. And she were with her nice mate from the Academy. Taking a break from the tour of Southern England with that ballet company. Then they're off abroad. Japan, I think she said. Doing ever so well, she is.'

'Really?' Silver was nonplussed. God only knew what web of lies Sadie Malvern had woven about her career. 'Where? And which mate was it that she mentioned?'

'What's her name again, Colin?' The woman looked at her son. 'I can't quite— Was it Mary?'

'No, Ma.' The pale-faced youth rolled his eyes at Silver, seeking male camaraderie now.

Silver gave an encouraging half-smile.

'It were Meriel. Meriel Steele.'

SATURDAY 22ND JULY
CLAUDIE

Down on the high street I hailed a cab, hastily applying mascara and blusher as I sat in the back, remembering the club-owner's scorn last time, trying to make my hair look wild and tousled rather than like I'd just literally fallen out of bed.

I arrived at London Bridge around six and made my way past Southwark Cathedral. It was Evensong; the girls' choir singing, the purity of their voices floating out into the dusky sky. For a moment I could almost believe that there was peace in this city. Then the air was riven by a siren, and I turned my back on the church, making my way to the club.

'Can I see the American please?' I asked, relieved it was a different doorman. He was white, shaven-headed and thickset, with tattoos on his neck. 'Larry,' I said as confidently as I could.

'Wait here,' he ordered. He had a strong accent that sounded something like Russian. I leant against the wall outside watching a malevolent shark of an aeroplane track the sky, expecting to be turned away again. I was surprised when, five minutes later, I was let down into the club.

I walked down the stairs and it was like entering hell: all red velvet and dim light, and hot beyond belief. I peeled off my parka and sat at the bar as instructed. A small redhead was up on the mirrored stage, upside down on the pole most of the time, giving her dead-pan all to Lady Gaga's *Poker Face*; other half-naked girls were dotted around the place, talking to the punters, laughing, simpering, taking money, dancing at tables or leading groups of men away to the side booths.

I glimpsed Larry at the side of the stage, beckoning the sweating redhead as she finished her set; the music changed and the next girl arrived on stage, scowling provocatively at the audience who whooped. The redhead slipped her skimpy black dress back over her head and followed Larry. It looked like he was reprimanding her for something. She seemed truculent at first, and then she changed tack; she started laughing, stroking his chest, looking up at him like a little girl and batting her lashes. But for all the coquetry and the flirting, she was holding herself too rigidly. She's scared of him, I thought.

After about five minutes he let her go, and she disappeared into the club, which was slowly filling up. A large stag party arrived and took over a couple of tables in front of me; they were in their late twenties and thoroughly over-excited. 'I'd hit it,' I heard one of them proclaim with relish, pointing at the nearest girl, a pneumatic blonde with breasts so high and round they were like bread rolls. 'I'd fucking hit it hard.'

'We all would.' The rest guffawed loudly, ordering champagne and beer. 'Let's have it, boys.'

'Andrei says you want a job.' Larry was suddenly beside me, wiping his forehead on his jacket sleeve. He snapped his fingers irritably at the pretty black waitress. 'Get me a soda.'

He didn't offer me anything.

'Not really a job—' I began, but he was staring at me now.

'Did we meet before?' he asked, his tiny eyes narrowing.

'No,' I lied, smiling my best smile.

'If you don't want a job, honey, what the fuck *do* you want? I'm a busy man.'

'I just wanted to ask you a few questions. It's about my friend, Tessa—'

'Never heard of her,' he said too quickly, grabbing the Coke from the waitress and draining it in one. Then he slammed the glass on the bar. 'Listen, darling,' he was millimetres from my face now and spitting. I shut my eyes. 'One thing I hate is journalists. I fucking hate journalists—even more than I hate feminist fucking do-gooders with their

244

moustaches and their hairy twats.'

'I'm not a journalist. I swear.'

He glared at me, and then he grabbed my face.

'Ow!' I protested.

His warm, fat fingers sank into my jaw-bone. 'I don't believe you.'

The tiny redhead arrived back now, neatly side-stepping the stag party who were getting more raucous by the minute. She had freshened up, changed into a see-through silver dress, reapplied her magenta lipstick, and she was waiting just behind him, drumming her nails anxiously on the bar.

'I'm not. I just—my friend died, and I—'

'Listen, lady.' He was hurting me. I caught the redhead's eye; she looked away. 'I don't care who you are. I don't know your dead friend Tessa and I suggest you fuck off. Right now.' He was angry; he pulled me off the stool so I tripped and fell against him, my wrist still in his vice-like grip.

'Ow!' I complained again. 'You're hurting me.'

'Get the fuck out of my club now.' He pushed me back against the bar. He was about to blow, I could sense it. 'I'm sick of you lot snooping around.'

'Larry,' the redhead spoke now, she had a rasping little voice, a broad cockney accent. 'I'm sure she don't mean no harm.'

'Who the fuck,' Larry wheeled round, his impressive bulk hard to turn, 'who the fuck asked you, Paige, baby?'

She shrugged and dropped her gaze, but not before she had caught my eye and flicked her gaze urgently towards the stairs.

'The boss is waiting,' he spat at her. She strolled over to a table in the corner where a plain man in shirtsleeves sat behind an open laptop, head down in concentration. He was wearing a flat cap and drinking Perrier. He wasn't watching us, but I had the feeling he had taken in every action, every word. Paige stood in front of him, obscuring his face from me as Larry started to propel me towards the exit. When I looked back, Paige and the 'boss' had both vanished. Andrei was at Larry's side now; he practically lifted me from the ground, carrying me towards the exit.

'I only wanted to ask about my friend Tessa,' I protested, but my heart was beating so fast now it hurt, and I was scared too. I'd hit a nerve somewhere, and these men were dangerous, that was obvious. I'd stepped straight into a wasps' nest.

Andrei carried me up the stairs and out into the warm Saturday night—but he didn't let me go. He kept on going, down a stinking back alley, and now I was truly frightened. I started to struggle frantically.

'What are you doing?' I kicked my legs like a child, one foot coming into contact with his shin. He swore in Russian and dropped me in front of him so I fell on all fours, my knees making painful contact with the concrete ground, and then he kicked me again so I went right down, the air leaving me like a burst balloon. I was lying next to a dumpster and the ground was filthy; the smell of urine overwhelming, ammonia pungent in my nostrils. I tried to scrabble to my feet but before I managed it, Andrei had kicked my arms out from beneath me.

I lay still now. I thought for a moment my arm might be broken, and I'd bitten right through my lip; I could taste the blood. I wondered if he was

246

going to beat me properly, or kill me even, and I was filled with a pure terror, and then a surge of something I didn't recognise for a moment. The will to live. And for a strange out-of-body second, I wanted to laugh; I felt the laugh build in my throat. I wanted to live. I hadn't felt this since Ned had died, but now I was threatened, I could feel the blood pumping round my body and pure adrenaline in my veins. I was filled with the knowledge that, whatever else happened, right now I didn't want to die.

With a concerted effort, I managed to roll over and pull myself to a sitting position.

'Please,' I struggled to remember my attacker's name. 'Please, Andrei, don't kill me.' I had read somewhere that you needed to bond with your aggressor. 'Please, Andrei,' I said his name again.

'Kill you?' the Russian said, and then he spat on the ground beside me. I could see a tattoo on his throat, creeping up from his coat collar, something like the top of the Virgin Mary's head, and I thought, I have seen that somewhere before. He cracked his knuckles, and I saw the odd symbols that decorated his fingers, and I thought of the man in St Pancras whose face I had never seen. A great wave of fear washed over me. 'I won't kill you now, little girl. But you need to go home and you need to not come back here. You understand me?'

I stared at him.

He prodded my ribs with his boot. 'You understand?'

I nodded fervently. 'Yes.'

'Good.' He eyed me, and then he leant down and pulled me up to my feet. I had a head rush so intense I thought I'd fall again. 'Now, go.' He pushed me out into the street, and then he threw my jacket after me. 'Go home. Before I change my mind.'

So I did what I was told. I went home—only someone else had got there first.

SATURDAY 22ND JULY
SILVER

Silver left the Malverns' smelly little house with a huge sense of relief. Standing on the pavement outside, the bastard Beer called him loudly and he found he had the most overwhelming urge to go to the pub.

So he did.

He parked the car up on the top of Craddock Hill and walked the fifty metres down to the Mock Turtle, the drizzle stinging his face. The landlord had changed, he could see that from the name over the door, and he was secretly relieved; he didn't need any painful reminders of a bygone time; any familiar faces watching him falling off the wagon.

He sat on a bar stool and ordered a pint of bitter. Then he sat and stared at it for a good five minutes. Five years, four months— His phone rang. It was Kenton.

'Ah there you are,' she said, and she sounded inordinately relieved. 'Did you get my messages?'

'No.' Silver eyed the pint warily. 'Phone doesn't work well up here. Crap reception.' Actually, he hadn't checked it since he'd left the debris that was Brenda Malvern's life.

'Do you know about the burning girl?'

248

'Yeah, I spoke to Malloy last night.'

'Right. Meriel Steele. I've got to—'

'What?' Silver pushed the pint away and stood now, almost banging his head on the beam above the bar. 'Meriel Steele? Are you sure?'

'Well, she's cinders, literally, but some students taped her as she set fire to herself.'

'Nice,' Silver grimaced. His mind was ticking furiously.

'Yeah, pretty bloody grim, as you can imagine. Looks like it's pretty much definitely her, but we're waiting for forensic confirmation.'

'OK. Well, I've just been to see Sadie Malvern's family.'

'Right.' She cleared her throat tentatively. 'Why are you so concerned particularly about Sadie, guv? Do you think she's got something to do with Berkeley Square? Or that she might be one of our unidentified dead?'

'She can't be. The family said she's not missing, they've spoken to her since the explosion. She's got no boyfriend, which I don't believe; she's on a "retreat". Apparently she was with her little mate. Meriel. So yes, perhaps there is a link.'

'Oh.' Kenton absorbed this. 'Wow.'

'Yeah, wow indeed.' Silver pushed his way out of the pub now, and he actually felt a spring in his step. Lana was fine, the kids were all right, and they had a lead. Maybe he could go back down to London now and get on with his job. 'So we need to treat the Academy as a central link between these girls.'

'Where and what was this retreat?'

'They weren't exactly sure, that's the problem. Somewhere on the coast, somewhere that might

249

have begun with H.' Silver doubted poor Brenda Malvern had ever been further than Leeds.

'That doesn't really narrow it down much, does it? Hull?'

'Sadie says it's dead gorgeous where she is now,' that poor washed-out woman had said, with a touch of envy.

'No. You couldn't call Hull dead gorgeous could you?'

'Never been, guv.'

'Yeah, well, don't bother.' Silver walked back up the hill to his car. 'Look, we need to talk to the Steele girl's family immediately. They might have an idea. There's something fishy going on here. Too many bad eggs in the Academy.' More eggs. The metal of his car key dug into Silver's hand. 'And who the hell are these Archangel and Prince characters? Sounds like a bloody fairytale. There's got to be a connection somewhere.'

'I'll get back on to Devon and Cornwall.' Kenton sounded quite excited. 'I've put a call in to Mrs Steele, but they're the ones who actually dealt with family notification. Craven and Tina've gone back to the Academy to speak to the head honcho.'

'OK. I'll try and get back by tomorrow.'

'Really?' Kenton sounded doubtful. 'Is everything OK at home then?'

'Yeah,' Silver grinned, 'everything's fine.'

*　　　*　　　*

But Silver wasn't smiling back at Lana's house when he realised leaving the children again wasn't going to be as easy as he'd imagined. Molly, in her filthy jodhpurs, was already welling up at the kitchen

250

table, having learnt that her mother wasn't coming home yet, and Matty, running in from playing on his skateboard to eat a ham sandwich his grandma had just made, was attempting great stoicism, but failing badly. Thank God Ben was out. Silver couldn't deal with three broken hearts all at once.

'You cannot just go and leave those poor kids again,' Anne was whispering furiously at him in the utility room. 'You're their dad.'

'Yeah, and Lana's their mum—and where the hell is *she*?' but even as he said it, Silver knew it was unfair. She had undertaken the majority share of child-care since they split. He *had* done his bit before the divorce, during Lana's probation period when she'd escaped prison by the skin of her perfect teeth, largely because Silver's boss had been persuaded to pull several strings, which had caused huge animosity in the local community, and shame in Silver's heart. Admittedly he'd had a lot of help from extended family, but nonetheless Silver had cared for the children during Lana's various rehab stints. But since the divorce, however dutiful he was about paying his maintenance on time and speaking to them on the phone, Silver hadn't been around much for his family. A fact he was more than painfully aware of right now.

'Look, Anne,' he changed tack now. 'You're doing such a fantastic job. They feel secure with you and I don't need to go immediately. I *will* come back again.'

'Don't you try and sweet-talk me.' Anne began folding towels like a machine. Snap snap went the fabric as she pulled it tight. Silver couldn't help thinking she might be imagining inflicting some sort of injury on him as she did it.

251

'Your soft soap won't wash. It never did with me. The little 'uns need you, Joseph.' Snap went the towel. 'Just like they did last time. Pass me that stuff from the dryer.' She didn't bother with 'please'.

'Sure.' He pulled out a bunch of clothes and began to make piles; an activity he found quite soothing. Halfway through, he realised he had no idea what garment belonged to whom, other than the pink pants and socks that must be Molly's.

'Maybe I could take Molly down to London with me,' he mused.

'Don't be so ridiculous.'

'I'm not. She could come and stay with me at Philippa's. Ben won't want to come now he's got Emma.' Ben had recently started seeing his first serious girlfriend, and he was awash with hormones and young love. 'And Matty—'

'Exactly. What about Matty?' Anne folded the final towel and placed it on her immaculate pile. Then she grabbed Molly's underwear from him, as if it was somehow inappropriate for him to hold it. 'You can't just leave him here. He'd be so upset.'

'I thought I was doing quite well there,' Silver observed mildly, but he let her finish the job. 'Well, I could take him too.' But he knew in reality this was impractical. He sighed. 'OK, you win. I'll stay a few more days.'

'A few more? You've only been here one.' Her mouth was pursed so tightly it had almost disappeared.

'A few more,' he repeated, 'while I work out what's to be done.'

He stalked out of the room to see his children. But his mind was full of Meriel Steele, and what

252

the hell Sadie Malvern was doing on this bloody retreat, other than finding her inner child.

SATURDAY 22ND JULY
CLAUDIE

'I've been so worried about you,' were Francis's first words when I found him in my flat that evening. He had stood as I had staggered in, feeling very much the worse for wear, and then I had stood too, frozen with fear. He had come towards me, hands extended—and I had found myself unable to move. 'Since last week. I felt bad I didn't contact you to see if you were OK. And now I see I was right to be worried. What on earth's happened, Claudie?' He moved as if he was about to touch my face; instinctively I side-stepped.

'Are you hurt? You're bleeding.'

My hand was clamped tightly round the phone in my pocket. 'No, I'm fine.' Which was quite obviously not true. I could barely stand upright.

He stepped towards me and I noticed an overpowering smell of lavender, and that his smiley blue eyes were a little tired today, the skin around them dry and seemingly more lined.

'Francis, sorry,' I tried not to stutter with shock, 'it's nice to see you and everything, but how did you get in?'

He smiled, and I thought for the first time that his beard looked strangely like groomed guinea-pig fur, Natalie's favourite pet of choice when we were kids.

'Your charming sister was here. She let me in.'

I looked around, and I noticed the Le Creuset

casserole dish had been refilled; that there was a note on the side in Natalie's girlish scrawl.

'She seemed to think I was someone called Rafe.'

'Really?'

'She brought you Stroganoff. She said to make sure you heat it through properly. Smells delicious doesn't it?' He smiled again, his mouth almost lost in the brunette guinea-pig fur. I shuddered.

'She thought you were Rafe?' I'd never bothered to introduce my sister to my new boyfriend. Natalie was disapproving—well, I was still married—so I hadn't seen the point. She had raised an eyebrow when she realised he was an MP but her interest in politics was non-existent; she rarely bothered to vote and she only read women's magazines, and I'd stringently avoided further conversations on the topic once she'd reproached me for dating again. I wanted something that was just mine, that no one else interfered with. Especially Natalie. 'Didn't you set her straight?'

'I didn't think it mattered. One love, love all,' he smiled beatifically, and I felt my gut twist with anxiety.

'Francis, I have to tell you—I'm—' I took a breath to steady myself. 'You're frightening me a bit.'

I remembered the photo of him and Tessa I'd seen in her flat; and I realised how little I knew of this man who'd been treating me, and I felt the cold press of fear.

'I'm sorry to hear that, Claudie.' His face fell. 'I really don't mean to. I come in peace.'

'Well,' I edged slightly nearer to the door behind me, 'I mean, you must realise it's not very normal to get into someone's flat under false pretences and—'

'Not false pretences,' he frowned now. 'Just an

254

honest mistake.'

'Whatever,' I shook my head with frustration. 'Anyway. As you can see, I'm fine. So you can go now.'

He stepped closer to me. My clothes were covered in dirt from the alley behind Sugar and Spice and I could hardly stand straight, I was in so much pain from Andrei's dig in the ribs. My face was probably bleeding again where the graze on my cheek had reopened, and my left hand was badly bruised. I must have looked a complete state; I certainly felt like one, and the cab driver who'd finally stopped for me had asked to see my money up front, eyeing me warily in his mirror the whole way home as if I might suddenly combust.

'You look—hurt. I can give you a treatment now if you like,' Francis offered. He started digging around in his canvas knapsack. 'I've got some calendula somewhere, and also some arnica. Brilliant for bruising. You know, homeopathic medicine can be really very effective.'

'Francis. Please. I really would just like you to go now. I appreciate your kindness coming here but—' I could hear the hysteria building in my own voice. 'Really. I'm fine.'

He stared at me and for the first time since I'd met him, I found his gaze eerie, the eyes too intense. I could almost feel him sizing me up.

'All right, I'll go. But really, Claudie.' He looked so hurt, like a droopy Bassett hound. 'I mean you only good.'

I stepped back so he could pass; my palms were sweaty and I found that I was holding my breath.

'Francis?' I said as he opened the door.

'Yes?'

'How did you meet Tessa? Was it on that yoga retreat?'

'I can't remember,' he frowned. 'I think I was recommended by a friend. That's usually the way.'

'What friend?' I asked.

He shook his head. 'It's hard to think now. So many spirits come and go.'

As he reached the door, he paused.

'I answered your phone, by the way.'

'I really wish you hadn't,' I said. I needed to sit down.

He started to say something about St Thomas's Hospital ringing to speak to me about contra-indicated results, but I wasn't really listening. *Just go, just go* I willed him silently, and he looked at my face, and he stopped talking and went.

As soon as he had left, I finally exhaled. Then I locked and bolted the door, and I stood, back against it, heart thumping—and I realised with a blaze of something, how angry I was. And then I thought of Amanda Curran's words, of the man she'd met with Tessa.

Over on the sideboard, I found the card that the nice woman officer with the soup-coloured hair had left, DS Lorraine Kenton, and I rang her number. She didn't answer, so I left a message asking for her to call back.

Then I went into the bathroom, took two strong painkillers for my bruised ribs, and got into the shower. And that was the last thing I remembered for a while.

SATURDAY 22ND JULY
SILVER

Molly and Matty were watching *Doctor Who* in the living room and Anne was changing bed linen upstairs when Ben arrived home. Silver called his eldest into the kitchen before his grandmother got there first.

'Good innings?' He thought his son had been watching the County Cricket down at the Youth Club, but from the way Ben was blushing, Silver would hazard a guess he'd been up to something different altogether.

'I see.' He grinned at his lanky son. 'She's a cracker, that Emma, isn't she?'

'I'll say.' Ben opened the fridge, immediately scavenging for food, his tousled dark hair falling across his face as he leant in to look for spoils.

Silver remembered kissing an enthusiastic Ruthie Burton round the back of the Mock Turtle on a boiling summer's day, just before he met Allana. He grinned. 'Her mum wasn't bad in her day either.'

'Yeah,' Ben smiled pleasurably at the thought of his sunny-faced girlfriend, and ripped a leg off the roast chicken Anne had served up for tea. 'She said she knew you. She's still not bad for an old bird. I can't believe my luck, Dad.'

'Why not? You're a good-looking lad.'

'You sound like Mum.' Ben's handsome face darkened. ''Cept Mum don't think Emma's good enough for me.'

That made sense. Allana was never going to let

her boys go gently.

'*Doesn't* think, Benjamin. And you've been with her now? Emma?'

Ben nodded shyly.

'So you're—you know,' Silver poured his son a glass of juice. 'You're being careful?'

'Dad!'

'I'm serious.' Silver wiped the rim of the glass. Anne's washing-up left something to be desired. 'Embarrassing or not, you do *not* want a puking baby at home at the age of seventeen, believe me. Even if you do think Emma's *The One*.'

'I hear you, Dad.' Ben drained the juice so he didn't have to look at his father.

'So you're taking precautions?' Silver thought he'd better try and emphasise the point now he'd started.

'Dad. We've done all this at school, all right? In Pshe.'

'What the hell's that?'

'Durr,' Ben pulled a face. 'Sex education, Dad. You know, birds and the bees—'

'All right, wise guy.' It sounded plausible. 'It's just—I'm not ready to be a grandfather yet.' Christ, what a terrible thought. Silver looked out at the darkening Moors and wondered where on God's earth his life had slipped away to when he wasn't paying attention.

'Don't worry about it,' Ben muttered. 'I'm—we're sensible.'

'Grand. Now, look. I've got a proposition for you.' Silver opened the door quickly and checked up the hall that Anne wasn't about to come flouncing in with some new complaint. Then he leant against the worktop and eyed his son. He couldn't believe Ben

258

was so tall, taller almost than him. How the hell had that happened? It seemed only yesterday that Ben had been the mewling baby on Lana's lap, muslin cloth firmly tucked around him so he couldn't ruin her pristine skirt. 'I've got to get back to London, to this case.'

'The bomb?' Ben tore into the chicken now.

'Sort of the bomb,' Silver agreed. 'But your gran doesn't want me to leave the kids.'

'She'll go mad if you do, Dad.' Ben gnawed the meat down to the bone, flecks of chicken falling to the floor.

'Yep, I know.' Wincing, Silver shoved some kitchen towel towards his son. 'Wipe the floor, mate. So I thought, as long as you were all right up here with your Emma, I might just take them with me.'

'Who?' Ben was lost.

'Matthew and Molly.' Silver took the kitchen towel from his son and shoved it in the bin.

'Take 'em where?'

Silver concentrated on wiping the bin lid. 'Down to London with me.'

'What about school?'

'What about it?'

'Dad! Don't be—' Ben struggled for the word.

'Difficult?'

'Difficult, yeah.'

'Obtuse?'

'Dad!' Ben grinned. 'Yes, obtuse.'

'Look.' Silver took his son by the shoulders and held his gaze. Ben's hazel eyes were on a level with his now. 'Matty's just finished his exams, and Molly breaks up next week. It's not going to hurt her to miss a day or two. And they could do with it.

They're missing Mum.'

'Well, when's Mum coming back?' Ben looked wary suddenly. His relationship with his mother was tense at the best of times; they had clashed badly since Ben hit puberty; which had coincided with the car crash. Ben had been seated next to his mother, in the passenger seat, directly in front of Jaime who had died almost instantly. And of course Silver had always thanked God, however much guilt he'd felt, that his own kids had been unhurt—but he'd also always worried that Lana's latent hostility to her eldest son was his fault. Molly was the only girl, and Matty was Lana's baby boy, but Ben—Ben was very much his father's son, from his lopsided smile to his single-mindedness. Silver knew too that Ben had never forgiven his mother for that dreadful day. The boy may have walked away pretty much unscathed on the outside, but the inside was a different matter.

'I don't know, son.' Silver heard the bastard Beer whisper quietly in his ear again at the thought of Lana. 'I wish I *could* tell you. She'll be gone till she's sorted herself out, I guess.'

'And when will that be?' Ben's jaw set rigid and he flung the stripped chicken bone in the bin savagely.

'Soon, I hope.' What more could Silver say? He really didn't know what had got into his wife; whether this disappearing act precipitated some sort of breakdown, or whether it was just a bid for freedom. Only time would reveal the answer.

'How long you planning to go for, Dad?' Ben eyed him suspiciously. 'Really just a day or two? All the way down there?'

'OK, a week or two, maybe. It'll be good for them.

See the sights, broaden their horizons. Realise there's a world beyond Frogley.'

'That's exactly what Mum *doesn't* want them to realise.'

Silver was impressed by his son's sense of perception. 'Well, Mum's not here is she?'

Ben stared at him and then a grin spread over his handsome face. 'You're serious, aren't you?'

'So, do you mind? Or do you want to come too? Plenty of hot chicks in London town, you know.'

'Hot chicks?' Ben was incredulous for a second, then he creased up laughing. 'God, Dad. You're so—old.'

*　　　*　　　*

He knew he would pay for the decision for the rest of his life, but Silver waited until Anne had 'popped home to get some bits' and then he bundled the kids in the car with some crisps and Coke and a hastily packed bag. Matty had been totally unfussed, 'As long as I can bring my skateboard, Dad?'; Molly a little more tearful, clutching her old teddy bear, her lip trembling below the gappy top row of teeth.

Ben insisted he would stay and talk to his grandmother.

'You don't have to, lad.' Silver felt a pang of guilt. 'I'll just leave her a note.'

'Dad. I don't mind. And you have always told me I'm man of the house when you're not here.'

Silver smiled ruefully, feeling yet another pang of guilt. What damage had he and Lana done to these kids during their own private hell? he wondered. He pulled his lanky son into a bear-hug. 'And if you change your mind—'

261

'Nah,' Ben patted his father's back as if he was the child and stepped out of the embrace. 'I've got Emma, and my job at the Hebdon Arts Festival next week. I'm happy here for now. Plenty of time for London town.' He winked at his father. 'And hot chicks.'

And so Silver hit the Southbound M1 with his daughter asleep in the back, and his younger son's inquisitive freckled face pressed against the glass window, searching the dark countryside for something intangible.

Silver shoved his Dean Martin CD in and cranked up the volume to sing along to *That's Amore* as they always had done on long journeys.

'Remember this?' He ruffled his son's curly mop. 'What adventures we're going to have, big man.'

Matty waited precisely ten seconds before turning Dean off.

'Don't sing, Dad,' he grimaced. 'It's embarrassing. Can we have Eminem?'

SUNDAY 23RD JULY
KENTON

Lorraine Kenton felt pretty chipper this Sunday morning, it had to be said, having managed a full night's sleep followed by an early morning breakfast with Alison that had led to—well. She smiled at the memory as she tried to tidy her desk a little. She'd also heard from Silver; he'd be in this morning, and she was relieved—but also proud. She didn't think she'd done too bad a job without him. She'd spoken to the local constabulary in Devon and Cornwall who had gone to break the news to Meriel Steele's family, and she was awaiting records from Steele's dentist to pass to the pathologists. She didn't know what to do about questioning the parents about the girl's whereabouts before her death though; she was waiting for Silver to arrive first. And she was desperately going through the cuttings again for any mention of a man called Archangel, or latterly, since Silver had spoken to the little red-haired lap-dancer again, the Prince. So far, nothing. The link at the Academy was defeating her still, though she thought that if she could track down the Archangel, all would become clear. Someone at the Academy had been up to no good, spreading a deep malignancy; who though, wasn't yet clear.

Whilst Kenton grafted Derek Craven strutted around the office with photo-fits of dead girls, giving it the big '*I am*'. Talking a lot and achieving precisely nothing, as far as Kenton could see. He'd returned from the Academy with some kind of theory but he refused to share it with the rest of the team, though Kenton assumed it would be to do with the mysterious Lethbridge. Kenton watched him now, pontificating in Malloy's office, his big belly almost wobbling as he paced the room.

Yawning, she fetched herself a cappuccino from the coffee machine, avoiding the still teary Gill McCarthy as best she could, and then cursed her own stupidity for actually believing it might taste something like coffee. She filled it with sweeteners and played her messages. One was from the St John's Wood nursing home, St Agnes, saying that Edna Lamont was on the mend, if she would care to visit now. And then a woman's voice, young-ish, frightened. Cross, perhaps.

'Could you call me back please? I'm worried about this man I have just found in my flat.'

Claudie Scott. She left a phone number.

Kenton frowned. Claudie Scott—why was that name familiar? She scrabbled through the notes on her desk. Of course. Tessa Lethbridge's friend. The girl with the faraway stare.

Kenton called the number, but she just got an answer-phone. She left a message, apologising for taking so long to get back to her.

'Hope all is OK. Let me know the details, Claudie.' She rang off, and had a tentative sip of her cappuccino, wrinkling her nose in distaste. When Silver got in, they could go and visit Edna Lamont. Kenton's pulse quickened slightly. This was why she had joined the force. This was proper detective work.

Craven left Malloy's office, and swaggered past her desk, having the audacity to actually wink at her. She bit her lip.

'Kenton,' Malloy stood at his office door. 'Can I have a minute?'

Kenton's stomach rolled uncomfortably. Frankly, her big boss terrified her. Even if all the others said he was just blarney and not brimstone, he didn't half shout a lot. Kenton, who came from a very small, mild family of church-goers, who raised money for the local hospice every year with their own bring and buy sale in their own front garden, and who never, ever raised their voices, was always worried by him—particularly the ripe language.

She sat tentatively on the chair in front of Malloy. He chucked a copy of *News of the World* on the desk. There was a picture of the rather solid Steele in a pink tutu aged about twelve, arms above her head like the fairy in a jewellery-box; another more recent but rather fuzzy picture of her, pouting suggestively. And then a blurry grab of the girl on fire in Trafalgar Square.

DANCER DIES IN DEATHLY BLAZE the headlines screamed. *GIRL IGNITES HERSELF IN HORROR FIRE: WHY?*

'How the fuck have they got hold of this footage?' Malloy glowered at her. 'Any ideas?'

'No sir.' She pulled the paper closer. You couldn't call Meriel Steele a looker, that was without doubt. She was rather potato-faced, sullen even. And those boobs. Wow. 'Someone else must have got a picture. Everyone uses their mobile phones these days, don't they?'

He ignored her logic.

'Right.' He picked up a shiny green pencil and turned it over and over in his hand as he spoke. 'So, DCI Silver has crawled up the fucking M1, as we know—'

She dared to interrupt. 'He'll be back this morning, actually, sir.'

'Good. About fucking time.' He stabbed the pencil into the newspaper. 'Craven has just drawn my attention to the fact that Meriel Steele is not the only girl from the Academy up to no good. We have Sadie Malvern—aka the sometime lap-dancing Misty Jones—who is still missing.'

'Actually, Silver has—'

Malloy didn't stop to listen. 'And we have the little girl on the CCTV footage, Anita someone, who presumably is in kingdom fucking come. And then we have the bloody dead, lying, dance teacher with a fake name. What the fuck is going on, Kenton?' He glowered at her, holding the pencil

265

so tight that at any moment it was going to shatter into a thousand pieces. 'Why does it take Craven to point this out at such a late date?'

'Sir, I am fully aware of these girls and the connection, and—'

'I don't care what you're fucking aware of. Get down to that ballet school and find out what the fuck is happening.'

'We have been already, a few times. And it's Sunday, sir.' Kenton realised too late that this explanation was a bad move, but she'd started so she'd have to finish. 'I think you'll find—'

'What?' He stood now, slamming his chair into the desk and crossing to the window. 'That they're all at fucking church? Saying their prayers and singing *All Things Bright and Beautiful*? Pull the other one, Kenton. They're up to no fucking good, these bloody ballet fools, and I need to know what the fuck is going on, Sunday or no bloody Sunday.'

Kenton stood now, understanding she was dismissed.

'Yes, sir.' Her mouth was dry and her heart was thumping and, as she backed carefully towards the door, she thought that if she saw that bloody traitor Craven in the next five minutes, she wasn't sure what she'd do.

SUNDAY 23RD JULY
SILVER

At 9 a.m. on an already sweltering morning, Silver took the call that finally confirmed it was Academy student Anita Stuart who had blown herself up

266

in the doorway of the Hoffman Bank. One of the builders who had been hospitalised with shrapnel injuries after the attack had been trying out the camera on his new mobile phone before the explosion. His wife had only just gone through his phone last night, and found the brief clip of footage; it was jumbled and unclear, but it had captured the moment when Anita Stuart had reached inside her bag and detonated a bomb. It also showed the shadowy image of another woman behind Anita moments before the explosion, and Stuart shaking her off as she ran towards the bus stop, the phone camera tracking her as she screamed 'Now now now!' before opening the bag.

The implications of the bomber being one of the Academy students were huge, Silver realised without a flicker of doubt. McNulty from the Explosives team was still cursing as Silver hung up from the call and leant his head against the cool window for a second, listening to the children thunder downstairs for their breakfast. It didn't make any sense to Silver. Why the hell would a genteel little ballet student choose to blow herself to pieces? More to the point, who had persuaded Anita Stuart that it was a good idea to die so dramatically aged only seventeen?

Silver left a sleepy Molly and Matty in front of a lavish fry-up courtesy of Philippa, the air in the kitchen thick with grease and the stink of bacon. His landlady seemed more than happy to distract the ever-moody Leticia with the new arrivals. She'd apparently confronted her middle daughter about the internet whilst Silver had been up North. Consequently, this morning Leticia wouldn't speak to him at all, however hard he tried to make her laugh with his silly jokes. But she didn't seem to mind Matty. No one minded Matty, that was the truth—he was a genuine old soul in a young body, his trusting freckled face inviting friendship from most, his tawny hair sticking out at all angles as he ate his bacon fat with enthusiasm and pulled silly faces at the girls.

Whilst Precious showed Molly her collection of something hideous and pink called Bratz, Matty and Leticia logged into You Tube on her laptop.

'Biggest mistake of my life, letting Marlon buy her that bloody machine,' Philippa muttered as ever, but she looked pleased the two children were bonding—until she realised it was over footage of fatal shark attacks.

'Come now, Letty,' she pulled a face at her daughter, who blatantly ignored her and clicked on another Great White mauling a surfer.

Late already, Silver watched them all for a moment from the doorway. On a whim he dashed back into the room, and kissed each of his children on the head.

'Dad!' Matty ducked, horrified, rolling his eyes at a smirking Letty, though Molly was still quite happy to accept her father's affection, thank God, her wide face beaming.

An hour after he'd left Yorkshire, Anne had rung to berate him, and he knew he was being entirely cowardly by not yet returning her call. He'd texted her and Ben to say they'd arrived safely in London; he'd also rung Lana to tell her he'd taken the kids with him, but he'd only reached her voicemail again. He wasn't expecting a call back any time soon.

When he arrived in the station car park, feeling

rather bleary and in need of caffeine, Kenton was outside, waiting for him, her face slightly flushed.

'Malloy's on the warpath. Can we go straight to St John's Wood please?' Kenton's voice was tight. 'We can talk to Edna Lamont now she's well enough.'

'Sure,' Silver was aware of a tension in his young partner. 'Everything OK?'

'Fine,' Kenton lied, sliding into the seat next to him. 'Have you seen the headlines?'

'Meriel Steele? Yes, I have. Pretty unavoidable. Have you reached the family yet?'

'Lesley Steele's coming up today—Meriel's mum. Dad's poorly and house-bound apparently. And there's no body to see, poor lady. Should be here around three.'

'Right. We need to push the connection between these girls. And the Prince character? Or the Archangel? Anything?'

Silver had phoned through the information Paige had given up on Friday night. He felt she knew far more than she was saying; he guessed it was about the club's mafia connections, but he hadn't yet thought of a way to persuade her to speak out. She was scared, that was clear, and she wouldn't speak until she thought she'd be safe.

'Roger's looking into it. Nothing specific yet, though. Sorry.'

'God.'

He decided not to push Kenton on whatever was upsetting her. She'd tell him in time, if she wanted to. He unwrapped a stick of Orbit and switched the stereo on, Eminem's vitriol filling the air.

'Sorry.' He grinned at Kenton, who gave him a begrudging smile. 'Kids' favourite.'

'No worries. Didn't think it would be yours.'

'So. St John's Wood, then, kiddo. Posh land.'

*   *   *

The nursing home was a large, grand house, set back from the road in a pretty garden. Very different from the place his own mother had ended up in when dementia struck her quite suddenly ten years ago, Silver thought, feeling a sudden melancholy as he parked on the end of a row of expensive cars.

Kenton was sneezing ferociously on the doorstep as a pretty Asian nurse let them in. 'Hayfever,' she sniffed miserably, indicating the huge oak tubs of yellow petunias and pansies on either side of the door.

'CID,' Silver showed his badge, smiling politely at the nurse. 'We've come to see Edna Lamont please.'

'Oh,' the nurse frowned. 'I'm not sure she's well enough—'

'I had a message saying she was,' Kenton said firmly, blowing her nose. 'Last night.'

'She may have taken a turn for the worse again, I'm afraid.' The nurse showed them to a seat in reception. 'If you don't mind I'll just check with my colleague.'

'Flipping typical,' Kenton muttered. 'One step forward, four steps back.'

'What's wrong?' Silver muttered back. 'You're not your normal sunny self, Lorraine.'

Girlfriend trouble, he thought knowledgeably.

'It's—' Kenton didn't know what to say about Craven. She knew Silver wasn't that enamoured of the man either, but it wasn't her place to speak badly of her superiors. There was a line, and she

270

had to tread it carefully. 'Can I tell you later?'

'No problem, kiddo.' Silver discarded his gum into the bin contemplatively and wondered if the home had a vending machine.

The nurse came back. 'If you can get everything you need in five minutes—'

'Five minutes?' Kenton expostulated.

'Five minutes is ample,' Silver smiled again at the nurse, whose name badge read Pritti. She melted slightly at that lopsided grin. 'Ta very much, Pritti.'

She led them down the hushed corridor, the silence broken only by the snores of one patient and the intermittent cries of another who, every now and then, shrieked 'Let me go' loudly.

'That's Ruby,' the nurse whispered sadly. 'She's got early onset dementia. We're waiting to move her.'

'Move her?' Kenton repeated. 'Why?'

'We don't really nurse, or deal with the terminally ill. It's a shame, because a few of us have specialist psychiatric training.'

'So why not use it?'

'We're more for—pastoral care.'

'Great,' Kenton muttered again as they waited outside Edna's room. 'They get sick or mad, they get turfed out.'

Silver patted her shoulder. 'Your job's not a moral crusade, kiddo. Calm yourself.' But he admired her passion.

Edna Lamont was a delicate-looking old woman, fine-boned and obviously once rather beautiful. She lay very still in her bed, a pink blanket pulled up almost to her chin, despite the warmth of the day; her elegant liver-spotted hands folded above the blanket, a pale green bed-jacket laced up to the

271

chin. She looked aristocratic, and ancient, as if a single gust of wind would blow her clean away.

'Joe Silver, Metropolitan Police.' Silver offered her his hand and then sat beside her. 'We won't take up much of your time, Mrs Lamont.'

'Miss Lamont. I was never married.' She turned rheumy eyes the colour of faded jade on him. 'Or just call me Edna. How can I help you, Mr Silver?'

'Thank you, Edna.' He didn't correct her. 'It's just—I wondered if you could have a look at a photo for us? We'd be very grateful.'

Silver looked at Kenton, who retrieved the picture of Tessa Lethbridge from her bag.

'Do you recognise this as being your niece, Rosalind?'

The old lady peered at it for a long moment, then reached her hand out for the photo. It quivered as she brought it nearer to her face.

'It's hard to say. It's been so long since I saw her. She fell out with my brother, you see. Her father, Edward.' She dropped her hand back onto the blanket, as if she was exhausted already. 'Edward hated Rosalind's politics. They had the most terrible row the last Christmas they spent together; he called Rosalind a communist and she renounced him for his consumerist ideals. He was the most ghastly bore sometimes, I have to admit, but it was all silly dramatics, if you ask me. And they never made it up. Rosalind left the country soon after. He never saw her again.'

'She left and went where?' Silver and Kenton exchanged glances. 'Can you remember?'

'It's hard to say.' The old lady shook her head. 'She was always travelling. I used to call her a free spirit. I know she went to Africa for a while. Lived with the Ashanti tribe in Ghana for a while. Studied with their witch-doctors apparently. Learnt all about healing herbs. She sent me a bone once. Her mother was quite hysterical with worry.' She patted Silver's hand; her skin was paper-dry. 'I'm sorry, Mr Silver. My memory is not what it was, I'm afraid.'

She began to cough. Pritti cleared her throat pointedly, and checked her watch.

'I think,' she said gently, 'we should finish. I'm going off shift now, and Edna is tired.'

'You've been very helpful, Miss Lamont.' Silver stood now. 'We won't take up any more of your time. But if you remember anything else, perhaps you could ask the nurse to phone us.'

'There was something else.' She coughed again, her delicate body shaking gently. 'When Edward died, we had to try to reach Rosalind to return for the funeral. She refused of course. She was so far away, she had just been in a car accident herself in—what do they call it? That big place. Open space, with the dreaming men.'

Edna shut her eyes for a moment. Kenton looked at Pritti. Had Edna fallen asleep?

They waited.

'The outback.' Edna Lamont's eyes snapped open again. 'Australia.'

SATURDAY 22ND JULY
CLAUDIE

When I woke, I found I couldn't breathe—and so I fought to. The panic reminded me of my last day

273

with Ned. I had struggled to breathe then, or maybe I didn't want to breathe—and I didn't know where I was, or what time of day it was—or even what day or month or year it actually was.

Two days after Ned died, they found me in the garden. I had taken a great spade apparently, and dug up half the back lawn for some reason. When they discovered me, I had my hands shoved into the earth.

It took such a long time to clean that dirt off.

I think I believed that perhaps I could bring him back, if I dug down deep enough; that I would find him somewhere. But I couldn't. I didn't. He was gone. My guffawing son with mischievous eyes the colour of chocolate. Eyes forever shut. I had watched them close the final time and I had wanted nothing more than to die myself.

I had howled to the heavens, and then the heavens howled back. Rain fell, thick and fast. My life was over. Everything I cared about had been stolen from me.

Absolutely beached by my sorrow, I had lain on my bed in the old house for a fortnight without moving, except to the bathroom. My mother and Will and sometimes Zoe and Natalie had forced me to eat; sat with me and talked to me, and through the bleakest hardest time, they had not given up hope. But I had.

A long time after, I realised he was only mine to borrow, my baby. My tiny little boy. Only mine to borrow for such a very short while.

Now I lay in the gloom, fighting for breath, my head throbbing like something was alive inside it, and I thought of my son, the fighter, and I tried to sit up. I couldn't. I hit my head on something hard.

Then I realised my hands were tied.

I laid my head down again. I felt sick, waves of nausea rolling over me, and I needed to think.

There was a noise underneath me; I couldn't think what it was for a time; and then I realised. It was the whisper of tyres on a road. I was in the boot of a vehicle, and we were moving.

SUNDAY 23RD JULY
SILVER

'Doesn't get us very far, does it?' Kenton opened the passenger door in the nursing-home car park. 'I mean, nice old lady, and all that, but—' She looked downcast. 'You know.'

'No,' Silver agreed. 'But it's better than nothing.'

As they left, Edna Lamont had promised to ask her neighbour to bring photos from home. 'They will give you a better idea of Rosalind's appearance, I suppose, though they are all really rather dated now.'

Kenton checked her watch as Silver pulled out onto Abbey Road. 'It's nearly two. Lesley Steele should be arriving soon.'

Two Japanese students stood on the zebra crossing immortalised by the Beatles, pulling silly faces for the camera. A sudden breeze blew one girl's tiny ra-ra skirt up, revealing a lacy thong.

'Blimey,' Silver braked just in time. 'Could have been a Hard Day's Night.'

Kenton grinned. 'What—not She loves you, yeah yeah yeah?'

Lesley Steele had arrived earlier than expected, and by the time Silver and Kenton had crossed London again, Craven had got his claws into her already, much to Kenton's dismay.

Mrs Steele was a small, round woman, a little like two circular loaves of bread stuck one on top of the other. Her greasy hair was pulled back tightly in an old-fashioned bun, and her face was devoid of make-up, her eyes like two tiny bloodshot currants in a lump of raw pastry. But still, despite the extra weight and the tear-stained face, Kenton was struck by how very like her daughter the older woman was.

Craven had made her tea and sat her in an empty office, where he was pretending to empathise with her.

Silver opened the door.

'Mrs Steele? I'm so very sorry for your loss,' he said seriously, offering her his hand. Kenton was impressed with his natural manner. 'Cheers, Derek, I'll take over now,' he murmured.

Craven was put out. 'But I've already—'

'No worries, Derek. If you could get on to the paperwork for pathology, I'd be grateful.'

Craven shut the door very hard behind him as Silver slid into the seat opposite Mrs Steele, Kenton hovering behind him. She remembered not to put her hands in her trouser pockets, though they were itching to go there.

'Are you able to shed any light whatsoever on the tragic occurrence?' he asked. 'Had Meriel been in touch at all recently?'

'No,' the woman shook her head. Her expression was hard to read; a mixture perhaps of shame and

276

confusion. 'We honestly thought she was still at the Academy. We hadn't seen her for a while. She hadn't told us any different.'

'A good while?' Silver consulted his notes. 'Over nine months, I believe?'

'Well, we thought she was having a whale of a time,' Lesley Steele was defensive. 'She was bored with our little village; she had been for years. It's ever so quiet, and she seemed to be living the high life up here. And in the limelight. She never wanted to come home.' Her face crumpled, and she started to sob quietly. 'We were so proud.'

Kenton stared at the woman, who was only now starting to realise her daughter would never come home, and she knew where she'd seen Meriel Steele before. Of course, how stupid!

She must have made some sort of noise, because Silver glanced round. Lesley Steele was bowed over the table, her forehead in her hands, tears splashing down onto the formica. Kenton raised her eyebrows at her boss and tried to mouth 'Sugar and Spice' but he just shook his head at her.

'In a minute,' he murmured.

'Mrs Steele, it would really help me and any other girls who might also be in trouble—'

'Trouble?' the woman said, looking up now.

'Yes, trouble. I don't know why Meriel did what she did yet, but I imagine someone else must be involved. It's our job to find out why.'

'Yes,' the woman latched on to this. 'Yes it is.'

'So', Silver was calm, 'do you know where Meriel was just before she died?'

Lesley Steele flinched at the word. 'No. Like I said, we thought she was in London.'

'Did she have a boyfriend?'

277

'No.' Lesley Steele shook her head fervently. 'I would have known.'

Silver bit back the retort on his lips. 'You're sure of that?'

'Positive.'

'Was she friends with a girl called Anita Stuart?'

The woman's face stretched taut. It had been all over the morning news. 'The one who blew up the bank? I'd never heard of her before. She wasn't Meriel's friend. I'm positive.'

'And she hadn't told you of anywhere else she had visited recently?'

'I can't think,' the woman was getting flustered now. 'We spoke so rarely. She was always so busy.'

'Do you know Sadie Malvern?'

'That little minx?' Lesley Steele sat up straighter and dried her eyes on a sodden tissue. 'Yes, I do. A very bad influence, my husband thought.'

'We have reason to believe the two girls might have been together before Meriel died.'

'Really?'

'Yes. Can you think of anything at all Meriel said about any kind of outing?'

'She did tell me one thing,' Lesley Steele said slowly. 'About a day trip they did to some film location.'

'Film location? Can you be more specific?'

'Somewhere with a long beach that was in a film. Meriel didn't like it because she had to walk so far to get to the sea.' Lesley Steele suddenly looked triumphant. 'It was a Gwyneth Paltrow film, I know that much.'

'Right,' Silver looked defeated. 'OK.'

Kenton saw Lesley Steele out five minutes later whilst Silver spoke to Philippa.

'Kids are fine, Joe, getting along famously. All good,' she said cheerfully. 'One thing though. How long they staying? Because I—'

'I'll talk to you later.' He saw Kenton practically skipping back across the office. 'Gotta go.'

Silver hung up knowing Philippa would no doubt be cursing him.

'I knew it,' Kenton said breathlessly. 'I recognised Meriel Steele from that club Sugar and Spice, when we went in on Friday. I've only just realised. She had totally different hair. A black bob. Must have been a wig.'

'Right.' Silver straightened his cuff. He thought fleetingly of Paige.

'So we'd better get down there, yes?'

'Yes,' Silver agreed. He had a heavy feeling in his gut about life right now. 'Yes I suppose we'd better.'

Stepping through the door, Anne rang his phone again. He pressed *Reject*.

SUNDAY 23RD JULY
CLAUDIE

I must have passed out again because when I came to, we had stopped moving. It was very quiet, wherever we were, and then I heard the sound of footsteps, heavy boots on concrete, and then there was light, just for a second, and I was wincing, screwing up my eyes against the unnatural brightness—and then someone put something over my head.

I struggled desperately, but it was a horrible

effort because I was sore and sick and unbalanced because of my tied hands and feet. And then a voice was speaking, and quietening me, a female voice, and then in the background I heard another voice, telling her to bring me in and I thought I'm sure I know that voice, oh Christ I've heard it before, but I couldn't place it. I could hear birds singing and I even heard a cow or a sheep or something farm-like but I was so disoriented that nothing made sense. I was stumbling, and then they took me into a building, and I could smell sweet essential oils—and a familiar acrid smell that I couldn't immediately place, and then they took the cloth off my head.

'Where the hell am I?'

'My poor child.' The woman with bushy brown hair who held my hands smiled benevolently at me. Her nose was rather like a snout and her eyes were sore and pink, as if she were allergic to something. 'You don't look very well. Sit down, please.'

I stared at her, trying to focus, and I felt sure we'd met before but I couldn't think where. There was a girl with her, standing behind me, so I couldn't see her face properly. She helped me sit down. I looked around. I was in a kitchen, a farmhouse kitchen by the looks of it, with a flagstone floor that was freezing under my bare feet, and an Aga that was giving off no heat. I had the most terrible pains in my stomach. I tried to lean forward, to somehow alleviate them, but the woman was still holding my hands.

'Oh gosh, poor Claudie. Sadie, untie her please. We've had a long journey. Claudie, my name is Miriam. So lovely to meet you.'

Sadie Malvern. The missing dancer.

She was wearing a long, purple dress, tied with a halter-neck, and she had bare feet, which were filthy. Her pretty, heart-shaped face was totally unmade up, her long blonde curls tumbling over naked shoulders, and she had a rainbow tattooed on her hand.

'Sorry,' she smiled at me beatifically as she untied my own hands. 'I don't want to hurt you.'

I was utterly bewildered now.

'Where am I?' I croaked, and then I leant forward, and I was violently sick all over her feet.

The woman called Miriam smiled as Sadie leapt back; smiled again at her protestation.

'Come on, flower. It's all in the name of love and unity.' She fetched me a glass of water from the sink. 'Here.'

I drank greedily. Sadie had disappeared now, and the other woman wiped the floor and my feet, very gently, and then led me to a sofa at the other end of the room. I was freezing cold now, and shaking, and then I saw all the light in the room was moving in slices above me, and I followed the slices, and I felt my eyes growing huge with wonder.

'What's happening?' I said, and she laughed and said 'Only what's meant to be happening. What will follow on from last week.'

'Last week?' But now I didn't care really about last week; I simply felt euphoric and like I wanted to hug her. And then I didn't remember anything any more.

*   *   *

When I woke again, I was lying on something hard and I was in a dark place, a different place, and

281

someone else was in the room too. I tried to focus. After a while I realised it was Sadie moving around quietly, balletically you could say even; she was closing the curtains at the small casement windows, and I said, 'Why are you here?' and she looked round at me like I was mad.

'I'm closing the curtains so you can sleep.'

'No,' I said, 'I mean, why are you *here*. In this place?'

'Because we belong here.'

'We?'

'We are the absolutely good, and the absolutely good belong here.'

She came and stood at the end of my bed now. I tried to sit up, but it made my stomach hurt again.

'Belong where?'

'Everywhere.' Her hands were clasped across her breast as if in prayer. 'Here, there. Together. Together we will show the world how corrupt it has become. How everyone has begun to live only for themselves. How we have to listen to the corrupters and take the pain; how we have no choice. We must return,' her pretty face was fierce now, her blue eyes blazing too brightly, 'we must return to the good place. The right place. We are teaching them a lesson.'

'We?'

'We. The Daughters of Light. One by one we fall for our cause—and then we rise to our heaven.'

'Fall?'

She shrugged. 'Die, if you like.'

'What are you talking about?' I whispered, and tears were gathering in my eyes and I had those terrible griping pains in my stomach again. I felt dirty, like worms were crawling in my veins; like my

282

whole system had been poisoned.

'Die,' Sadie repeated. 'Only it will be the start of eternal life; our saving of the world. We are sent here to die for our cause. I am waiting for my turn. When the Archangel says so.'

'Archangel?'

'Michael, Gabriel, call the Divine what you will.'

The Archangels.

'Whatever you want to call the Divine,' she shrugged those delicate porcelain shoulders again, 'we shall follow. You will follow too,' she patted the coverlet down, and walked to the door. 'When the time is right. I am sure.'

She blew out the candle.

SUNDAY 23RD JULY
SILVER

Who the hell went to watch lap-dancers on a Sunday, Silver wondered as Kenton buzzed the intercom at Sugar and Spice. Sundays were meant to be for family and friends, log-fires, roast dinners and football in the park, too much wine at lunch and Lana throwing the Yorkshire puddings at him, the peas rolling all over the floor, the kids trampling them underfoot as they ran for cover whilst their parents screamed blue murder.

Sundays now were empty, lonely days, reminding Silver only of the disintegration of something, of something he wished he'd worked harder to maintain. Something that had ultimately seemed beyond his control.

He wished he was at home now in New Cross

with his younger children. He checked his watch as Kenton buzzed again.

'Perhaps they're shut?' She pulled a face. She thought of her own Sundays as a child, with her parents at the parish church, neatly be-skirted and gloved until she'd rebelled at eleven and worn trousers for the first time. She imagined her mother's face if she saw this place; she shuddered.

'They're not shut,' Silver indicated the opening times on the wall beside them. 'They just don't want to talk to us.'

Eventually a thickset Russian with a crew-cut and a tattoo on his neck let them in. His unpleasant smile displayed two missing front teeth as he led them downstairs. A woman with a mop and bucket was cleaning the stage, and Larry was sitting at a table near the bar with a bespectacled middle-aged man, greying and rather ordinary. By the look of the receipt-books and calculators, they were going through some kind of accounts.

Larry stood and came forward. 'Now what?' He held a toothpick in his fat hand, which he rammed into his back teeth. 'It's Sunday for Chrissake. Can't a guy get a bit of peace?'

'Meriel Steele,' Silver said coldly.

'Who?'

There was a discarded *Sunday Mirror* on the bar. Kenton picked it up and held it in the man's face. 'This Meriel Steele.'

Larry actually blanched. It was the first time Silver had seen any reaction from the man at all during their investigation.

'Ah yeah.' He removed the toothpick. 'Meriel. Poor kid. We knew her as Cindy.'

'Dear Lord,' Kenton muttered, refolding the

284

horrific image. Was no one here allowed to be themselves?

'And you last saw her—?' Silver leant against the banquette behind him. 'Exactly when?'

Larry shrugged. 'Probably a week or so ago.'

'Try Friday. Two days ago. When we were here last.'

'Right. Well, it's hard to know. So many of them come and go.'

'We've reason to believe she's friends with the missing girl. Sadie Malvern. Or Misty Jones, as you apparently know her.'

'Maybe.' Larry's little eyes were darting back and forth now between the police officers.

'And yet you didn't tell us that, even though Meriel was dancing that day. It could have been very helpful. Did you employ Anita Stuart too?'

'Who?'

'The dance student involved in the Hoffman Bank explosion.'

'No,' Larry Bird shook his jelly chins definitively. 'Absolutely not.'

Silver felt a rush of repugnance for this man, for the whole set-up. Girls were starting to trickle through the bar now on the way to the changing room. They looked so normal—nothing like what half an hour in front of a mirror would help them become. They were wives, daughters, mothers. Sure, some of them were in control—but how many? They were manipulated and used, and they let themselves be because they didn't know any better, because they needed the money. What was it that Paige had said about pimping them out?

'In fact,' Silver stepped nearer the American. He wasn't the tallest of men himself, but he had a good few inches on the barrel-esque Larry. 'In fact, you could have prevented her death. So,' he glanced at Kenton, 'I want to impound all accounts. I want a list, including phone numbers, of every single girl that has danced here in the past six months. And I want it NOW.'

Kenton suppressed a smile. She'd rarely seen Silver angry, but now he was, it was stark and impressive.

'Lorraine, get on the phone and get uniform down here—'

'You can't do this!' the American expostulated. 'There'll be trouble. My boss is extremely well-connected—'

'Do you think I care?' Silver hissed, but he didn't doubt it. There were reasons why places like this were allowed to get away with working as high-class brothels.

'Larry,' the man at the table spoke now, in a low, warning tone. He had a very slight Transatlantic accent that Silver could not place, though he looked terribly British in his attire. 'Just do what the officer ordered. Get him a list.'

'And you are?' Silver looked over at this mild-mannered character.

'John. John Adamson. I'm just the accountant.' He smiled a calm rather superior sort of smile.

'Just the accountant?' Kenton repeated. 'So what exactly are you accounting for, Mr Adamson?'

'Oh, you know, just the usual.'

Silver left Kenton to wrap up the paperwork and headed towards the changing rooms. He knocked tentatively at the door; there was no queue today, he guessed it was too early.

The tall, black girl who had boasted about all the

men who wanted her opened the door. She didn't look so cheerful today, in baggy jeans and Ugg boots. With no make-up or emerald contact lenses, she looked ordinary—drab even.

'Yeah?' she gave him the once-over and sighed. 'Old Bill again is it?'

'I was looking for Paige.' He unwrapped a stick of gum.

'Paige?'

'Small, redhead. Lots of freckles. Was here last time.'

'Oh, you mean Rachel.'

'Surname?'

'Rachel Johnson, I think. I've not seen her.' The girl frowned. 'In fact, she left early last night. Didn't finish her shift.' She shrugged. 'Ask Larry.'

'I will.' What had the girl said at the hotel the other night? She had been apprehensive, and she had given him information, useless as it had been so far, and he hadn't taken her fear very seriously. The sinking feeling in his stomach joined the raft of worries there. 'Cheers, kiddo. If you see her, ask her to call me?'

The girl shrugged again. 'OK.'

He rejoined Kenton. He didn't want to flag up his interest in Paige to Larry; he feared he might have done enough harm as it was.

'Uniform are on their way.'

'Fucking Jesus,' Larry muttered and slammed his hand on the bar. 'Get me a soda,' he snapped at the bartender. 'Now.'

John Adamson was wrapping up, calm and quiet in his plain button-down shirt.

'Look,' Silver was worried. 'Can I leave you here, Lorraine? There's something I want to check out, now.'

'Sure.' She glanced at him, the almost-handsome face wearied, the shadows under his hazel eyes belying his energetic air.

'Cheers.' He ran a hand through his short salt and pepper hair. 'Call me when you leave. And if you get an address for a girl called Rachel Johnson, let me know immediately.'

And he bounded up the stairs, out of hell, horribly aware it might be too late already.

*   *   *

Back in the land of the living, Silver tried Paige's number but it just rang out. Walking back to the car, he phoned through to the station.

'Can you try to track a number for me? I need the billing address.' He gave them Paige aka Rachel's number. 'It's urgent.'

He rang Philippa. 'I'll be home in an hour. Can we have a chat then?'

Next he rang Anne. 'I'm sorry,' he cut across her furious invective. 'I know you think I'm irresponsible, but I have a duty here too. The kids will be fine with me. Is Ben there?'

'No,' she sniffed derisively. 'He's always with that Burton lass.'

'Well,' Silver grinned. 'Young love, Anne. You must remember. You and Tony.' His late father-in-law, a gem of a man. Passed away, thank God, before Lana's disgrace. 'You met at school, didn't you?'

He felt Anne hesitate. He sensed her soften slightly. He took a deep breath now himself.

'And Lana?' He felt himself tense. 'Any word?'

'She left me another message. Said she's getting her head together.' He heard the quaver in Anne's voice. 'I'm scared, Joe.'

He was taken aback by her admission.

'Anne,' he wished for once that they were in the same room, 'she'll be fine. I'm sure. She's just—' he watched a young mother in a red sun-dress lean over her pushchair, cooing at her fat-faced baby, 'she's never recovered from that day. She's still dealing with it. Badly, it would seem. And there's nothing we can do, other than support her, I guess.'

'I suppose,' Anne sniffed again, but this time she was fighting the tears. 'I just—I don't know what went wrong, Joe. I—I tried so hard.'

'It's not your fault, Anne.' He paused outside the grocers on the corner. 'And it's not mine.' He'd needed to say that for a while. 'It's no one's fault except Lana's. Lana got addicted, and she got sick. And she made her choices. Now all we can do is help her live with them.'

Silver hung up soon after and walked into the shop; plucked a can of diet Coke from the fridge. He realised at that moment, icy tin in hand, that his life was going to have to change immensely. He paid the money and left.

MONDAY 24TH JULY
CLAUDIE

Some time shortly after dawn, a sombre Asian girl opened the curtains and woke me. She presented me with a bowl of runny porridge and a cup of tea, and I forced myself to eat despite the foul appearance of the food, because I felt so weak and light-headed. I hoped it would help.

'The Archangel, our true Bringer of Light, will visit you soon,' the girl said joyfully.

'Who?' I answered, spooning the thin slop near my mouth and then dropping the spoon in repulsion.

'I think you will be most pleased to be reunited,' she smiled. She was quite pretty, but she had a very hairy face, I thought absently; hair grew on her cheeks in swirls beside her ears, joining her hair-line eventually.

'I don't know what you're talking about.' I tried to lever myself out of the bed. I stared at her dove pendant as if it would give me clarity, remembering the necklace the intruder had dropped in my hallway. I clutched my own locket. 'I think I should ring home now.'

But who would I ring? She looked at me with pity, as if she knew there was no one.

'This is your home now,' she said.

I flopped back on the bed. I kept smelling that odour I'd smelt on my arrival, and then in my mind's-eye suddenly I saw the ruined note that Tessa had left with Mason the day before she died. *'Take'* and *'necklace'*. That was what the smell was: the same as the herbs in the locket Tessa had given me months ago.

Frantically, I pulled at the chain round my neck, chafing my skin as I did so. *'Take the necklace off*—is that what she'd written? The smell of the herbs had always been noxious and yet I'd believed, because she'd told me, that they were spiritually good. But looking at these girls and their pendants, I felt a huge shiver go through my body. What if it wasn't good at all? What if it was very, very bad?

*   *   *

I lay there trying to piece it together. What did they mean 'reunited'? I felt something around me I could not quite pinpoint; like a thin black shadow that constantly vibrated, and I realised after a while it was fear. They were crazy, that was obvious, but they were so convinced that what they believed was right—and that was terrifying.

Who was the Archangel? Some time during those dark hours, I had a sudden fear it was Will. My beautiful sometime husband whom I had loved so very much, who had been driven from me by our worst nightmare becoming real. And then I thought, that's stupid, it could never be Will. Never mind that I didn't really know where he'd been for the past year, that he'd suddenly turned up all angry and sad. He was a good man, if a weak one. Wasn't he?

And then I remembered Francis, and the way he'd appeared in my flat two nights ago—or maybe it was longer, because time was becoming nebulous; and I shuddered again, and I thought of his zealous belief in the 'other life', which I'd ignored for the release his tiny needles brought. I thought about the fact that Tessa had been far closer to him than I'd ever realised, and I wondered why I'd let myself believe in them when they were so obviously not who they proclaimed themselves to be.

And I began to cry, because I saw how lost I had been, and how empty my life had become since Ned had died, and I wondered if this was my punishment for not being able to save him; for giving up on my

291

own life.

With some sense of relief, I remembered ringing that policewoman, so perhaps someone would look for me, someone might realise I was gone.

There was some kind of commotion downstairs. I tried to sit up in bed, but I felt so very weary and like I'd been drained of everything I had.

Then Miriam came in, followed by the Asian girl carrying a projector, and they pulled the curtains shut again and played this against the white stone wall.

'I've missed you, Claudie,' a voice said. 'I sincerely hope you'll stay.' Then the film cut to a small dark glowering girl, reading from a piece of paper. Anita Stuart.

'We are getting nearer.' Anita looked up at the camera, and her eyes blazed with something near mania. 'We are achieving our goals every day. The world we live in today is a terrifying place, I'm sure you'll agree. It's full of people who only care about themselves, and so the answer is to make people sit up and take notice. Before it is too late.'

Now she stopped reading, and started to recite, faster and faster.

'This world,' she declared, 'this mad world we live in where money means everything, this world of the machine and climate change and neon light; this world where we rush, rush, rush,' her eyes were shining now, and Miriam had sat forward in her chair, 'this world where no one stops and no one listens—well, it will IMPLODE.' Anita threw her arms in the air. 'It is screaming in our faces, and all I have done is taken the evidence and used it to our best advantage because we must purify, we must purify the world.' There was spittle on her chin.

292

'Or we will be left sitting in the debris—or maybe we won't. Or maybe there will be nothing left of us either.'

'Hallelujah!' agreed the women in the room fervently as Anita bowed her head, and the end of the film rattled into nothing.

'I'm lost,' I said faintly.

'Exactly,' the Asian girl cried with triumph, 'and we can save you. All the lost souls will be saved.'

'Oh Christ,' I muttered.

'No, not Christ,' her face darkened. 'It is not religion. Religion only divides. How badly we have seen that since the days of 9/11.'

'But—the Archangels?' I mumbled. 'Redemption and Daughters of Light?'

'Merely symbols.' Miriam stepped forward now, her brown hair tumbling round her face. 'I am serving *my* God, Claudie, and it takes what it takes.'

'Hallelujah!' repeated her accomplice, rocking in her chair. I nearly told her to shut up, only I feared the consequences.

'We are sacrificing ourselves to save the world.'

'And it is your free will,' I said slowly, 'or what your orders are?'

'It is one and the same,' Miriam said calmly, and I didn't argue.

Why would you argue with a psychopath?

MONDAY 24TH JULY
SILVER

Silver was up at six, having spent the latter part of the evening playing Scrabble—badly—with

Molly, Leticia and Matty. He couldn't remember the last time he'd played a game with his children. What took him aback was how much he enjoyed it—despite all the cheating and misspelling and attempts at swear words. And at least Leticia had deigned to speak to him again now, although there was an awful lot of eye-rolling during the game, and breaking off to text.

Philippa's son Raymond was away at university, so Molly and Matty had taken over his room. After they'd gone to bed, Silver had sat down at the kitchen table with his landlady and had a long chat over a pot of rather stewed tea. They had agreed that, for a little extra cash, Philippa and her eldest daughter Melody, who was at drama school in central London, would keep an eye on them and that Matty was old enough at fifteen to be left in charge of his little sister if both women were out. Fortunately, Philippa largely worked from home in her capacity as a senior adviser on adoption rights.

'But they're gonna get well bored, you know, Joe,' Philippa had pointed out, shelling peas for tomorrow's risotto. 'It'll be OK for a day or two, a week maybe, cooping them up whilst you're working. I'll get Melody to take them out when she's around, see a sight or two. But,' she sucked her teeth just like Leticia had the other night at Silver, and sliced a pod neatly with her mauve thumbnail, 'but then what?'

'Then,' Silver put the bastard Beer back in his mental fridge. 'Then I'm going to have a make a decision or two, P.'

A decision or two that he should have made a long time ago.

Kenton's text woke him at six:

Call me asap. I know where the retreat is.

'That location.' She was babbling when he rang her. 'It must be Holkham Beach. Gwyneth Paltrow walks across it at the end of *Shakespeare in Love*. It's in Norfolk, I think. I couldn't sleep so I Googled it. Stupid, because we watched it the other night actually—' She cleared her throat. 'Me and Alison. And she'd been there, so she knew. Alison. She'd even mentioned it. Good film,' she finished abruptly.

'Obviously,' Silver said dryly, thanking God for the fact that women had such an appetite for celebrity trivia, though he was a little surprised that Kenton was like all the rest. 'Well done, Lorraine. Get on to Norfolk Constabulary, can you. I'll see you in an hour.'

*   *   *

Silver arrived at the station around eight to the sight of Craven and Kenton hissing at each other like alley cats, right in the middle of the open-plan office.

'Listen, missy,' Craven spat, his domed forehead shiny with sweat. 'I've been in this job for a damn sight longer than you. I don't need some dykey upstart to come and tell me what to do.'

He was furious, his eyes bulging with anger. Kenton had drawn herself up to her full height, which wasn't very full, and was squaring her shoulders at her superior.

'I understand, DI Craven, that you have a

problem with me, and it would appear to be a) because I am female and b) because you have trouble with my sexual orientation. Which is nothing—' she was so angry she couldn't get her words out, was turning scarlet herself now with badly suppressed fury, 'absolutely *nothing* to do with you. Or my job.'

'Understand this, Kenton,' Craven leant over her until she started to back away, jabbing his finger in her direction, 'you don't teach your father to fuck. Capiche?'

'Jesus!' she exploded. 'My father? You don't deserve to be in the same room as my father. Who the hell do you—'

Silver spied Malloy through the door.

'Right, ladies and gentlemen,' he said calmly, 'we need to stop this. Now.'

'But—' Kenton spluttered.

'Leave it, Lorraine.' Silver turned to Craven. 'We'll talk about this later, Derek. I don't know what your problem with Lorraine is, exactly, but we need to get it sorted.'

'My problem, DCI Silver,' Craven spelt the letters out so they dripped with sarcasm, 'is—'

'Save it,' Silver snapped. 'I'm not interested right now. Let's just get our heads down and then we can all have a nice group hug later. I want a recap of exactly where we are. Get Roger and Tina over here, now.'

Kenton called them and then sat down heavily at her desk, her scarlet face clashing with her dyed hair. She waited for Silver to give her the nod, and then she began to tick her list off on her square fingers.

'I'm waiting for Edna Lamont's nursing home

to get back to me re her photos of Rosalind. I've spoken to Norfolk Constabulary who are fully aware of the situation and are patrolling the area. But identifying possible retreat locations around Holkham, well, it's a problem. It's a hugely popular tourist destination. There are masses of holiday lets, so I'm not sure of the next move.' She sneaked a glance at Craven to see if he was going to react to her admission.

'If we can determine what type of retreat it is that might help, but my feeling is it'll be these mad bastards, the Daughters of Light.' Silver leant on the desk and eyed Craven, who was still sweating profusely. 'Derek?'

'The lab's formally confirmed the dead girl is Meriel Steele—or what's left of her.'

Kenton butted in. 'I think we need to go back to the Academy and try and find out what's going on down there—'

Craven shot a look of such venom at the young woman that it was surprising she didn't wither on the spot. 'I've been back down there.'

'But we're not any nearer understanding the link, Craven, unless it's Tessa Leth—' She checked herself and put her head down. She stared at her knees whilst the younger officers listed their doings for the past day.

'Right.' Silver checked his pocket for change. 'Kenton, fill in the board.'

She stood, whiteboard marker in hand, finally looking more cheerful. In the centre, the Academy was represented by a square; a picture of Tessa Lethbridge on one side, with the name *Rosalind Lamont?* beneath it. On the other side, she lined up the photos of Anita Stuart and Meriel Steele.

Deceased was written beneath them in red letters. Now she moved the picture of Sadie Malvern underneath the word 'Archangel', next to which was written *Michael Watson?* On the right of the board, Sugar and Spice was represented by another square. Meriel and Sadie's names were also written there. So far, there was no reason to think that Anita had anything to do with the club. What *was* the link between the Academy and pole-dancers?

'Derek, was it you who spoke to Anita Stuart's family?'

'Yeah. Complete shock and nothing else concrete, apart from a bit of an obsession with that teacher Lethbridge.' Craven lifted his bulk from the chair and adjusted his trousers, standing splay-legged in the centre of the room. Kenton looked away. She rarely hated anyone, but she hated him.

Silver thought again of Paige's words about the boyfriend 'the Prince', about 'Archangel' and Sadie becoming evangelical about the world. *Fuck*, Silver thought. He thought of Lana and then of Brenda Malvern: he really didn't need Sadie to die now, on top of everything else.

'Someone is coercing these girls to do what they're doing. We know that Sadie possibly had a rather charismatic boyfriend. We know that the Purity Alliance was set up by Rosalind Lamont and Michael Watson. We haven't tracked either down yet—which is useless.' Silver pulled his cuffs down, one after the other, straightening them as he thought; as he slowed his brain. 'So what *have* we found out so far?'

Roger Okeke, the fresh-faced black DC put on the Archangel research, was dying to speak. He coughed and shuffled his papers. 'I have done an extensive search on the character—'

'It's not fucking *Mastermind,*' Craven muttered.

'And so far I haven't found much, I have to admit,' Okeke dried up, embarrassed.

'But?' Silver prompted. 'It all helps, Roger.'

'But—well, in the transcript of the anonymous call that Tina took on Friday, the caller says this,' Okeke looked down to read aloud, *"We're alive and remain and shall be caught up together in the clouds."'*

'So?' Craven was determined to be belligerent.

'So,' the young policeman was defiant. 'The whole quote is from the Bible. *"We which are alive and remain shall be caught up together with them in the clouds to meet the Lord in the air."* Thessalonians 4:17. About the Lord speaking in the voice of the Archangel.'

'Bingo,' Silver said.

'Also,' Okeke was stammering slightly now, with enthusiasm, 'he mentions the Sons of Light. That's the name of the Archangels in the Bible.'

'Hal-e-fucking-lujah,' Craven muttered under his breath. Silver was increasingly aware he had a problem on his hands with Derek Craven, a problem that needed sorting.

'Nice one, Roger. We really need to nail this Watson character. Is he the Archangel?'

Craven sat heavily as Silver continued.

'Something links these three girls: Anita, Meriel and Sadie. Is it just the mysterious Lethbridge at the Academy? Did she have some hold over them? Tina, can you speak to Lesley Steele again, please. Press her again on boyfriends. We didn't get that far with her yesterday, poor woman's so shocked. Then start talking to Meriel's friends—if

299

she had any; to the other ballet students, to anyone basically. How are we doing with uncovering Lethbridge's true background?'

Press assistant Jo Reid wiggled past and Silver sensed a loss of concentration from at least three of his team: Craven, whose tongue practically fell out of his head, Okeke and Kenton. Silver watched Reid go and then cleared his throat loudly. Personally he thought her charms were a little— obvious, and she had made it abundantly clear that his own charms hadn't escaped her.

'Er—Lethbridge?' he prodded.

'I'm waiting to speak to the police in Australia again. I'm expecting a call in the next hour,' Kenton murmured, tearing her eyes from Jo and thinking rather guiltily of Alison. 'And I'm waiting to speak to the real Tessa Lethbridge, hopefully this morning. I'll fill you in as soon as the guy in Canberra calls back.'

Silver could see his boss hovering in the back-ground, on the phone. The Met were taking a serious bashing from the press. They were being accused of responding too slowly to the Berkeley Square tragedy. The families of those still missing were furious that it was taking so long to identify the dead; the police were trapped in a mire of human tragedy and botched bureaucracy. And heads therefore must roll; of this, Silver was more than conscious. He could see Malloy cracking his knuckles again. Never a good sign.

'Tina, there *must* be more stuff out there about these Light nutters. Roger, check out the background of that fat American tosser who runs Sugar and Spice, Larry Bird, and I want details of who he answers to there.'

Roger nodded eagerly. 'No worries.'

'And someone bloody well trace Michael Watson, for Christ's sake, even if it is only to eliminate him. Derek, you liaise with Norfolk.'

Craven pulled his plastic cigarette out of his shirt pocket and lumbered off. Silver felt a stab of pity. The truth might be as simple as Craven just not being up to the job; as simple as being left behind by these bright young things.

'Lorraine, I'll meet you downstairs in five, all right, kiddo? I want to talk to Lucie Duffy again. I've got an idea she knows a damn sight more about Sadie's disappearance than she's letting on.'

Having bought himself a can of diet Coke from the machine, Silver took the back stairs to the car park. Halfway down, he took a call from the back room.

'You wanted an address for a Rachel Johnson?'

Finally.

'Yes, please.'

A street in Bethnal Green. Silver tried calling her again: still nothing. He had a bad feeling about the little redhead. He had a very bad feeling about the whole bloody matter, right now.

MONDAY 24TH JULY
CLAUDIE

I have dreams unlike any I've ever had. Afterwards, this is what I remember.

Ned's hand in mine. Warm hand curled between my fingers. Looking down. Laughing. Safe, inside and out. A feeling I had finally come home.

A day when it all changed. A fall into the pit. A day when coming home meant darkness and a deadening, stabbing loneliness. A day when coming home meant half a bottle of vodka or some pills. A time when I stopped remembering so well. A time when I didn't exist. A time when I broke from reality, through necessity. Thoughts of death; my own death, all the time.

My husband, crying. My husband, leaving.

My life, empty. Without meaning.

*   *   *

At some point I wake up and I remember what's missing and I feel like someone has squeezed me out of my own skin. I know I will never be the same again, I will never recover from this deepest hurt, this deepest cut I can never heal; the edges will never join again.

And all the time I feel like this I want to die. I don't want to be party to this pain, this pain that envelops and suffocates me; this pain that threatens to extinguish everything.

I feel Ned's hand in mine. I feel his presence and he is there and I will never, never let him go and I will never, never see him again and I am screaming, screaming into the void again.

It is my fault: I let him go. I couldn't hold on long enough, I couldn't pull him back from the brink again. I couldn't save my child. I carry the full weight of a mother's guilt. It is crushing me.

*   *   *

When I woke properly, sweating and dry-mouthed

and shaky, the older woman, Miriam, from the first day was in the room.

'Where is everyone?' I croaked, and she smiled and brought me water.

'Around.'

I drank. The sun was setting through the window, the colours sliding into one another. I stared at the window. There were iron bars on it. It struck me properly for the first time that I was a prisoner here.

'Why is it so quiet?'

'They are preparing.' The woman took my glass and refilled it with water from a cracked china jug on the windowsill. Her hair was like a wiry brown halo.

'What for?'

She passed me a plate of something. Rice and vegetables.

'I'm not hungry.'

She frowned. 'You need to eat. We owe it to the Archangel to keep ourselves strong and fit.' She looked at me doubtfully. 'Maybe it will take you some time.'

'Maybe.' The rice had a bitter taste. I put it down again. 'Preparing for what?'

'For the final divine message.'

'Right. And what would that be?'

She smiled at me. 'We will know when we hear it.'

My stomach rolled. I looked again at the plate of food. There were tiny white flecks of powder on the chopped carrots. I looked again. Perhaps I was seeing things.

Tentatively, when she was not looking, I licked a piece of carrot. It was sour and strange-tasting. Of course. How could I have been so dense?

They were drugging me.

MONDAY 24TH JULY
SILVER

Silver sent Kenton down to the Academy to question them further about the girls and the lap-dancing club.

'There must be some link somewhere we're missing. And we need a confirmed bloody ID on the Lethbridge woman, now.' He rummaged through the papers on his desk. 'And who is this joker with her?' He shoved the photo he'd pinched from Tessa's flat at Kenton. 'Let's clarify everything.'

Kenton pocketed her phone; she had been trying to ring the troubled Claudie Scott again to no avail. Presumably the crisis was over, whatever it had been.

'I'll get on to Edna Lamont again; see if she's got those photos yet. And I've emailed a picture of Lethbridge to that Martin woman. Not that I expect her to be much help.'

'Who?' Silver looked distracted.

'The one-time secretary of the Empathy Society whom I met. The sour one.'

Kenton didn't mention that it had taken some powerful words, all of which she had taken great relish saying, to force even Jan Martin's email address out of her.

'It's private property, not property of the state,' Martin had started with. 'It's an order, and that's the end of it, or you will be charged with obstruction,' Kenton had ended with. Martin had eventually capitulated; but not without inflicting several minutes of moaning about infringement of civil liberties and the like on Kenton.

Silly cow.

'Nice work, Lorraine. I'll call you as soon as I've made this visit.'

Silver put Billie Holiday on the stereo and drove to Bethnal Green. The singer's mournful tones seemed horribly appropriate somehow.

Paige's address was a terraced Georgian house on Cambridge Heath Road, smart and fairly genteel-looking, despite a vandalised bus shelter housing various homeless situated directly outside.

A Slavic-looking girl in a pink kimono answered the door.

'I'm after Rachel. Or Paige.'

The girl looked at him blankly. A skinny man appeared behind her, half-dressed, doing up his shirt buttons.

'Can I help?' He pushed the girl to one side. 'Sorry. Katya doesn't speak very good English.'

'I'm looking for Paige—Rachel Johnson? Small redhead.'

'Oh, Rachel.' The man glanced up the stairs. 'I haven't seen her for a few days actually. This is a house share, so you can imagine. We come and we go. We're all pretty busy; we're a bit like ships that pass in the night.'

'I'd like to check.'

The man's eyes narrowed slightly. 'Well—'

Silver flashed his badge.

'Sure,' the man stood aside to let him in. Silver thought he saw a pair of pink fluffy handcuffs protruding from his pocket.

Paige's room was immaculate; spangled dresses hung on a rail, rows of shoes below it on a rack, higher than the average woman's; a futon with a flowery duvet and a fluffy polar bear on the pillow. Stripy pyjamas flung on the end of the bed; make-up above the washbasin in the corner. Books on the shelves; Noam Chomsky, a few reference books about Accounting, a big red ring-binder. She was studying for something. A William Boyd novel by the bed. A Miro poster on the wall. *'Still waters'* Silver remembered her saying, and felt an almost palpable sense of regret.

He hoped to God it wasn't too late for Paige.

*   *   *

Kenton was eating a KitKat with something akin to fervour when they met up in the foyer of the Academy.

'I've been talking to Mason Pyke, the secretary here.' She snapped a chocolate finger off and offered it to her boss. 'She's a piece of work, I have to say.'

'No thanks.' He shook his head at the biscuit. 'Why?'

'Oh I don't know. Gives off air that she knows everything, but actually knows nothing. But Tessa's mate in that photo is her acupuncturist apparently, and she did tell me Sadie Malvern's got an ex-boyfriend though. He's coming up in a minute.'

Two painfully thin students in white tights and running shorts squeezed past them. Kenton looked at her chocolate bar ruefully and then down at her own chunky thighs.

'Not much hope for me in a place like this.'

306

'Not much hope for them if they don't eat something soon.' Silver thought of his ex-wife weighing every calorie religiously when they were first married. Still, it wasn't until after the kids were born that she'd given up food for the pleasures of annihilation.

A handsome boy bounded up the steps now, two at a time.

'Those fat cows need to eat a few less Big Macs,' he'd caught Kenton's words, 'then I'd stop straining myself on the lifts.'

His eyes were like green glass, chilly and hard. Billy McCorkdale was a pretty, blond, scholarship boy from Manchester with the talent of a young Acosta but a chip the size of Oldham, according to Mason Pyke. If he could rein in the tantrums, he'd go far.

'Oh I don't know,' Silver said mildly, 'most of these girls look like they need building up a bit to me. So, you dated Sadie last year? You did well— older girl, young lad like you.'

'Sadie Malvern aka silly bitch,' the boy shrugged.

'Why are you so cross with Sadie?'

'Because. She were a two-timing cow. And cos she let that stupid bitch Tessa Lethbridge tell her what to do.'

'What do you mean?'

'Lethbridge told her she was throwing herself away on me.' He ran a hand through his blond curls. 'Look, I know she's dead an' all, but Lethbridge properly wound me up. Thought she were so grand, but she were useless. Ask any of the lads.'

'Can you expand a bit?'

'Well, she weren't really ballet, were she, after

all that. Don't surprise me. Her teaching was cack. And she had too many favourites.'

Silver grinned. 'My teachers always had favourites.'

'She were no good, if you ask me. She just liked the girls. Mebbe,' he leered like a naughty schoolboy, his accent thickening, 'mebbe she were just an old lezzer.'

Silver couldn't face looking at Kenton.

'Anyway,' Billy went on, 'she told Sadie I'd ruin her career and about a week later, she stopped seeing me.'

'Why would you ruin it?'

'Because,' his voice tightened now. 'Just because Lethbridge didn't like me.'

'And was that the only reason, do you think?' Kenton tried to keep her voice level.

'I don't know. Perhaps.' There was a pause. 'But I think Sadie were seeing someone else,' he said quietly. It was obvious he'd really loved her. 'I followed her and Tessa once. They met a bloke downstairs in a wine bar. Older.'

'Can you describe him?'

'Not really. Just old. Grey. Sadie looked well smitten.' His face closed down again. 'Silly bitch. Anyway. She got what she deserved.'

Silver's ears pricked up. 'What do you mean?'

'Look at Sadie now. Getting her tits out for the lads. What ballet dancer would ever do that? It's an art form, and she's showing her arse crack to the world.' Pain was scrawled across his handsome features. 'Good riddance, I say.'

*   *   *

'Sour grapes?'

'Maybe.'

'Another thing the Pyke woman said,' Kenton scrunched up the biscuit's foil as Billy left them, girls' eyes following him down the corridor, 'Lucie Duffy's the star of the show tomorrow afternoon at the Royal Opera House. There's the premiere of *Swan Lake*, and then a party; charity event. Big occasion. A few minor royals and the Prime Minister might even be there.'

'*Swan Lake*?' Silver peered over Kenton's shoulder into a classroom, watching a group of first years practise a complicated sequence of barre work.

'The dying swan.'

Silver was none the wiser.

'Odette and Odile? The beautiful swan girl and the evil one, who pretends to be the goodie to get the prince.'

Mason Pyke suddenly appeared at the top of the stairs beside them. In her grey pinafore and knee socks, she looked like an elongated and rather horrifying schoolgirl.

'I forgot to say, Officer.' She pulled that letterbox smile at them, flattening her fringe with one hand. 'You should talk to our physio Claudie Scott again about Tessa Lethbridge. They really were thick as the proverbials and there was something very odd going on last Thursday. You know, the day before the *bomb*.' She dropped her voice reverently. 'As they say, "*Cowards die many times before their deaths.*"'

'Well, we'll talk to Scott now. Where is she?'

'You can't actually,' Mason looked almost pleased, her spindly hands folding her pinafore

309

pleats. 'She's not in today. Not sure why—she should be.'

Kenton turned slowly, a look of horror crossing her pleasant face.

'What?' Silver asked her.

'Oh, God. Claudie Scott. That is one coincidence too many.'

*　　　*　　　*

By the time she arrived back at the station, Kenton had a message from Natalie Lord, Claudie Scott's younger sister.

'I found your number by her phone in the flat,' she explained rather tearfully when Kenton rang back. 'And your message on the answer-phone. I'm really worried, Ms Kenton.'

'DS Kenton,' she corrected gently. 'When did you last see your sister?'

'On Wednesday. Then I popped round on Saturday to leave her a casserole, but she was out. She doesn't look after herself properly since Ned's death.'

'Ned?'

'Her son. He died two years ago.' Natalie started to cry properly now. 'Claudie's not recovered yet. He was only three.'

'Oh dear,' Kenton felt a genuine rush of sorrow. 'Yes, of course, I remember now.' She thought of Scott's slightly bewildered and detached air the day they had interviewed her, of the hands she'd scratched the whole time they spoke to her.

'And then she was caught in the explosion,' the sister went on. 'You know, the one near her work.'

'Caught in it?' Kenton didn't remember Claudia

Scott mentioning that. 'And where do you think she may be?'

'I feel so daft,' the other woman's words were speeding up, coming out garbled. 'When I came round, I let this man into her flat. Brendan says now I was mad. But he definitely knew Claudia, this man. And I just thought it was her boyfriend.'

'Who is her boyfriend?' Kenton frowned. 'Have you not met him before?'

'No. Well, I wasn't very—' Natalie sought the right word. 'I wasn't very approving. She's still married. Only, after Ned's death and everything, her and Will, well they, they just sort of fell apart.'

'So,' Kenton prodded her carefully back onto the right track. 'The boyfriend?'

'He's an MP. Rafe Longley, his name is. Terribly respectable, I'm sure, but just not—well. You know.'

'Right. So you hadn't met Mr Longley.'

'I chose to ignore it, I'm afraid. And I'm not much good on politics anyway. Don't know my cabinet ministers from my cabinet makers.' She seemed almost defensive. 'I leave that kind of thing to my hubby. Anyway, I did look him up this morning, on the computer, after I went round and Claudie was gone, when Brendan said I was stupid,' she sniffed, loudly, 'and I realise now he wasn't the man I left in the flat. It was someone else altogether.' She began to wail. 'Oh, God.'

'Please, Mrs Lord,' Kenton was firm. 'Calm yourself. What makes you think your sister is missing?'

'Her shoes. She hasn't taken her shoes, or her bag. Her purse is here. So's her phone. And her bed—' Kenton could hardly understand a word

311

now, she was crying so hard. 'Her bed is unmade. Claudie always, always makes her bed. Even when Ned died, she made her bed. Once she got out of it.'

MONDAY 24TH JULY
CLAUDIE

I realised that I had to get out of here. I had to tell someone about this evil; this final 'divine message'. I made it as far as the window. The sky seemed vertical almost, it was so immense, and the moon floated, suspended between banks of cloud. All I could see was the perimeter of the farm we were on, and the broad sweep of the land beyond, no buildings, no road. Somewhere, not so very far away, was the sea; I could sense the salt in the air.

I tried the casement window. It opened a little, but not enough to get through, even if I could unscrew the bars. Down in the yard, an old white Golf was parked beside an ancient tractor. I wondered who had the car key.

I tried the door. It was locked.

I sat back on the bed. I read a pamphlet so thoughtfully left for me.

UTOPIA vs. DYSTOPIA? it screamed.
Some people call it brain-washing: this is undoubtedly an evil concept. We come together to celebrate life, and to rid the world of its narcisstic content. We are ruining this planet, this earth, soon there will be nothing left, if we don't act NOW!!

Narcissistic was spelt wrong.

I thought about the memories that I was struggling with. I had been brainwashed perhaps, hypnotised somehow. I thought of last Thursday night, of coming round in Rafe's porch. I thought of Rafe.

Rafe.

I had a sudden feeling of absolute horror. He had been at the Academy's charity event at Sadler's Wells. He had access to the students. Then I pushed the thoughts away. It couldn't be Rafe. But I saw the lost souls he'd described; I saw that smooth charm at work, the easy interest he had in everyone; the beguiling way he drew you in.

Rafe couldn't be the Archangel—could he?

And where did Tessa fit in? Had she been part of this too, a Daughter of Light?

I wondered how many more girls the Archangel had got his claws into. Why?

Why had been a big question in my life since Ned died. Why him? Why us? Why not someone else?

All the days after, it had ricocheted round my brain, that tiny word, until I could have screamed with the pain of it bouncing off the sides. Relentless, small word, banging off my skull.

With growing dread, I contemplated the hours I'd lost the morning of the explosion.

What had I done?

*   *   *

Sadie brought me soup the colour of mud—lentils apparently—and some kind of fresh juice. She sat at the end of my bed until I attempted to eat a little, but again it was largely unpalatable, and anyway, I

313

didn't trust them now. As soon as I raised the spoon to my mouth, she stood again, and I slid the bowl away.

'How long have you been here?' I asked her as she wafted around the room, fiddling with things, as if she were a house-proud mother.

Sadie shrugged. 'Time is immaterial. It counts for nothing.'

Oh, God.

'I bide my time and I wait.' She gazed out of the window. 'I can sense the sea you know, from here. It is so beautiful. The true universe.'

Something jarred.

'So, you believe in purity?'

'Yes.' She turned back to me. 'It is our creed.'

'I see.' I knew I had to phrase myself carefully. 'So, if it is your creed, do you think you could explain something to me; something I don't understand? It would really help me.'

'Sure.' She sat at the end of my bed now. On the back of her left hand some kind of intricate flower was drawn in henna.

'What's that?' I pointed.

'That?' She looked down and extended her hand towards me. 'That is the lotus flower. The symbol of pureness.'

'I see.' I didn't see at all. 'So my question then is. I think you were dancing—dancing at the club called Sugar and Spice?'

'Sometimes, yes,' she nodded earnestly.

'But that—I mean, you can't call that club a "pure" place? It's a money-making, sleazy, sexist empire—' I saw her frown. 'Sorry. I'm just—I'm not very keen on them. I think they exploit women.'

'Only if they let themselves be exploited,' she

snapped, her Northern accent suddenly harsh, and for a second I glimpsed a little of what I remembered of Sadie from the Academy.

'I see.'

'Anyway,' she regained her equilibrium quickly, 'I did it for the cause.'

This girl *had* been truly brainwashed.

'For the cause?'

'Any money I made went to the cause. I give myself wholly.'

'Who took you there?'

'What do you mean?' She looked impatient.

'Who persuaded you to dance for "the cause"?'

'Ah,' she smiled now, slowly. 'That would be telling. All will become clear, Claudie, all will reveal itself when the time's right. Now,' she held out my glass. 'Drink your juice. It's good for you.'

I saw myself standing at the bar in Sugar and Spice with the fat man, Larry. I saw myself on my hands and knees being kicked down by an indifferent tattooed Russian called Andrei. *Kick a dog when it's down . . .*

'You know all those nicknames the Archangel uses,' I said slowly. Automatically I took a sip from the glass.

'They're not nicknames, Claudie,' Sadie looked sorrowful, as if I had misunderstood, 'they are the true being.'

'Right. Whatever. I think I know another one.' I tried to pull myself up to a sitting position. I was starting to feel a little floaty again myself. 'The Pied Piper. Right?'

She stared at me with her slanted blue eyes, and shook her head. 'No. I've never heard the Archangel called that. Never. That was Tessa.

Tessa brought us to the Archangel. And for that we were grateful. Until she changed her mind.'

MONDAY 24TH JULY
SILVER

Claudie Scott's flat did indeed look like the home of a woman who had left in a hurry. It was rather empty, as if she was merely passing through, and very tidy—except for one kitchen cupboard that had been upended and a carrier bag lying on the floor with just an old receipt in it. There was no doubt that all the everyday things—purse, credit cards, phone, keys, were all still there. She, on the other hand, most definitely wasn't.

Natalie Lord was waiting for them. She was a tear-stained pregnant mess, wringing her plump hands over and over, her jaunty little silk scarf askew.

'What can you do?' she kept asking. 'My sister's obviously been kidnapped.'

'That's a big conclusion to come to, Mrs Lord.' Silver led her to a chair and made her sit whilst Kenton, who'd filled him in briefly on Claudie Scott on the way there, started to search the flat. 'What makes you think that?'

'Well, just look. And the water was still running in the shower when I got here.'

Not much to go on, thought Silver, given that we don't actually know she's been taken. But he had to agree, it was one missing female too many.

'We'll put her description out immediately, nationwide,' he soothed Natalie. 'And we'll be calling a press conference as soon as possible. But

316

first, I need you to give me some details. Tell me a little about her, and what's been happening in her life recently.'

'I don't really know,' Natalie sniffed. 'She's so private, my big sister. Very independent. Since Ned died, and she and Will split up—'

'Ned was her son, yes? And Will?'

'Will Scott. Her husband.'

'Can you give me details?' Silver pressed her. 'Where does he live?'

'In their old house, I think. In Richmond. He's been in the States working. Claudie—' she started sobbing again. 'Claudie couldn't bear to be there any more. In that house. She's been pretty—sick.'

'Sick?'

'She's been under, you know. Psychiatric care.' Natalie looked apprehensive; embarrassed even. 'She—had a kind of breakdown when her son died. It's hard to explain.'

A warning bell sounded with Silver. A grieving mother who'd had a breakdown was not the same MO as the missing dancers. He thought fleetingly of his own wife.

'Sir,' Kenton was behind him in the galley kitchen. 'Look at this. The same as in Lethbridge's flat.'

She came round the breakfast bar to show him the framed tract she'd just found in the drawer.

THE SUN MAY STILL SHINE
BUT IF YOU DO NOT ACT
SOME DAY SOON
THE END WILL BE THINE

'Any ideas?' Silver asked Natalie.

She read it, then shook her head vehemently.

317

'None.'

'Is Claudie the religious type?'

'Not at all.' Natalie adjusted her little scarf fussily. 'In fact, she refuses to ever come to church with me. And believe me,' her mouth formed a funny little circle of outrage, 'I have tried.'

I bet you have, Silver thought.

'Right,' Silver stood. 'Let's get cracking. We'll give you a lift home, Mrs Lord. And I need details of the husband, the boyfriend and the psychiatrist, please.'

*   *   *

'Claudie Scott did mention the psychiatrist when we questioned her about Lethbridge,' Kenton said, after they'd dropped Natalie Lord home. 'She was fairly reticent, and it had no relevance to anything at the time. But now, if she's missing, well, maybe the shrink can shed some light on her disappearance. You know, her mood or something.'

'I don't care about her bloody mood, Lorraine. We just need to trace these fucking purity nutters before anyone else disappears off the face of the earth.' Silver was thoroughly fed up and Kenton was shocked that he'd sworn; it was so unlike him. He banged the steering wheel with the flat of his hand. 'Why is this investigation moving at a snail's pace?'

He sounded like Malloy, he realised, but the frustration was killing him, not to mention the pressure from above. He had a horrible feeling that if something didn't click soon, another girl was going to die. He checked the time. Where the hell had the day gone?

318

'Husband or nut doctor?'

'Husband I'd say. Plus,' Kenton indicated the Sat Nav, 'we can pop in at the nursing home en route. Jan bloody Martin's gone awol though, surprise surprise. She's not returning my calls.'

'And what about this Watson bloke? Are we any nearer at all?'

Kenton shrugged. 'He seems to be a clever guy. He's covered all his tracks somehow.'

As they pulled into the forecourt of St Agnes's, a hearse was blocking the drive.

'Another old dear checks out.' Silver pulled the glove compartment open and dug around for gum. 'Come on, Kenton. Let's get on with it before Malloy's head explodes.'

The sombre Asian nurse Pritti was following a covered stretcher down the front stairs.

'Hello again,' she was so demure. 'I'm so sorry, but I'm afraid Edna passed away a few hours ago.'

Kenton gaped at her. 'Really?'

'Was that expected?' Silver snapped his gum in half rather savagely. 'It seems a bit sudden.'

'She had been very sick.' Pritti shook her head sadly. 'It's heartbreaking, of course, but now she will be at one in the clouds.'

'I don't suppose she got those photos she mentioned before she died?' Kenton asked.

'No, I'm sorry. I don't think she had the chance to make that call.' Pritti bowed her head. 'I was only with her right at the end though.'

She had a strange look on her face. It was almost smug, Kenton was just thinking, when Silver spoke. He was staring at Pritti, who was fiddling with something at her neck.

'Can you repeat that please?'

'At one in the clouds?' Pritti smiled with something close to rapture.

'Why do you say that? That's a Biblical quote, no?' Silver asked her, his eyes narrowing. 'Are you a practising Christian?'

'No. But I studied the Bible of course, in school.'

'What do you know of the Purity Alliance?'

'Who?' Pritti said, but a shadow crossed her face.

'The Daughters of Light?'

'I don't know what you mean.' Beneath her neatly buttoned grey cardigan, the silver dove was just visible.

'I think you do.'

A look of alarm crossed the nurse's face. And then another look settled there. She gazed at the policeman and his partner. Her gaze said 'I am ready'.

'Kenton.' Silver felt his pulse accelerate. 'Speak to the undertakers and to Forensic Pathology *now*. We need a post mortem on Edna Lamont asap. You know the drill. And take her in.' He nodded at the nurse.

DS Kenton looked alarmed. 'On what grounds?'

'Suspected murder. Put her in an interview room and grill her.'

Pritti didn't blink, she just stared at her feet.

'And where are you going?'

Silver put a call through to the station.

'I want to speak to Claudie Scott's boyfriend and the husband, before someone else dies.'

MONDAY 24TH JULY
CLAUDIE

I hadn't eaten enough for the drugs to take hold properly this time, but it meant I was empty and weak, too. I slept for a bit in an attempt to raise my strength. Later, when Sadie took me to the bathroom, I concentrated on working out the layout of the house a little better. The narrow wooden stairs were only feet away from my room; I guessed the kitchen was beneath it because I could often hear the low rumbling of voices through the bare floorboards, though never clearly enough to understand exactly what they said.

'Sadie,' I heard the woman called Miriam call. 'I need a hand to prepare the package.'

'I'll be down now.' Sadie was vague, distracted.

'The package?' I asked innocently. 'What's that?'

'*That,*' she turned to me, 'is the answer.'

She left the room.

It was dark outside, and I heard the patter of rain beginning.

I didn't know how many women were in the house, or how hard it would be to escape them, but it was clear to me that if I did not act, a new atrocity was about to be carried out sometime very soon. My hands were untied now and they, apparently, were busy with their package.

I had nothing to lose.

I had to make a break for it.

MONDAY 24TH JULY
SILVER

Silver was unimpressed by Will Scott, Claudie's husband. Weak was the word he'd have used to describe him. Even his face seemed a little feeble—mouth too girlish, sandy hair too long and all on end, his eyes wary.

'It seems indisputable that Claudie has disappeared,' Silver informed the man brusquely.

'Disappeared?' Scott paled. 'Are you sure?'

'It definitely looks that way, I'm afraid. And we need any clue whatsoever to help find her. When did you last see your wife?'

'I've only seen her once in the past year,' Will Scott was immediately defensive. 'Last Friday.'

'And that was because—?'

'I wanted to talk. I suppose I—' He trailed off.

Silver waited. He had learnt over time that silence was more likely to encourage people to open up and talk.

'I suppose I thought perhaps we'd get back together.'

'But?'

'But that's not going to happen. We've both moved on.' He fiddled with his pencil sharpener.

'I believe Claudie has a new boyfriend.'

'I don't think I'm the person to ask about that, DCI Silver.' Will Scott's fingertips went white where he was holding the pencil too tight. So he did care. 'I've never met him, anyway.'

'Claudie's sister Natalie thinks she's been kidnapped.'

'Natalie always did have a sense of the dramatic.' Will rolled his eyes.

'Did you think she might be—suicidal?'

Now Will Scott looked really shocked. 'Claudie? I bloody hope not. No, not now, I don't think. She's pretty tough. Even if she has lost it a little.'

Charming, Silver thought.

'Sorry, not lost it.' Too late, Scott looked sheepish. 'You know what I mean.'

Not really, thought Silver. He waited again.

'I just couldn't reach Claudia after the death of our son,' the other man went on. 'No one could really. It was like she shut down.'

'Blamed herself?' Silver asked carefully. He thought of Lana. Perhaps he *did* understand.

'I guess. But there was nothing she could have done. He got ill, a rare genetic disorder, nothing could be done—and that was that. Ned.' Will Scott looked out of the window, his hands clenched tight. Silver gave him a minute before continuing.

'And the psychiatric help?'

'I helped find Helen Ganymede just before I left for America. She was recommended.'

'By whom?'

'I'm not sure now. There were so many names mooted.'

'Really?'

'Whatever you may think of me,' he met Silver's gaze now, almost challenging him, 'I was worried about my wife. Helen's an expert in her field; she's even written books about disassociating.'

'Disassociating?'

'Trauma causing the brain to shut down. It can lead to something called multiple personality disorder—though I don't think it ever manifested itself that badly in Claudie.' He looked thoroughly uncomfortable. 'But she became very remote, and she lost periods of time.'

'Lost?'

'Couldn't remember stuff. At all.'

'Right. And when you saw her, did she give any indication she might be planning to go away?'

'Not to me.'

'Have you heard of the Daughters of Light?'

'No,' Scott shook his head.

'The Purity Alliance?'

'No. Why?'

'Because two girls from the Academy where Claudia works have died in self-propagated incidents. A third is missing, as is your wife. We believe they've come under some sort of—cult influence.'

'What, and you think Claudie might be next?' her husband scoffed. 'Pull the other one. She's hardly a suicide bomber.'

'I'm rather more afraid,' Silver said seriously, 'that she might have found out something that put her in danger.'

'I see. Well, there was the break-in—' Will Scott spoke slowly.

'What break-in?'

'The night I went to see her. Someone had got into her flat. Nothing was taken, but they wrote something on the wall. From that Ring a Ring o' Roses rhyme. She didn't seem very rattled, that's what I thought was odd. She just scrubbed it off again.'

'What did he write?'

'I'll show you. I took a photo on my phone.'

He reached for his iPhone. Typical, Silver

thought. Scott was exactly the type of man to own one.

'*Atishoo Atishoo, We all fall down,*' Silver read. The rhyme, he knew, was written about sickness; influenza, he had a vague inkling.

Promising death.

* * *

Craven called Silver just as he was clearing Security at the Commons.

'Wait till you see what we've just got our hands on,' Craven was more revved-up than he'd been in the past few days. 'That little bitch's suicide message.'

'Whose?' Silver held his arms up so the guard could swipe him down.

'Stuart's. Anita fucking Stuart. Fucking DVD, just like the Jihadis. Eyes blazing, the whole shebang. Only she's not doing it for seven bleeding virgins. She's doing it for the greater good of the world.'

'Where did it come from?' Silver was perplexed. Why send it so long after the event?

'There's a note with it, guv. From whoever's pulling the strings. Promising retribution for the destruction of the natural world.'

* * *

Claudie Scott did not have particularly good taste in men, Silver thought, as he sat opposite Rafe Longley in his House of Commons office. He could see that Longley was good-looking and from the way he spoke on the phone, undoubtedly charming. But there was something fake about him, and

325

something rather peacock-like. Silver was surprised the man wasn't a Tory.

'Sorry,' said Rafe, hanging the phone up with a smile Silver did not believe, pushing back his thick hair. Forty-something, and trying for thirty-five. 'Busy busy busy. Only just got back from my constituency.'

'Which is where?' Silver enquired politely.

'Norwich North.'

Silver's ears pricked up. 'Norfolk?'

'Yes.'

'Nice picture,' Silver indicated a colourful Russian icon on the wall behind Rafe's desk, absorbing the man's words.

'Just something I picked up on my travels. Visiting St Petersburg for work, I believe.'

And no doubt worth a fortune. Longley had an invite on his desk to the Royal Opera House event on Tuesday 25th July, Silver noticed.

'Ballet fan?'

'Not really, but the department likes to be— diverse. Martial arts and comedy are more my cup of tea—but it pays to be fair to all.'

'So you're in the Culture Department?'

'If you can call it that,' the other man joked. 'Culture! It's a broad remit these days. Fancy a toilet as art?'

Silver didn't laugh. He didn't like Longley, he knew that much already.

'So. You met Claudie Scott where?'

'At a do in January. Sadler's Wells, I think.'

'How?'

'Someone introduced us.'

'Who?'

'God,' the other man narrowed his eyes as he

326

contemplated the question, 'it's hard to remember. Someone from the Academy possibly.'

Silver was very careful not to show a flicker of emotion. 'Not the teacher Tessa Lethbridge by any chance?'

'That odd bod? No,' Longley shrugged. 'But I did meet her later, through Claudie. She was very—passionate, shall we say. About ballet—and about Claudie.'

Silver kept hearing this.

'And you last saw her when?'

'Who?'

'I meant Claudie, actually, but you can tell me about Tessa too.'

'Tragic that she died,' Longley went for sincere now. Unconvincingly. He had a slight look of a young Blair, Silver observed. 'Funny old bird. All those lies. I wasn't entirely surprised, I must say.'

Silver drew his Ace from the pack.

'Did you know Claudie was missing?'

'Missing?' Rafe stared at him. 'No. Are you sure?'

'You really didn't know? I thought you were an item.'

'We—er,' guilt crossed his face. 'We were never really—exclusive.'

'Exclusive?' Silver shook his head, pretending ignorance, enjoying seeing the other man squirm.

'You know. I mean, we went out for a while, but—'

'Oh, I see.' Silver was patronising. 'You mean you had an open relationship?'

'Well,' Longley stacked the papers on his desk fussily, 'maybe open would be describing it a bit—being a little—strong, you know. But Claudie never seemed that interested. In commitment. I mean,

327

she'd been married. Still is married, I think.'

Which was doubtless what Longley liked about her: she wouldn't get clingy. Amazing what you learnt from asking the simplest questions. Silver felt a sense of satisfaction. Battle of the Alpha males, Lana would say. And Silver loathed infidelity. It had scarred him deeply when he realised his wife had been sleeping with another man, let alone a friend. He would never be able to trust a woman in quite the same way again, he was pretty sure; he hadn't yet.

'So when did you last see her?'

'On Thursday night, I think. Over a week ago.'

'And what happened then? You split up?'

'No, not then.' Longley was increasingly disconcerted, that was obvious. His handsome face didn't change, but there was a look in his eyes that Silver recognised. 'I found her unconscious outside the flat, actually. It was a bit scary.'

The look of a cornered animal before it attempts to flee.

'Unconscious?' Silver frowned. 'Is this normal behaviour for Claudie Scott?'

'No, absolutely not.' Longley was vehement; finally telling the truth. 'We were meant to go out to dinner and she never turned up at the restaurant. When I got home, having not reached her on the phone, I found her slumped in my front porch. She suffered terrible migraines sometimes. I just thought she'd taken too much medication and passed out.'

'So then what happened?'

'I put her to bed, and in the morning she was fine.'

'Fine?'

'Well,' Longley's discomfort was almost painful now. 'I say fine, she seemed fine. I left her asleep and probably went to the gym before coming to the House. I do most mornings.'

'I see. And that was the last you saw of her?'

'Yes. Oh no—wait,' he paused for thought. 'I popped round to see her in the week. Wednesday, perhaps? I felt bad. She's a lovely woman. Just a bit—damaged.'

'We're all damaged, aren't we, Mr Longley?' Silver smiled pleasantly. 'I'd be worried if an adult over the age of twenty-one didn't have some kind of—what do they call it now? Baggage.'

'Yes, well,' Rafe Longley frowned. 'Claudie more so than most, I'd say.'

'She lost a child, Mr Longley, I believe. No worse trauma for a parent.'

'Yes, of course.' The MP shot his cuffs in a gesture that Silver recognised in himself. 'I wouldn't know. I don't have kids yet.'

Silver could believe it.

'Claudia was last seen yesterday afternoon, in her flat, where a man whom her sister believed to be you was waiting for her.' Silver scrutinised Longley's face as he spoke. 'She hasn't been seen since.'

'Me?' Longley stared at him. 'Sorry—I don't understand.'

'Her sister Natalie, having not met you, believed him to be you when he arrived. He was tallish, over six foot, with dark hair, and a beard. He let her call him Rafe. Does that description ring any bells?'

'No,' Longley shook his head, looking, to his credit, more than a little upset now. 'I feel terrible now.'

329

'I need any pointers you can give me.'

Longley stood now, clearly agitated, knocking a greeting card on his desk onto the floor. 'Christ. Poor Claudie. What do you think's happened to her?'

'That, Mr Longley,' Silver gave him the benefit of a half-smile, and picked up the card, 'is what I need to find out as soon as possible.'

The card showed Raphael's 'The Annunciation', the Angel Gabriel talking to Mary. Silver recognised it from taking Ben round the V&A last October half-term for his history of art A level.

It was signed 'With thanks from Tessa'.

'For my namesake,' Rafe Longley smiled uneasily. 'The picture. I got her in to have tea at the Commons. You know what these foreigners are like. Old-style crazy.'

*   *   *

Silver left the House of Commons in the drizzle, wondering whether he could take Rafe Longley in, but he had no real evidence other than a few bits of circumstantial. He headed for Helen Ganymede's house in Hampstead. When he'd called her at nine, she had been understanding about the lateness of the hour.

'Of course you must come now,' she said. 'If Claudie is in any sort of danger at all, I'd like to help.'

Helen Ganymede's house was the kind of house featured in television comedies about happy families, or adverts about tired, dirty teenagers returning home from Glastonbury to their patient mum. It was large and solid and homely, unlike

Helen, who was slight, almost ethereal, her skin pale and lightly freckled, dressed elegantly in a silk shirt and trousers. Silver tried to guess her age, which was hard; older than him, he thought; probably around fifty. For a moment he wondered if they'd met before, but he knew they hadn't.

She offered Silver coffee, which he accepted gladly. 'Long day,' he murmured.

'What's happened to Claudie?' she frowned as she percolated a fresh cafetiere.

'She's disappeared. Of her own volition, or because she's been taken, I'm not sure yet.'

'Taken?' Helen looked up, shocked.

'We're concerned she may have become mixed up in some kind of cult preying on Royal Ballet Academy students. The two girls who have killed themselves, Anita Stuart and Meriel Steele, there are definite links; and another girl's missing.'

'I see.' Helen pulled her grey hair into a graceful knot. 'I have been a little worried again recently about Claudie, it has to be said.'

'Why?'

'A few things.' Helen poured the coffee into fine white bone china. 'Cream and sugar?'

'Cream would be nice, thanks.'

She opened the fridge. 'For instance, she had a fantasy about being chased the other day. First time she's had one of those in a while; probable paranoid delusion. And I've been aware the thing with Tessa Lethbridge might be problematic. They were very close. I think Claudie felt—betrayed.'

'By her mistaken identity?'

'Yes. Can't say I blame her.'

'You knew Tessa?' Silver watched the cream swirl neatly round the cup.

331

'I met her once when she came to see if I would take her on.' Helen was matter-of-fact. 'I couldn't, because she was such good friends with Claudie. It's unethical, you see.'

'So you wouldn't have a feeling about how involved she might have been with this group the Daughters of Light?'

Silver heard the front door opening, and glanced round as Helen lifted a hand in greeting. A man in a flat cap and mac was shaking an umbrella in the hall behind them; he grunted a greeting back.

'Dog walking waits for no husband, rain or shine,' she said with a smile, though Silver thought he sensed a new tension in her slight frame. A small spaniel bounced into the room and bounced out again, leaving dirty paw-prints on the gleaming tiles. The man in the hallway called him.

'Kipper. Here, boy.'

'No, I can imagine.' Silver turned back to Helen, who was pulling faces at the mud on her perfect floor.

'I'll sort it out in a sec. Sorry, you were saying?' Helen sipped her own coffee, fiddling with the tiny gold doll on the chain around her neck. 'Daughters of Light?'

'Yes.'

'Tessa certainly never mentioned anything about any group when I met her. It was very brief, of course. Our meeting.'

'And Claudie?'

'Claudie might be the perfect victim for a cult. They tend to pick on people who have lost something—or who are just lost generally. You know about Claudie's son?'

'Yes,' Silver nodded. 'Tragic, poor woman. And

332

I understand this provoked some kind of serious psychological reaction?'

'Yes exactly,' Helen looked almost enthused. 'That's why she came to me in the first place. Her husband Will sent her, before he left for America. She suffered from severe disassociation when Ned died. Which means that she would split from her consciousness. And that's what I'm afraid might have been happening again recently. You know, suffering delusions, that kind of thing.'

'Trauma's a powerful thing.' Silver thought of his own wife. He'd love to ask Helen a few questions about Lana now. 'But she didn't ever mention the cult?'

'No. I don't think so.'

Silver's phone rang. It was Kenton. 'Sorry, do you mind?' He stood, moved to the side of the room to answer it, gazing at the banks of framed photos on the sturdy Welsh dresser.

'Eureka moment!'

He could tell Kenton had been dying to say that for ages.

'Pritti Vershani has just given up the location of the retreat. It's a farmhouse on the Holkham estate.' Kenton was almost breathless. 'What do you want me to do?'

'We'd better get up there. Do you have an exact address?'

'Kind of. Shall I call Norfolk?'

'Yes, but I want to be there.' The adrenaline began to pump into his bloodstream. The thrill of the chase. 'How long will it take to drive to Holkham?'

'About two hours apparently, this time of night.'

'Well, nothing's likely to happen in those two

hours is it?' He looked out at Helen's garden, shrouded in darkness, the rain driving at the window now, wondering if he could take the risk of not sending uniform round there immediately. He *needed* to be there, that was the truth. 'I'll pick you up. Anything else?'

'I finally got hold of Jan Martin. She has confirmed that Lethbridge *does* look like Lamont.'

'Right. Any news on Watson?'

'No, guv.' Kenton was rueful. 'He's a sticking point still.'

'Good news?' Helen asked as Silver hung up. 'Have you found her?'

'Claudie? Possibly. Not sure yet. Have to go to Norfolk and look.'

'I wonder—' she began, then broke off.

'What?' He took a final swig of coffee, standing beneath the huge Renaissance print on the kitchen wall. Too many fat little cherubs for Silver's taste; a huge blue sky and wispy clouds.

'Should I come with you? Would that help?'

'I'm not sure.' He looked at the woman, calculating; he glanced at the photos on the side while he contemplated her words. 'We have no guarantee that we will find Claudie, of course.'

'Of course. Oh, but I hope you do. I'd hate for anything to happen to the poor girl.' Helen's grey eyes were filled with hope. 'I've become so fond of her. I really would be glad to accompany you.'

'Come on then, Mrs Ganymede.' Silver made a snap decision. 'Let's get cracking.' He could ask her thoughts on Rafe Longley as they travelled.

She smiled with relief. 'Brilliant. Let me just tell my husband, and I'll be right with you.'

MONDAY 24TH JULY
CLAUDIE

I crept down the stairs, the flagstones freezing beneath my bare feet. I could hear them talking in the kitchen, the low murmur of women's voices, and then Sadie, louder, getting upset about something, her high voice raised, querulous now.

'I'm just not sure—' I heard her say and I wanted to hear more, but then someone dragged a chair across the floor noisily and I thought, I have to go now, or I will miss my chance.

But the front door was locked. I rattled it as hard as I dared without attracting too much attention: it was definitely both locked and bolted. I heard the chair scrape again and someone say 'I'll get it'. In the nick of time, I ducked down behind the stairs.

The woman called Miriam stomped out looking bad-tempered. She had a key round her neck on a grubby bit of ribbon, which she used to unlock the front door. Then, at the last minute, she was struck by something, some kind of thought. She walked back, her foot on the first stair. Please don't go up, I prayed desperately. Please. She paused—and then turned and went out of the front door, a blast of cold air making me shiver, leaving the door ajar behind her.

I knew I only had one shot at escape; I peered round the door into the yard, the voices in the kitchen now beginning to escalate in a way that suggested the start of a row. 'Why have they left it so late?' I heard Sadie say, 'the rest of them are—'

I had to go. Wearing only the thin summer

pyjamas they had dressed me in when I arrived, I stole across the courtyard, round the back of the old white Golf, keeping as close to the buildings as best I could, watching for Miriam. I wondered if that was the car that had brought me here.

The fresh air was a shock to me after a few days inside, the smell of countryside, manure and grass so strong I could almost taste it; my heart was beating so fast that it hurt.

Something screeched and shot out of the undergrowth beside me and I nearly screamed, realising at the last minute it was only a skinny old farm cat. I would have laughed at myself, only right now it didn't seem all that funny. I spotted Miriam far on the other side of the yard, through the open door of one of the dilapidated barns. She was gathering bottles of what looked like bleach into a cardboard box, with her back to me.

The moon was on the wane but I could see the five-bar gate now; the night was bright enough for my eyes to adjust quickly to the dark, and I sped up now, my feet squelching through God knows what, and I saw tiny lights in the distance and realised it was a road, and from the other direction I heard the sigh of the sea, and I climbed the gate, tearing my pyjamas on the wire that held it shut, and I was down on the other side, and I started to run, run, run . . .

MONDAY 24TH JULY
KENTON

Kenton was more excited than she'd felt in years. This was it—her first big arrest! As soon as she got off the phone from Silver, she'd called Norfolk Constabulary and they had agreed to flag up the perimeter of the farmhouse building Pritti had identified on Google Earth—after a lot of crying and hand-wringing and coercion.

Waiting out in the station forecourt, Kenton rang Alison to share her news—it seemed a good reason to call. But Alison didn't answer. Kenton hadn't spoken to her since she'd left her bed yesterday morning and, try as she might, she had a slightly sick feeling in her stomach that it had all happened too fast—the falling into bed—and Alison had lost interest already. Surely she should have heard from her by now? Kenton left what she hoped sounded like a breezy message on Alison's voicemail, trying not to let the doubt creep into her voice, and pocketed the phone. Hopefully Alison would ring back before Silver arrived, and set her mind at rest.

She didn't. As Silver pulled up, Kenton could see there was someone in the car with him, a middle-aged fair woman wrapped in a pink pashmina, who smiled at Kenton and moved into the back seat as soon as he stopped the car. Silver introduced them quickly; Helen Ganymede, Claudie Scott's psychiatrist. The two women exchanged brief greetings as Kenton buckled up, pushing the guilt she felt about Scott down as hard as she could.

337

'So,' Silver pulled off again, heading for the A12. 'What exactly did Pritti say? What made her change her mind?'

They spoke in low voices, although Helen was already dozing in the back.

'She was totally reticent at first, until eventually we showed her the pictures of Meriel burning. Eventually she cracked and broke down completely.'

'Nice work.' Silver's face was grim. 'If that's what it takes. Did she shed any light on the Archangel idiot?'

'No. She just refers to him as the Divine One or "our leader".' Kenton shivered. 'Scary, really. It's like—she's not there any more.'

'Not there?'

'Like, not in her body. Brainwashed. She's just repeating—you know. Clap-trap she's been taught. I left Craven with her though.'

'Poor girl,' Silver muttered. 'Is there any gum in the glove compartment?'

Kenton rifled through it. 'Anything from Claudie's husband or boyfriend?'

'Husband's a hopeless arse and the MP's a charlatan, but that doesn't necessarily make him a kidnapping nutcase—though he has been up in Norfolk and he has some kind of link with Tessa, too, that he's lying about. I've asked Roger to check him out, but my gut says he wouldn't have the time to be the Archangel, in between shagging women and sorting the country's cultural desert out.' Still, there was the Lethbridge link. Bloody woman, kept cropping up. Silver fell into a reverie as Kenton surreptitiously checked her phone for the tenth time since leaving London. She definitely had a full signal and no messages. Damn.

'Do me a favour.' Silver tossed his own phone at her now. 'Text Philippa and explain I'm going to be working all night. You could even,' he grinned at her now, showing those perfect white teeth, 'you could even do one of those daft smiley faces at the end. Might soften the blow.'

As they drove up the empty A12, Kenton leant back and shut her eyes. She had found the images from the explosion had started to haunt her again during the past twenty-four hours: the body cleaved in two in the middle of the road, the whimpering and crying. Tessa Lethbridge's white face in deathly repose. She needed an end to this case now, have some kind of closure, some kind of retribution for those killed and wounded right before her very eyes on Friday 14th. And then she needed to sleep.

*   *   *

The traffic was light and the flat Norfolk roads empty. They arrived at the grand entrance to Holkham Hall in good time, next to a pretty pub called the Victoria, the kind of place where middle-class couples took mini-breaks. There they met with the local Chief Superintendent, a tired, balding man called Ellory, who was very much of the old school. He had a year until retirement and wanted no bother on his watch.

'We've got cars and uniform at every strategic point around the building you identified.' He looked concerned. 'But I have to say, I am not convinced it is the correct location.'

'Really?' Silver frowned. 'Why?'

'Farm concerned is owned and let by a local

family, the Thomases. It's rarely if ever empty; and there is a tenant farmer in residence right now, I understand, who has been working the land as they would expect.'

Silver felt the cold plunge of disappointment, but they had no choice but to plough on. Helen had woken up now and stood shivering by the car, the fringe of her pashmina blowing in the wind.

'You need to stay here,' he explained, and she nodded, looking rather frightened.

'Of course.'

Silver grabbed his torch. Kenton resolutely shoved her phone in her pocket and followed him as they walked to the perimeter of the farm, tracking across lumpy gorse land.

They circled the building and moved forward slowly on the word of the Chief. Lights blazed in the downstairs windows and a dog was barking out in the yard, getting more and more frenzied as he sensed the police approaching.

A man appeared in the doorway. The Archangel? He was silhouetted against the electric light behind him; Silver could make out the shotgun in his hand.

'Mr Gordon?' Silver called out now. 'Len Gordon?'

'Yes?' The man stepped forward, the dog jumping at his feet now. 'Who wants to know?'

Silver could hear the trepidation in his voice.

'Police. Can you drop your firearm please?'

Slowly, the man lowered the shotgun to his side.

'We need to search your premises immediately.'

'Search them?' The man held a hand over his eyes to block the torch-light that was now blinding him. 'Go right ahead. What are you looking for, mate?'

Silver met him in the farmyard now, by the gate,

and extended his warrant badge. 'Missing girls.'

The overweight farmer stared at him in shock, and then began to laugh. 'I should be so bleeding lucky. Wife left me three year back; last girlfriend didn't like getting her feet muddy. Stuck-up cow.'

Silver could smell the whiff of alcohol on his breath, and recognised the slight stagger.

'Look away.' Len Gordon stepped back and extended a thickset arm, gesturing at the outbuildings. 'You'll be lucky if you find so much as a female rat round here.'

They searched. There was nothing. The farmer watched them as if they were entertainment especially for him, red nose bulbous, chuckling, whisky glass in hand.

'Have you tried down the lane?' Gordon enquired, as they regrouped in the yard.

Silver frowned. 'The lane?' The bastard Beer was whispering as he watched the gold liquid in Gordon's glass tip perilously. The man gestured unsteadily down the track.

'Disused farm. Last owner shot himself in the head.' Gordon rubbed his jelly nose, then downed the contents of the glass. 'Don't bloody blame him, personally. Considered it myself once or twice.' He picked up his gun, cradling it like a baby in his big arms, the thick fair hair there glinting in the torch-light. 'Have a look down that way. There's either ghosties camping out there, or my eyes have been playing tricks on me recently. Lights in the windows and that. Cars back and forth.' He shrugged. 'I thought it were gyppos.'

'Did you report them?' Silver asked sharply.

'Leave 'em to it,' Gordon turned back to the house. 'That's my motto.'

341

Hope is a double-edged sword, lacerating us when it proves futile.

Down the lane, they were too late. The decaying farmhouse was empty, Kenton realised with a thump of frustration—but it hadn't been until recently.

No Sadie Malvern, no Claudie Scott—though Sadie's bag was still in the kitchen, an expensive leather affair with a Mulberry tag, which definitely looked more lap-dancer than religious zealot. The old metal kettle was still very slightly warm, which meant they couldn't have left that long ago.

'Damn, damn, damn.' Silver stood stock still by the door, above which someone had painted the words:

DADDY'S GONE A-HUNTING

Kenton sensed his deep anger, though he still managed to contain it.

'How the fuck did they know we were coming?' Silver rubbed his face with his hands. He looked exhausted.

'God knows.' Kenton gazed up at the scrawl. 'Perhaps they saw us at the other farm. That's from a nursery rhyme, isn't it? My sister always sings it to my nephew.

> *Bye, baby Bunting, Daddy's gone a-hunting,*
> *to get a little rabbit skin to wrap the baby Bunting in.'*

'Is it?' Silver rubbed his face again, trying to rouse

himself, but he felt tired beyond belief now. He had a sudden image of Lana cradling one of his babies, swaddled, singing quietly. He shook his head against the maudlin memory. 'So who and where is Daddy?'

Kenton shivered. 'It's really creepy, isn't it?'

Helen Ganymede entered the house now with a WPC.

'Any sign of poor Claudie?' she asked anxiously.

'No, none.'

But that wasn't quite true.

Upstairs on the single made-up bed lay a locket, the thin silver chain broken. A locket that Kenton remembered seeing round Scott's neck. It was full of acrid-smelling brown twigs.

'What do you think it is?' Kenton smelt it cautiously.

'I don't know. But we need to find out. Bag it.'

Silver looked out of the little casement window, across to the dark sea must be, whispering in the distance. Sure, he was worried about these missing women, but he realised with a shock that shook him almost viscerally that he was in the wrong place.

His phone began to ring.

'Silver,' he snapped. He listened for a minute, then looked up, his hooded eyes blazing.

'And you're sure it's her?'

He hung up.

'Sir?' Kenton held the little locket by her side.

'Claudie Scott. They found her on the road, about a mile from here, wandering round in her pyjamas.'

Helen sat heavily on the old wooden chair in the corner. 'Thank God.'

TUESDAY 25TH JULY
CLAUDIE

I sat in the interview room and waited for them. I was freezing, I couldn't warm up, despite all the hot drinks they brought me; I had been walking for what seemed like hours, but I'd lost all sense of time. I wanted to explain how messed up these girls were. But I was so confused again, I could hardly think straight, and I was in pain. Worse, I was frightened. I thought someone was going to come after me. I thought the police were going to blame me. I was losing my will to fight; I just wanted to close my eyes and to sleep now.

TUESDAY 25TH JULY
SILVER

'Something's not right,' Claudie Scott said, as soon as he came through the door.

He leant on the wall and looked down at her. She was still shivering, a blanket wrapped round her shoulders, her blonde hair all on end, tangled and tousled where she'd been forced to lie down, big brown eyes staring up at him like a child's. Haunted eyes. He thought of the photos in her flat of the little boy, the son she had lost. They looked remarkably similar, and Silver felt a stab of pity he didn't know how to convey.

'I see. Are *you* all right though, Claudie?'

She kept her hands in her lap beneath the table,

344

but he knew she was tearing at her own bloodied skin.

'I—I'm not sure.' She eyed the toast warily. She wasn't going to eat it, he could tell, although her face was hollowed, as if she had not had a square meal for weeks. 'I think I will be OK.'

He sat now, opposite her, and he studied her. The circles below her eyes were dark and ingrained, her pallor tinged with grey. She was a pretty woman, but she was destroyed, it was absolutely obvious. What could he do for her?

'Have we met before?' he asked.

'I don't think so.'

'You look a little familiar.'

She shook her head. There was a pen on the table; he turned it round neatly, thinking, and then he gave her a reassuring smile.

'So, Claudie. In your own time, I need you to tell me why you're here. How you came to be all the way out here. Did someone bring you?'

'Yes,' she nodded. 'And something's not right,' she repeated.

'What?' he said now. He could sense how frightened she was. 'What's not right?'

'I can't—it's hard to explain.'

They locked eyes. He desperately wanted to help her. Something in her vulnerability reminded him of Lana. He thought of the two men he'd met earlier, Will Scott and the suave MP. How they'd failed her. He could see her attraction for Longley, who obviously liked lost causes.

'That sounds stupid, I know.' She was stuttering slightly. 'I mean, I can't quite put my finger on it.'

'On what?' He willed her on.

'I think I might have done something bad. The

345

Friday before last.'

'What kind of bad?' Silver asked. He thought about unwrapping his gum, but it seemed a little inappropriate. So instead, he sat back in his chair and looked at her. He knew he had to wait, and eventually she would tell him.

'Very bad,' she muttered. She stopped again. He could hear the scratch scratch scratch of fingernails on dry flesh.

'Do you know my name?' he asked.

She shook her head. 'Sorry—I can't remember.'

'It's DCI Silver.' He wanted her to know he was a friend. He spoke gently. 'Joe Silver.'

Kenton walked into the room now. She smiled at the woman and Silver remembered they'd met before. Claudie gazed back at Kenton. She might have attempted a smile, but her face was so stricken it was hard to tell.

'And what happened to your face, Claudie?'

She raised her hand to her cheek. 'Berkeley Square.'

'Berkeley Square?' Silver sat up straighter. 'The explosion?'

She nodded.

'OK, Claudie,' he flicked the gum away and smiled at this broken soul again, 'why don't you start from the beginning? Who brought you all the way out here?'

'I think I might have done something terrible,' she repeated. She met his eyes this time. 'I think I might have killed a lot of people.'

TUESDAY 25TH JULY
SILVER

Silver drove Claudie Scott back to London early that morning after they had all had a few hours' sleep in a local hotel. Claudie was exhausted; nervy and obviously frightened, and Silver couldn't help feeling that, given her history, she certainly did appear a little delusional.

In the early hours of Tuesday morning, she had seemed convinced that she had had something to do with the bombing in Berkeley Square, that she had been there or if she hadn't, she should have been. But her memory was patchy, her brown eyes wide and staring, her raw, cracked hands shaking with an almost constant tremor. She had rambled about the Queen of Hearts and choppers chopping, and she kept saying 'as you like it' until Kenton and Silver's worried eyes met above her head.

The police doctor in Norwich checked her over and said that apart from some bad bruising and a cracked rib, she seemed all right; although she was also complaining of stomach cramps, which he gave her some medication for. He took some blood too, but they'd have to wait a day or two for the results.

She's under-nourished, that's for sure,' he explained. 'There's ketones in her urine. She's been starving.'

They couldn't persuade her to eat though; she kept muttering about poisoning and pushing food away. Helen Ganymede sat with her for a bit, until she slept, and Claudie seemed pleased to see her, which Silver hoped was a good sign, for Claudie's sake.

On the plus side, she was able to tell them that she had seen Sadie Malvern at the farmhouse, and also Pritti Vershani, whom she identified from a photo. Silver felt a burst of relief at the news of Sadie's presence, which didn't last long when Claudie informed them she thought that they were preparing for something big.

'They mentioned a package,' she said. 'I think Sadie is the one who is meant to be responsible.'

'And the man in your flat, Claudie? Who called himself Rafe to your sister?'

'Who?' She stared at them, dry lips cracked. 'Oh, you mean Francis Watts. He's my acupuncturist. Bit weird, but harmless I think. Friend of Tessa's.'

Not long afterwards, Claudie collapsed, doubled over with stomach pain.

'I'll accompany her to hospital if you like,' Helen offered. 'I'd be glad to.'

'We'll send a plod down too, to keep an eye for a bit. It's hard to know what she's dreamed up and what's real. Her sister will be here in a while.' Silver contemplated the situation. 'Kenton, find this Watts bloke and bring him in for questioning.'

'Where are you going?' She frowned at him.

'To the Royal Opera House.'

Silver was concerned he'd dismissed Rafe Longley too quickly. Okeke had brought him pages of a biography on the hot-shot MP, pointing out with some excitement that his full name—Rafael— was the same as one of the Archangels.

'I don't think he's old enough to be Michael Watson,' Silver shook his head. 'And the press would have got on to a minister having a dodgy background like Watson's'. Silver was desperate to

348

return home, shower and change, but the station bathroom would have to suffice for now. His worst nightmare was wearing the same shirt two days in a row; no matter how scrupulous he was it was impossible to keep white cotton as crisp and pristine as he liked over two outings.

He plucked the shaver from his desk drawer and took it to the window; watched Claudie Scott being helped into the ambulance, Helen Ganymede stepping in after her. He didn't for one moment think that Claudie had anything to do with the bombing; it concerned him more that it had served someone well to let her believe she might have been responsible.

Silver could sense Kenton steeling herself for an argument. He fixed her with a look.

'Look, I know you want to come, kiddo, but I need you to bring in the acupuncturist,' he murmured to her. 'It could be crucial.'

'OK,' she shrugged, her eyes filled with disappointment.

Silver addressed Okeke over the buzz of the shaver. 'What time's the Royal Opera House event start?'

'Four.'

It was already two.

'We need to be there if Longley is. Check with his office. And have we verified his movements in Norwich during his last constituency visit?'

'Yes, they largely check out.' Okeke perused his notes. 'But his next-door neighbour did say she saw him with someone late on the Saturday night.'

'Someone?'

'A young lady. Small and dark. Pretty. They were rather—enamoured, apparently.'

Silver grinned. Okeke's speech was so courtly and proper. 'Doesn't surprise me.'

TUESDAY 25TH JULY
KENTON

Craven saved Kenton the trouble of picking Francis Watts up. She was just finishing her double espresso from the canteen (marginally but not significantly better than the machine's coffee), and determinedly not checking her phone, wondering why Alison *still* hadn't called, when a shadow loomed over her.

'Derek,' she said wearily without looking up.

'Lady-boy to see you,' he sneered, jerking his balding head in the direction of the interview rooms. 'Don't say I never do anything for you.'

'Lady-boy?' she frowned.

'Name of Francis. Friend of Tessa Lethbridge. Sticks needles in folk for fun.'

'Francis Watts?' Kenton sprang to her feet. 'Nice one, Derek.'

They made a strange triumvirate in the bleak interview room.

'So, Francis,' Kenton said carefully as Craven fiddled with his plastic cigarette. She *really* didn't want to blow this. 'What were you doing in Claudie Scott's flat and how did you know Tessa Lethbridge?'

'I met Tessa when she contacted me through my website.'

Kenton frowned at Craven. 'What website?'

'I don't run it any more, but I did for years. It was the old Empathy Society one,' he sighed, running

350

his fingers through his horrid hair. 'Tessa read about us in some New Age journal—*Crystal Life*, I think. I haven't run the Society for years but I'm not ashamed of what we stood for.'

'So your name is not really Francis Watts.'

He sighed again. 'No. It's not. It's the very ordinary Michael Watson.'

Kenton tried to hide her excitement.

'And you say Tessa and you only met—recently?'

'Last year some time.'

'And Tessa is not Rosalind Lamont?'

He stared at Kenton and then began to laugh. 'Rosalind? Tessa? Are you out of your tiny little tree? Hardly.'

Kenton bit her tongue. 'So would you mind telling me where Lamont is?'

'I have no idea.' Watson ran his hand through his nasty little beard and added sorrowfully, 'She lost her way some time ago. We had a lovers' tiff or ten, and she went abroad for a while. Then she married into money and we fell out. We began to move in totally different circles.'

'Money?'

'Some banker type. Foreign, I think. Possibly Russian.'

Russian . . .

'His name?'

'I don't make a habit of remembering my ex-girlfriends' husbands' names.' Watson fiddled with the black rubber circle that stretched a great hole in his lobe. Kenton suppressed a shudder. Did he really think a tribal earring looked fitting on a fifty-year-old? 'Sorry.'

'So why change *your* name?'

'That's what we did, my love.' He looked down

his beaky nose at her. 'We were activists. We were undercover half the time. We didn't want to be hounded by the fascist state. We wanted to be free.'

Echoes of Jan Martin, Kenton thought wryly. The man smelt like a scented candle. Utterly distasteful.

'We took our names from the great classics. It was a game really.'

'Gabriel Oak?'

Watson looked amused. 'Very good.'

'So you haven't seen Lamont for—how long?'

He squirmed slightly. 'Years.'

He was lying.

'Mr Watson, I suggest you tell us the complete truth.'

He sighed heavily. 'I saw her some time last year, for about five minutes. She booked an appointment at my clinic under a false name.'

'What name?'

'Bathsheba something'.

Craven let out a snort. 'Bath-whatty?'

But Kenton had done her research this time. 'Bathsheba Everdene—from the Hardy novel?'

'Yes,' Michael nodded slowly. 'I guess so.'

'And what did she want?'

'She wanted me to join some mad society of hers. She brought leaflets but I chucked them all in the bin. I can't remember its name, before you ask. I was worried by her, to be honest. She was a little— possessed.'

'Not the Daughters of Light?'

'Possibly,' he shrugged. 'I didn't take much notice to be honest. She was raving, I thought. I asked her to leave, and she told me I'd be sorry.'

'Can you explain why you were in Claudie Scott's flat, uninvited, last Saturday?'

Now he looked uncomfortable for the first time. 'I was worried about her.'

'Really?' Craven spoke now, his disdain obvious. 'Not because you wanted to make her disappear?'

'Why would I want to do that?' Watson frowned. 'I'd been treating her for some time. I care about her.'

'But she was frightened of you. Frightened enough to ring us. Why was that?'

'I don't know.' Watson toyed with the shark's tooth round his neck. 'She seemed quite paranoid. When I treated her the last few times, I knew something was wrong. Her system is utterly clogged. Her eyes were dilated recently, her blood pressure is too low. There's something very wrong, but I haven't been able to work out what.'

'And that must be frustrating for a specialist like you?' Kenton interjected.

'Well, let's just say I wasn't surprised when the hospital called about the contra-indications.'

'You've lost me,' Kenton shook her head.

'I took a call for Claudie when I was at her flat. She'd had some kind of test at St Thomas's. They said they found contra-indicated drugs in her bloodstream.'

'Contra-indicated?'

'Drugs she should not have been mixing. I wasn't surprised. Claudie's system was getting so weak. And with Tessa's tragic death—'

'Tessa who wasn't actually Tessa.' Craven scowled at the other man and shoved the plastic cigarette in his pocket. 'It doesn't really stack up, mate, if you know what I mean.'

Kenton was amazed that for once she and Craven appeared to be singing from the same proverbial song sheet.

'Look,' Watson sighed. 'I met Tessa because we shared an ideology, but one that I have no active part in any more. You have to believe me. I left all that rubbish behind me years ago. I have no interest in politics now. I retrained. I just,' he smiled a truly sickly smile, 'I just want to help people now.'

'And your relationship with Tessa?'

'Friends. Sometime lovers,' he shrugged. 'Love one, love all. She was a lost soul too.'

'So you know nothing about the Daughters of Light?'

Again, Watson looked uncomfortable, squirming slightly under their scrutiny.

'Well—'

There was a sharp knock on the door and Tina Price entered the room.

'DS Kenton, I need a word.'

'Now?' Kenton pulled a face.

'Yes, now, please.'

Kenton stepped outside the room as Craven took up the baton. 'So, about these bleeding Daughters of Light—'

'So?' Kenton could feel her own agitation; she wanted to get back in there with the two men. She had a sudden vision of Craven producing the result she'd worked so hard on, without her.

'Tessa Lethbridge,' Price said, her pleasant face eager beneath her shining bob. She would look much better once she got rid of the thick metal braces, Kenton thought absently.

'What about her?'

'I think we know who she is.'

TUESDAY 25TH JULY
CLAUDIE

I woke in the back of the ambulance and for a moment I thought I was trapped in my own worst nightmare again. Frantically I looked around for Ned; but he wasn't here; it was me on the bed this time.

Helen was here though. She was sitting beside me, holding my hand as we rattled over speed-bumps. The paramedic was fiddling with something in the corner, and Helen smiled down at me.

'Nearly there,' she said. 'You've done so well, my love.'

She bent her head nearer to me. 'I never thought you'd be so strong. You really have fought it every step of the way, haven't you?'

'Fought it?' I shook my head, the oxygen mask bound to me. 'The splitting, you mean?'

She gazed down at me. Round her neck was a locket, very similar to the one Tessa had given me. The tiny gold doll I'd seen before hung there, a Russian nesting doll, I'd had a set as a child. And entwined with it swung the locket decorated with a tiny little bird—a pigeon, perhaps, I thought, sleepily.

The paramedic glanced over and smiled at the touching picture we appeared to make.

'Nearly there,' he shouted over the engine's roar.

'I was just saying how well Claudie's doing,' Helen spoke up now.

'I'm sure she is,' he nodded in agreement, and

355

looked back at what he was doing. 'Not long now.'

A dove.

I struggled to sit up, but the blanket was trapping one arm, and Helen was holding the other.

'I don't feel well at all,' I mumbled.

'No, I'm sure you don't, my dear,' Helen smiled and squeezed my hand. 'Don't worry though. It'll all be over soon.'

TUESDAY 25TH JULY
SILVER

If the crowd at the Royal Opera House were your typical ballet connoisseurs, then DCI Joe Silver was very glad he was not one of them.

He'd tried to catch Rafe Longley at the Commons, but his secretary said he hadn't come in today, so Silver had no choice but to go straight to Covent Garden. Okeke pulled in behind a bashed-up white Golf and let Silver out whilst he parked the car.

By the time they met at the front of the Opera House, the place was packed; fur stoles, face-lifts and beige wool a-plenty; Jaeger and Jimmy Choo and everything Lana would have killed for. Okeke was impressed, Silver could sense, as he asked to be taken through to the Green Room where Longley was apparently preparing his speech. But the room was empty apart from a dumpy middle-aged woman with a bush of hair manning the tea and coffee urn. Her name-badge read 'Miriam'.

'I've not seen him,' she smiled politely, and Silver shut the door behind him.

He checked the time; this would be an opportune time to catch up briefly with Lucie Duffy. The stage manager was outraged that the soloist was going to be interrupted so near to her performance, but Silver was adamant.

'Police business can be crucial, kiddo, I think you'll find,' he drawled at the irate woman, whose purple crew-cut reminded him of one of Molly's fuzzy-felt boards. 'It goes like that, art or no art.'

Lucie Duffy's dressing room was round the corner from the Green Room. Silver knocked at the door and didn't wait for a reply. Okeke was standing behind him as Silver opened the door to find the MP for Norwich North with his trousers round his ankles, entangled between a gasping Lucie Duffy's muscular legs, her stiff snowy-white tutu adrift, at right angles with the floor.

'Oh my big prince,' Lucie was moaning. She caught Silver's eye and smiled triumphantly. 'You king,' she murmured again in Longley's ear.

Tutu must be scratchy, Silver thought.

'Excuse me.' Silver shut the door smoothly, hiding his grin. Okeke was embarrassed, on the other hand, deeply embarrassed; he'd already backed about twenty feet down the corridor.

'Perhaps, sir, we should come back.'

'No way, Roger,' Silver shook his head. 'No time like the present.'

He waited for a minute and then gave a short, sharp knock and reopened the door. Longley had managed to re-zip his trousers, a little red in the face, whilst Duffy looked utterly unruffled as she rearranged her skirts.

'I always find a few endorphins sharpen my performance,' she purred, moving to the dressing-table to fix her thick make-up, little tendrils of hair damp against her long neck. She caught Silver's eye again in the mirror. 'Don't you think, Officer?'

'Mr Longley, I'd appreciate a word.' Silver stood by the door, watching the MP tuck his expensive shirt back into his suit trousers.

'Right. Now?' Longley was sweating slightly, not as blasé as yesterday. Hard to be with Duffy's make-up smeared across one cheek.

'Yep. Now,' Silver nodded, narrowing his eyes at the other man. 'Prince.'

'Fine,' Longley was almost sulky, like a schoolboy. 'Where?'

'Don't mind me.' Duffy batted her lashes.

'In private, if you don't mind.' Silver smiled pleasantly at the young ballerina, extending an arm towards the door to show he was waiting for Longley.

Longley pushed past Silver, the smell of sweat and Gucci aftershave thick in the air.

'I have to make my speech in five minutes,' he grumbled.

'You were cutting it fine,' Silver observed mildly. 'I'll walk down with you.'

The two men took the back stairs to the auditorium, Longley fumbling for his notes in the inside pocket of his jacket.

'I hate these bloody events,' he muttered.

'Have you ever met a woman called Rosalind Lamont?'

'Never,' Longley shook his head.

'And your girlfriend calls you "Prince",' Silver remembered Paige's words from the hotel. 'Very noble. So you know Lucie's flatmate Sadie?'

'The blonde girl? I met her once or twice.'

Silver stared at him. 'Screwed her, you mean.'

The man cleared his throat. 'No.'

'Sure about that?'

'I might have—kissed her once.' Silver met his eye as they took the last corner of the stairwell. 'She was a very pretty girl.'

'Was?'

'Is.' He was defensive. 'I don't disguise my delight in attractive women, DCI Silver.'

'What was your connection with Tessa Lethbridge again?'

'None. Met her through Claudie. Have you found Claudie?'

'Yes. She's all right.' Silver thought of the lost soul he'd last seen being escorted into an ambulance. 'As all right as we'd expect right now, anyway.'

'Thank God. Where was she?'

'In a retreat. A messed-up kind of commune.' Silver smiled icily at the other man. 'In Norfolk, funnily enough. And you say you have no involvement with the Daughters of Light?'

'None whatsoever.'

'Well, we're just checking that out now.'

'Feel free.'

They reached the wings of the stage now. Longley swept his hair back, finding a small comb in his back pocket, and giving it a quick pass through his luxuriant mane with a somewhat sheepish smile. 'Pays to look one's best.'

'Really.' Silver raised an eyebrow as if he'd never checked his own appearance in a mirror.

The Chief Executive of the Royal Opera House was on the stage now, welcoming the gala crowd, thanking them for their attendance, bowing to the Royal Box where the Duke of Kent sat, and then welcoming Longley.

Longley took to the stage now, explaining fluently the necessity of the arts in today's society, thanking Sheikh Zayid, Prince of the Emirates and the Chairman of Shell BP for their sponsorship.

'We know art plays a major role in our lives, but without the money to back it, without the oil that runs through the very veins of our society, we would not be here today.'

Lucie Duffy was behind Silver now, a fluffy fleece wrapped round her sinewy frame.

'Sadie should be here somewhere, you'll be pleased to know.' Lucie unzipped her top, stretched out her feet with great delicacy and removed woollen legwarmers. 'She's coming today.'

'Coming today?' Silver frowned. 'Are you sure?'

'Yeah,' Lucie nodded, throwing the fleece on the floor next to the rosin box and bending to attend to the ribbons on her pointe shoe. 'She asked for back-stage passes.'

'You should have bloody let me know,' Silver snapped at her. 'Christ, Lucie, I told you, if you heard anything—'

Recriminations were pointless now; action was necessary. Silver summoned Roger Okeke who was hovering nearby, listening to Longley's speech.

'Roger, we need the Explosives team here like yesterday.'

Duffy's grey eyes widened in shock. 'Explosives?'

'Where's your phone?' Silver demanded. 'In your fleece?'

'No,' she shook her head. 'It's upstairs.'

'Do you know Sadie's number?'

360

'No. Sorry. No I don't. What's she done?'

'Right.' Silver was thinking on his feet. He knew his own phone didn't work in the depths of this great building. 'We have a problem.' He snapped a stick of gum in his pocket. 'A major problem.'

He needed to get everyone out of the Opera House immediately. He didn't know how much truth Claudie Scott had spoken; there was a fair chance she was suffering some form of delusion, but he couldn't take the risk. In Norfolk she'd definitely mentioned both a package and Sadie, and that could only mean one thing if Malvern was following the example of the other girls.

'Would she come in the main doors?'

'No,' Duffy shook her head, 'she'd come up through the artists' entrance.' Where they wouldn't search her.

Fuck. Silver grabbed the stage manager who was gathering Lucie's cast-off garments. 'I need to get the venue cleared—NOW.'

'Are you mad?' She frowned at him. 'I'm afraid that's not going to happen.'

On the stage, Longley was wrapping up and the *corps de ballet* were preparing for their entrance with a last-minute warm-up, bending and stretching gracefully as the orchestra began to tune their instruments.

'Bloody do it,' he grasped her arm harder, 'or I'll arrest you for manslaughter.'

Okeke ran back down the corridor. 'Explosives are scrambling now.'

'OK. Roger, we need to start clearing the—'

Duffy grabbed Silver's hand, digging her sharp little nails in so hard she drew blood, her face pale beneath the make-up.

361

'There she is,' she pointed into the opposite wing. 'Sadie.'

Sadie Malvern stood, dressed in a long, mauve dress. She was filthy, her long curls tangled, a beatific smile on her pretty face, a hand-drawn banner slung across her body that read *IN BEAUTY WE BELIEVE*.

She opened the white shawl she held closely across her breast. Round her slim waist was strapped a badly-made explosive belt.

THURSDAY 24TH JULY
KENTON

Kenton yawned widely, deeply frustrated that they'd had to let Francis Watson go for the time being.

'Nice try, Derek,' she gave her colleague a thumbs-up as he walked back into the office from seeing the man out. Maybe it was time to let bygones be bygones.

'Should have left me in there alone.' Craven pulled his top lip back like an old horse, his teeth like yellowing tombstones. 'Would have got a result that way.'

Price and Kenton exchanged glances as he wandered off. Price was busy downloading the information on Tessa Lethbridge from the PDF the Australian High Commission had sent, once their records had been checked and the name change registered. Not Tessa Lethbridge at all, of course, but plain Elaine Jensen, born in a tiny village just outside Queensland's Brisbane forty-nine years ago, with not a formal ballet qualification to her name.

Kenton pulled an A4 bit of paper out of the printer and made a list.

'*Queen of hearts*; *Daddy's gone a hunting*; *Atishoo atishoo we all fall down.*'

All nursery rhymes; all some kind of code. Representing people, Kenton was imagining—certainly the first two.

But who was the Queen of Hearts—and who the hell was Daddy?

'What does "*as you like it*" mean to you, Tina?' She glanced over at the young policewoman. 'Anything? Another kid's rhyme?'

'No,' Tina shook her head. 'It's a Shakespeare play. Celia and Rosalind in the Forest of Arden. I did it for A level English. Good play. About hidden identities. Subterfuge and disguise.'

Kenton wished, not for the first time in this investigation, that she'd paid more attention in English Literature instead of mooning over Diana Grills.

'Homoerotic you could almost say,' Price was warming to her subject. 'I think—'

'Rosalind?' Kenton sat up. 'Are you sure?'

'Oh yes, absolutely,' Tina nodded with some enthusiasm.

> '*From the east to western Ind,*
> *no jewel is like Rosalind.*'

Kenton's phone rang. Alison! At last. She felt a shiver of anticipation.

'I'm really sorry,' Alison said. 'I left my phone at my mum's on Sunday evening, and I've only just got it back now.'

'No worries,' Kenton breezed. Alison wasn't to know she'd been praying for her to ring for virtually seventy-two hours. Kenton smiled as she listened to Alison's story of woe, tucking the phone beneath her ear as she typed *As You Like It* into the internet search engine. She scanned the first synopsis of the play that came up.

'Christ,' she sat up straighter, 'I don't believe it. Alison, I've got to go.'

Kenton stood, grabbing her jacket.

'You come with me.' She flung the phone at Tina. 'And get me Silver on the phone, right now.'

TUESDAY 25TH JULY
CLAUDIE

They left me in a room with only Helen for company, and a policeman outside the door.

'I'm her psychiatrist,' she smiled at the nurses when I tried to tell them my fears; but they just thought I was rambling. 'Don't worry. I'll sit with her while we wait for the family. I'm afraid she might have to be sectioned again. She shouldn't be alone.'

'Who are you?' I gazed at her as I struggled again in the bed, but the drips were restraining me. Why did I still feel so damn ill and weak? 'You're one of them, aren't you?'

'You can call me Rosalind if you like.' Helen pulled her hair back, smiled that crocodile smile. 'You know, I never thought you'd be able to function for so long with all those drugs pumping round your system. Hang on a sec.' She plumped up

364

my pillow for me.

'Drugs?' I couldn't speak properly; my voice was just a croak.

'Fentanyl is such a brilliant invention. Over eighty times stronger than morphine. Those "nicotine" patches.' She smoothed my hair back. 'It was like giving candy to a baby. Bye Baby Bunting,' she smiled again. 'My God, what a stroke of genius. You didn't know whether you were coming or going, did you, dear?'

'I feel terrible,' I murmured.

'You're in severe withdrawal, I'm afraid.'

'Oh God.' The cramps, the sweating. It made some kind of sense. 'But why?'

'God had nothing to do with it—only playing God perhaps.' she patted my hand. 'I did hope you'd join the cause but I realised some time ago, you were too far gone. I thought Tessa would have been able to bring you in, but she failed, in your case, quite spectacularly.'

'The cause?'

'And then I feared you knew too much. You were an interesting experiment really, my dear Claudie. John said I'd never be able to control you so well, but you just rolled over, really.'

'What are you talking about?' I was aghast. 'Who's John?'

'Tessa was not so easy, because she changed her mind. I believe she even tried to contact the police at the last minute. Fortunately they thought she was mad, and it was only luck that the blast still took her. Let the great spirit protect her. But you—you were a pushover, your system is so weak,' she smiled, and her fair-tipped lashes covered her treacherous eyes as she searched for something in

365

her bag. 'The Midazolam was a genius stroke after you spoke to Tessa on the Thursday night. Thank goodness you were overheard.'

'Midazolam?'

'It's a powerful drug, my dear Claudie, usually used on anorexics. It causes what we term anterograde amnesia. You had no chance of remembering anything. Of course, Miriam phoned you a few times to check.'

I remembered the threatening phone calls; the voice I hadn't recognised.

'Tessa.' I stared at her. 'Did you kill Tessa?'

'No. Tessa killed herself. Trying to stop brave little Anita.' Helen gazed at me. 'Or rather, you could say *you* killed Tessa.'

My worst fears realised.

'Did I—' I could hardly force myself to say it. 'Was I there? In Berkeley Square?'

'No, Claudie. You were not there. You didn't make it. You were undoubtedly trying to reach Tessa to help her, but you failed. We removed you from Tessa's flat and made sure you wouldn't remember—though you did try so valiantly. You should be very proud of yourself.' Helen looked less amused now. 'In fact, you were a complete pain in the backside. Running all over the place, trying to find out what happened to your stupid friend. John was quite angry. With me, actually.'

She shot me a look as she fiddled with my drip now.

'So *how* did I kill her?' All the moisture was leaving my mouth. 'What do you mean?'

'You warned me of her fears. In our penultimate session. Don't you remember? Told me how strangely she'd been acting, and then Anita

366

confirmed it. I realised that Tessa had cold feet; that she might sing like a canary, as they say. I'd only been controlling her by threatening to expose her lies the last few weeks—and then she swiped my old passport from my office and tried to blackmail *me*. As if she could have.' She laughed with incredulity. 'So sad. She'd lost her faith.'

Vaguely I thought about the text message on my phone; of talking about Tessa during the session.

'But you hardly knew her.'

'That's what it suited me to have you believe. But I knew her before I knew you. It was she who recommended me to your delightful husband.'

'To Will? Don't tell me he's involved.'

'Of course not. But they were sworn to secrecy; Will because he thought he was doing the right thing in a "counselling" sort of a way. That you shouldn't know you had been discussed by your friends. His guilt manifesting itself, basically. And Tessa, well, she was key to the whole operation. She brought John the girls.'

'Who is John?' I asked again. I was nearly crying with frustration now.

'My husband. Ivan Adanov. He was a celebrated professor of politics back in Russia, where we met—before he was enticed into the capitalist world of banking and clubs. My one-time partner in the cause—though he chooses to take a back seat now.' Her forehead wrinkled unattractively as she frowned. 'I fear our paths are diverging now too, and that saddens me deeply.'

'The cause?'

'The Daughters of Light. Tessa believed so vehemently at first. My Queen of Hearts, bringing me the tarts. She was that kind of woman, led by

367

whoever was around. Poor plain Elaine Jensen.'

'Elaine?'

'Weaving a fabulous fictitious life around herself: deaths, and babies, and drama. Utterly pathetic. And then you. Annihilated by loss.' She patted my hand. 'But then,' she found what she'd been looking for in her pocket, something small and shiny, 'you did need help.'

'I thought it was your job to help people?'

'I don't care about individuals any more.' Helen stood now. 'No one can empathise today. I'm tired of listening to my patients bleat on about their pathetic little lives. Everyone's so wrapped up in their own mess. But I care. I care about this world that we are so busy ruining. I don't have the energy to worry about the individual now—I'm looking at the bigger picture, Claudia.'

'And what's that?'

'The planet, the world. That was my original quest, with Michael, until he reneged on it. And if something doesn't happen soon, if no one takes action, it will be too late forever.'

'Too late?'

'For the world. Forever. It's almost too late, but there is still time.'

'I don't know what you're talking about,' I croaked. 'Who is Michael?'

'Michael Watson. You know him as Francis. My original partner in crime. Before I met my destiny in John.'

I thought of the man in my flat, his guinea-pig beard, his hands on my body. I shuddered. 'He's part of this too?'

'No. No, he has become spineless. Although it was Michael who introduced me to Tessa, albeit

368

inadvertently.'

My head hurt. 'How?'

'I visited him last year. I wanted him to join me again; I needed a partner when John wavered in his belief. Tessa and I met in the changing room of Michael's clinic. We "bonded" immediately. Poor foolish Tessa. Afterwards, I forbade her to tell Michael of our allegiance. It was fortunate,' she smiled a rather ghastly kind of smile, 'that she generally did what she was told.'

'And Franc— Michael?'

She sniffed. 'He "found himself", the poor fool, by the time I found him again—he'd quite lost the will to change society.'

'By killing people?'

'It wasn't ever about killing people, Claudie.' Helen gazed at me and her face had a sheen of perspiration over it. 'It is about standing up for what you believe in. Making a difference. Blowing the lies open. I chose you, each of you, so weak, so empty. Empty, gaping vessels.'

'Empty?' I whispered.

'Yes. The dancers, broken by years of teaching by terror. Tessa brought them to me and John; she thought she was helping them find a new path. They were easy; never felt they were enough, never good enough, always striving for something. John used them as dancers and whores, and I trained them for the cause. It suited us both. And Tessa, she was easy too. With her pathetic web of lies which I unravelled in two sessions.'

I stared at her rabid face. 'And you?' I asked. 'Why did you do it? What broke you?'

A smile flitted across her neat features. 'I am not broken.'

369

'Oh yes,' I said, looking up at her. I summoned every single last ounce of energy I owned. 'You most definitely are. That is quite obvious. You reject this apparently narcissistic world—and yet this is absolutely about you. About control, about mirroring your image.'

'No,' her voice was shrill now, her serenity dissolving. She stepped back. 'It's about saving the world.'

'Pull the other one, Helen,' I said. 'There are better ways of saving the world than coercing young girls to kill themselves for your ideals.'

'Well,' she stared at me. 'We'll have to agree to differ on that.'

She moved back to the drip, fiddling again.

'What are you doing?'

'I'm helping you on your way. That's what you wanted, wasn't it? You gave up a long time ago, I realised that.' She sat on the bed, and took my hand. 'I felt for you, Claudia, I did really. I still have *my* empathy. I saw you were destroyed. Now, you can sleep.'

And she was right. I was destroyed. I tried to pull my hand out of hers, but I couldn't, it was too heavy. My body was becoming impossibly heavy.

'It's too late, Claudie. You rest now.'

'Too late?' My mouth hardly moved. It was as if I had been turned into air. I was air.

'Think about it, my love.' She stroked my hair behind my ear. 'There are far far worse ways to go.'

She stood by the door, ready to leave, and I gazed at her. I moved my dry mouth to form words—or maybe I didn't, maybe I just thought them.

'It's fine,' I said. 'You are mad, and you will be caught, and I will join Ned. I am more than happy

to join Ned.'
My eyes closed.

THURSDAY NIGHT, 13TH JULY
CLAUDIE

I get off the bus and I am retching into the gutter, I feel so sick—and then it passes. I sit on a bench under an elm tree and I am sweating and trembling, but the nausea at least has passed. My phone bleeps. It is a text from Tessa.

'I need to talk to you, Claudie, please. I am terrified, and I have a confession to make. You will hate me— but I need your help. Something very bad's about to happen and I don't know what to do.'

* * *

I flag a cab down in the sultry evening, and I try to catch my breath. I go to Tessa's. I buzz the intercom; she lets me up. Only it is not Tessa who opens the door. It is a woman I do not recognise. She has a mass of bushy hair and a horrible snout nose.

'Tess has had to go out,' she says.

'Oh,' I say. I feel uneasy. 'Do you know when she's back?'

'No,' she smiles. 'Soon. Why don't you wait?'

'I left something behind,' I lie, 'a dress I lent Tessa. I'll just fetch it.'

I go into the bedroom; I feel as if she might be hiding in here, but of course she's not. I ring her phone; she doesn't answer. I scribble Tessa a note.

As I prop it on the mantelpiece and walk through to
the living room, Tessa calls back.

'I'm at the Academy. Can you meet me here?'

'I'm at your flat. Are you coming home? I can wait.'

'Oh God,' she says, and she sounds scared. 'At my
flat?'

'Yeah, in your flat. Your friend let me in.'

'Claudie,' and she is whispering, 'get out of there.
Come and meet me here. But get out of there right
now.'

I hang up the phone. As I turn, the woman is standing
very near me. Too near.

'I have to go,' I say, 'I have to meet my boyfriend.'

'That's nice. Does he live near?'

'Not far.'

She stares at me expectantly.

'Maida Vale.'

'In the posh bit?'

'The new bit. Clifton Towers,' I say absently. My
mind is whirring; what is not right here? Who is she?

With a sense of relief, I open the front door.

'Oh, it's lovely there isn't it? Very grand.' She grabs
her tie-dye bag. 'I'll come down with you. I need some
cigarettes anyway.'

In the lift, I notice she smells of stale sweat. I try not
to wrinkle my nose. My head hurts still. Outside the
flats a beaten-up old Golf is parked.

'I can give you a lift,' the woman says, opening the
passenger door, and I start to demur. She is scrabbling
around in her bag now, and there is another figure
walking towards us very fast from a huge black Range
Rover parked on the other side of the road, a figure I

372

think I recognise from the corner of my eye, I think it is Helen, and I start to turn, to say 'No, really, thank you, I'm fine' but the snout-faced woman is stepping right up to me; she has something in her hand, she is bringing it up to my face, and I try to duck my head, hitting my hip on the open car door and then . . .

FRIDAY 14TH JULY:
THE BERKELEY SQUARE BOMB
CLAUDIE

When I got off the bus from Rafe's flat—fell off the bus even, the sirens started. Their electronic drone pierced the air like a screeching choir and God I'd never heard anything like it. Police cars and fire trucks and ambulances. The driver of the bus was being radioed constantly, and the passengers were starting to panic, and mutter, and the bus wasn't moving at all any more. I saw that the road had been shut off: police bikes and vans were parked haphazardly across the tarmac so it couldn't carry on.

I tried to push through—but a uniformed policeman stopped me.

'You can't go in there, love,' he said, and I thought I could smell burning in the air. 'Whole area's sealed off.'

'I work at the Academy. Just round the corner. The ballet school on Berkeley Square.' I checked my watch frantically. I had a knot in my stomach that said I was late. Too late. Though it was still only 7.41.

I had to meet Tessa. I couldn't remember why or where she was, but I was sure she had asked for my help.

373

'I have to get to work,' I cried. 'It's vital.'

'I don't care where you work, madam, you need to turn around now. The police cordon is being extended as we speak.'

A group of angry pedestrians had gathered behind me, and were starting to push and shove, and I was at the arrow-head of the crowd, and suddenly I found myself slammed into the policeman's serge chest.

'Easy, love.' His arms went around me for a moment and I felt strangely safe, like I could just stay here and see out the storm we were caught in, but then he was pushing me back, and depositing me beside him. 'Get back,' he bellowed at the crowd, and now other officers were appearing, and a loudspeaker was being used.

'We need everyone to evacuate this area immediately. Please leave the area, calmly and quietly. There is no need to panic,' said a woman's voice, but by now quite a lot of people were panicking.

'It's just like bloody 7/7,' a young Asian man with long hair and a saggy red jersey said mournfully. 'This is what happened that day.' And people picked up on that, and '7/7' went rippling through the crowd. A woman screamed and a couple of children started crying and I thought, something is very wrong, but I couldn't think what. My head was throbbing so badly, and I just kept thinking of Tessa waiting, and I had a sudden surge of energy. I tried to break through the crowd with some vague idea I'd make it through the cordon, but I tripped and went flying over someone's briefcase, and I fell awkwardly on the pavement, my cheek scraping the ground painfully, making my eyes water. Or maybe I was crying.

A couple helped me up, and asked if I was all right; and I felt wetness on my cheeks, blood or tears I didn't know, and a band of iron was tightening around my

374

chest and I realised if I didn't get out of this crowd, I would start screaming.

I put my head down and held my bag in front of me like a shield, and I managed to push my way out, away from the cordon, away from the smell of diesel fumes and the burning. When I was a bit further away, down by John Lewis, I turned round and looked in the direction of Berkeley Square and I saw a dark plume of smoke feathering up into the air over the rooftops and my stomach clenched again.

I tried my mobile phone. I would phone Tessa to explain, or Mason, and find out if everything was OK in the Academy—but there was no network, everyone was on their phone and the lines had all gone down.

I started to run. I ran straight into the path of a frenetic cyclist at the junction of Regent Street. And then I was not running any more.

TUESDAY 25TH JULY
KENTON

Kenton was sweating profusely when she reached the hospital reception.

'Claudie Scott.' She could hardly speak, she was so desperate. 'Just brought in by ambulance.'

'Are you family?' The blank-eyed receptionist gazed at Kenton, tapping bejewelled pink talons on the desk before her.

'No, I'm police, and I have reason to believe her life might be in danger. I need to find her NOW.'

But by the time Kenton reached Claudie Scott's room, Helen Ganymede was nowhere to be seen and Claudie Scott was sleeping.

'Stop everyone leaving the building,' Kenton instructed the policeman who had been stationed outside Claudie's room—but she knew it was too late. She sent Tina Price to check the hospital CCTV, but she knew that Ganymede—aka Rosalind Lamont—would be long gone.

Natalie Lord arrived as Kenton tried to reach Silver; he didn't answer. Kenton went into the little room where Claudie was asleep.

'I can't wake her.' Natalie was holding her sister's hand, which was entirely limp, her broad brow furrowed with concern. 'She seems very deeply asleep.'

A middle-aged nurse with exhaustion written all over her face arrived in the room with Claudie's medication.

'Is my sister all right?' Natalie asked the woman. 'I can't wake her at all.'

The nurse checked Claudie's pulse, frowning as she did so. She called her colleague who was at the nurse's station outside.

'Her BP's incredibly low. And someone's been fiddling with this drip.'

The other nurse frowned and pressed her pager.

'What's wrong?' Kenton took a step forward.

'I'm not sure.' The first nurse looked up at her colleague. 'Her breathing's very shallow; bp 70/40.'

The nurse tried to smile at Natalie, but she was obviously tense. She kicked something inadvertently as she leant over Claudie. Kenton swiped it off the floor.

'What's this?' Kenton asked.

The nurse took it.

'It's a morphine vial.' The woman pressed the emergency button by Claudie's head over and again. 'But not one of ours. I don't know what the hell's happened here, but we need a doctor, now. She's crashing.'

TUESDAY 25TH JULY
SILVER

Silver and Sadie stared at each other across the great stage.

'Sadie,' he was calm. 'Don't do anything silly, lass. Let's have a chat, shall we?'

Silver yanked Lucie Duffy with him as he slowly stepped towards the girl.

'You need to speak to your friend,' he muttered. 'Quickly.'

'Bring down the safety curtain now,' Okeke snapped at the stage manager. 'Now!'

For once, the fuzzy-headed woman did as she was told, eyes wide with fear. 'Is this a prank?' she mumbled.

'Does it look like one?' Okeke muttered back.

On the other side of the stage, the white-faced dancers in their courtly dress were frozen in fear behind Sadie.

'Sadie,' Silver said quietly. 'We need to talk. Can you walk towards me please? Just a little.'

'Come on, Sadie,' Lucie's voice was thick with fear. 'What have you got on? Doesn't go with your dress, babe.' She faltered. Silver squeezed her hand hard. Silver heard her inhale. 'I'll lend you the Westwood.'

Sadie took a few steps towards the middle of the stage, Silver and Lucie walked slowly to meet her.

They faced each other.

'What's this about, Sadie?' Silver asked the girl. Up close, she didn't look quite so calm, her whole body was trembling, her feet filthy and bare, her eyes wild.

'The Archangel has spoken,' she said. 'I am here to deliver us from evil.'

'Evil? Look where you are, lovie,' Silver was gentle, like he was coaxing a child or a nervous animal. 'There's no evil here. This is what you loved, isn't it, Sadie?'

'Sadie,' Lucie Duffy was trying not to cry, her terror was so immense. 'If you stop being so silly, I'll get you a part in the ballet. I swear. I'll talk to Monica Mason. She needs dancers like you. Don't do this, Sadie.' Lucie started to cry, tears rolling through the thick make-up. '*Please* don't do this. I don't want to die.' She was sobbing properly now.

Sadie was faltering, shaking, unsure what to do. Silver knew she was terrified.

'Sadie.' Silver took another small step towards her. In the wings, behind her, Okeke was moving the dancers slowly away. 'I saw your mum a few days ago. She's dying to see you.' A better choice of words would have been preferable, he thought, too late. 'She's waiting to see you. She's so proud of you. Think of Colin and your mam. Think of,' he took a deep breath, it was a risk, he knew. 'Think of little Jaime. She wouldn't want this, would she? Her big sister dying in agony?'

'Jaime?' Sadie frowned. 'What's Jaime got to do with it?'

'She loved you so much, Sadie, and she wouldn't want you to die. Not so young. Not with so much life to live.'

378

'But it's a bad life.' Sadie stuck her chin out in defiance. 'We need to take the message to the world.'

'And who told you that?'

'The Archangel.'

'And is the Archangel dying, Sadie? No, I don't think so.' Silver had nearly reached her side by now. 'No, he's sitting pretty, watching you do his dirty work.'

'Not he,' Sadie corrected carefully. 'She.'

'He, she,' Silver reached out for her hand. 'Whoever. Listen to me, lovie. Meriel's death wasn't pretty, Sadie—and it was entirely pointless. She died screaming. It will achieve nothing, lass, your death. It might be headlines for one or two days. And people won't understand, and they won't change their lives. But we want you to live. Don't we, Lucie?'

Lucie was crying so hard now she could hardly speak, but she nodded her head vehemently.

'Of course,' she managed. 'Please, Sadie.'

'Come on, Sadie.' Silver took her freezing hand in his. 'Let's take this silly thing off, shall we?'

And Sadie stared up at him, and he held her gaze, and he saw all of humanity's frailty reflected in her frightened eyes.

TUESDAY 25TH JULY
CLAUDIE

I am in the kitchen and there you are; you come trundling round the door, following the cat, and you are grinning in a way that means you have done

379

something naughty.

'Thomas through the flapjack,' you chuckle, a single trail of dribble on your chin, and you have put your Thomas the Tank Engine train through the cat-flap so it's fallen down into the mud. And I laugh, and scoop you up, your fat tummy swelling in your starry pyjamas, and I kiss it, and you chortle.

'Through the flapjack, hey?' I say, 'how about that?' and I press you to me and you smell so nice, you smell like life, and I hold you tighter, your pudgy wrist; I bury my face in your soft hair, and it tickles my nose.

And Helen always said the pain would lessen, and for all her madness and evil, she had helped a little. But the pain always comes again suddenly so I am transfixed by it, by a state I thought had lessened; that doesn't ever die down, that takes me by surprise, knocks me off my feet, comes in great waves like a wild sea; rendering me breathless and momentarily desperate. Trapping me as if I was in a small room pushing at each wall, only to find there was no way out. There is no way of winning, I know that now.

'Where do you go?' Will kept saying to me plaintively after you finally went, and I couldn't explain. But now I know. I went to the place where I could grab at ghosts.

'It will die down in time,' Helen had said, 'the pain.' But do you know, it never really has—and so I am happy to go now.

I am not coming back. Not without you.

TUESDAY 25TH JULY
SILVER

They laid the crude belt down on the stage and after a while, the Explosives team came to disarm it.

Silver took a still-shaking Sadie Malvern to sit in a dressing room whilst he waited for uniform to finish dealing with the evacuation of the building. Okeke was with Rafe Longley; Silver had asked him to hold him in the Green Room for now. It was apparent that Lucie Duffy, once she had stopped hyperventilating, didn't know whether to be glad that her friend had made the right choice, or angry that her chance to shine in front of minor royalty had been thwarted. She stood in front of Sadie for a moment, hands on her hips above her snowy tutu.

'Honestly, Sadie, are you completely mad?' She glared down at her. 'Actually, don't answer that. It's quite bloody obvious.'

The last Silver saw of Lucie Duffy was her stomping upstairs with her partner Kiko, intermittently swearing like a trooper and sobbing, her thick, black eye make-up running down her face in rivulets. As usual with Lucie, Silver was unsure of how pure her motives were.

'Would you like to speak to your mum?' Silver asked Sadie gently. 'We can call her if you like.'

Sadie shrugged her narrow shoulders, a birthmark the shape of a love-heart adorning the left one. 'Not really.'

'Oh come on,' Silver coaxed.

'It's not me she really cares about. Me mam.'

'I'm sure that's not true,' Silver frowned. He took

381

off his jacket and wrapped it around her shivering
shoulders. He noticed his own hand was trembling
slightly.

'She never cared much, not since our Jaime
passed.' Sadie turned those huge blue eyes on
him, like fog-lamps they were, or scraps of sky. 'I
recognise you, don't I?'

Silver shifted uncomfortably. 'Yes, kiddo, I'm
afraid you do.'

Sadie shrugged a tiny shrug. 'Best off away from
that lot, I am. I've got a new family now.'

They sat in silence for a minute.

'What's going to happen to me, Mr Silver?' she
said eventually.

'I'm not exactly sure, Sadie.' He weighed up
the truth; whether it was worth telling. 'You'll be
charged with attempted murder, I imagine—but
there might well be extenuating circumstances.'

'Like what?' The girl gazed at him.

'Well, who made you do this? Was it Longley?
Your boyfriend? The Prince?'

'No.' She shook her head fervently. 'He's not my
boyfriend. He's been shagging Lucie, but he's nowt
to do with me, that Rafe. He's a stuck-up tosser.'

'So,' Silver prompted gently. 'The Archangel, who
is he? Do you know his real name?'

'*Her* real name,' she reproved him. She wound her
friendship bracelet, a little string of sky blue, round
and round her wrist until it was tight. 'I told you.
Her.'

'Who is she?'

'John's wife. Helen.'

Silver stared at her. 'Helen? The psychiatrist?
Who's John?'

'John?' Sadie blinked up at him. 'John's Helen's

382

husband. I think she is going to leave him though. She is so—pure and he, he is about money and stuff she hates.'

'Sadie, love, you've lost me. Why does she call herself the Archangel?'

'Because she is leading the revolt in heaven.'

'And John? The husband? Is he in heaven too?'

'Hardly,' Sadie's lip curled. 'Only when he's fucking young girls. It's not his real name. His real name is Ivan Adanov, Helen told me, but he'd kill you if you called him that. John owns Sugar and Spice. He used to be the same as Helen but she says he's changed. Still, he lets Helen do what she likes, and she looks the other way.'

Craven arrived at the door of the dressing room now, lumbering like an old bear in a zoo.

'We picked up a woman called Miriam round the corner; she was driving the white Golf from the CCTV footage. And Kenton's trying to get hold of you, guv. Urgent.'

The white Golf. Of course. Silver stood now. 'Where is Kenton?'

'At the Royal Free Hospital. The girl Claudie Scott,' Craven was mumbling now, he could see the distress on Silver's face and for once he was sensitive to it. 'I'm afraid it's not good news, guv.'

Silver thought of the psychiatrist's perfect house, of the Renaissance print of the Archangels' battle in heaven, of the photos on the sideboard. Of the husband with the dog. The husband whose face he thought he recognised in the photos; of the man sitting in Sugar and Spice quietly adding up figures. Of the instinct Silver had ignored when he chose to fly down to Norfolk that night.

'Fuck.'

383

'Stay with her,' Silver ordered Craven, indicating Sadie who was staring at the ceiling, murmuring quietly to herself, and he walked out of the room. He kicked the next door along the corridor so hard that it cracked. Then he kicked it again. He walked down the hall and the bastard Beer was screaming in both ears, and he knew he'd messed up fatally.

TUESDAY 25TH JULY
KENTON

Kenton took the call from Silver as she was leaving the hospital.

'Get to Helen fucking Ganymede's house now and check the bitch isn't there. I doubt she'd be so stupid—but you never know with a lunatic like her. Apparently she is the infernal Archangel!'

'Gladly, sir.'

Price put the blues and twos on and they drove, sounding like banshees from hell; from the hospital to Hampstead Heath. They skidded down Ganymede's road and Kenton took the drive corner far too fast and they—

They hit Helen's Range Rover head on.

Of course, Helen was far too elegant and restrained to even show the tiniest amount of terror or regret, and she certainly wasn't about to try to run. But Helen Ganymede—aka Rosalind Lamont—had finally slipped up. She should never have gone home, but she was exactly the kind of solipsistic sociopath who would believe she could get away with behaving however she wanted. Her black Range Rover was packed to the hilt,

384

and they learnt later that she had locked up the house, alone apparently, and was about to head for the Eurotunnel when Price and Kenton had apprehended her. She had greeted them with a smile as she stepped down from her car, holding a book carefully against her leather jacket, and had remained entirely calm during her arrest. As Kenton thought of Claudie Scott lying in that hospital bed, she felt hot tears spring to her eyes.

'How could you?' Kenton said as she escorted Helen to the marked car that had just arrived. 'She trusted you, absolutely.'

'She was right to trust me. She has gone to the best place, poor Claudia,' the woman smiled beatifically, and ducked her head gracefully as she was pushed into the car, and Kenton found that she had no strength left to argue. Because who was to say that Helen wasn't right? Claudie Scott had lived in purgatory; she had given up the fight for life the day her son died. As Kenton went to shut the door, Helen held out the old book she had been clutching. It was a dog-eared volume of nursery rhymes.

'It was mine when I was a child. I don't need it any more,' Helen said as Kenton flipped open the front page. *Rosalind Lamont* was scrawled there in spindly writing, the ink faded. 'I never had my own kids,' Helen blinked once, twice. 'So I was mother to those poor lost girls instead.'

Kenton slammed the door hard.

She gave the book to Price and walked off for a moment. She stood on the edge of Hampstead Heath as Helen was driven away, hands deep in her pockets, and she breathed a huge breath—but still she felt she couldn't drag enough air into her lungs.

She was exhausted, right down to her trainered toes. It was the end of a truly terrible day, and she didn't trust herself to speak to anyone right now; but at least they had apprehended the chief suspect.

Uniform had gone straight to Sugar and Spice. The club had been closed and the entire contents of its offices impounded. But Kenton had a nasty feeling that they would find nothing much. Already the Russians' lawyers were screaming, forming a pincer-like movement around the police investigation; already the Chief Superintendent's phone was ringing. Kenton had learnt from Silver that Lamont's husband was John Adamson, aka Ivan Adanov, formerly of the Hoffman Bank, now partnered with two Russian oligarchs in Sugar and Spice. Apparently they enticed various girls into their ring of vice. But of Ivan Adanov, aka John Adamson, there was as yet no trace.

Francis Watts had apparently told the truth; that he had been approached by Helen soon after he'd met Tessa when Helen had tried to coerce him into joining her and the Daughters of Light. When he refused, she had used Tessa to demonstrate her power, although Francis swore he had no idea. To Helen, it was obviously all a game. Just like the name changing was a game long indulged in by the pair, since student days. Lamont and Watson, changing their identities to fit with their favourite books. Michael Watson, sometime Gabriel Oak, now Francis for the reprobate Captain Francis Troy in *Far From the Madding Crowd*. And Ganymede— Rosalind's alias in Shakespeare's *As You Like It*; the whimsical code Tessa Lethbridge had faithfully recorded as she tried to crack it.

Further lost souls Sadie Malvern and Pritti

Vershani languished in the cells at the police station, poor misled girls. The post mortem on Edna Lamont had showed an excess of diamorphine in her blood; the implication was that Vershani had been coerced into administering it by the Archangel. She had met Helen Ganymede at the clinic they both worked in a few years ago, and Ganymede had got her a job at the nursing home to keep an eye on her aunt. A fatal eye, as it turned out; disposing of the old lady when she threatened to reveal Ganymede's true identity. Too late, Henrietta Lamont, Rosalind's younger sister, had flown in for the funeral. Too late for Claudie Scott.

Kenton yawned and pulled her jacket tighter round her in the chilly damp evening. If Kenton had anything to do with it, Jan Martin would also be brought in tomorrow for wasting police time. Despite her protestations, she had deliberately lied to protect Lamont's identity. Once Lamont had realised she'd been questioned, she had visited Jan Martin in Spitalfields and persuaded her that she was doing the right thing throwing the 'fascist police' off the scent.

She thought of Claudie Scott, lying motionless in the Royal Free. This wasn't the result Kenton had anticipated; it was far far worse.

Tomorrow, she knew, the Royal Opera House incident would be all over the papers . . . *Here comes the chopper to chop off your head.*

Tomorrow she was going to interview Helen's sister Henrietta, forty-eight hours too late, and then she would learn what she could have done so desperately with knowing last week.

* * *

387

Rosalind Lamont's younger sister looked just like her older sibling, only less expensive and less washed out, with her sunburnt complexion and thick brown eyebrows. Whilst Rosalind had eschewed the hippy apparel of her youth, Henrietta had apparently embraced it, clad now in a paint-stained fisherman's smock and old denim flares. Her thin hands were coarse and scratched; when she saw Kenton glance at them, she laughed and splayed them out before her.

'Nature of the beast, I'm afraid,' she said. 'Farming in Nova Scotia is not for the faint-hearted, I've learnt in the last five years. Bloody exhilarating sometimes, but exhausting.'

But when she heard the nature of Helen's crimes, Henrietta stopped laughing, her ruddy face appalled beneath the shock of grey hair.

'Are you sure?' she kept repeating at first, though to whom it was unclear. '*Killing* people?'

'I'm afraid so,' Kenton nodded gravely, and waited for Price to bring the woman sweet tea for the shock before they continued talking.

Henrietta was at least able to shed some light on Helen's marriage to the mysterious John Adamson.

'Ivan? Ros met him about eight years ago when she was travelling. Just before she retrained as a shrink.'

'She wasn't a proper psychiatrist, was she?'

'Wasn't she?' Henrietta shook her head. 'I assumed she was. She did so well in everything she set her mind to.'

Like killing innocents. The thought obviously crossed her sister's mind too as she looked blankly at Kenton, fear in her eyes.

'No. You have to be a doctor first. Her credentials don't check out, I'm afraid. Why did she want to retrain?'

'Said she wanted to "help" people. Had a lot of therapy herself. She was born with a terrible stammer; was teased dreadfully as a child before she overcame it. But I never really bought the helping people line, I have to say. I think it was always about—knowing more than the next person.'

'And the husband?' Of whom there was still no trace. Kenton held out little hope that he would be found easily.

'Russian fellow, apparently related to the Tsar. Ooh, she liked that, my big sis. A snob to the end. A white Prince, she used to boast. My father was so appalled, he kept it from the rest of the family. Damned commies, he used to say.'

'*Was* he a communist? John—Ivan?'

'God, no, I doubt it. He was a professor of politics back in Moscow, but he seemed more intent on capitalism after some time in London. I know Ros thought he'd renounced his principles. Scared me really, the few times I met him. He was very—cold. He would look through you as if you didn't exist. And as far as I could see,' Henrietta practically harrumphed, 'he had no interest in anything but making his next buck. Very clever man, but—you know. Jeremy detested him.'

'Jeremy?'

'My husband. Couldn't stand all that—wealth. You know, ostentation. Common as muck, really. What do they call it? Eurotrash.'

Kenton didn't bother to point out Russia wasn't in Europe.

'And to be honest, Ivan didn't want to be Russian

389

any more. He changed his name when they married, when he was naturalised.'

And he had covered his tracks very cleverly, Kenton thought, there was no doubt he paid someone at the Deed Poll service to 'lose' his original identity so the police could not follow his trail.

'But why would someone like Helen—sorry, Rosalind—be interested in a man like that?'

Henrietta stared at Kenton. 'Power, my dear. He was utterly powerful—and utterly deadly I should say. And Ros is all about power. Forget about those stupid hippy ideals—that was all about ruling the world too.' The woman broke off, gazing into space for a moment. 'I can't believe it.' She shook her head again. 'I mean, she was always wild, but this—' She clasped the scratched hands tightly before her. 'Christ. Thank God my parents are dead. Thank God. Because this would have killed them both.'

For a second her face crumpled, the thick eyebrows drawing in like two teacher's ticks. 'I still can't believe it. How absolutely ghastly.'

TUESDAY 25TH JULY
SILVER

Silver had been heading back to the station to interview Helen Ganymede when he had taken the call from Philippa. In an instant, his world turned on its head with such alarming speed that it knocked the very wind from him; it turned in a sickening way that made everything else seem entirely irrelevant.

He couldn't get to the hospital quickly enough.

Okeke drove him, blazing down the wrong side of the road, the siren blaring, and Silver couldn't speak; found himself praying, his hands clenched so tightly that they hurt for hours afterwards. If he didn't get there in time, if he didn't—he couldn't countenance the thought. An image of Claudie Scott cartwheeled through his aching head, and he thought of her lying prone on the other side of town, the opposite direction to where he was now headed. And the pity he'd felt in that Norfolk interview room for a woman destroyed by the loss of her child became a pain in his chest so intense he almost couldn't breathe for a moment.

'Roger,' he muttered.

'Boss?' the other man said, without taking his eyes from the road. They ran the next red light, and the next.

'Hurry up, for Christ's sake.'

TUESDAY 25TH JULY
KENTON

Kenton breathed the thick London air down into her lungs and turned back to the car. Right now, she needed some respite, and she needed it fast. She called Alison.

* * *

Alison brought a copy of the *Evening Standard* to the noisy pub.

'Bad day?' She handed Kenton a pint and ruffled her hair affectionately. 'Have you seen this, by the way?'

In the paper there was an article about Tessa, the headline beside an old, grainy shot of the woman, her hair much shorter, her smile almost tremulous.

'The fantasy life and lonely death of the ballet teacher killed in July 14th bombing.'

Kenton read the piece, heart thumping.

How the Australian primary school teacher Elaine Jensen managed to steal the identity of ballet teacher Tessa Lethbridge and pass herself off as a leading light at our esteemed national ballet school, the Royal Ballet Academy, has caused all sorts of questions to be asked within that organisation. As Jensen's father Peter arrives in London today to bury his daughter, the tragic irony is that if Jensen hadn't been killed in Friday 14th's explosion in Berkeley Square, the truth might never have been unearthed.

So what prompts someone to use an entirely stolen identity? Ordinariness, it seems. 49-year-old Elaine Jensen apparently led a lonely and rather sad life in Melbourne suburb St Kilda, until a chance meeting with the real Tessa Lethbridge at a charity event in the city's Arts Centre descended into a form of hero-worship. The real Lethbridge is a highly qualified and well-regarded teacher who trained alongside various stars in the late 1980s, and once headed up the prestigious Melbourne Ballet School. But when Jensen became obsessed with her, Lethbridge took out an injunction to stop Jensen hounding her, after she was found by police in the other woman's flat.

Colleagues of Jensen's in Melbourne primary St Fitz's have been commenting on the elaborate stories she would tell, culminating in a fake pregnancy and a death notice that she placed in the Australian Times.

'She was a perfectly nice woman,' said Rebecca Learfont, 'but there was always some drama going on which became ever more complicated. In her last year here, Elaine told us she had had twins in the summer holidays who had then died—but we hadn't even known she was pregnant. In the end, we began to doubt the veracity of pretty much everything she said.'

In Britain, Academy staff are reticent on the subject of colleague Lethbridge; shock has undoubtedly set in and whilst they mourn her death, it is undoubtedly a strange position to find yourself in when you are not sure who exactly you are mourning.

Elaine Jensen. Even the name had turned out to be ordinary. Kenton chucked the paper back on the table.

'Shall we get out of here?' she asked Alison, and Alison stood, shaking back her black curls, and held out a warm hand.

'Come on then.'

TUESDAY 25TH JULY
SILVER

Lana and Ben walked through the ward doors in King's College Hospital, and Silver stood. Lana went straight to Matty's side, and Molly was there too, crying, sobbing now she'd seen her mother, plaits all awry, burying her face in her mother's hip as Philippa melted away discreetly.

'He's going to be all right, Lan,' Silver said, looking down at his sleeping son, normally so full of life, and he felt very old, so old at that moment. 'They've done the CT scans. There's no traumatic injury to the brain. He's going to be fine.'

Lana stared at him. 'Are you sure?' she whispered. Her big blue eyes were filling with tears now, and he reached out his hand.

'Yes, Lan.' She let him take her hand. 'They've assured us now. He'll be fine. They sedated him to do tests, but he'll wake up soon.' He felt a huge lump at the back of his throat, and he swallowed hard. 'I did tell him to wear that blasted helmet when he was on the skateboard. I kept telling him.'

'You know what kids are like, Joe,' she said, and he felt a throb of relief that she wasn't angry. 'It's not your fault.'

For a second they locked eyes over Matty, and Silver tried to smile, before Lana sank down onto the bed, beside her youngest son, and she buried her head in the blanket, and she sobbed. 'Thank God,' she sobbed, 'thank you, my God.'

Later Lana would explain where she had been this past week; how she had started to find hope;

394

how she had sworn to start afresh with her family. She had always feared this was her end; that this was what would happen. Since the day that she'd made the worst decision of her life, since she rolled that bloody car, since the day Jaime Malvern's little life was snuffed out, all down to her, she'd known that one of her own kids would be taken from her as payment, to avenge her sin. She had drunk more at first to block that thought and in doing so she had annihilated her own life, she had hidden in the gutter until she couldn't get up again.

Eventually she had seen some sense, and she had come back to her children. But she daren't love them too much: although she *did* love them more than anything. She loved every hair of their heads, every bone in their body, every freckle, every finger-nail, every lost tooth and scraped knee; it didn't matter if they argued or bickered, it didn't matter if they never picked up their dirty socks or made their beds or lied about where they'd been or kissed the wrong girl, she loved them so fiercely that it threatened to destroy her sometimes. Only she didn't dare show them; she didn't dare show Him up there, in case He realised and He took them from her.

Lana had been doing her deals with the Devil and her deals with her Maker since the day she got sober; only it hadn't brought her solace or peace.

Two weeks ago Lana had finally decided perhaps it was easier for everyone for her to end it. She'd sat on that beach last week and thought of walking quite calmly into that freezing sea. Until that man had been silhouetted on the cliff, and she had thought for a moment he'd come to claim her, to do away with her—until she realised he was a priest.

And Silver had to walk away himself for a moment, up to the vending machine, his arm round Ben, almost his height now, warm and sinewy beneath his father's arm.

'All right, son?' Silver said quietly, and he heard the slight catch in his own voice. 'Are you OK?'

'Aye, Dad,' Ben nodded his head, stuck his lean chest out manfully. 'Now our Matty's OK, so am I.'

Silver found himself craving open space, fresh air.

'I'm going to go outside for a minute. Want to join me?'

Ben shook his head. 'I'm going to call Emma, if that's OK.'

Silver made his way out of the sterile building, past the pictures painted by ex-patients called Hope and Despair, feeling a wave of emotion more powerful than any he'd felt in a long time. He walked away from the neon-lit entrance, leant against the wall in the darkness, and he looked up for the stars—but there weren't any. The city's pollution hid them.

Silver had had enough of London for a lifetime at that moment. He found his gum in his pocket, but all he really wanted was a cigarette. He didn't remember a craving this bad since the day of Lana's court hearing.

The truth was he felt heart-sick. He knew he had messed up. He had been distracted by Sadie Malvern; driven by his own guilt. He should have sussed Helen Ganymede; he'd ignored his gut instinct and chosen glory. At this moment, he utterly despised himself.

His phone bleeped. 'Silver.'

'All right, DCI Silver?' A little, rasping voice. Paige.

396

'I heard you was looking for me.'

He felt a rush of relief. 'Where are you?'

'I thought it was a good idea to keep my head down. Those Russians. Well. You never know.'

'Any idea where John Adamson is?'

'So you worked it out finally. You don't want to mess with them, know what I'm saying? That Ivan was a twisted fucker.'

'Will you go on record about that?'

She laughed. 'You're a trier, aren't you? I admire that about you.' There was a pause. 'I think you're a good man, DCI Silver. And believe me, there ain't many about.'

'Really?' He cleared his throat.

'And if you change your mind about that washing-up . . .' she tailed off. 'Well. You've got my number.'

Silver took a big breath of dirty air and walked back into the building. Ben was hunched over the pay-phone in the corridor, mumbling sweet nothings by the look of his flushed face.

Silver stopped at the drinks machine. A blonde woman stood beside it, searching her purse for change.

'Don't suppose you've got two fifties for a pound?' she asked ruefully. 'I really begrudge giving them any extra.'

She grinned. She was very attractive, Silver noticed absently. His eyes were gritty with exhaustion.

'You're in luck,' he said, digging in his pocket. As he handed her the coins, he realised that his hand was shaking slightly.

And as the woman thanked him, he heard the squeak and slam of the ward door as it was flung open fast.

'Daddy!' His daughter was there, tripping over her own feet, all breathless. 'Dad—Matty's awake!'

DCI Joe Silver was more tired than he ever remembered being before; more traumatised by a single day's events than he had been since Lana's accident; but at that moment he could have jumped for sheer joy.

Silver called Ben and then he hurried his pace; walked back down the hall to be with his family.

CLAUDIE

I dream you, and you are here, shadow made real. Like a great white bird, I scud over the land like passing cloud and it is night; I see you in the moonlight and I swoop down to fetch you. I gather you to me and this time, I will never let you go.

Come with me.

I fly to the end of the land and then I fly on. You are gathered to me, safe. I fly on, with you, into the night sky.

We don't look back.

*Read on for an exclusive
short story by Claire Seeber*

THE MIDDLE OF THE BED

How easy is it to shift into the centre of the bed? Impossible, you're finding: you do not belong there. For eight years you slept perched on the left side of the big mattress, only your breathing tangled together at night. Now you force yourself, you try; you keep edging towards the middle—but the human-shaped hole left there rolls you right back again, so you end up where you started.

Since. Since he went, you drink a lot of tea and eat a lot of biscuits: too many biscuits, you are vaguely aware. You're not even sure you like tea. You do not answer the phone or go and see Jane or Debbie, or his mother. Least of all his mother: you cannot bear the pain etched across the handsome face. You keep eating the biscuits at home for a while and then you move on to wine. Your heart feels like something raw and flayed, hanging in the butcher's shop. You're not sure it feels like part of you any more; it's separate. You appear to have separated.

And in between waking—never in the middle of the bed—and craving night again, somehow the days still begin and end. The sun rises, the sun falls. Somehow you feed the girls and put them to bed and get them up again. Somehow you talk and play and even keep on breathing.

Mrs Tanqueray from opposite stops you at the front gate one summer morning.

'Young widows,' she says sorrowfully. She has a slight accent you cannot place and her chest is all crepey; you don't want to stare, but Mrs

Tanqueray's gold crucifix attracts your eye, sways inside her flowery turquoise dress. You look down at the top of Tabitha's head instead; it's shiny, her parting a white road between blonde slopes. 'I was one too, you know,' the old lady says, her brown eyes hooded but kind. Gently she pats your hand that rests on the gate-post. 'A long time ago. If you ever want to talk.'

You force a smile; today, you do not care for conversation. You make a polite excuse; you walk to the shops. You are still numb; you find you crave fig-rolls. They suggest holidays in Greece before you had Tabitha. You see him reaching up and grabbing a fig, he held it to your lips and you felt a great wave of anxiety that you were supposed to do something with it that you did not really understand. 'Oh figs, aren't they an aphrodisiac?' he said, with a glint in his eye, and you tried to suck it in a way that would make him believe you knew about the world, about this scary world, only suddenly a big wasp crawled out of the fig and instead you gasped and dropped it. It splattered on the ground. He wasn't cross; he took your hand and you both stepped over it on the way down to the white-stoned beach. Only as you struggled into your polka-dot bikini, under that glaring midday sun, you felt you'd failed him somehow.

When you bring Geri home from nursery, Mrs Tanqueray waves from her window; her net curtains are quite grubby, you notice, inside her peeling blue-framed windows, although the glass itself sparkles. Her tortoiseshell cat sits beside her, alert on the inner sill. You nudge the girls: you all wave back.

You feel the odd one out now in the tidy

little street amidst the proper families; as the fathers pack up Volkswagens for shiny weekend jaunts, ruffling their toddlers' hair, a little too jovially, whilst the mothers in Birkenstocks bring sandwiches and gleaming three-wheeled scooters out. You know what the neighbours think: they murmur, 'Poor things. Life will never be the same again.' You do not fit: you are the shortcake in the packet of bourbons.

Only sometimes when the three of you are traipsing to the park again, you see those cars pull off to begin the weekend jaunt, and the fathers' faces are snarling, pulled back angrily over yellowing teeth. You can't hear what they're saying to their wives, whose taut faces are often shielded by large sunglasses. You shudder and hold the girls' hands harder. Sometimes you fear that if you ever let them go, you'll lose them too; that you will watch from the ground as they float off into the clouds, like little helium balloons, out of reach forever.

Autumn nears; the leaves tumble from the trees. You think of him only a fraction less: you do what the Buddhist books instruct. You sit into your pain, you breathe as deep as you can; you ride those waves. Only some days you are pressed down with the most incredible weight that won't let you up again. Sometimes you wake and find both girls breathing quietly beside you, and you are still perched precariously on the very edge of the bed.

One night near Christmas, after Jane's seventh call this fortnight, you finally shake yourself from your torpor. It has been ten months: you must go out, you realise that, or you'll become as one with the old red sofa, which you've sat on so long you know every sag and dip: every faded edge and how badly it needs re-covering.

Upstairs, your toddler sleeps whilst Tabitha is spinning in her bedroom, round and round she goes. Clemence, the sylph-like teenage babysitter from next-door, claps her on, languid in stonewashed jeans.

'Mummy,' Tabitha giggles, falling across her small bed in zebra pyjamas, 'my head feels all crazy.'

You kiss the girls goodnight. There is ice on the pavement and you walk slowly, carefully, glad you eschewed heels. You catch the train across town.

Christmas, it's nearly Christmas, the goose is getting fat. Outside snow foams across the front gardens, in places bulbous and pristine. You slipped and slid here, you forced yourself out, you didn't even wash, it was too cold, you pulled your holey leggings on beneath your party dress, you sprayed the perfume on and you boarded the train. You had to make the effort, you couldn't stay home again. For all the numbness, you needed adult company.

On the train you sat beside a young family and they were laughing about the pantomime they'd just seen, and you were transfixed for a moment. They were everything you had lost; that you couldn't have now. That you'd tried to have but failed.

Jack is at this party, laughing in the corner. He is challenging you, this man you met two hours ago, who you did not really notice at first; you just saw that smile, that silly face, those button eyes, eyes that are button-bright from the nursery rhymes your grandma sang.

He takes your hand. Ready? Are you ready? No! screams your muffled intuition but you have drunk

404

a bottle and a half of sparkling stuff and at some undetected point you slid out of your body, you are absent now. In your place, in your place is a brave woman who has survived; a woman who twists and writhes beneath the party lights. Who laughs and throws her head back and takes her cardigan off to display arms someone once called elegant, who secretly banks on her appeal to work, to appeal to someone, some time.

Do not go home with Jack. It is a bad idea isn't it? It can only ever be a bad idea.

You don't remember what to do. The drink has hit a spot, what spot? A spot you have forgotten. It overtakes you so you stumble. You look around for something, for something you're unsure of; solace or perhaps comfort. And all you know is you don't want to be alone again tonight, trying to reach the empty middle.

You go home with Jack. You find yourself in his flat in the eastern suburbs of the city and you are unsure how you got here. It is a dump of a bed-sit with a folded-out sofa and dirty sheets; a perilous tower of computer books leans by the smelly ashtray. You are so drunk you feel nothing much when he kisses you, though you wonder when you last shaved your legs; and afterwards you fall asleep so that when you wake, you are terrified you're lost. Where the hell are you in fact? You realise you are right on the edge of the thin mattress, peering into the abyss.

You ring Clemence; it's 2 a.m., she is asleep on the red sofa.

'Sorry,' you mumble and you call a cab, and Jack doesn't look so cheerful now in the half-light, his button-bright eyes dulled. You pull on the leggings

405

with the hole in the seam and you don't really say goodbye; you run downstairs for the cab. You lean your head against the cool damp glass and watch the city night slide by. You thank God you were both so drunk you failed to actually do it.

In the morning you have a hangover so bad that you feel sick each time you move. You force tiny discs of aspirin down and cook eggs and bacon and big mugs of tea; you make the girls eat with you. Afterwards, replete and stunned by food and warmth, you go out to the shed that hasn't been opened since Johnny died. This is your job now, you think, as you extricate the wooden sledge from beneath the flower-pots and dead spiders. Their legs are rigid, angular slants that protest furiously of death.

Up the quiet road you three go, wrapped up to your noses, little triumvirate tramping through the snow. The silence seems immense and you savour it. Clemence's mother is clearing her path with a broom, all pursed lips and beret and muttering. She sees you and looks away.

But Mrs Tanqueray, dressed in navy polo-neck, waves from her window. Her tortoiseshell cat pours itself off the fence, picking its disdainful way through the snow before you. You wave your woollen-gloved hand right back at the old lady, and you find a smile more easily today.

In the park you sit on the sledge with the girls at the front and you fly down the small hill and you laugh, and you laugh, the wind whips your hair in your face, the snow stings your cheeks, and you feel fifteen. And as you retrieve Geri's hat with the pink bobble from the slope, you know somewhere deep in your belly, it will all be all right.

On the way home, Mrs Tanqueray still sits by her window, flanked by the grubby nets. You open your gate, pushing the splintered wood through the snow, and then you stop. You retrace your steps, fitting your booted feet into old prints like a child, and knock on her door: you say 'Would you like a cup of tea?'

You cannot miss the way her eyes light up. Slowly Mrs Tanqueray fetches her stick; 'Don't rush' you say, helping her on with the black coat adorned by cat hairs. She comes now, following faithfully beside you, clutching a packet of mince pies, 'From Marks', she apologises. 'My hands are too stiff to make pastry now.'

You cross the road together, towards your little girls whose heads are turned up to the sky, who are catching snowflakes on their tongues. Underfoot, the snow creaks.

'My name is Violet,' the old lady says, and for a moment you wonder about the girl she once was, the girl with the hooded brown eyes and the pretty name and the young husband who, like yours, floated off somewhere too soon.

'Call me Em,' you say, and you hook your arm through hers. 'In the spring-time, Violet', you confide, 'I always wash my curtains. It's a kind of ritual. Shall we get yours down as well?'